BURNING SHAKESPEARE

To Mary —

BURNING SHAKESPEARE

always lovely to see you!

A.J. HARTLEY

best wishes — A.J. — Hartley

Charlotte, NC

FALSTAFF
BOOKS

WWW.FALSTAFFBOOKS.COM

For Finie and Sebastian. Always.

PROLOGUE

"The villainy you teach me I will execute,
and it shall go hard but I will better the instruction."
(*The Merchant of Venice*, 3.1.67-9)

London, 1600

Consider this man climbing the wooden stairs to his bed chamber. He is white, neither old nor young, clad in the fashion of his day, the colors muted but the cut stylish, and the whole a little more than he can realistically afford. As he walks, he frees himself of his doublet and peels off the sleeves one at a time, careful to keep the fabric away from the candle flame. Under the doublet is a smock shirt with loose unadorned sleeves stained with spots of black on the right cuff. Ink, perhaps.

A writer then, though whether that makes him a secretary, a lawyer, or something else entirely is not immediately apparent.

His beard and moustache are neatly trimmed, and he wears a pair of simple gold earrings, which make him look quite dashing, though his hair line is receding fast. In another year or so he will be quite bald on top, and he looks older than his thirty-seven years. Weariness comes off him like smoke from a banked fire, and his dark eyes are fathomless.

1

In his room he clambers out of his remaining clothes and considers the manuscript pages bound with ribbon on the deal table beside the low-slung bed, the only furniture in the tiny, erratically angled room. Wind thrums the thatched roof above him and, for a moment, he reflects upon the sound, wondering how to phrase it. For a long moment in which he might almost be asleep already, he sits quite still, poised to reach for the pen. He blinks, as if leaving a trance, and considers the guttering candle before, with palpable reluctance, blowing it out, and collapsing onto the stuffed, uneven mattress. Even in the dark, which is utter, the kind of darkness subsequent periods generally find only far away from human settlement, his eyes sparkle black. Despite his tiredness he lies awake for several minutes as if waiting for something to happen.

The eyes close at last and then, in almost the same instant, another pair open. They belong to something at the foot of the bed, something visible only as a deeper hollow in the darkness. They glitter with malice like the eyes of a predatory beast, but the rest of the body is strangely inconstant. It shifts like smoke or the currents of deep, black water, eddying and rippling, a swirling chaos seeking shape as something not yet fully formed. It exudes malice, a wild and aimless impulse to violence and destruction, a need to devour, to violate, to undermine whatever is good and true, whatever might bring joy. It is an appetite, voracious and insatiable, but—as if already gorged and stuffed—it wants to spew hatred, to sew discord like poisonous wheat. It swirls and seethes, surging, snatching, clawing for what will give it the form to walk abroad...

On the bed, the writer starts from his sleep and sits up. As his eyes snap open, the creature perched gargoyle-like at the foot of his bed vanishes into nothing.

Biding its time.

ACT ONE

"A sad tale's best for winter. I have one of sprites and goblins."
(The Winter's Tale)

ACT ONE, SCENE ONE

"In this though I cannot be said to be a flattering
honest man, it must not be denied but I am a
plain-dealing villain."
(*Much Ado About Nothing*, 1.3.28-30)

Northside College, Boston. 11:36 a.m. Today.

Bliss

Now entertain conjecture of a time rather later than our last little slice of excitement—assuming you read the prologue—and on a different continent entirely. We have left what, for convenience, we will call simply *the past* and move into what we might think of equally simply as *the present*. Neither term is precisely accurate, but are, as they say, good enough for government work. We have moved through a little more than four centuries and crossed the chilly reaches of the Atlantic into the heart of what is known, in ways managing to confuse both history and geography, as New England. We are in a generic conference room in Northside College, one of Boston's smaller and less renowned schools of higher education. A meeting that has been tense as a drawn bow is coming to an unhappy end.

"The motion fails," said the secretary, unable to stop her gaze from flashing anxiously toward the Chair of Northside College's Board of Regents. It was her job to say it, though the raised hands around the table seemed to be bellowing the result into the awkward silence. She moistened her lips and said in a quavering voice, "Eight to one."

The hands lowered. The board considered each other, their faces carefully blank. No one looked at the Chair, the man who had proposed the motion, the man who ruled the College from the shadows despite the apparent importance of Chancellors and Provosts, the man who—quite frankly—scared the holy hell out of them.

His name was Robert Bliss, entrepreneur, businessman and—more recently—self-styled public servant, specifically in bringing his understanding of what he called "market forces" and the "labor economy" to higher education via Northside College's Board of Regents, of which he was the chair. This last he had achieved by advocating for the popular position that colleges and universities were far too expensive—which was undeniably true—and that what they taught was largely useless—which was undeniably false. Bliss was immune to arguments to the contrary, of course, because he assumed—like many a self-styled public servant—that the sole purpose of higher education was to get students jobs when they rejoined what he liked to call *the real world*. That learning might have something to do with life as well as a living had never occurred to him. Once, when one of the board—a retired anthropology professor who wore flowing skirts he suspected she wove herself—had suggested that education's capacity to "expand minds" was a social benefit, even a necessity, for a healthy and happy democracy, Bliss had reached unsteadily for a glass of water, torn between the need for a cooling drink and the desire for something to throw at her.

It was Bliss' conviction on such matters that had pushed the recent (failed) measure to come to vote in spite of all previous debate. The humanities and social sciences were largely disposable, he argued, and while he was realistic enough to know that he could not simply gut those departments at a stroke, it would be a good "proactive" measure to announce the college's attitude to those fields of study that were not clearly vocational. Today's business landscape had no place for the esoteric parsing of obscure language, abstract philosophizing or trendy theory. It particularly had no use for art or history, and where those things coalesced, lines should be drawn. Shakespeare, the Venn diagrammatical center of all the above, should therefore be eliminated from the English and theatre department curriculum.

The board had been quietly horrified. Even those who shared Bliss' skepticism about what went on in some of the humanities classrooms, with their liberal preoccupations and their burrowing into the arcane and bewildering as if it all somehow Mattered, balked at cutting The Bard. He was Great Literature. He was Culture. He was Tradition. They didn't especially like or even understand why people cared about Shakespeare, and they'd no more read or attend one of his plays than casually visit Neptune over the weekend, but eliminating him from the curriculum? It seemed...a Bit Much. A Bit Incendiary. There would be people who cared about this stuff, old-school blue bloods who had gifts to the school pending, donors who might seize on this as a reason to direct their cash toward Harvard or BU. Wasn't one of their most famous faculty a Shakespeare professor? Lestering, his name was. Tobias Lestering. Wrote books that got reviewed in the fancy New York papers. The board got where Bliss was coming from, they assured him, they really did, and if they thought they could strip Northside down to its Business School and its football team without jeopardizing its existence they'd be right there leading the charge, but at this point in time, given the lie of the land, and weighing the pros and cons, cutting Shakespeare was, they said—borrowing from Bliss' own vocabulary—lousy optics.

Bliss didn't care. It was time Northside showed the world it was serious about education that had real "use value," that its students would thrive "where the rubber met the road," and that the board were thinking "impactfully" and "outside the box." He pontificated, he badgered, and when they pushed gently back, insisted they take the vote anyway.

As has already been made clear, he lost. Completely. He lost so utterly that a few members of the board thought with a little heart-patter of greedy anticipation that he might, after some serious raging, resign on principle, leaving the Chair open to someone better suited to lead Northside into the next decade...

But Bliss didn't quit. He frowned. He became eerily silent. He sat so still in fact that he might have turned to stone, transforming into an abstract statue, not so much Patience On a Monument as Displeasure, or Ambition Thwarted And Seriously Pissed Off. Something like that. He sat there glowering at no one and everyone simultaneously, but he did not quit, and that scared them all the more. Like seasoned animal trackers putting their ears to the ground and spotting a hundred elephants approaching at speed, they sensed retribution coming, because Robert Bliss, whatever else he was, was a revenger straight—ironically—out of Shakespeare. His unnerving silence confirmed in their minds that most terrible of prospects: Robert Bliss had a Plan B.

The board, rarely right about anything, had that one bang on the money, though if they had been forced to speculate on said plan, they could have sat there till doomsday and never guessed right. Like so many other things in the universe, this was also almost, but not quite, ironic.

Bliss was a medium-sized white man in his early sixties, medium height, medium build, neither athletic nor noticeably overweight. His slowly receding hair was a medium brown. Robert Bliss was nondescript in almost every detail.

Almost.

Pass him on the street and you would never know the man existed, but make eye contact with him in an otherwise empty elevator and you would have a markedly harder time getting to sleep that night. His eyes, though unremarkable of themselves in terms of color (they were a medium blue, which in some lights could pass for green or even brown), exuded a chill blankness that spoke of absence within. No life, no fire, no—for want of a better word—soul. His staff looked down when they spoke to him, fearful of staring into those empty depths and the strange, furtive coldness that seemed to lurk therein, but sometimes, when he barked his outrage at one of his employees, they would find themselves meeting that empty gaze and it was like standing on the edge of a dank and misty precipice whose sides were sheer and whose bottom unfathomable.

One of those staff now saw him coming, returning to his office like a storm cloud on a mission likely to bring thunder and lightning into someone's life and, with a commendable sense of self preservation, she hung up the phone and flashed a professional smile that almost masked the panic in her eyes.

"Welcome back, Mr. Bliss," she said. "Is there anything I can do..."

"I'm going to be busy for a while," he informed her. "No calls. No visitors."

He didn't need to add the "or else." The secretary had seen him angry before a thousand times, but this was different; he had a contained, frozen look, a bomb caught in the act of detonating, and his eyes were fixed on the office door in front of him like a javelin in flight. She nodded quickly and lowered her eyes to her computer keyboard.

Bliss slammed the reinforced door of his office so that it clanged shut and reverberated through the building like the gates of Hell. He crossed the vast central space with its aggressively inappropriate tiger-skin rug and flicked a switch on the wall. The windows, which looked down the river to the Citgo sign, were steadily veiled by heavy, floor-length drapes of steel grey, droning faintly as they closed. Soft fluorescent light flickered on in their place, and shadows dwindled to nothing under their artificial glow. Then he turned and started.

A hooded figure stood at his desk, its eyes burning red, its claw-like, skeletal hands clasped.

"Jesus!" Bliss exclaimed.

"Hardly," it replied.

"You wanna cut the dramatics?" Bliss remarked.

The dreadful figure passed a bony hand over the horror that was its face.

"As you wish," it said.

It became a late middle aged white man, distant, cold, very slightly amused in an arid kind of way, but a man nonetheless. Its name, as Bliss well knew, was Belial.

"Better," said Bliss, shrugging out of his unease like a man wriggling out of a tight jacket. "Are we all set?"

"I take it your venture was unsuccessful?" replied the devil.

"It's fine," Bliss lied. "We have a contingency, right?"

Belial nodded fractionally.

"A passage has been prepared," he said, his words soft and grey, "and, thanks to a textbook summons, we have impunity to act as we wish."

"To change history?" Bliss pressed. This was crucial.

"If that is still your plan, yes," said Belial. "I am...yours to command."

"Don't you just hate that?" Bliss said, his good humor returning like a stab of lightning.

"I'm not going to dignify that with a response," said the devil.

"Still, I love to see you jump when I give the word."

"I am never far away," said the figure, his voice at once intimately close but seeming to come through some dense mist. It was an agreement, of sorts, but it held a touch of menace. "You have probably begun to wish I were."

"Why would I do that?" asked Bliss, moving to a chrome chair and leaning against it.

"You will," said the hooded figure, "when the time comes..."

"It hasn't," Bliss cut in. "Not yet. And it won't come for a long time, maybe longer than you can wait."

"I have passed eons of which you know nothing," the other replied darkly. "Doubt not that I can wait."

"Whatever," said Bliss. "So why do we need this summons thing?"

The demon relaxed as he considered the logistics of their task.

"It's a legal loophole," he said. "It allows us to alter the past because someone from that period actually invited us in. Normally even devils are subject to laws, and tampering with the past is strictly forbidden. But when a demonic summons is made from the period in question, we have impunity to enter and act as we wish."

"Change the past?" Bliss clarified.

"Not just the past," Belial whispered. "For all things have consequences in normal time. We alter the past and it produces a ripple throughout history changing all which follows. Our actions in the sixteenth century cannot but alter the eighteenth, the twenty first, and all that follows."

"And this is all legit because some sixteenth-century Satanist invited us in?"

The devil's ancient head tipped from one side to the other and he made a *not exactly* face.

"*Satanist* is an inappropriate term in the circumstances..."

But Bliss was impatient to get started.

"Yeah, yeah," he said, waving the nuance away as he waved all nuances away. Robert Bliss was a man who thought in bold strokes. Nuance was for wimps, academics, and liberals, and in his experience the three often came in a single package. "Whatever. We good to go, or what?"

Belial winced at the phrase but assented.

"We are."

"Then what are we waiting for, devil?" he demanded. "Cut the crap and get on with it."

"You seem to forget who I am," said the demon.

Bliss sighed.

"You are Belial," he said, "captain of the hosts of Satan who fell with Baal and Dagon and who is forever damned with Lucifer and—this here is the real kicker—is *my servant* for twenty four years, for which he gets..."

"Your soul."

"Eventually," Bliss added. "Should such a thing exist. Now: about our mission."

"To erase the works of Shakespeare."

"Right," said Bliss.

"Violating all principles of time and space," said Belial.

"You got a problem with a little rule breaking?"

"I'm a devil," said Belial. "It's kind of what we do."

"So the big deal is?"

"Well..." said Belial, uncertainty and the merest whiff of critique oozing through his butlery manner like a spreading stain on a crisp shirt. "It just seems so..."

"So what?" demanded Bliss, leaning in with a touch of glee.

"So unnecessary," said Belial. "I mean, why? A few old plays... Why do you care?"

"Let's just say I'm doing the world a favor," said Bliss darkly.

"By eradicating one of the world's cultural monuments?"

"Millions of people are about to breathe a sigh of relief," said Bliss. For a moment he looked almost contemplative. "Students especially. High school kids. College kids..." He smiled. It was, Belial was surprised to notice, a thoughtful smile that was very nearly kind.

"And it will be one in the eye for all those professors you loathe," the devil added.

Bliss rediscovered his grim pleasure in a heartbeat.

"Absolutely," he said.

"Except, of course, that it won't," said Belial, incapable of letting the man's satisfaction go unchallenged.

"What do you mean?"

"The students won't feel relieved at not having to write essays on Shakespeare," said the devil. "They won't feel grateful to you."

"I don't want their gratitude."

"And the faculty won't resent you," Belial went on undeterred. "No one will feel anything about the disappearance of Shakespeare, because for them he will never have existed. There will be a moment in which their lives are stuffed with quotations from *Hamlet* and *Macbeth,* and then there'll be a moment in which they never were. They won't remember, because the entire timeline will have altered. Shakespeare's name will mean nothing to them."

Bliss had been looking to argue, but his face got that satisfied look, which was almost beatific, as if he were gazing out over a glorious vista of flowered meadows or wide blue waters.

"Yes," he agreed dreamily. "Won't that be something?"

Belial considered him, then gave his old-retainer shrug of resigned agreement.

"If you say so," said the devil.

"I do," said Bliss, snapping back to reality like a triggered rat trap. "And they might not remember all those tedious puns and preposterous speeches, all that ancient rubbish packed up and lugged around as if it's worth something, and maybe they won't feel the moment that the bag is lifted off their shoulders and they are freed to do something fun or useful for once, but *I'll* feel it. I'll know."

He smiled then, an improbably wide grin that seemed to split his nondescript face like a shark swallowing a seal. His eyes had something of the shark about them too, a blind, rolling ecstasy that flashed suddenly and unexpectedly of madness. Robert Bliss was poised to consume a sizable portion of the world, and the prospect thrilled him with tormented delight. Belial, who had seen a great deal of (self) destructive obsession in his considerable time, nodded thoughtfully, taken aback by the force of the man's determination and the dark torrent of fury that drove it, but he couldn't resist pushing the needle in a little further. He was, after all, a devil.

"So, all this work," he said, "not to mention throwing away your prospect of eternal life, is so you can get your own back on the literary and educated world..."

"Just trying to make a point," Bliss remarked with would-be casualness.

"As am I."

Bliss paused and looked the devil in the eye.

"You want my soul or not?" he said.

There was a ghastly pause and the devil's face seemed to flicker with a hundred emotions, all muted, stifled. When he spoke, it was with a kind of resigned sadness.

"It is my only joy," he said.

Bliss smiled grimly.

"Then move your demonic ass," he said.

The devil made a flicking gesture, and a shimmering rectangle of light, just large enough for a man to pass through, opened in the office like a door. From the recesses of his robes he plucked a gold stopwatch whose dial told twenty-four hours, then motioned Bliss to step into the light.

At the exact moment that the chair of Northside College's Board of Regents stepped into the shimmering rectangle, the watch began to tick.

ACT ONE, SCENE TWO

"Here can I sit alone, unseen of any
And to the nightingale's complaining notes
Tune my distresses and record my woes."
(*The Two Gentleman of Verona*, 5.4.4-6)

Boston, Massachusetts: Commonwealth Avenue. 11:58 a.m. Today.

Our Heroes

Come with me.

It's not far: only a few hundred yards from Northside College, in fact, and this moment follows directly from the last one, so there's no hopping about in time to trouble us. After the dark confines of Mr. Bliss' office, the change of air will be refreshing.

See? Even with the faint tang of car fumes in the wind, it's a relief to be outside. We are on the platform of an urban railway system watching three people who have never met but who are about to become, for want of a better word, entwined. Their lives, I mean, but other bits as well.

One is Xavier Greenwell, a spruce looking young Black man, who has spent the last five years in mergers and acquisitions at FDL Financial Services, though his mind is currently on the prospects of the Boston Red Sox's first baseman. I will spare you the precise nature of his sporting ruminations because the player in question, and I want to make this very clear, is of absolutely no importance in what is about to happen.

Some twenty three yards down the platform is a young white woman in jeans and a hooded sweatshirt, one Rose Matthews, a student and the aunt to three-year-old Tracey with whom she has been shopping. I will return to these shortly.

For now, devote your attention to the third member of this unlikely trio. He is a slightly slovenly white man in his late thirties, slim to the point of wiriness, smelling faintly of sweat and store-brand shampoo, and his mind is, ironically, musing on the past and the future, specifically his. Why this is ironic will become apparent in the future you will reach in about twelve pages.

Till then, bear with me.

The man is flicking through his wallet with a dissatisfied air, though my use of the word *his* is both a little misleading and central to his dissatisfaction. The wallet belonged to one Tobias Lestering, professor of Shakespeare at the nearby Northside College, but the man currently thumbing through the good professor's belongings is Jimmy O'Rourke, known to some of Boston's less respectable businessmen as Jimmy Fingers for reasons which you are probably already surmising. Thirteen minutes ago, Jimmy slipped into the college on a whim, scoping for open offices, preferably those featuring unattended laptops. He had found one, had pilfered the tweed jacket hanging on the back of the chair (discovering the aforementioned Disappointing Wallet), and snagged a bookbag before the office's owner had returned from the room where, according to the sign on the door, he was taking a rest.

The book bag, Jimmy had discovered to his further woe, contained books. Nothing else. The bag he had already dispensed with, but the incriminating wallet still needed a home unaffiliated with the current owner. Jimmy peered along the platform for a trash can into which he could dump his ill-gotten (and mostly useless) trophy, but there weren't any. Which was a disgrace, he observed privately. How were you supposed to keep the city clean and tidy without basic sanitation? What was the world coming to?

In fact, the world was coming to an end: not the whole world, just Jimmy's corner of it, but let's not get ahead of ourselves.

Boston's green line trolleys (to continue our little rumination on history) are like comets must have been to Medieval man: they appear without warning, create a great deal of excitement, and just when you think there'll never be another, you see four. Jimmy O'Rourke reached the conclusion that, owing to some baffling malfunction in the mysterious netherworld of the Boston Mass Transit system, he would probably be walking home and finding somewhere to relieve himself of his meager profits for the day en route. He had other things on his mind, things of significance, next to which the question of how he was going to get home was of little consequence. Jimmy had made a decision.

Or perhaps the universe had made the decision for him. Either way.

He had been working the area off and on for ten years with limited success, generally staying out of the watchful eye of the authorities and limiting himself where possible to activities that might be called misdemeanors rather than outright felonies: no violence, no brandishing of weapons or indeed "possession of burglarious tools," and mostly generating the kind of haul whose absence might not be noticed for a few days. Or at all. Which was part of the problem. It was not unusual for one of Jimmy's raids to produce little more than cross-town bus fare. Thus sailing close to the windy side of the law rather than charging cheerily through the gale like a pirate, all guns blazing, he had managed to stay mostly out of trouble but had also managed to avoid getting rich. Or close to a living wage.

Simply put, Jimmy Fingers was the city's most risk-averse criminal, something his shady friends who gathered for a pint down at the Purple Briar Taphouse often linked to the fact that he was also the city's *least successful* criminal.

It was time, Jimmy had decided that morning, to up his game, take some chances, and score some serious profits, hence his foray into the Northside College English department. And hence his disappointment. He had gleaned precisely seven dollars from Tobias Lestering's wallet, and while there were two credit cards on which he might venture a little shopping spree, Jimmy—essentially an old-fashioned thief and pickpocket—was nervous around anything electronic. Fingerprints, he understood. But the footprints of little ones and zeroes that trailed you after you messed with computers were inexplicable and terrifying. Give him a poorly lit alley, an open window, or an old-fashioned lock any day.

But, in keeping with Jimmy's new impulse to up his pay grade, he had tried the good professor's ATM card. It hadn't gone well. His one shot at the required pin number had been the professor's birthday digits —cleverly deduced from the purloined driver's license at the back of the wallet—but that had been a bust. Jimmy had tried it twice, then pushed a few random keys, as if the machine might give him some money out of pity alone, squinting at the screen till it beeped at him.

Meanwhile, a line had started to form behind him. He could feel them shifting irritably, watching him with annoyance and contempt. His shirt had started to feel curiously small and his face was hot. He tried a few more random keys, tapping them rapidly like a demented woodpecker as if that would make it look like he knew what he was doing, but that had triggered something terminal in the infernal machine. It began spitting slips of paper and squeaking incessantly. It was at this point, as the grumbling from the line behind him got louder and Jimmy tried to seem as if he was the victim of a technological fiasco rather than its architect, that he remembered that ATMs had cameras. He fled—fled *the scene*, he thought grimly—leaving the bookbag behind him.

Thus safely up to speed, we can return our attention to the railway platform.

"Excuse me, sir?"

Jimmy spun round, finding a tall Black man in a suit who had appeared at his elbow. The suit looked civilian, not official, which was to say, not a uniform. Still, being addressed as "sir" alarmed Jimmy. It usually came with remarks like "is this your vehicle?" "are you sure you have never seen these (non-consecutive) bank notes before?" and "show us your hands," this last followed by the production of the kind of bracelets not sold in jewelry stores.

Jimmy panicked. He stared at the distant tunnel mouth, but the trolley that would take him away from all this was nowhere to be seen.

"Yes?" he managed.

"You left this." Xavier Greenwell's voice, like his bearing, was strong and confident, precise and without notable inflection or accent. This is the African American banker I alluded to earlier. He was perhaps thirty, athletic, and dressed with panache. The dark blue suit was cut slim, and the tie was bold but not loud. He was brandishing the open bookbag from which the spines of its disappointing treasure protruded. "You left it at the ATM."

"Did I?" said Jimmy stupidly. He was stalling, but the effect made him look befuddled.

"Yeah, man," said Xavier, confused but kind, as if he might be dealing with someone not entirely on top of things. "See?" he said, sliding a heavy-looking volume out and flipping the cover open. "Professor Tobias Lestering," he read. "That's you, right?"

Jimmy blinked, considered, and chose.

"That's right," he said. "Of course. That's me. Professor Tobias Lestering," he added ponderously, drawing himself up and trying to look as he imagined professors looked. "My books. Thank you. My good man," he added after a fractional pause. That seemed the kind of thing a professor would say.

Xavier peered at him doubtfully but gave him the bag.

"You're welcome," he said.

"I am most glad to receive them again," said Jimmy, warming to his role. He was leaning back a little so that he peered down his nose and his accent had developed a mid-Atlantic hauteur. "What would I do without them?"

"I'm sure you'd manage just fine," said Xavier in the slightly furtive tones of someone keen to be done with the conversation.

But Jimmy was on a roll.

"Where would I be without my..." He glanced at the uppermost book in the bag. "My Shakespeare?" A memory chimed and with it, miraculously, came words he hadn't thought of for years, arriving whole and unbidden in his mind. "*Tomorrow and tomorrow and tomorrow*," he intoned, "*creeps in this petty pace from day to day, to the last syllable of recorded time.*"

"Right," said Xavier, his eyes flitting from side to side as the other people on the platform started to pay attention.

"And all our yesterday's have lighted fools the way to dusty death."

"Okay. Yes. *Macbeth*," said Xavier backing away. "Good one."

"Excuse you!" said Rose Matthews, the aforementioned college student with her three-year-old niece. In his hurry to get away from the guy doing Kelsey Grammer impersonations, Xavier had backed into her.

"Sorry," said Xavier. "I didn't notice..."

"Oh, for crying out loud!" exclaimed Rose as a Stop and Shop bag slipped from her grasp, spilling packages of chicken thighs and a bag of onions onto the platform.

"Sorry," muttered Xavier, stepping on one of the packages and rupturing it.

"Look out!" she blurted, trying to scoop the contents back into the bag with her one free hand as her niece looked on, intrigued.

"Out, out, brief candle..." Jimmy went on, gesturing wildly and enjoying himself for the first time that day. *"Life's but a walking shadow."*

"Would you mind not doing that?" said Xavier, voice raised, hands pressed to his temples.

"A poor player who struts and frets his hour upon the stage and then is heard no more..."

"I wish you were heard no more," Xavier muttered, turning so quickly back to the girl he had bumped into that he inadvertently stepped on the onion bag, crushing one and sending the rest shooting out like billiard balls. The three year old laughed, got free from her aunt, and pursued one of the errant vegetables to the edge of the platform.

"It is a tale told by an idiot..." boomed Jimmy.

"You're the idiot!" Xavier shot back.

There was a deafening blare from the trolley horn as the train came speeding up from the tunnel under Kenmore Square. People who had been mildly diverted by Jimmy's antics now returned their eyes to the long-awaited train with a sense of God being in his heaven and all being right with the world. On the side of the trolley was a poster advertising The American Repertory company's production of William Shakespeare's *Love's Labour's Won*. Had Xavier seen it, it may have afforded him another rush of irritation, which would have helped his situation not one jot. As it was, he was hopelessly attempting what the TV pundits call *damage control*.

"*Full of sound and fury...*" Jimmy went on.

"Tracey!" called Rose. "You get over here right now."

"*Signifying...*"

Xavier spun to address this, and put his foot on another onion, this one barely larger than a shallot. It rolled under his weight towards the platform edge. He sprawled over, clutched for something solid to slow his fall, and found the hand of the Manic Shakespearean. Momentum, as sports writers are fond of pointing out, is like a freight train, an analogy which, had he thought of it, would soon strike Xavier as oddly apposite. But by then, other things would be striking him less metaphorically so his mind was likely to be otherwise engaged.

"*Nothing!*"

Rose Matthews' niece ran giggling toward the two men whose slow-motion fall was taking them down onto the trolley tracks.

The horn rang out again, a note of desperation creeping in this time, but there was no escape. Rose dived into the path of the trolley as its brakes slammed ineffectively on, shoving her niece clear of the rails but taking the full force of the train along with the two men.

In the accurate but uninspired words of Officer Edward Grady, who had been proceeding in his cruiser only a few hundred yards down Beacon Street and was the first policeman to arrive on the scene, they didn't stand a chance.

CHANCE IS, they say, a fine thing, whether you stand one or not.

Jimmy Fingers' last thoughts were that Macbeth's eulogy, which he had been rehearsing for the exasperated banker a moment before, was, as an assessment of his life, right on the money: bad acting and nonsensical blather, signifying bugger all. He considered this dimly as the eternal second unraveled, but by then the steel of the train was introducing itself to the small of his back so he wasn't in the mood to develop the idea.

In any case, the stray quotation from what theatre types knowingly call "The Scottish Play" caught the ear of a slender, serious-looking woman who was currently occupying a seat in what can only be called an other-worldly space.

It was exactly what she had been waiting for, and it raised that fine chance that Jimmy and co. so badly needed.

In seconds the woman, and I use that term not so much loosely as completely inaccurately, crossed dimensional lines to attend this auspicious railway accident. Despite the journey, she was, on the whole, quite pleased.

ACT ONE, SCENE THREE

"Were I chief lord of all the world,
I'd give it to undo the deed."
(*Pericles*, 4.3.5-6)

The Rose Theatre, London. July 15, 1594. 3:23 p.m.

Ned Alleyn

We tend to assume that history is a series of events—births, coronations, battles, inventions, and such like—all lined up nice and orderly like people in a queue at a deli, all patiently waiting their turn, their chance to reshape the world a little. It's not. It's more like a packed bar at one in the morning where an over-worked bar tender serves whoever shouts loudest or waggles the most money, and then gives you a hilariously named cocktail with an umbrella in it when what you asked for was two pints of lager. Then, as you are trying to return the drink, which tastes like a cup of sugar stirred into lighter fluid, the bar unexpectedly turns into a bank, or a clothes shop or, just occasionally, the Ottoman Empire. The problem is that narrative history, the kind you get in textbooks that always seem so orderly, so cause-and-effecty, is something that happens to other people after they're dead. When you are actually living in it, just trying to get from one day to the next and hoping to make a little sense out of the process, it's total bloody chaos.

The world's Great Thinkers have expended massive intellectual energy trying to make sense out of history if only to see if we might do a better job with the present, but most people would rather focus on getting their two pints of lager. Some of the aforementioned Great Thinkers believe that human history (which is pretty much everything that happens after the first ape descendent decided he had a way to make everything better, mostly for him) hinges on the activities of Great Men and (when they can get a word in) Women. Others view individuals as largely irrelevant, mere flotsam on the great sea of time, all the really big things of history being determined by shifts in thought and economics, culture and environment, which happen not just because someone gets up one morning with a bright idea, but because the tides roll the boat a little and a lot of people lean one way, changing the speed and direction of the vessel or, if your bit of the history wave is an unfortunate one, capsizing it and killing everyone.

Probably, it's a bit of both.

I mean, there's no denying that lots of individual people took very particular actions that defined the explosion of art, commerce, and science in the European Renaissance, but they wouldn't have had the necessary money and resources available to them if a quarter of the population hadn't just dropped dead from the plague, an event planned by nobody. And let's not forget that history isn't so much about events as it is about the story surrounding those events: not precisely *what* happened, but what was *seen* to have happened and was spottily documented by the kind of people who give eyewitness accounts to the police and can't agree on whether the car in question was a dark blue Toyota, a pink Cadillac, or a stainless steel DeLorean. Combine this with the notion of a multiverse in which all possible variables all occur, generating an infinite number of new realities in the process, and the conundrum, as it were, deepens. The resultant difficulty of figuring out how history might have evolved differently had certain key events not happened is, as the Great Thinkers would say, a bit of a bugger.

Which is as good an introduction as any to what is about to happen, and when I say "about to happen," I am, of course, referring to some-thing that happened a long time ago. To be precise we are in one of the recently constructed commercial theatres in late sixteenth-century London, a timber-framed building on the smelly South Bank of the even more smelly river Thames. For now, let us step away from these macro ruminations on the nature of time, history, and the cosmos and focus on a single person. His name is Edward Alleyn, and is, he is fairly sure, the most famous actor in the world, though in the early 1590s that is saying less than you might think, acting for money being a comparatively new profession and one that might still get you fined and beaten for vagrancy if you don't have the protection of a powerful local patron.

Either way, Alleyn had never been more sure of his fame than now, standing at the very lip of the stage with a sea of faces turned up to him. There was a clap of theatrical thunder from the tiring house, upon which cue he raised his head, his expression grim. The crowd had been settling noisily, muttering amongst themselves and milling around in search of ale and apples, not sure whether they would eat them or throw them, but now a great stillness descended on the audience. This was what they had come to see: Christopher Marlowe's outrageous words in Alleyn's mouth, worth more than a couple of pennies of anybody's money. The timbers of the crowded galleries creaked once, then the silence was complete. Backstage, Philip Henslowe, the company manager, slightly shady entrepreneur, and father-in-law to Alleyn, paused in his counting of the door takings and looked up expec-tantly. It was a warm summer's day and the sun was high, throwing short shadows beneath the stage canopy, but Alleyn's words were, figu-ratively speaking, about to plunge the theatre into deepest darkness:

"Faustus," he began, addressing himself by name, "begin thine incantations

And try if devils will obey thy hest,

Seeing thou hast prayed and sacrificed to them."

Alleyn paused significantly, and looked at the stage floor, allowing the terrible impact of his words to settle. Faustus was his most ambi-tious role since Tamburlaine and it was even more shocking: a hell-bent scholar who sold his soul for earthly power. It was no wonder the author had come to such a messy end the year before. The death of Marlowe was another one of those little historical events about which historians and enthusiastic cranks would bicker for generations, one of whom would build compelling evidence for the idea that Marlowe was not actually murdered, but escaped in the disguise of a Siberian washerwoman, later opening a fish and chip shop in Blackpool and writing all the major lyrics for Kool and the Gang.

But I digress. Alleyn, who was less easily distracted, got on with things thus:

"Within this circle is Jehovah's name
Forward and backward anagrammatized,
Th' abbreviated names of holy saints,
Figures of every adjunct to the heavens
And characters and signs of erring stars,
By which the spirits are enforced to rise:
Then fear not, Faustus, to be resolute
And try the utmost magic can perform."

There was another thunder clap and a palpable ripple of unease through the spell-bound audience. Alleyn spread his arms, the folds of his scholar's robes opening like bat wings. He struck a pose, legs apart, hands raised, and eyes turned heavenwards as his great, booming voice rolled out the Latin incantation:

"*Sint mihi dei Acherontis propitii! Valeat numen triplex Iehovae! Ignei, aerii, aquacti, spiritus, salvete! Orientis princeps, Belzebub, inferni ardentis monarcha, et Demogorgon, Propitiamus vos ut appareat et surgat Mephostophilis!*"

The crowd didn't understand a word of it, of course, except for the devil's name at the end, but that didn't matter. It was all about the drama of the thing, and that Alleyn had in spades. He also had help from the special effects boys. There was a brilliant flash and a deafening report like the bellow of a great cannon. Many of those standing in the yard ducked and covered their faces with their arms, but Alleyn stood impervious, arms outstretched, daring the universe to do its worst. Around him great gouts of smoke came billowing up from the stage trap and firecrackers exploded in the floor beneath him.

And as the smoke gusted apart, a beast was revealed, larger than a man and distorted far from humanity, with clawed leathern wings and the head of a dragon, greenish and serpentine. Smoke rushed from its nostrils in a loud, menacing hiss, and a woman in the yard gasped. It

25

wasn't especially realistic, but so long as Alleyn treated it as if it were, he could keep the laughter at bay for a few minutes, and it wouldn't be on stage anything like that long.

Alleyn looked the painted paper mâché beast up and down, careful not to rush the moment, then spoke.

"I charge thee to return and change thy shape,

Thou art too ugly to attend on me.

Go, and return an old Franciscan friar:

That holy shape becomes a devil best."

They liked that. The crowd, delighted by Faustus' mastery of the devil and his stab at the loathed continental Catholics, roared with laughter and burst into applause. It didn't matter that the audience had been Catholics themselves until about twenty minutes ago: Catholics were now for mocking and, if you could get your hands on one, burning. No one was entirely sure why this was the case, but it gave them a warm feeling of belonging even when they weren't standing very close to the pyre.

"I see there's virtue in my heavenly words," said Edward Alleyn bowing slightly to the pit, before proceeding:

"Who would not be proficient in this art?

How pliant is this Mephistopheles,

Full of obedience and humility.

Such is the force of magic and my spells."

At which point, the trap door creaked again and a figure cowled like a monk was lifted onto the stage. The dragon mask and costume had been discarded but, Alleyn noted, the boys below had not been able to resist throwing in some more smoke and fumes. It annoyed him a little, and not just because the special effects took away from him and his words. The whole point of the devil's return was that he came back in the likeness of an ordinary person, not reeking of sulfur. He concealed his irritation and waited for his cue.

Before the smoke had cleared completely, the figure spoke.

"Now Edward, what would you have me do?"

Alleyn froze. *Edward?* The idiot! How could he call Alleyn by his real name instead of addressing him in character? He was Doctor John Faustus!

The effect was ruined. Audiences have a knack of smelling out mistakes, and this was no exception. There was a ripple of amusement, and an apprentice in a greasy apron yelled, "Methinks the devil would know the doctor's name!"

A guffaw broke from the wit's associates, and someone called from the first gallery, "Perchance Satan did not read the play bill."

Another general shout of laughter and Alleyn winced. He was no comedian like Dick Tarleton, gaping and bandying with the audience. He was a serious tragedian. Things were slipping away from him. The actor playing the devil said nothing to save the scene and, as time passed agonizingly slowly, Alleyn decided that the only thing was to do the line again himself: properly, this time. He glared at the cowled figure as the smoke gathered in a pall over their heads and whispered between his teeth, "Now *Faustus*, what would you have me do?"

The monkish character stepped towards him and shrugged out of his hood, revealing a pale, hairless head with dull red eyes set in cavernous sockets. Alleyn gasped.

"Master Alleyn," said the nightmare figure, offering a skeletal hand to the actor. "Mephistopheles couldn't make it, I'm afraid, but I am delighted to meet you. My name is Belial."

There was a profound silence that lasted barely a second before shattering like an immense pane of glass and, with a swelling shout of alarm punctuated by shrieks of genuine terror, the crowd stampeded out of the theatre as if Hell itself were at their heels. Which, in a manner of speaking, it was.

ACT ONE, SCENE FOUR

"No, 'Tis not so deep as a well, nor so wide as
a church door, but 'tis enough, 't will serve. Ask for me
tomorrow, and you shall find me a grave man."
(*Romeo and Juliet*, 3.1.95-7)

Rose

Rose Matthews, being a keen English major with an ear for words, had always thought the term "restaurant" a bit odd when applied to fast-food, hamburger-serving...*establishments*. See? Even "establishment" was a bit of a reach. She had once tried the term "eatery" to refer to a McDonald's in a freshman comp essay and her teacher had put a little exclamation mark in the comments as if she'd cursed, which in hindsight, might have been better. *Eatery* was a Rose word, a cautious attempt at precision that came out sounding almost but not quite ironic enough to make her cool, a word suggesting that she had been born a century earlier than made any kind of sense. But what was the right word? A "restaurant" suggested, Rose argued with herself, a maître D' with an accent and a wine list longer than her honors thesis, not Formica, plastic palm fronds, and piped elevator music. It wasn't a "diner" because that had a counter, a waitress who called you "hon," and a jukebox that played Elvis and Patsy Cline. Nothing seemed to fit the generic, brightly colored buildings with their equally generic fare and, as a result, Rose Matthews was having a hard time putting a name to the place in which she appeared to be standing.

"Well, here we are."

This singularly unhelpful comment was uttered by a lean, earnest-looking person with olive skin and long black hair gathered at the back. A woman, Rose thought, though she wasn't absolutely sure. She had high cheek bones sharp enough to cut you and a chiseled jaw. She might have been forty five. Or seventy. It was hard to say. She might have been North African or Arabian. Persian? Rose looked at her and opened her mouth to speak, but the part of her brain which usually selected and arranged words—carefully, like an archaeologist dusting off artifacts—had shut down in disbelief. The woman(?)'s voice, like her features, was androgynous, soft but low. She smiled one of the least convincing smiles Rose had ever seen and shuffled. Rose, a mistress of shuffling and unconvincing smiles, as is often the case with shy people who are a little too smart for their own good, continued to imitate a rather slow gold-fish, mouthing soundlessly. Then, since she was getting nowhere like a wide receiver with a tail wind, decided to look elsewhere.

She was standing in a generic hamburger...*place*. She was, more to the point, in line to buy something: a hamburger, presumably.

This was curious, and not just because she was more of a Caesar salad (dressing on the side) kind of girl. She looked toward the smoked glass doors but couldn't see what was outside.

"I came through those doors," she told herself silently and without any degree of conviction. "I must have." She had no recollection of doing so. Indeed, she had no recollection of anything since...

Since...

Something significant was eluding her.

Rose turned to look at those in line with her and started. One was a Black guy, probably only a few years older than herself, who seemed distantly familiar. A grad student or TA, perhaps? No. His suit looked too businessy though his tie had some kind of cartoon character on it. He was gazing about him as if suspicious and slightly dazed. Like her, in other words. Behind him stood a lean, middle aged, white guy who was cradling a large book as if it were about to explode. They both looked at her and their eyes registered the same thing: utter bewilderment, the shadow of an ungraspable memory, and an edge of hostility.

The vaguely Middle Eastern woman—the only one of them who looked even slightly at home here—was wearing a black suit with a slim skirt and sported, somewhat bizarrely, a gold pocket watch on a chain. The suit was well-cut and classy, so that Rose felt unaccountably underdressed, despite their unprepossessing location. The woman's face was serene, placid as a mountain tarn, a metaphor that pleased Rose because she liked the word. *Tarn.* It was an almost onomatopoetically calm word, and in other circumstances would have spread peace through Rose's mind. But the woman's eyes were silver-gray which was...odd, and overturned all Rose's tentative attempts to fix her ethnicity.

Afghan? Kazak? She had no idea.

"So here we are," the woman said again. It hadn't calmed them the first time, but the effect this second time was, if anything, worse. Finding something threatening in the sinister repetition, the older guy with the book slid it up his chest as if it were a shield. Rose's eyes widened. It was a complete Shakespeare, exactly like the one her English professor used in class.

"I'm glad you kept hold of that," said the mystery woman. "It's *relevant.*"

Rose and the other two considered her warily, and she smiled as if she had offered a truth about the nature of causality, natural harmony, or the precise scale of the universe. Rose's tarn-like calm rippled with unease.

"I remember you," said the businessman to the guy with the book, and though he didn't seem sure of the memory, he was clearly not feeling nostalgic. "You...pissed me off. Somehow."

"Yeah?" said the other. The word came out with blustering hostility, the sinewy man drawing himself up to fight, but the aggression never reached his eyes, and he deflated almost immediately, looking unsure. "Yeah, I do that. Sorry."

"It's cool," said the guy in the cartoon tie. "I don't really remember..."

"Can I help the next person, please?"

Rose wheeled in panic. A girl behind the counter dressed in a red and green striped shirt with matching skirt and peaked cap was smiling perkily at her. She was wearing a large round button pinned to her uniform. "Hi!" it said, "I'm SALES ASSISTANT. I can't wait to serve you!" Rose stared.

It's like *Alice in Wonderland*, she thought wildly. This is the tea party with the Mad Hatter and the March Hare. When her soda arrived, there'd be a dormouse asleep in the cup. Rose wasn't sure exactly what a dormouse was but figured she was about to find out.

"What'll it be today, Rose?" chirped SALES ASSISTANT.

"Well..." she managed.

"Have anything you like," inserted the probably-not-Afghan woman, over her shoulder, in an accent that was as unfixable as her appearance. She sounded like a movie star from the forties, one of the cool, unconsciously sensual ones who only seemed to exist in black and white.

"Well..." Rose repeated. She seemed on pretty safe ground with "well." It didn't really constitute an utterance and thus bought her more time.

"Gimme one of those combo things," inserted the skinny man.

"The Super-dooper Barrel o'grub Special?" SALES ASSISTANT enthused.

"Yeah, whatever," he replied. "The number three. I'm starving."

Rose watched, impressed by her companion's decisiveness, but instantly confused by why she thought a stranger who happened to be in line with her a *companion*. SALES ASSISTANT's fingers flew over the till keypad and a series of square greenish zeros flashed up in the register window.

"That will be nothing at all, Tobias," she said, happily.

"Huh?" said the man whose name, apparently, was Tobias.

"Special offer," said SALES ASSISTANT.

"I meant, why did you call me that?" asked Tobias.

Odd name, Tobias, Rose thought vaguely. It reminded her of something, but she couldn't think what.

"Because it's your name, sir," said SALES ASSISTANT.

"Right," said Tobias, though he didn't seem convinced. "Okay. Thanks."

"All part of the service," said SALES ASSISTANT.

"I don't know what that means," said Tobias. His confusion developed a new wrinkle, and this time the word that popped into Rose's mind was *furtive*. Tobias (and what *did* that name remind her of?) was looking shifty.

"Can someone tell me what exactly is going on here?" Rose asked the...er...*eatery* in general.

The woman in the suit frowned thoughtfully and looked about to reply when another (suspiciously similar) SALES ASSISTANT appeared from the back with a tray of food.

"One Super-dooper Barrel o'grub Special, number three for Tobias," she sang, smiling broadly enough to show each one of her perfect teeth. "And you'll find a clockwork toy in the plastic bag. If there's anything else I can do for you, just holler. Everything's free today. Next guest! What can I get for you, Xavier?"

The businessman winced at the use of what was apparently his name—though his bewilderment was without that tricksy layer that Tobias had—and turned to Rose.

"Where the hell are we?" he muttered.

"Hell?" said the unplaceable woman, amused. "Oh no. Quite the contrary."

At this peculiar remark, the three people in line all turned their backs on the SALES ASSISTANTS and stared at her. Tobias froze in the act of shoveling fries into his mouth and said, "And that means what exactly?"

The woman tried another encouraging smile, but she read their faces and it died—ironically—as if a train had hit it.

"Why don't we sit down," she said, motioning them towards a plastic booth.

They moved like puzzled sheep.

"There now," she said as they took their seats, speaking in the measured tones of a yoga instructor or, Rose supposed, a therapist. "That's better, isn't it? Sitting down. Hamburger-type foodstuffs to consume and soft jazz playing. How relaxing it all is!"

"Tobias"—Rose wasn't sure why she thought of his name in inverted commas like that—put down his hamburger-type foodstuff quickly.

"Why do I feel like you know what's going on," Xavier began, giving the possibly-Kazak lady a steady look, "and these two don't?"

Rose felt slightly affronted by this presumption of her ignorance, but she couldn't argue the point.

"Well," the woman replied, monkishly calm, "this place is not what it seems to be."

"I'm not sure what it's supposed to be," said Xavier.

"There's no need to be personal," said the woman, suddenly brittle. "A lot of hard work went in to making it like this."

"Why?" asked Xavier.

"For your comfort. It was deemed better suited to your lives and would thus make the...*adjustment* easier, less stressful."

"Adjustment?" said Rose. "What adjustment?"

"The *necessary* adjustment," said the woman in the suit, gliding like a swan on still water. "The period in which you grow accustomed to the subtle shift in the dimensional quality of your existence."

"Which means?" demanded "Tobias."

"Just what it says," said the woman. Her serenity had buckled for just a moment, as if she was baffled or irritated by their failure to grasp what she was saying, and though she returned to her easy calm, she now reminded Rose less of a monk and more of a kindergarten teacher trying to get her imbecile charges to paint within the damn lines for once. "I understand your confusion and how hard it is to take all this in, but we *are* trying to make things nice for you. This isn't even part of my job description. I'm only here out of the kindness of my... I'm trying to ease your adjustment."

"To the subtle shift in the dimensional quality of our existences," said Xavier.

"Exactly."

"And in words of one syllable," said "Tobias" who struck Rose as someone accustomed to dealing with bureaucratic evasion, "why don't you tell us what the hell you're really saying?"

The suit lady knitted her brows and seemed to consider her options. She drummed her fingers on the table for a moment. Like the rest of her, they were long and slender, exquisitely delicate but also strong.

"You're dead," she said.

Rose blinked but said nothing. The words meant nothing. How

could they? "Tobias" gaped like a stranded carp. Xavier's face puckered into a scowl of dismissive bafflement that anyone would say anything so palpably stupid.

And yet.

Rose considered the impossible burger...*bistro*, struggling to patch together her strangely insubstantial memories. It was like trying to sew water. There had been class with Dr. Haverstock who Grets (Gretta) Lewis thought was too cute for his own good (and theirs). She had a paper for him on the *Faerie Queene* due next week. She had been itching to get started on it but had promised her sister to take her niece shopping...

"Oh, my God!" she exclaimed. "Tracey!"

"Your niece is perfectly fine," the other woman said.

"Fine?"

"Alive, I mean." She smiled, as if this would clear up the problem.

"She must be terrified!" Rose said, her voice strained and brittle. "I have to get back."

The other woman sighed heavily. "You can't *get back*," she said.

"I have to!"

"Your niece is a little distressed perhaps, but otherwise..."

Rose clapped a hand to her mouth to hold in a sob.

"I told you," said the woman. "You're fine. You're just, you know, dead."

"Get. Me. Back."

"I can't do that!" exclaimed the other with a smile that utterly failed to lighten the situation. "Going back is not an option available to us. Look, I really don't understand what all the fuss is about. It's just an alteration to your state of being. Don't be so *linear*. You're here, conscious as before, aren't you? I really don't see the problem."

She glanced for support at the two men. They met her eyes, and her benign liquid smile froze.

"Not only should you get her back," said Xavier menacingly. "You get us all the hell out of here by whatever means you got us in. I don't know who you are, but this crap about our being dead is just about the stupidest thing I *ever* heard. So why don't you just tell us where we are and how we can leave?"

The woman blinked. She looked at their faces and seemed, for a moment, as stunned as they had been moments before.

"You don't *believe* me?" she said, amazed.

"You bet your ass I don't," said Xavier, meeting her eyes and holding them.

"This is absurd," said the lady in the suit, languidly.

"You got that right," said Xavier.

"So where do you fancy yourself to be?"

"I'm in some sorry-assed burger joint listening to one of the dumbest piles of *Twilight Zone* horse shit I ever..."

"Joint," said Rose dimly. The others turned quickly to her for clarification. "This is a burger *joint*," she said. She thought about it as the others stared, and her enthusiasm faded. "At least it is when he says it."

There was a long pause. Xavier opened his eyes wide and blew out of puffed cheeks. It was a comment, of sorts, one which suggested that Rose was not firing on all cylinders.

And who could blame her? Dead? It was preposterous. She had a niece to play with. A paper to write...

"As I was saying..." Xavier went on.

"Fine," said the woman in black, and now Rose could almost see the swan's legs furiously paddling beneath the effortless glide. "You don't believe me. You think this is some kind of elaborate prank for my entertainment? Fine. Then tell me what you see."

Her right hand flashed out with astonishing speed and clamped itself over Xavier's face, fingers spread. Xavier's head snapped back and for a second he remained like that, with the woman leaning over him, her face fixed. Then, as suddenly as she had made the strange movement, the woman released him. Xavier stayed as he was for another moment, his eyes closed but their lids flickering as if he were dreaming. Then they flashed open, wide and staring, and his mouth fell open in horror.

"What?" demanded Rose. "What did you see?"

There was a long silence.

"You," said Xavier in a low, hesitant, and dragging whisper like wind in dead leaves. His eyes, though open, were unfocused, as if he could still see whatever it was the strange woman had shown him somewhere off in the distance; it was not a pleasant sight. "I saw you," he went on, "and you," he added, turning and looking through "Tobias." "And I saw," he paused and breathed in, a long tortuous gasp that filled his chest, "me."

"And we were...?" said Rose, hesitantly.

Xavier nodded slow and glazed.

"A train," he concluded with awful finality.

And Rose remembered. A split Stop and Shop bag spilling onions. The blare of a horn. A jumbled chaos of skylight and noise and sudden, blinding pain.

How could she have forgotten?

Rose stopped breathing. She sat very still, eyes blurring, unaware of her tears or what she was thinking. For a long moment she simply was, and then they came, the panic and regret, the shattered hopes and ambitions, the grief that hit her like a tsunami wave, the kind that carries cars inland and pushes down buildings, wild, indiscriminate, and unstoppable. She didn't weep for herself, exactly, for what she might have become, the many, many experiences she would never have. She wept that she would never see her clumsy, well-meaning father, her critical but loving mother, her cool sister, her niece, her college friends: Gretta, who had bought her a toaster oven for her dorm room; Tony Ramirez, who she had fallen in and out of love with a dozen times in the first month of the semester; Sonya Redmon, the only person as nerdy and obsessive about books as she was, who could match her quote for quote on anything from *Sense and Sensibility* to *Buffy the Vampire Slayer*... The wave lifted and carried her away from all of them. Or rather *they* were carried away from *her*, pulled by the flood while she was left behind, reaching for them, screaming, watching them drown.

"Tobias," who still looked dazed rather than grief-stricken, leaned over and patted her hand vaguely. His hand was small and pale, callused but tender. Without thinking she took it and held it, avoiding his eyes, till she had recovered some measure of self control. Doing so didn't mean moving past her feelings so much as funneling that entire tsunami into a bottle and corking it tight. It would have to do. For now. Her life—or whatever it was she was in now—had grown too strange for sorrow.

She looked at Xavier, the only one of them who had actually seen the site of the accident. It is said that seeing is believing, that a picture paints a thousand words. Rose wondered if she might have been able to do more with her feelings than bottle them up if she had been able to see what Xavier had just seen.

No. She registered the man's punch-drunk face and was glad not to know precisely what her death had looked like.

"Quite," said the woman in the suit, speaking in a tone that made the word boom like a church bell. They looked at her as her former serenity returned like sunrise. "Ask not for whom the bell tolls, it tolls for thee. *Tolled*, I should say. Several minutes ago. Now," she said, business-like, "can we get on?"

"Oh my God," whispered "Tobias," gazing at the woman with a stricken but clearly excited look. "You're Death!"

"What?" asked the woman in black. "No. That's not how it works at all. There's no Death—capital D—just, you know, *death*. Small d."

"Oh," said "Tobias," deflating. "Right."

"Very well," said the woman in black about whom the only thing they knew definitively was that she was Not Death. "Let's leave all the pointless agonizings over your half-fulfilled ambitions and dreams for the future and get on with business."

"Business?" "Tobias" echoed. Rose was still paralyzed, her eyes bright with tears, but Xavier looked ready to throw a punch.

"Yes," said the woman, "business."

She picked up the collected Shakespeare and tapped it significantly. "This," she said. "We have to save the works of Shakespeare."

As the other three stared at her in disbelief and confusion, the woman in black picked up the hamburger-type foodstuff Xavier had abandoned and considered it.

"I do wish *I* could salivate," she remarked wistfully.

ACT ONE, SCENE FIVE

"The heavens themselves, the planets, and this center
Observe degree, priority and place,
Insisture, course, proportion, season, form
Office, and custom, in all line of order."
(*Troilus and Cressida*, 1.3.85-8)

Gladys

Rose was not entirely at fault for struggling to identify the age, gender, and ethnicity of the "vaguely Middle Eastern" "woman" in the black suit, because in real terms she didn't truly have things like ethnicity or gender. She did, however, have age. Lots of it. She might not look like it, except perhaps in the depths of her curious grey eyes, but she bore centuries on her back, ages in what, for want of a better word, we will call her heart, and epochs in her mind. No one could say precisely how many because while she was not quite as old as the earth itself, she was certainly older than humanity. She had had many names over the millennia, but they had always had more to do with who was talking about her than who she actually was, varying by region and period: others of her kind did not need something as banal as a name to know who she was. It was thus only recently, when she had undertaken the particular task that led to the creation of the afore-mentioned burger...er... *joint*, that it had been deemed appropriate to give her a human name. The Nomination Assignment Department had initially suggested good old names full of unlikely letter combinations and apostrophes ripped from the "What To Name Your Baby" pages of the *Mesopotamian Evening Standard* 2500 BCE ("now in friendly demot-ic!"). While she agreed that these had an appropriate sense of heavenly gravitas positively reeking of Thrones, Dominions, and Powers, they didn't exactly put twenty-first century North Americans at their ease. She had requested "Roshunda," which she liked to say because it sounded like a mighty, pyramid-levelling storm coming rapidly in your direction, but was told that this might cause Confusion and Offense. No one seemed precisely certain why, other than pointing out that she didn't "look like" a Roshunda. This seemed to her a weak excuse, since she could look like pretty much anything she felt like if she made the effort, but forms had already been stamped and that was that. At last, in a tasteful if bureaucratic ceremony, she was officially named... (*drumroll, please*)

Gladys.

That she looked no more like a Gladys than she did a Roshunda seemed to trouble no one, so Gladys she became, assuming—incorrectly as it turned out—that this simple descriptor would make her interac-tion with humans easier. Because, as has probably become apparent, she herself, as it were, wasn't one.

Now, as she considered the confused and baffled resentment on the faces of Tobias (no inverted commas for Gladys, thank you very much), Xavier, and Rose, she felt the eons pressing on like the spar down the middle of a fold out couch. She had seen it before, but it always produced the same remote sense of failure. It wasn't entirely her fault, of course. A project of this scale is never the property of one celestial attendant, especially one of Gladys' relatively low standing. But she had been integral to the Heavenly Burger proposal, so it was difficult not to take its palpable deficiencies personally.

She considered the recently deceased humans around her, processing their defiance, confusion, and futile desire to make sense of their predicament, with the kind of weary patience only found on the face (simulated, obviously) of an entity that had been doing the same thing for millennia. The impact of what had happened to them would take some time to sink in. In fact, it might never fully register, though that wasn't entirely a bad thing. Humans, Gladys had observed, being accustomed to think in the very short term, were oddly protected against the horror of what eternity is really all about. As they aged, and time seemed to them to pass faster and faster, measuring out their lives if not with coffee spoons then in seconds, minutes, and hours rather than decades or—as in Gladys' case—millennia, it became paradoxically harder and harder for them to think of a state outside time. Consequently, Gladys decided, they seemed to think of death as somehow temporary, like a vacation: a state that terminated with the return to normal existence. The idea that they were dead *forever*, rather than for, say, the next two weeks on a Mexican beach sipping colorful drinks, required the unlearning of a lifetime.

"Shakespeare?" said the youngest—Rose—as if she had misheard.

"That's right," Gladys replied cheerfully. "William. The writer."

Xavier, he of the profession that commanded the most respect among humans because it involved large amounts of money even if he didn't actually own much of it, peered at her as if trying to assess which of them was most clearly out of their minds.

"If you don't mind me asking," said Tobias, Gladys' mission-critical lynchpin since they would be depending on his expertise as a Shakespeare Professor, "if you aren't Death then who, or *what*, are you?"

"A fair question," said Gladys. "I am Gladys. I am what you would call an angel."

Had Gladys anticipated the effect that this kind of remark would have on humans, she probably would have spent more time at cocktail parties. There was an awed hush. Then Xavier found a little residual skepticism.

"You're an angel, called *Gladys*?" he said.

"That's right."

"You don't look like any angel I ever saw," he replied.

"Seen many, have you?" said Gladys, with a slightly frigid politeness.

"Pictures. Movies," Xavier hazarded, a little uncertainly.

"Ah, the wisdom of Hollywood," Gladys remarked dryly.

"I don't believe in angels," said the man Gladys thought of as Tobias (no quotation marks), who clearly felt this point should be made before things got away from him.

"And yet here I am," said Gladys.

The professor blinked, momentarily flummoxed.

"Well, you must admit, you don't exactly look like a Michelangelo cherub," inserted Rose, her attention remaining fixed on Gladys like one of those laser-sighted weapons by which the period had become so fascinated.

"There's no need to be personal," Gladys replied. "I'm here to help ease your adjustment to..."

"The subtle shift in the dimensional quality of our existence?" Xavier volunteered.

"Right," said the angel. "I keep an eye on things here and, if necessary, I take steps."

"What kind of steps?" Rose demanded.

"Well, it rather depends. In this particular instance, I have assembled a kind of task force to operate on my behalf."

"So, we're in Heaven?" inserted Tobias, looking doubtfully around him.

"No," said Gladys.

"I mean," Tobias persisted, "we're not in Hell."

"No," said Gladys, glad she could answer something clearly.

"Well that's a relief," said Tobias. "I mean, I've never been very religious..."

The unfinished phrase hung awkwardly in the air for a moment and then he looked at his shoes.

"So, what's Hell like?" Rose wanted to know. Or pretended to. It was as if she had forced the question out to prove to herself that she was present and engaged, that she was an interested party gathering —as they say—*intel on the situation*, rather than a child trying to think about something else so that she wouldn't cry. Gladys wasn't fooled for a moment, but it didn't help her navigate the question. She sensed that for a second there she had looked less like an angelic being than a dog who had been left to guard the house but had then eaten the couch.

"Rather like this, actually," she confessed. "The adjustment room part of it at least. I don't think they have ketchup though."

"That's the difference between Heaven and Hell?" Rose gasped, suddenly absolutely present. "*Ketchup?*"

"I don't really like ketchup," said Tobias.

"I don't think that's the point, do you?" Rose shot back, releasing his hand.

"Probably not."

"Well?" said Rose, turning on Gladys. "How can they be the same? Hell is supposed to be fire and brimstone, devils and pitch forks, and..."

"Yes, yes," the angel huffed, irritation taking the place of discomfort, "some of it is like that. Part of the time, at least. Or it certainly used to be. But when we came up with this half-way house idea..."

"Half-way house?" parroted Xavier.

"This intermediate...place...where the dead can get, you know, adjusted to their fate...or lack of it, it seems our marketing people must have poached the idea from theirs, or the other way round and..."

"Marketing people?" Rose repeated, incredulous. "The after-life has marketing people?"

"In a manner of speaking," Gladys persisted, amazed at how difficult this was all turning out to be. "But anyway, both parties got hold of the same idea one way or another. Probably they were just chatting about current projects over lunch..."

"Angels and devils have lunch?" gasped Xavier.

"Well," said Gladys, "when I say *lunch*... I mean, they don't really consume in any way you could comprehend..."

"But whatever they do," Rose pressed, "they do it together?"

"Sometimes, yes," the angel snapped. "Heavens to Murgatroyd![1] Are you going to let me finish this story or not?"

"No," said Rose forcefully. "I don't see what any of this has to do with us and I think you had best explain what is going on."

"I thought I had," said Gladys.

"No," said Rose with cool hostility. "You haven't."

"I told you," the angel answered with a labored intake of what, for want of a better term we will call *breath*, "I organize task forces that operate on behalf of the angelic order in human affairs."

"So?" Rose persisted. "I don't see how that involves us."

"Well, you're it," said Gladys, surprised that all was not crystal clear. "The task force, I mean. You three."

"Excuse me?" said Rose.

"It's all rather complicated," said Gladys, "but the gist of the thing is that there are certain things I can't do: like involve myself in the lives of humankind in a direct, interventionist fashion. In real time, as it were. You can."

"But we're dead," said Xavier.

"At the moment, yes," said Gladys, her petulance leaking out. "But the task I have for you involves working in the past. So," she concluded as if the implication were obvious, "as long as we are dealing with a period before noon today, you are alive."

The humans (or former humans, if you want to be precise, humanity being intrinsically bound to, you know, *being alive*) considered this for a moment before finding something else about which to be hostile.

"What on earth—or wherever we are—makes you think we'll help you?" said the newly feisty Rose, staring at the angel.

"I work with time," said Gladys, laying her hands palms down on the plastic tabletop. "The 12th century is only a hair's breadth from the 23rd in my line of work. I could take you from Middle Kingdom Egypt to Dickensian London in the blink of an eye. If you complete the assignment I have for you, I can bring you back by, say 11:55 today. Then, rather than hanging around the Commonwealth Avenue trolley platform waiting to be mown down by a passing train, you might step into *Au Bon Pain* for a croissant and a cappuccino."

"We'd come back to life?" said Rose.

The angel made a face and shrugged. "Not really."

"But you just said..."

"I mean that the moment of your death would not occur," Gladys explained with studied patience. "It would not *have occurred*. So from that moment you would go on with your lives, fulfilling your dreams and ambitions as best you could for whatever span of time is allotted to you. Of course, if this proposal doesn't interest you..."

"Go on," said Xavier, "we're listening."

"I have a better idea," said Gladys. "Give me your hands."

ACT ONE, SCENE SIX

"But I have done a thousand dreadful things
As willingly as one would kill a fly
And nothing grieves me heartily indeed
But that I cannot do ten thousand more."
(*Titus Andronicus*, 5.1. 141-4)

Bliss

Permit me a change of focus, and not just from our plucky band of unwilling heroes. We are moving again, in space and time, landing squarely here:

London. 16th July, 1594.

Forgive me. I know this jumping around is unseemly and frowned upon by the better class of writer, but it is necessary and I hope you can get used to it, because it's going to happen a lot.

We have left said plucky heroes behind in present day Boston, but it is a truism of a thousand mediocre writing seminars that the villain is the hero of his own story. Never was this more true than of Robert Bliss, Chair of Northside College's Board of Regents, and now—literally true in one sense and not at all in the other—Renaissance Man.

He was picking his way around puddles of sour refuse, faintly nauseated as much by the insistent pressure of his newly acquired stockings as by the fly-blown mounds of trash, bones and God alone knew what else that was heaped by the walls of houses and shops. It was a warm day by English standards, muggy and unpleasant, the kind of weather civilized societies counter with air conditioning, but we are centuries away from that, and even when humanity gets it, the English don't. A long shadow fell on Bliss from the tower of St. Peter's Church, and he shivered at the sudden coolness and at the impression of holiness in architecture. This latter he shrugged off, consulted a file of notes, and stalked around some particularly muddy holes in the dirt road like a punctilious spider, scanning the lurching wood and plaster buildings around him. He muttered to himself as he read off the erratically spelled names on the sign boards, checked his notes once more, and homed in on the establishment of one Thomas Millington, likening himself to one of those laser-sighted weapons on which Gladys had recently been speculating.

He had just identified the shop he had been looking for when a man and a woman who had apparently just bought something at the window turned and barreled into him with such force that he was driven back, off balance, and sliding into the mud. He landed squarely on his butt in a puddle of brown, lukewarm water.

"God damned Dark Age idiots!" he roared after the people as they vanished up a neighboring alley without so much as a word.

Bliss drew himself up, smoldering and dripping (the former metaphorically), and tried the door in as foul a temper as he could muster, which, for the chair of Northgate College's Board of Regents, was going some. It was locked. He cursed under his breath and knocked again. A middle-aged man in a coarse smock belted at the waist appeared at the window—apparently the business end of the establishment—and asked Bliss how he could help him. Actually he said, "Now, master, what do you lack?" in a dialect so broad with sprawling, mouth wrenching vowels that Bliss was caught momentarily off guard and could think of nothing to say. The shopkeeper, a large man with a florid face, eyed him steadily, waiting.

"Oh," said Bliss, starting. "Right. Well, I hear you sell plays."

The face behind the counter wrinkled with confusion as he tried to figure out what had just been said.

"Plays," repeated Bliss, hopefully. "Drama. Theatrical texts. You speak the goddamned English language?"

The shopkeeper's face clouded doubtfully but less with confusion than with suspicion, and his gesture to a stack of paper pamphlets carefully arranged on the folded down shutter showed that he had understood perfectly. Bliss grinned as he flipped through the heap of booklets, conscious of the shopkeeper's eyes riveted on the top of his head. He had to stoop slightly to the casement-counter and did so cautiously, half expecting his hose to enact some hideous form of half nelson on his genitals, but on succeeding without apparent injury he perused the titles of the stacked plays.

They were quartos: small, single volume editions, about seven inches by five and covered with a soft blue paper wrapper. Bliss passed over their titles (*A Knack to Know a Knave, Friar Bacon and Friar Bunghay, Edward the Second*) until he found what he was looking for: "THE First part of the Contention betwixt the two famous Houses of Yorke and Lancaster, with the death of the good Duke Humphrey: And the banishment and death of the Duke of *Suffolke*, and the Tragicall end of the proud Cardinall of *VVinchester,* vvith the notable Rebellion of *Iacke Cade: And the Duke of Yorkes first claim vnto the Crowne.*"

"Catchy title," said Bliss dryly, picking up what was known to later centuries as *Henry the Sixth part Two* and composed by, among others, William Shakespeare.

"A shilling," the shopkeeper growled from behind the counter.

"I thought they were six pence each?" said Bliss indignantly.

"Ay," the other returned, his face expressionless, "marry, that be for an honest citizen o' the city, not some Dutch Knave."

If this was an insult, Bliss missed it, merely shrugging in response and gathering up all the copies of the play left in the pile. These he shunted across the counter, cursing while he located the purse that hung from his belt.

"How long before you backwards yokels invent pockets?" he muttered, placing a gold coin on the oak top. The shopkeeper's eyes widened, staring first at the coin, then at Bliss, who met his gaze with irritation.

"What?" he demanded. "Don't tell me it's not enough."

"Nay, forsooth," managed the other, "'t will more than suffice, your worship."

"Funny how quickly one loses one's Dutch Knavishness when large amounts of cash change hands, isn't?" said Bliss.

"Begging your pardon, master, but your accents seemed so unfamiliar-strange, that..."

"Yeah, yeah," drawled Bliss. "Whatever. Just give me the goddamned plays then go and evolve."

The shopkeeper, who had placed one hand deliberately over the coin and left it there, now used the other to gather the papers awkwardly and push them towards Bliss in a teetering stack.

"Thank you *so* much," said Bliss. "You've given me new insight into the term 'service economy.'"

The other, unabashed by this bewildering remark, nodded and managed a kind of earnest smile, saying, "I warrant thou wilt enjoy thy reading."

"I wouldn't warrant much on it if I were thee," said Bliss acidly. "I've no intention of reading this tedious horse shit. I'm going to burn it."

He left, the play books bundled under his arm.

The shopkeeper watched him go, his right hand still held fast over the coin in case his customer thought better of it and came back for change. He watched the stranger turn a corner and disappear before a broad and cunning smile spread across his face. Only then did he turn his greedy eyes on his open palm. Where the gold coin had been, a small olive-colored toad squatted, pulsing slightly. The shopkeeper's cries drew the tenants from next door, but by then Robert Bliss was nowhere to be seen.

ACT ONE, SCENE SEVEN

"Give me life, which if I can save, so;
if not, honor comes unlooked for, and there's an end."
(*Henry IV part 1*, 5.3.59-61)

Boston. The very near future, or one of them, at least.

Jimmy

Jimmy felt Gladys' grip tighten suddenly and something like a wave of energy passed from her to him, through his other hand to Xavier and, presumably from her other hand to Rose. Everything went white, there was a momentary sense of being in an infinite number of places at once and then normality returned like a dog that has just knocked over a Ming vase. Feeling as if he'd just gotten off a particularly nasty roller-coaster, Jimmy sat down on the floor heavily, clutching his stomach.

Xavier cut to the chase—something, Jimmy imagined—he did a lot.

"Where the hell are we now?"

Gladys smiled.

"The 'now' is more appropriate than the 'where,'" she said, unhelpfully.

"Meaning?"

"We are in the College Library about four hundred yards from the site of your little encounter with Boston's mass transit system."

Jimmy got to his feet and tried to look natural. Just a regular guy materializing in a library after having been run over by a train.

Think calm thoughts, he told himself. *She's an angel, not a cop.*

This didn't really help. After all, if he really was dead, angels were about as near to law enforcement as made no difference.

"Library," he said, nodding sagely and forcing a species of smile. "Oh yes. Spent many a long hour in here."

Xavier gave him a look.

Too much? Maybe he should dial back the professor accent thing he was doing.

"Why are we here?" said Xavier.

"I'm trying to respond to your cripplingly sequential notion of time in like terms," said the angel, clearly put out. "I have positioned us geographically (in the College Library) and temporally, using the coordinates of your accident as a starting point. It is twenty minutes since your tragic demise."

She consulted the ornate fob watch.

"Now, look at the books around you."

Jimmy did so, and his heart sank.

"*Timon of Athens,*" said Rose, baffled. "*Pericles, Prince of Tyre,*" she read from another book spine in the same tone. "*Antony and Cleo...*oh! Shakespeare!" she exclaimed with sudden realization and a glimmer of pleasure. "*A Midsummer Night's Dream. Henry the Fifth... Corio...lanus,*" she intoned. "Don't know that one. *The Tempest. Romeo and Juliet.* I read that in high school. *Macbeth.* Cool."

Shakespeare, Jimmy thought. *God.*

"Oh yes. Excellent," he said, gesturing vaguely as if he had written the damn books himself.

Xavier turned on him.

"Shakespeare?" he demanded, his voice loaded with accusation. "This is all because of you, isn't it?"

"Well, now, I hardly think..." Jimmy began, but Gladys the angel cut him off.

"Yes," she said, smiling. "It is."

49

Xavier reached for Jimmy's lapels and pushed him into the shelves.

"I knew it!" he declared. "If it wasn't for you, we'd be fine," he said, nodding at Rose. "We'd be walking around, alive."

"What?" interjected the angel. "No! I explained this already. It's because of Tobias that you're here, on my team, but it's not his fault that you're dead! His expertise as a Shakespeare scholar attracted my attention—those lines from *Macbeth* spoken with your dying breath was an especially nice touch—but it's because you got hit by a train that you're dead. I thought that was clear."

Jimmy, AKA Tobias, felt like he was back on the rollercoaster: with each phrase of the angel's speech, he shot up to joy and relief, then crashed down into guilt and dread.

"Don't be angry with Professor Lestering," Gladys concluded. "It's because of him that you all get a second chance at life."

Xavier frowned, then grudgingly released Jimmy and smoothed the wrinkles out of his jacket.

"Sorry," he muttered. "But you can see how I might have misread... Sorry."

Relieved to be at this point of the rollercoaster ride, Jimmy rallied.

"Don't mention it old boy," said Jimmy, acting his proverbial ass off. "Water under the bridge."

Rose, however, was eying him shrewdly, and Jimmy, plunging back down the rollercoaster track and going through some bowel churning corkscrew move, recognized the signs. He was rumbled.

"You are Professor Tobias Lestering?" she said. "The Shakespeare scholar?"

Jimmy faltered, his eyes flashing between Rose and the others. He could bluster it out or he could confess. But then what? What if they only had another shot at life because the angel had misidentified him? What if he came clean and they all got just a momentary impression of falling under the green line trolley followed by...nothing. Or worse. If angels and devils were real, as seemed likely, maybe there was an eternity on the end of a fiery pitchfork awaiting him for his life of (petty) crime, the last beat of which had led him into this particular moral quagmire...

He opened his mouth to speak, far from clear as to what he was about to say, when Gladys held up a warning finger.

"Hush," said the angel glancing up from her watch. "It is beginning."

~

Rose

WHEN YOUR WORLD IS UPENDED, and the most precious things are taken away from you, it makes a sort of sense that familiarity of any kind brings a kind of relief. Rose's attitude to the plays themselves was complicated, but evolving—or had been until a few moments earlier. In high school she had actually despised *Romeo and Juliet,* or rather the way it was beaten into her as a Great Work of Literature on which she was to be Graded. But on becoming an undergraduate, the plays—well taught and seen on stage a few times—had started to worm their way into her mind and even her heart. It was, therefore, unsurprising that the sight of them had sparked a flicker of joy in her now, and not only because when you've been killed by a train and transported (ha!)—via a poor imitation of Burger King—on a time travelling jaunt with a group of total strangers, one of whom is not actually human, you hold onto what you can.

The last play on the list was one she particularly liked: a tale of blood and kingship, violence and witchcraft, passion and ambition. She had enjoyed it almost secretly in school when Liking Shakespeare was not high on the list of things that made you popular, but had reveled in it and a handful of other Shakespeare plays she had read in her first year Brit lit courses at Northside. Then she had discovered *A Midsummer Night's Dream* and *As You Like It* and *Twelfth Night,* glorious, silly, clever, and sometimes touching plays she had encountered at the feet of a truly amazing teacher, not just an academic but an enthusiast who genuinely loved what he did; his name was Professor Tobias Lestering.

She remembered now. It had come back to her so bright and clear that it seemed impossible that she could have ever forgotten, even for a moment. Professor Lestering was her Shakespeare teacher and in no way did he resemble the "Tobias" who was now mouthing vaguely at her, his face flushed with the scale of his lies.

"Look now," said Gladys.

~

Xavier

Xavier looked and, at first, saw nothing. Then Rose made a noise, half gasp, half squeal of alarm. The red, hardbound cover of *Macbeth* that she was holding had begun to fade. The color bled out of the book as if it had been left in the sun. Xavier reached for it, snatching the volume from her like a member of a magic show audience, determined to see how the trick was done.

"Hey!" exclaimed Rose, but Xavier didn't take his eyes from the fading book. He felt its weight evaporate in his hands and found himself looking at his fingers *through* the pale volume. The title became illegibly faint and the whole thing suddenly collapsed in on itself in a tiny shower of dust that vanished before it hit the floor. The book was gone.

So long, Shakespeare! thought Xavier. He had to suppress the impulse to giggle. Partly it was the profound weirdness of the situation with a whole bunch of attendant stress, but it was also because Xavier had never been what you might call a Shakespeare fan. He had Views on Shakespeare's part in what he called The White Cultural Machine and on one play in particular.

He glanced at the shelves to see if the text in question was also turning to dust, spotting it just as the words faded.

Othello.

There for a moment, then gone.

Good riddance, thought Xavier with a thrill of somber glee. *Into the void with you, you racist piece of...*

But it wasn't just the Shakespeare plays that were fading to nothing. It was all the books. The shelves around him were emptying in the same fashion, turning to the merest scintillation of dust caught in the softest of breezes—as if the universe, after a long day's cosmic operation, had finally sat down, put its feet up, and sighed—blowing every visible stack empty. Nor was it just the books. Soon the shelves themselves were becoming indistinct and fragmentary, then the walls, the ceiling, the floor: all collapsing in on themselves as the great sigh continued, blowing out the very fabric of the world till there was nothing but light.

The four figures stood as they had been, but any sense of place was gone. Any sense of *anything* was gone. They were in the middle of nowhere. And while Xavier may have said that of, say, wandering around New Hampshire, this time it was literally true. He was standing on what felt like solid ground, but could see no sign of it, nor was there anything below, above, or around him. There was only a brilliant emptiness. Xavier glanced down, stared at the absence beneath his feet and became very still.

"Damn," he said.

"Quite," said the angel.

~

Gladys

GLADYS WAS BEGINNING to find these mortals rather tiresome. They hadn't even begun their mission yet and they were already getting on her last metaphorical nerve.

"I don't understand," said the Shakespeare professor.

"I'd tell you to get used to it," said Gladys, "but you won't."

"Hey!"

The angel shrugged.

"The universe is a complicated place," she said. "The sheer enormity of what humans don't understand is staggering. Some of the edge wears off after a few centuries, but there is just so much you will find absolutely and utterly incomprehensible that the novelty of your own ignorance is unlikely to wear off."

"Great," said Tobias miserably.

"Where are we?" Rose demanded. Her voice had both an edge and a crack.

"Where we were a moment before," said Gladys with ill-conceived impatience.

"No," said Rose reasonably. "Before we were in a library. Now we are in a nothing."

"The two are not mutually exclusive," said Gladys, her lips twitching into a slightly smug smile. "We are where we were, but the library is no longer here because the books are no longer here. No point having a library if you don't have any books, am I right?"

The jokey tone didn't work, and Tobias eyed her narrowly.

"So," he said. "You wanted us to see some books vanish, why?"

"I can't tell you all of it," said Gladys breezily. "There are elements of what is happening here that I am forbidden to pass on to the living."

"We aren't living," Xavier reminded her, glancing furtively around as if looking for something to hold onto.

"Not now you're not, no. I'm aware of that, thank you. But you will be, hopefully, so I can't, as it were, *impart these mysteries unto you*," said Gladys, hoping that her vaguely Biblical diction would give her explanation credibility.

"You're being vague," said Xavier.

"Well, if I tell you specifically what I'm not going to tell you then I will have told you, won't I?" Gladys snapped. While they silently unraveled her syntax, she pressed on, forcing herself to calm down in the process. "The Shakespeare volumes that were on the shelves have disappeared not just here but everywhere. The works of Shakespeare have ceased to exist as of this afternoon."

~

Jimmy

"I DON'T UNDERSTAND," Jimmy said. It was becoming his mantra. He suspected he should be saying as little as possible so as not to give away that he wasn't who everyone but the girl thought he was, but he couldn't help himself. For a professional thief, Jimmy was fundamentally and inconveniently honest.

His remark wasn't just about the Shakespeare business. It was also because the nothingness around them had started filling in, as it were, the light turning to something pale and powdery beneath their feet. In seconds what had been mere emptiness moments before was now an infinite expanse of rolling white sand dunes under an equally infinite blue sky. There was no sun, no wind, or movement of any kind, and the place was eerily silent except from time to time when grains of the fine sand fell upwards into the sky in little streams, like bubbles rising from a glass of soda water.

"Since the place where we were no longer exists," said the angel as if this was perfectly normal and self-evident, "we have moved to a temporal space, a kind of pocket in the universe, less a location than a holding pattern."

"The sand is falling up," said Jimmy, as if she might not have noticed.

"The usual rules of physics do not apply here," she replied.

"Oh," said Jimmy, nodding if this cleared everything right up. "Okay then."

"This makes no sense," said Xavier.

"Heavens to Murgatroyd!" Gladys exclaimed.

"You said that before," said Jimmy suspiciously.

"So?" replied Gladys. "It's just an expression."

"It is," said Jimmy, "if you're a sixties cartoon character."

"Will you just shut up and listen?" said Gladys. "The books are gone, and the disappearance that you just witnessed is only the end of a time-line. History itself has changed. We saw the moment in which that change reached what you consider to be the *present*," she said. "But the past prior to that moment has also altered. As of this afternoon there is no Shakespeare and there wasn't any yesterday, five years ago, or a hundred years ago. For the present inhabitants of the twenty-first century, the works of Shakespeare never existed."

"But," said Jimmy, still fogged, but using his professorial voice, "I've been teaching them for years."

"About that..." said Rose.

"You were part of a different timeline!" Gladys cut in, to Jimmy's relief. He was, he thought miserably, going to have a little word with Rose, though what that word would be he had no idea: *please*, proba-bly... "The three of you died before that timeline altered!" the angel was saying.

"So history has been altered," Jimmy said. "But shouldn't one set of books just turn into another set? Different books, I mean. Why did the building disappear?"

Gladys squeezed her eyes shut as if fighting a headache, then spoke with pained clarity. "Because the timeline you were in has ceased to exist," she said.

～

Xavier

"Bullshit," said Xavier, leaning forward and fixing the angel with his dark, unblinking gaze, "the disappearance of a few plays leads to...?" He gestured vaguely at the pale emptiness around them.

"Yes," said the angel. Xavier, who was still a little giddy at the sheer madness of their situation, thought she was looking a little less unflappable than she had, and the word made him want to giggle again. "The reality of the space we were in was defined by Shakespeare's historical presence. Remove him from the past and the contingent reality in the present unravels."

"No way," Xavier said. In spite of everything, he was feeling punchy. "When Marty McFly's parents don't get together, he doesn't get born. That makes sense. But people can't read *As You Like It* so Boston turns into a desert?"

"Marty McFly?" asked Gladys.

"*Back to the Future*," Rose supplied. The angel looked bemused, but Xavier waved the point away.

"I'm just saying: a few books disappear and then...this? It doesn't make sense. They're only plays!"

Gladys cut in decisively. "No. They are the single largest cog in the Western cultural machine. Whatever he had become in your era, Shakespeare was once the cornerstone of art, literature, education, religion, and politics. His works influenced the way societies developed. They were woven into the language and culture of the present because they shaped the cultures of the past. They defined the things people thought important, and they became the foundations of things that go far beyond the plays themselves."

"They defined what *some* people thought were important," Xavier cut in.

"Yes," Gladys agreed. "People with money and power and weapons who were currently shaping the world in their own image. But if they didn't have Shakespeare, would the Victorians have had theatre? Would they have developed schools and libraries? To have such things you have to also have something you want to pass on. Shakespeare was central to that impulse. They weren't just plays; they were an index of the way the world shaped itself, the things it valued, and the things it did not. Shakespeare, from a certain standpoint..."

"A white imperialist standpoint," Xavier inserted, but Gladys barely even hesitated.

"...was Britain's greatest export, the demonstration of its cultural superiority, which it beat into its empire for a hundred years and which became the bedrock of English-speaking society. Shakespeare was the principle cog in an engine connecting popular culture to high art and education. Without that cog..."

"The machine breaks?" Jimmy ventured.

"And turns into other things," said Gladys.

"Okay," said Xavier, shrugging and saying what he had been busting to get out since the angel began her Western Civ speech, most of which he was surprised to find he had agreed with, even if it had led him to the opposite conclusion. "Maybe the world will be better off without Shakespeare."

Rose gaped at him, but he gave her the kind of firm "best I can do" look he used when negotiating with hostile clients.

"Well," said Rose, turning pointedly back to Gladys, "leaving *that* aside for a moment, this isn't *something else* that the world has turned into. It's nothing."

"Because the timeline you were in ended," said Gladys. "Other timelines came into being in its place, timelines which have been developing and complicating and dividing for four centuries, all without Shakespeare. There are other Bostons out there, but you can't see them because they are not of your reality."

Rose

"Wait," said Rose, her mind racing. Much as it annoyed her to side with Xavier—whose anti-Shakespeare pronouncement had irritated her—this was all crazy, and even if it was real, it was happening too fast. She had been shopping. She was on her way home with her niece. They were going to play, watch *Peppa Pig*, and have dinner, and then she was going to work on her

Spenser essay. That was real and normal and manageable. It felt real. *This*, whatever *this* was, felt unreal, less like death and more like being dropped into a foreign country where she didn't speak the language and everything was baffling. She wanted to go home. But... "Our city is gone?" she asked.

There was a long silence. Gladys considered her as you might an animal in a zoo: something cute, but perplexing, like a platypus. She seemed to weigh a number of possible answers then said, "We're going to put things back the way they were."

"And then we get our Boston back?" Rose pressed.

"In theory," said Gladys. "I don't see why we wouldn't..."

"Promise," said Rose, staring fixedly at the angel, knowing that her eyes were suddenly brimming with unshed tears, but refusing to blink.

"Well, I can't guarantee anything..." Gladys began.

"Then you get nothing from us," said Rose.

"I'm trying to help you!" said the angel, indignation flashing from her strange, silvery eyes.

"And we'll help you, so long as you promise to get us back," said Rose.

The two men had grown almost respectfully silent and watchful, but their eyes were fixed on the angel and their faces were hard.

The angel sighed heavily.

"Oh, very well," she said. "If you can execute my instructions effectively, I promise—in so far as is possible—to get you your lives back."

"Not good enough," snapped Rose.

"It has to be!" said the angel. "I have power, but I am neither omnipotent nor omniscient."

"That much I'd already figured out," said Rose with a sideways glance at "Tobias." She may have no idea what was going on, but she knew one thing that the angel didn't and that was that their all-important Shakespeare expert wasn't one.

"I will get you back if I can," said the angel with the air of someone making a final offer. "Frankly, you don't have a lot of alternatives."

Rose considered this and nodded once.

∾

Xavier

"So these instructions of yours," said Xavier to the angel. "What are they?"

He had in no way shelved his misgivings about the Greatness of Shakespeare, but Xavier had reasons of his own for getting back. One of them was that he was days away from securing the Sveltzer contract—the culmination of weeks of research, meetings, and presentations—a career boost that would put rather more than a feather in his cap. Another was his father, Albert Greenwell, currently an in-patient at Mass General in the cancer ward. What with the craziness of work lately, Xavier hadn't visited for three days. He had called and his dad had said it was all right, but it wasn't—not really—and though he had managed to convince himself otherwise, Xavier found that his recently changed attitude to his own mortality had affected the way he thought about other people's. He wanted to go home. He wanted to see his dad. He wasn't about to tell anybody that, but he felt that sudden and unexpected longing like an open wound.

"Well," Gladys began, "we have to go back in time. Rather a long way back, actually. For you, I mean."

"How far back is a long way back?" asked Xavier.

"Speaking as one unused to time travel," said Tobias, "last Friday is plenty far back."

"Alas," said Gladys, dry as the desert surrounding them. "That will not suffice. It seems we will have to enter the mid 1590s..."

"No chance," said Tobias. The angel gave him a withering look.

"Look," she said, "if you want the last thing you ever see to have been the chassis of a Boston trolley, that's fine, but if you think the rest of your life might have proved even vaguely rewarding, I suggest you stop whining about a perfectly routine bit of time travel and get on with the task in hand." She gave Tobias a stern look full of teacherly disappointment. "I thought you of all people would jump at the chance! You get to see Renaissance England in the making: the period you have studied all your adult life! You may even meet Shakespeare himself!"

Xavier caught a frown from Rose, the student, who seemed to be fixing Tobias with a critical eye. Did she blame him for their predicament or was it something else?

"I just don't understand..." Tobias began again.

"So you keep saying," said the angel, sharply. "But you don't have to understand to do what I'm telling you. And anyway, it's all perfectly simple. Somebody," said Gladys darkly, "has been buggering about with the late sixteenth century and we have to fix it."

"Somebody?" said Xavier, somehow sure he wouldn't like the angel's clarification. He was right.

"Some*thing*, then," said Gladys. "A devil."

"A devil?" said Xavier, his eyes popping.

"A minor one," Gladys answered. "Up to a spot of mischief, I expect. That's why we can travel in time. There's a balance clause in the rules of temporal engagement. If the forces of darkness alter history, the forces of light are permitted a counter move."

"And if we don't believe in devils?" asked Xavier. "I mean, this is the twenty-first century."

"Really?" said Gladys, glancing around at the infinite expanse of nothing.

"Even so," Xavier persisted, refusing to understand the disturbing nuance of the angel's remark. "All that woo woo crap; I don't buy it."

"But I am an instance to prove the contrary," said Gladys with a long and exasperated sigh.

"So you say," said Xavier.

"Yes," said Gladys, "I do. Now, can we get on?"

"But about this devil...?" Xavier began.

"Look," said the angel. "It's just some misguided sprite tinkering with things he has no business with. No match for me."

"Then why do you need us?" asked Xavier.

"In the name of all that's holy," exclaimed the angel, "must you query everything I say? I need you because you have to put a couple of things back in place. Physical things. Things I can't touch. I'm not allowed... Only humans can alter extant human history. I can get you there, but I'm not permitted to act without human agents, see? I'll take you there, you help me put things back where they're supposed to be, and then I'll bring you back to your oh-so-fulfilling existences. Alright? Easy. The whole thing will take a couple of hours."

"A couple of hours?" Xavier said, head forward and eyes narrow with caution.

"Maximum," said the angel. "In return for which paltry labor, you get your lives back. I really don't see the dilemma."

Well, thought Xavier, *if you put it that way...* He shrugged and the others nodded. "Okay," he said. "I guess."

"Society and culture will be forever in your debt," said Gladys tartly.

~

Gladys

GLADYS HAD HAD ABOUT AS MUCH as she could stand of these bloody humans. She hadn't expected joyous gratitude but still... Actually, she *had* expected joyous gratitude. And why not? She was about to save their miserable lives in return for a little work: interesting work at that. Humans were supposed to love the idea of time travel. She had read that somewhere. And she was handing it to them on a plate! The professor at very least should be ecstatic. But it was, *we don't really want to,* and *what if it doesn't work?* Maddening. Unless that was a ruse and they had other concerns. She had been warned about the duplicity of humans, saying one thing when they were thinking something completely different: *lying,* they called it. Most unangelic. So maybe Tobias' apparent reluctance to go and see his idol at work came from more than fear about the logistics of the trip? Academics spent their careers in learned speculation, weaving pictures of moments from the past that they could not possibly see. Maybe he was afraid he would learn things that would prove his work wrong, all those years spent following the wrong critical path. That made a kind of sense. These humans! So limited in capacity, but so arrogant! Better keep things simple and straightforward so they don't get distracted.

"We have to get a copy of every Shakespeare play the moment they are printed," she said. "Before the opposition can destroy them. We get one of each and ensure its survival. Simple. There are nineteen single play editions printed before the rest appear in the 1623 Folio."

"What's that?" said Rose, her eyes swiveling toward Tobias, as if waiting for him to offer an answer. He didn't, so Gladys did.

"It's kind of a complete works edition. But we'll work our way through to that beginning in 1594."

"1594!" Xavier exclaimed.

"What did you expect?" returned the angel. "We'd save the works of a sixteenth century dramatist by watching Hendrix play at Woodstock?"

"And how do you think London in 1594 will feel about a Black man wandering around in a suit and tie?" asked Xavier.

"We'll adjust your wardrobe when we get there," said Gladys.

"So not my point," said Xavier.

"From 1594 we make a series of hops," said Gladys, determined to maintain the momentum of the conversation. "1597 for *Richard III* and *Romeo and Juliet*, 1598 for *Henry IV part 1* and so on. Till the Folio in 1623 when we can get all the plays that weren't published by themselves earlier."

"But if everything is in the Folio," Tobias said, "why can't we just save that?"

Gladys peered at him and, for the first time, something turned over in what she had in place of a stomach and sent a quiet little rumble of confused alarm to what she had in place of a brain.

"Because the quartos are often different from the versions that appear in the Folio," she explained pointedly. "As you know."

"Right," said Tobias sagely. "The quartings. Exactly."

"*Quartos*," said Gladys, considering the professor uncertainly. "The first printings are single volume texts called quartos. Yes? I thought this was elementary stuff for a scholar of your standing..."

"Absolutely," huffed Tobias. "Elementary. Quite so, my dear, er... Watson. Go on."

"We are trying to restore what you know as the present. That means the past must be preserved as perfectly as possible with all the variant texts preserved. Right?"

"Obviously," said Tobias, with an odd sort of bluster. Gladys was aware that Rose had fixed the professor with a penetrating stare, but she wasn't about to stop now. "Best case scenario, we save all the plays in every form in which the enemy might seek to destroy them."

"And worst case?" said Rose.

"Well, many of the plays exist in multiple early quartos. It might be all right if we aren't able to get every variant within the time allowed."

"Might be?" said Xavier.

"I can't see the future till it happens," said Gladys. "I can't be sure what will happen if we deviate from the past you know. Will the future change if we can't get the 3rd quarto of *Henry V*? Yes, there will absolutely be ripples in the academic world. Will it change contemporary Boston? No. Or at least, I don't *think* so. Not as much as losing the play entirely, certainly."

"That doesn't sound good," said Rose.

"The good news is that to be successful the opposition has to destroy everything, every version of every text *and* they don't know we're following. So as long as we make our jumps a fraction earlier than theirs, we should be able to get one copy of each play before they torch the rest. You give them to me and when the coast is clear, I put them back."

"I thought you couldn't alter history?" said Rose.

"I can't alter *extant* history but, according to the rather confusing terms of universal metaphysical law, I can restore something that was formerly part of the timeline. The snag is that in order to have the plays so that I can put them back, I first have to remove them, which is not allowed."

"Which is where we come in," said Rose.

"My head hurts," said Tobias.

"Doesn't sound too tricky," Xavier conceded.

"Finally," Gladys said, ignoring Tobias. "But there are rules. Missions involving time travel must take less than twenty-four hours."

She checked her watch.

"The incursion into the past by the opposition took place sixteen minutes ago," she went on. "If the twenty-four hours run out before we have restored the works of Shakespeare to the world, then you stay dead, and the present as you knew it ceases to be. Clear?"

In many respects, of course, she knew they weren't. But their experiences of the last hour or so had clearly rendered them largely incapable of rational thought, or at least had left them with the conviction that rational thought was of absolutely no use to them today. They exchanged anxious glances and nodded, convincing nobody.

Gladys, pretending this was a real decision, made a casual, flicking gesture, and a shimmering rectangle of light appeared like a door before them.

"I'm told that humans can find the journey a little unnerving," she said nonchalantly. "But the sooner we start, the sooner we'll be done."

They regarded the shimmering door with excitement and trepidation.

"Cool," said Xavier, apparently in spite of himself.

"Should we hold hands?" asked Tobias.

"If you wish," said the angel, smiling.

"Will it help?" Rose asked.

"Not in the least," said the angel.

"I'll pass," said Xavier.

Rose dropped her hands to her side and Tobias, finding himself with no-one to hold hands with, fidgeted for a moment, then "Shouldn't we prepare ourselves mentally somehow?"

"How?" asked the angel.

"I don't know, I've never done this before."

"Exactly," said Gladys, "so why don't you leave the mechanics to someone who has and see if you can be quiet for a moment."

"I was only trying..." Tobias began.

"Don't," said Gladys quickly, "unless you want to try and find your way back from bronze age Sumeria."

"Where's that?" asked Rose.

"*When* is that, more like," Tobias corrected.

"Will you give it a rest," Xavier muttered, "and let the woman, or whatever the hell she is, do her thing."

"Thank you," sighed the angel. "Now, as I said, brace yourselves. After you."

And they stepped through.

FOR A MOMENT the three humans all saw the sky over Boston, felt the trolley tracks against their skin, and the memory of pain caught them like a splash of frigid water. Then they were each careening back along the tracks of their own histories, friends, family, familiar streets, classrooms, ceremonies, and the flotsam and jetsam of their lives bundled into a millisecond swirl of images, sounds, and evocative scents that brought them to the edge of memory and then bore them past and back, further and further. Rose stared at her niece's tiny hands. Xavier smelled the burgers and ribs on the old smoker his father used to work. Jimmy saw the face of the woman who had almost been patient enough to stay with him in spite of everything...

Back they fell, through a gallery of forgotten faces and dead relatives, through school and childhood when the world seemed so much larger and full of promise. Then further still, dwindling, through soundless images of mothers' hands and moments clutching ice-cream and presents, then on through the dwindling albums of their lives, till like the picture that contracts into nothing on an old television, there was void, emptiness, and a dizzying, nauseating plunge through a time of which they had no memories to give it form.

It was a sickening moment that felt like hours, but the three mortals were too caught up with the surge of emotion to feel the extent of the nothingness. They felt not so much small as forgotten, ignored and insignificant, the history in which they had not been somehow passing comment on the irrelevance of the lives they had left. When they were able to open their eyes again, they each turned away to wipe the tears with which this curiously intense personal retrospective had left them: not sorrow or joy, but everything they had ever felt made stabbingly poignant by the sense of its having passed and been forgotten.

"There now," said Gladys when it was all over. "Not so bad, was it?"

ACT TWO

"Ay, now am I in Arden; the more fool I."
(*As You Like It*)

ACT TWO, SCENE ONE

"Now, by my life, this day grows wondrous hot.
Some airy devil hovers in the sky
And pours down mischief."
(*King John*, 3.2.1-3)

London, 1594.

Belial

Belial watched as Robert Bliss wiped the clotted mud from his face, his blank, soulless eyes lit by the firelight. The human smiled knowingly, and—wreathed in smoke and surrounded by tortured screams, as he was—Belial might have taken him for a minor managerial functionary in Hell itself.

But they weren't in Hell. They were at a public execution in Renaissance London, feeding pages from *Henry the Sixth part II* into the small fire, which the executioner, glad of the unpaid assistance, had lit in a handy metal brazier. Behind him, inside a ring of engaged on-lookers, a man who had been almost hanged to death was being cut down. You might be forgiven for thinking that this would have been a good thing, but a glance at the knives and poker thingies that the executioner was arranging like a punctilious hostess laying elaborate table settings for dinner would have told you otherwise. The half-dead victim did not need to be told and screamed with all the breath he still had in his body.

"You've got to admire the purity of it," said Bliss to Belial at his shoulder. "We pretend we're so much more evolved where I come from, but good God, if they could live stream stuff like this, the cable companies would make a god-damned fortune!"

"Must you use those terms all the time?" said Belial irritably.

"What terms?" asked Bliss, feeding the fire with another play quarto.

"God. Hell. God-damned."

"Why should you care?" shrugged Bliss. "I'd no idea the devil was so squeamish."

"It's a matter of invoking things of which you know nothing and with which you have no business."

"Whatever," said Bliss, invoking his favorite word instead. "I've brought the cheesy plays. Can we get *Macbeth* now?"

"Let me see what you have."

Belial could feel Bliss' eyes on him as he perused the papers. He had taken on a more conventional form than the one in which he had introduced himself to Edward Alleyn, causing the audience of the Rose Theatre to run for their lives. Then he had been a monster; now he was just a pale, slim man in his fifties, his hair dark but silvered throughout, tall and austere looking. Only a hollowed quality about his face, an almost unnatural thinness in his features and a cold, ancient sparkle to his black eyes hinted at what Bliss alone in the entire London population knew: that he was captain of the hosts of Satan who rose against the throne of God, and who fell with Moloch, Chemos, Baal, Astoreth, Thammuz, Dagon, and Rimmon, and now, eternally damned with Lucifer, conspired with Beelzebub and Mephistopheles to wreak ruin upon the world. Bliss had said he thought that was pretty cool.

"So this is our work for the afternoon?" Belial said. "*Henry the Sixth part Two*? Not exactly a massive blow to culture, is it? There are about half a dozen twenty first-century academics who will be very slightly peeved. And where are the rest of the plays? This isn't even the full printing. They must have sold a dozen. If *one* of those survives, we've wasted our time."

"We?" said Bliss. "You have done what our English friends and neighbors would call sod all."

"I brought you here, as you desired," said Belial, "and I think you ought to remember who you are addressing before you take that tone."

"Yeah, yeah," sighed Bliss.

The crowd cheered as the executioner held up a knife featuring little curves and spiky bits designed to make life just that bit less pleasant. Bliss grinned appreciatively. He liked a man who took pride in his work.

"You have no business sense," Bliss continued. "If you're the guy who sold me every copy of Henry the goddamned sixth, what do you do the moment I leave your shop?"

"I don't know," Belial shrugged. "Close up early and go to spend my unexpected profits on beer and women?"

"No," said Bliss. "You put in a call—or whatever the hell they do here—to your supplier to get another stack. If you can sell a hundred in half an hour, then the market has an appetite for more. So the printer is going to run off another couple of hundred copies, which I don't have."

Belial blinked.

"I don't think it works that way," he said unconvincingly. "I know where each play was printed and put on sale. We go to those places and buy up every copy in recorded history."

"But history is changing, isn't it? We are changing it. There are going to be more copies of this damned play in circulation by the middle of next week, but we'll have moved on, so we'll miss them."

Belial considered this uneasily. It seemed plausible, and that was going to make their job a lot harder.

"So what are you suggesting?" he asked.

"Well, I rather thought that was your department, but from a business standpoint it seems pretty clear: we have to stop making the printing of the plays profitable."

"And how would we do that?'

"Burn them?" suggested Bliss. "I don't mean buy them from the shops and then burn them. I mean burn the shops before anyone buys anything. Cut out the middleman."

"And be responsible for starting the Great Fire of London almost a century early?" said Belial. "I don't think so."

"Okay," said Bliss, ever the negotiator. "Well, we could start by simply not *paying* for them."

"Stealing, you mean?" said Belial, looking uncomfortable.

"Yes, devil. Stealing. Is that a problem for you?"

"Well," said Belial, glancing away as if it didn't really matter one way or the other, "I'd like to keep a low profile. Don't want to attract too much attention, do we?"

"I think buying all this crap is more likely to get us noticed than taking it while no one is looking," said Bliss.

Belial made an uncertain face as if weighing both sides of the argument.

"Tell me again who you are," said Bliss, watching him closely.

"What? You know who I am."

"I thought I did. I thought I'd allied with one of the universe's major mystical powers, a demon with a long history of mighty and terrible deeds to his credit, an entity of such horrible corruption that he wouldn't be seriously challenged by a crime not significantly different from a twelve-year-old snagging candy from the Pick 'n' Mix while the attendant is looking the other way."

"Right," said Belial, sheepish. "Of course. I'll get right on it."

"See that you do. How long before *Titus Andronicus* goes on the market?" Bliss remarked bitterly, "because that *really* sounds like the basis of a well-rounded liberal arts education." He had never read this particular play, but Belial's synopsis of the plot, with its rape and muti-lation and, (it seemed hard to believe), *children served to their mother baked in pies*, had left him vaguely outraged. "Children baked in pies. Very enlightening. No wonder the world is coming apart at the seams."

Belial gave him a considering look. He was having a harder time than expected pigeonholing Bliss' particular brand of evil. The devil was used to those who wanted wealth, power, and carnal pleasure in exchange for their souls. Bliss was different. His quest was almost ideological. Given that it would cost him an eternity in Hell, it was hard not to see something peculiarly selfless, even slightly admirable in that. Lunatic and wrong-headed, of course, but not entirely wicked, and nothing like the curious squirming prickle Belial had been sensing like an alarm on the edge of hearing ever since they had arrived. He felt its presence like something he should know but didn't. Something bad. Something demonic that wasn't either of them.

It was troubling.

"Well?" said Bliss. "*Titus Andronicus?*"

"Right," Belial replied, coming back to the moment with a start. "It will be delivered to the printer's in less than an hour."

"I hate this one-play-at-a-time, crap," Bliss remarked. "Why can't these imbeciles just print ONE book?"

"A Norton Anthology perhaps?" Belial suggested with the faintest quiver of a smile. "A Riverside edition, perhaps?"

"Don't be smart," Bliss warned. "I have Beelzebub on speed dial."

Belial shrugged as if he didn't care one way or the other whether Bliss went over (or is that under?) his head. That was a lie, of course, albeit a tacit one, and not just for the obvious reasons (Beelzebub being quite surprisingly unpleasant even to those on his own side). The prospect of Bliss checking in with Belial's superiors (inferiors, if you prefer), was the thing which most terrified Belial, and—given the things Belial had seen over the centuries—that was going some.

It was, of course, essential that the Chair of the Northside College Board of Regents did not recognize the devil's anxiety for what it was. Belial identified the part of his mind that had been hissing at him that this entire operation was a colossal error that could—at any moment—drop him up to his neck in hot pitch, wrestled it into a box, and sat on it. Even confined and ignored, however, the voice would not be silenced and seemed to resonate through whatever Belial had in place of blood, a constant whisper like the whine of a mosquito that wouldn't leave you alone, and though it spoke at the level of instinct, it said in no uncertain terms, *This is a Bad Idea.*

But then came the sound of an axe hewing flesh and bone, and Belial and Bliss found their thoughts derailed by the ongoing activities of the executioner. A fountain of blood splashed across the platform.

"And get me a helper," said Bliss, as if inspired by the horrid spectacle.

"What?"

"I can't be the only one who's done a deal with you and your Satanic buddies. Get someone to help me gather these damn plays together so I don't have to waste half my life here."

"I'll think about it," said Belial.

"Don't think, do," said Bliss. "That's my motto."

"Yes," said Belial. "It would be."

"And I want some real money," he snapped. "If whatever I pay out turns into wildlife, you can bet your ass the residents of this old timey hole in the ground will demonstrate their sophistication and broad-mindedness by burning me as a witch."

"Hanging," said Belial, watching the flames of the brazier as if wishing he were home. "If we were in Paris, they'd burn you. In London, they'll hang you."

"*Europe*," spat Bliss. "What a god-damn loser country."

ACT TWO, SCENE TWO

"What country, friends, is this?"
(*Twelfth Night*, 1.2.1)

July 16, 1594. Time remaining: 23 hours 41 minutes.
Plays to be saved: 19+*Folio*.

Gladys

Gladys closed the temporal door behind them and began talking before the mortals had begun to take in their surroundings.

"It's a curious sensation, is it not?" she remarked. The others didn't answer. "Probably even more so for you..."

She was going to say "mortals," but that seemed tactless, so she just let the sentence trail off into the air as she watched them wrestle with the people they had once been and all the hopes and expectations they had subsequently sloughed off like dead skin. The young man called Xavier was pulling at the starched collar of his shirt like a man who regretted every decision he had ever made. The young woman's face was hollowed out like a spent quarry, bereft of whatever had once made it valuable, and their Shakespeare expert looked merely stunned and stupid.

The business ahead might only take a half hour, but it was going to feel a lot longer. Watching them, the angel frowned to herself, caught between contemptuous resentment and something else she couldn't place: jealousy? That made no sense. She was an immortal, a creature of spirit for whom time meant nothing. She could sympathize with their limitations, as one might feel for the goldfish endlessly circling the same crudely molded plastic castle in a tiny bowl, but empathy wasn't identification. No one wanted to be a goldfish... She shook her head as if to clear it. They needed to get on.

Great Things were afoot. She wasn't exactly sure what they were, so the sense that she was at their heart was as disconcerting as it was exciting, but the humans didn't need to know that.

Keep things simple, she had told herself. That was how to keep them on track. And it made it less likely that she would have to face some potentially very awkward questions. That was very important. Keep things simple, small, and quiet enough, and maybe no one would notice... Something began to wriggle in the back of her mind, so she began to talk to drown it out.

"We shall have to make sure that the three of you are suitably attired," she said. "That should be our first priority. It's very important that you blend in. Now..."

The others were clearly not listening. They were gazing intently at something no living soul had seen for over four hundred years. They stood on a hillock on the South Bank of the Thames, which was teeming with boats of various sizes. To their right, London Bridge (at this distance, it looked more like a street lined with buildings) spanned the river to a sprawling mass of docks and shanties with steeply pitched roofs and chimneys smoking, the skyline occasionally broken by spires and the starkly imposing tower of St. Paul's Church, which reared up over the western part of the old walled city. But there were also trees, distant fields, and—in this comparatively unravaged landscape and less obviously warming climate—more birds than they had ever seen. It looked like a movie set or a theme park, but was, quite obviously, neither. For one thing, it was the kind of thing movies could only afford to do with models and computer graphics, and for another, it was too disorganized, sprawling, and dirty for a theme park, though there *were* lots of people wearing silly clothes and the food was appropriately terrible.

It also stank more than words could wield the matter. The place was a miasma of the foulest, most noxious aromas, particularly this close to the river, into which every gutter ran, every sewer poured, not to mention the accumulated piles of filth that threatened to block every street. Since the stench of corruption was, of course, also the stench of human bodies and their inconvenient mechanical processes, you might say that it was the stink of mortality.

But it wasn't just that. Under the smell, coiled inside it like a snake in the entrails of a mangled antelope, was...something else. It wasn't an aroma exactly, though it tasted like one. It was almost like fetid smoke, something rotten and burning that made you look around for the world's most loathsome barbecue, but though Gladys could feel it in an unspecific way, it was neither scent nor sight. She couldn't say how she detected it, but it was there and it was bad.

Very. Her angelic essence rebelled against the very possibility of it.

Gladys shuddered, then checked quickly to make sure the others hadn't noticed. The only way they were going to get through this was if they thought she was in control, that she knew what she was doing and wasn't terrified out of her mind. She pushed what she had tagged *The Sensation* out of her mind as best she could.

"What the hell is that?" said Xavier, a hand over his nose.

Gladys shot him a panicked look, then decided he was talking about the stink, not *The Sensation* beneath it.

"London," said Gladys, "obviously. 1594, if that helps. Does it smell? That's people for you."

Tobias turned to suppress a retch, but his eyes fell on the many-sided thatched structure at his back and he stared.

"Shakespeare's Globe!" he announced.

"No," said the angel, frowning at another dropped pass from her Shakespeare expert. This was not promising. "That's the Rose where Philip Henslowe has just begun managing the Lord Admiral's Men and where the demonic incursion occurred. Since it happened here, all our temporal jumps will bring us to this place. Over time the landscape will change and the Rose itself will disappear, but this will remain the point to which we will move each new year."

"We have to come back here every time we want to move to another time?" asked Xavier, his nose wrinkled.

"No," said Gladys. "We can jump *from* anywhere. But the jump will always bring us to this spot, regardless of the year."

Whether it was the prospect of returning to this spot over and over, or something else entirely, Gladys felt that foggy, nameless something uncoil a little in her head, and had to push it back down. It gave a reptilian hiss and squirmed. It was stronger than she had expected; even this early in their mission it was going to take most of her strength just to ignore it. And it would get worse, stronger...

"What if someone builds something here?" said Rose. "Like a house. Would we land inside it or, I don't know, on the roof or something?"

"On the *roof*?" muttered Gladys, as if this was the single stupidest remark anyone had ever made. "No, we won't *land* on the roof. We will *materialize* on this spot, and if that is in someone's living room in that particular period, so be it."

"But what if someone builds a dungeon here," Tobias persisted. "Or a...stadium where they fought animals? They had those back in the day. We could just, you know, materialize in front of a lion or something."

"It's not ancient Rome," Rose snapped.

"Well, the English equivalent," said Tobias, on his dignity.

"Oh, for crying out loud," muttered Gladys. "If you mean *bear-baiting rings*, they did indeed have them *back in the day*, but no one will build one here, alright? I've checked and this point will be totally bear-free for the next thirty years, which is all we need. Now, can we get on?"

"Yes," said Tobias sheepishly. "Right. Sorry."

"Fine," said Gladys. "Since we're covering logistics, I may as well tell you about the second twenty-four-hour rule. The first, which you already know, constrains all time travelling missions to a period of one day, hence this." She held up her gold watch. "The second says that we can only make one temporal incursion into any given day. So if we miss a text, we can't go back for it."

"And if we do miss one?" said Rose. "Do we have to save all... How many are there?"

"Depends how you count," said Gladys, glad of the kind of intellectual rummaging that meant she wouldn't have to actually think about *The Sensation*. "You get different numbers depending on whether you consider plays only partly written by Shakespeare, plays attributed to him but not actually by him, plays he was involved in but wasn't credited for, apocrypha, plays only recently assigned to him through stylometric analysis..."

"How many?" Xavier interrupted.

"Forty," said Gladys. "Give or take. Of course some exist in multiple variants..."

"Forty," said Xavier. "Okay. Let's get going."

"And we need all forty?" said Tobias. "We can't just get, like, twenty good ones?"

Gladys' faith in the Shakespearean took another hit.

"Some plays are more important than others," she acknowledged, "but it is the cumulative weight of Shakespeare's works that shapes culture. The only safe route is to get them all. If we can't save *Timon of Athens*, so be it."

"Never heard of it," said Rose.

"Which was, I believe, my point," said Gladys dryly. "Anything less than the entire Shakespeare canon will cause ripples through the timeline. What effect they will have you won't know till you go back home. Assuming it's still there."

"Forty then," said Xavier pointedly. "How do we start?"

"First we orient ourselves," said Gladys. "Over there and, Tobias will be pleased to note, at a remarkably safe distance, is the bear-baiting ring. Farther along the river bank the Swan will be built next year. Shakespeare's Globe," she continued with a censorious glance at Tobias who clearly didn't know any of this, "won't be built for another five years. Richard Burbage and the Chamberlain's Men are still at The Theatre, northeast of the city and with them is Shakespeare. I assumed you would already know all this," she added, still eying Tobias. "I hope you aren't going to let me down here."

The professor looked shamefaced but then drew himself up.

"Just getting the lie of the land," he said vaguely. "You can count on me."

"How?" said Rose sharply.

"For, you know, helping out," said Tobias. He looked oddly panicked. "Drawing on my expertise."

"In what?" Rose said.

"Now, now," Gladys said, pouring oil on troubled waters. "There's no reason to be rude. I'm sure Professor Lestering's insight will be of profound assistance as we..."

"He's not Professor Lestering," said Rose.

Gladys opened her mouth to contradict this, but it was if she had rolled over and found that the dull pain in her side that she had barely acknowledged but had been there all night was caused by a little plastic soldier left in her bed by her eight-year-old. Not that she had either. The point is that what she had been ignoring suddenly sharpened and became clear. Instantly she could sense "Tobias'" panic like she could sense the other, deeper wrongness about the place they were in, and it infected her immediately.

"Oh my God," she said, staring at him, aghast at the scale of her blunder and how long it had taken her to notice it. "You're not him, are you?"

The skinny man hung his head. "Not as such," he said.

"*Not as such?*" Gladys echoed.

"No," said the man who wasn't a professor.

"Tobias Lestering is my professor," said Rose.

"But that's the name in his book!" said Xavier. "I saw it when I returned it to him."

"Yeah, about that..." the other man began, and his voice had lost its learned hauteur and now matched his habitual slouch. "Not exactly my book. I sort of borrowed it. Not just that. There was some other stuff too."

"Like a wallet," said Xavier.

"Tobias" gave him a wan smile and a shrug. "Whatya gonna do, eh?" he said, as if stealing other people's things—clearly what he had done—was an accident that could befall anybody.

"So he's not the Shakespeare expert you thought you were getting," said Rose to Gladys, as if she had been considering this speech for some time. "And putting aside for a moment *how* you didn't know he wasn't who he said he was, just how badly screwed are we?"

Gladys gaped, first at the non professor, then at Xavier who was staring accusingly, and lastly at Rose.

The answer, Gladys suspected, was along the lines of "Majorly: we are *Majorly* screwed," but she didn't say that. Best not sew panic in the ranks.

"Well first," she said, stalling, "if you aren't Professor Tobias Lestering..."

"He's not," inserted Rose.

"Thank you, yes," said Gladys, fists balled. "If you aren't, then who are you?"

"Jimmy O'Rourke," said the man, seeming relieved to get the truth out there. "Some call me Jimmy Fingers."

"Of course they do," said Xavier miserably.

"Fingers?" said Gladys.

"Because he's a thief," Xavier explained.

"Easy!" said Jimmy.

"Are you a thief?" Xavier shot back.

"Yeah but..."

"Okay then," Xavier concluded before rounding on Gladys. "And you didn't know? He said he was a professor and that was good enough for you?"

"Not used to being lied to," Gladys muttered.

"I didn't lie to you, lady," said Jimmy. "I lied to *him*."

"And I was listening," Gladys replied. "I assumed you were speaking the truth."

"And this is Heaven's background check, is it?" said Rose. "Angels listening? Awesome. I, by the way, am a sort of feminist Mother Theresa and have spent my life doing good."

"Not how it works," said Gladys. "Not for End of Life Sorting. But that's not my department."

"We are so screwed," said Rose.

"Tomorrow and tomorrow and tomorrow," said Gladys. "He said it."

"That's a watertight means of identification," Xavier mocked. "If I'd been whistling a few bars from 'I Knew You Were Trouble,' would you have taken me for Taylor Swift?"

"Who?" said Gladys.

"Oh yeah," said Xavier. "We are in good hands."

"I don't think her ignorance of twenty-first century pop is necessarily a bad thing," said Rose.

"I think it's a positive asset," said the thief formally known as Tobias with a half grin. "I'm a Pogues fan, myself."

"And I grew up, much to my father's dismay, on Public Enemy," snapped Xavier, "but that so wasn't my point. I was saying that our angelic guide here is not exactly on top of things and I think we should take a moment..."

"To do what?" Gladys snapped. "To reconsider the plan you just committed to? Fine. Don't help. Bleed out on the tracks of the Boston mass transit system. See if I care."

"There really is no other option?" asked Jimmy.

"No!" said the angel in the tones of one answering whether the Taj Mahal might have been built by a team of ferrets. "You two happened to be thinking about Shakespeare when you died, which was what I needed. I thought it would ensure I had a suitable agent," she added miserably.

"Tomorrow and tomorrow and tomorrow," said Jimmy miserably.

"Quite," said Gladys.

"Ironic," said Rose sadly. "Since all we have now is yesterdays."

There was a pithy sort of pause, which made Gladys uncomfortable for reasons she didn't completely understand.

"Right," she said. "We need suitable attire."

"Must we?" said Xavier.

"Need to blend in," said Gladys. "Unless you want Rose arrested for prostitution."

"Excuse me?" said Rose.

"Your jeans," said Gladys. "Looks like you're wearing men's clothes."

"And that makes me...?" said Rose with bitter disbelief.

"It might," said Gladys, who always felt a little at sea when it came to the way humans built strict codes of conduct around the negligible differences between their appearances.

"Can't you just, you know," Jimmy said, fumbling for the right words, "*magic* us into the right clothes?"

"Magic?" said Gladys, midway between amazement and indignation.

"Yeah," said Xavier. "You being an angel and all."

"You think I'm some sort of side show act?" said Gladys.

"We should pitch a tent and charge admission," said Rose bleakly. "Magic tricks and a cross-dressing hooker. We'd clean up."

"So, these clothes," Xavier persisted, "where are they?"

"In a store of some sort, I imagine," said Gladys.

"You didn't bring any?" asked Jimmy.

"What?" replied the angel, instantly revising the question to "How? Where?"

At that moment the first actual Elizabethans they had seen so far, a couple in their thirties, rounded a bend in the road. They were suitably dressed for the period, which meant that the woman resembled an ornate cone travelling on castors, while the man, in hose and a cape, might have been the world's crappiest superhero. Both sported wide, stiff ruffs, which made it look like their heads were being served on plates. They stopped, staring fixedly at the visitors with expressions of horror and distaste.

"It's not me," said Gladys a trifle defensively. "They can't see me."

She felt it again, a deep sense of demonic wrongness, a vile and pointed impulse to hatred and destruction so strong she could almost smell its fulness. Gladys looked around wildly. The couple crossed the street, the woman gazing open mouthed over her shoulder at them while her husband, his hand on the fancy-looking rapier he wore at his waist, guided her hastily away. They were staring at Xavier.

"Keep hence, foul blackamore," warned the man.

"*Excuse* me?" said Xavier. "Did he say what I think he said?"

He took a step toward the couple, and the man's sword came out. It was long and bright and though it was certainly fancy—a gilded ornament covered in whimsical metal work and semiprecious stones—it was also a yard of sharpened steel designed, first and foremost, for killing people. Wisely, Xavier hesitated. In the same moment a group of boys kicking a ball came round the corner then stuttered to a pointing, jeering halt.

Now I am sure that some of those reading this book have been on the receiving end of this kind of petty nastiness and are aware that while a mean-spirited remark can be painful, it can also escalate into serious danger, so I'm going to interrupt this moment to assure you that, grim though this looks, Xavier will survive the encounter unscathed. Gladys, on the other hand...

And we're back.

"Oh, this is great," said Xavier, considering the malevolent and swelling crowd.

"Be gone, Barbary fiend!" warned the man, his sword point aimed at Xavier's chest.

"Ironic," Gladys remarked.

"That we've come to fight the devil," said Xavier, "and they think *I'm* the devil, or that you rescued us from death so that we could be butchered in a different century?"

"Either way, really," Gladys admitted.

Xavier had raised his hands and started to back off, but one of the boys picked up a stone and flung it at them. It hit Gladys, bouncing off her forehead, so that she yelped with pain.

Pain.

Angels don't feel pain. This is not because they are immured to it through centuries of mental discipline or a numbness to the various horrors mankind has visited upon itself in the course of human history. It is because they literally don't feel, can't feel, for the same reasons that Gladys was immune to the wall of stench that currently surrounded them: her body was essentially an illusion, a costume not unlike the preposterous ruffs worn by the racist Londoners currently glowering at them. She was, as has already been established, a being of air and spirit. She had no body. She did not smell (in either sense), did not taste (likewise), and absolutely did not feel pain.

So something was badly off kilter. She knew it as surely as she had recognized that other subtle wrongness about this place that had insisted itself upon her consciousness the moment they had entered the period. This was far more than some minor demon messing about with literary history. Something darker and more far reaching was at work, which meant that Gladys, a pain-feeling and therefore at least possibly mortal Gladys, was in far more trouble than she had dared to imagine. In other circumstances, the sheer scale of the disaster would have rooted her to the spot, but pain has a way of bypassing the mind and putting the all-too-physical body in charge, so, instead, she ran like hell.

ACT TWO, SCENE THREE

"The spirit that I have seen
May be a devil; and the devil hath power
T' assume a pleasing shape; yea, and perhaps
Out of my weakness and my melancholy,
As he is very potent with such spirits,
Abuses me to damn me."
(Hamlet 2.2.559-65)

London, 1594.

Shakespeare

The writer watched the actors' performance critically, though his gaze strayed as much to the house as it did to the stage. He listened for the gasps, the muttered agreements from the audience, the laughter, the spontaneous applause, and the tears. Those last were rarest, but worth the most. He watched when they fidgeted, talked among themselves, or decided to get a beer. It was like watching the surface of a pond on a windy day, ripples building to waves, subsiding, switching direction. By the end of the show, he had a kind of map of the play in his head, the cliffs and waterfalls, the blank and empty plains, the glorious vistas and the sucking marshes. In his mind he saw what the play could be, what it almost was. He had work to do before the next showing.

He collected the parts from the actors, warning those who should expect to see their roles swell or shrink in the next draft, both sets grumbling and rolling their eyes. Then he looked over the costumes to see what needed cleaning or mending—sets of lord's clothes (handed down from their patron's family and lovingly maintained) represented a significant percentage of the company's assets—and promised that the company would have their revised parts in no more than three days. He said it confidently, giving nothing away.

But the writer was afraid, and not just that he wouldn't meet his self-imposed deadline. Something had changed of late.

The words had always come to him easily. Too easily, some said. They flowed through him onto the page so fast that sometimes he was barely aware of thinking them before they appeared in ink, as if the talent was in his fingers, not his brain. Sometimes the actors—and other writers—said he should slow down, revise for clarity and brevity. He was too digressive, they said. Too easily taken on flights of fancy. They were probably right, but this was the only way he knew how to do it. It wasn't that he didn't think, didn't revise; he did. Extensively. But in that first blush of creation when the story was feeling its way into being, when the characters were telling him what they wanted and how they were going to get it, he wrote blindly, thoughtlessly, as if he were merely a vessel pouring the plays out like bright, clear water, or he was opening a cage and releasing something that was already alive into the wild. He wrote, his friends said, like a man possessed.

That used to make him laugh. Not anymore. Now he feared it was true.

He could feel the wrongness squirming like a sea creature in his mind, pulsing and writhing, a creature that spat and vomited the words he wrote. Words of power, for sure. But also words of malice, hatred, and destruction.

The writer kept his head down as he walked back to the garret where he wrote and slept, avoiding the eyes of passersby in case they saw something in him, something dreadful and dangerous, the same something, he feared, that made him Shakespeare.

ACT TWO, SCENE FOUR

"You shall find her the infernal Ate in good apparel. I would
to God some scholar would conjure her, for certainly, while she
is here, a man may live as quiet in hell as in a sanctuary, and
people sin on purpose because they would go thither; so indeed
all disquiet, horror and perturbation follows her."
(*Much Ado About Nothing*, 2.1.244-49)

New York, 2:30 this afternoon.

Cathy

T he audience applauded on cue, and the cameras homed in on
the tailored pink suit, bobbed blond hair, cloudless blue eyes,
and perfect teeth of Cathy Cornwall, bestselling author of
Being OK with You, and daytime TV's number one talk show host. She
checked the position of the microphone cable and, when she looked up,
flashed those teeth in a smile so broad, so genuine, that it broadcast
openness and generosity to each and every member of her audience, the
two hundred in the studio and the millions watching from home.

"Welcome back. Have you ever felt so hurt, so injured by someone,
that you wanted to strike out at them? Do you ever get so mad you can

barely think straight? Do you find that you have fallen out with people you used to love and don't remember why? Do you find yourself paralyzed by anger in ways that make you lose respect even for yourself? Today we are talking with some folks who feel rage, even hatred, toward people they once called friends; we are going to see if we can get everyone to talk, to put aside their differences and come back together. In the process they can learn to love themselves, which is, as we all know, the greatest love of all."

She paused, ending with another radiant smile and a knowing look to the camera so full of benevolence and wisdom that the audience broke into spontaneous applause.

"The first lady we are going to introduce to you is Francesca. Two years ago, Francesca was evicted by her landlord, Stan, when she couldn't pay the rent, which he had recently raised, forcing her onto the streets with her infant son. Francesca spoke about her experience at a town hall meeting, which is where we found her. What her words showed then was a person consumed with hatred and self-loathing, a person whose self-esteem was so low that she couldn't say anything without bitterness and resentment. Today that is going to change."

It was a textbook Cathy Cornwall show, containing all the ingredients necessary to fit the program's formula: shock, the spectacle of angry, hopefully violent exchange and, through the relentless badgering of the show's host, a tearfully joyous conclusion. It would end with hugs and the recitation of the show's moral agenda by each of the guests, first individually and then all together with the audience cheering them on: "I'm good." This final refrain would be chanted ecstatically as the theme music and closing credits rolled in.

Today the show was on eviction, but yesterday it had centered on high school kids outraged by the low grades teachers had given them, and had concluded with the teachers' vow to give A's to all as an affirmation of their own special talents regardless of what they had formerly considered "errors" in matters of math, spelling, the actual location of Mexico, and so on. Tomorrow it might be one of those "hard" subjects like sexism or racism, pitting carefully selected and malleable opponents against each other, only to reconcile them in a shower of glib poppsych that left the audience thinking that all the great problems of human society could be solved by Cathy Cornwall's magic wand smile.

In each case there was no overt political agenda, unless the refusal to have a political agenda can itself be called political. Rather, the goals of the show were a happy acceptance of all people regardless of their beliefs or actions and a rejection of the idea that an individual was in any way responsible for anything bad that ever happened to them or, for that matter, anyone else. It assumed that all the little horrors of twenty-first-century life could be fixed with a smile, a hug, and the absolute conviction that life got a lot easier if you were able to believe that you were never wrong and that other people's wrongness (or stupidity, or hate) was best ignored.

All opinions were equally valid. All beliefs were mere matters of perspective. All destructive or selfish acts were people being true to their needs. If they bothered you, you should seek your own happiness elsewhere. Someone evicted you to maximize his profits? Walk it off. Someone thinks you shouldn't be allowed to eat at the same diner counter because your skin is the wrong color or you sleep with the wrong people? Breathe in the joy of the universe. Beaten down by economic oppression, institutional racism, gerrymandered electoral districts, corrupt lobbyists, inequality of all kinds, educational inadequacy, the astonishing power of the very, very rich? Find your happy place. Go there and curl up with your warm, comforting thoughts about how valuable and important you are while the world outside burns.

It's all good, said Cathy.

Though the show went under her name, it was almost as commonly referred to as The Self-Esteem Show, and Cornwall was so pleased with the title that it was only her own self-esteem that had prevented her from renaming the show accordingly.

Her rise to fame had been meteoric. Only three years ago she had been largely unknown, an "expert" on the psychology of personal relationships who showed up periodically on breakfast shows around the country, hosting radio chat sessions and promoting her books: *Don't Let Them Tell You You're Bad,* and its outrageously popular sequel, *Don't Let them Tell You You Failed.* The way suitably (and plausibly) paved, she hit stardom with the colossal bestseller *Being OK with You,* which had stormed the bestseller lists two years ago and had loitered in its upper reaches feeling good about itself ever since. Some publishers had found the success of these later books difficult to account for since they were basically the same as their predecessors, which were, in turn, watered down, anecdotal versions of things the feel-good pop-psyche industry had been saying for years. Of course, there was a market for books that assured you that you were "a good person" regardless of what you actually did, but the extent to which Cornwall had been celebrated as a genius of the field was, to many, bewildering in ways verging on the mysterious.

The critic Charles Bryant had said exactly this in his largely ignored weekly column and had found himself the center of a Cornwall-show special on how negative judgments scarred people's sense of self worth: something Cathy was able to attest from personal experience in heart-rending sobs. The audience was soon clamoring for blood and Bryant, arriving at work the following day, found his office picketed by an angry mob, which had been carefully coordinated on Twitter, some of whom subsequently saw fit to destroy his car, break into his house, daub slogans in animal blood and human excrement on his belongings and, three days later, beat him to within an inch or two of his life. Other critics got the point and Cathy Cornwall's rise to iconic stature progressed apace, unimpeded by negativity.

Meteoric fame has its price, of course, and being besieged by well-wishers was one of them. Security backstage of the Cathy Cornwall show was uncommonly tight, at least in part because her followers possessed a self-esteem so unshakable that they naturally assumed that one of the most famous people in the country would like nothing better than to while away the day with them taking selfies. Fearing that repelling their adoration, gifts, and romantic propositions would get out in ways scarring her reputation, Cathy had insisted on a veritable army of security guards to do the job less personally, thereby preserving the privacy so essential to her own sense of self. She was thus surprised to find someone waiting for her amidst the bouquets that had transformed her dressing room into a kind of tropical paradise.

The man sitting at her dressing table, his skin pale and shrunken under the harsh lights, was slender and late middle aged. He was studying the card on what looked like a hundred long-stemmed red roses. Cathy, wounded that her security guards would be so thoughtless as to make a tender flower such as herself responsible for dismissing her admirers, pouted and was returning her hand silently to the doorknob when the man turned towards her. His face was hollow, his eyes sunken and burning red.

"Oh," she said, a trifle bored. "It's you."

"I need you to do something for me," said Belial, his eyes still on the roses.

"I'd love to," Cathy beamed, "but I am absolutely run off my feet today, so perhaps..."

"No. I need you to come with me right now."

"As I said," Cathy replied, smiling perfectly, "I'd really love to, but I'm preparing tomorrow's show and..."

"Ah," said the other, considering her thoughtfully, "the show. Yes. The wildly popular, the incredibly (some would say strangely) successful, and therefore lucrative, show. And the books, and the fans with their roses, and the adoring boyfriends lining up to satisfy your every desire, and the houses with their swimming pools and tennis courts, and the up-coming line of Cornwall cosmetics, the face on the cover of *Time*, the..."

"I'll come," she said quickly, her smile stumbling slightly and then recovering. "But I hope we can keep it brief. I have a lot to do and not much time."

"Time," said Belial, "is the one thing you need not worry about."

And so saying, they took a step eighteen inches to the left and into the late sixteenth century.

ACT TWO, SCENE FIVE

"This deed unshapes me quite, makes me unpregnant
And dull to all proceedings."
(*Measure for Measure*, 4.4.19-21)

London, 1594.

Gladys

We are told that exercise in general, and running in particular, is good for us. This is true, particularly when there are people running after you who want to kick you into the stone age.

Gladys, Rose, Xavier, and Jimmy ran through the streets, the hostile crowd at their heels swelling ominously at the prospect of showing some heathen foreigners a bit of good old British injustice. That they hadn't done anything deserving punishment didn't seem to matter so much as the fact that they were, in every sense of the term, strangers. Times change, but the impulse to target people who don't look or sound like you and blame them for all your little miseries never really goes out of fashion.

Gladys, being invisible and all, didn't really need to run like a cheetah with its tail on fire, but the pain she had felt when hit by the stone continued to gnaw at her, like one of those flesh-eating viruses that the twenty-first century had grown so fond of. Beads of perspiration had pricked out on her forehead and a chill was running through her flesh.

And there it was.

Because angels did not have *flesh* through which to feel a chill, and like certain southern ladies, they absolutely did not perspire. Now as she ran, she wasn't so much perspiring as sweating like a pig in a sausage factory, and she could feel every cobble under her all too corporeal feet as they sprinted down the street in search of cover. She slipped and sprawled heavily on the roadway and felt so many things so suddenly and sharply that she thought the sensory overload might just make her explode. Worse, when she glanced back at the mob, they made eye contact, so that Gladys was beginning to have grave doubts about a lot of things, not least of which was her own invisibility.

Something must have gone wrong in the time-journey. Was it connected to that festering sense of wrongness she had almost been able to smell ever since she arrived? Gladys' stomach wobbled at the thought. Something was rotten in the state of...well, London. And if Xavier's blackness and Rose's jeans were likely to be inconvenient for their mission, Gladys' oddly corporeal state might well utterly and completely bugger it.

Now, there had been times in her existence when the idea of having a body had seemed heavenly, or, more accurately, beyond the heavenly. A body would give her feeling, and through it she would enjoy physical pleasure. Even pain had seemed, from the intellectual and hypothetical stance of someone who never felt it, thrilling, something that defined existence and helped you assess it, something that feelingly persuaded what you were. Pain, she had reasoned, would let you know you were alive (which, in practical terms, she wasn't). But even in these abstract flights of fancy she had always come back to the fact that physical sensation meant corporeality, which, in turn, meant mortality. You needed a body to feel someone stroke it, to taste, or to know what it's like to have a favorite pet rub up against it, but to have a real body meant having something that could be damaged. If your body could be damaged, it could stop working and, eventually, would. A body—a real, flesh and blood, muscle and bone body—meant death.

Bruised and tiring now, Gladys realized that her interest in physicality had been extinguished like a snuffed candle. Her fall had cut both hands and one knee, and though the stumble had caused little more than grit-impacted grazes, the agony had been acute. Had each wound cost her a limb, she wouldn't have been at all surprised: at least then she wouldn't have felt obligated to keep trying to run, an activity that was, she now saw, a highly over-rated means of spending one's time.

Gladys had one recourse. Before making this little jaunt into the past, she had taken a precaution based on centuries of human squabbling over various culture-specific symbols of barter, investment, and status: she had gotten herself a little cash. A Spanish galleon, loaded with a vast cargo, much of it gold, had foundered in a storm and sunk off the coast of Mexico in June 1573 where—quickly buried by a great sand bar—it would lie undisturbed for all earthly time. The gold being thus forgotten, the angel reasoned, it was effectively outside all possible timelines and could thus be used by her agents without repercussion. A few handfuls of Spanish doubloons had thus materialized in her jacket pockets moments before she had brought the humans to merrie olde Englande and found it not very merrie at all. The coins made her clothes bulge, and she felt their weight as she ran, but they represented close to unimaginable wealth for sixteenth-century Londoners (though people were starting to imagine a good deal more than they once had), so that was probably useful.

She thrust a fist into her pockets, plucked about a dozen coins out, and cast them up into the air. The light caught them and they flashed as they fell tinkling in the street, where upon the crowd fell on them and, after a few moments of shocked scrambling around, on each other.

Gladys ducked behind a plastered stone wall, wheezing heavily, ran another hundred yards down an alley with Xavier, Rose, and Jimmy at her heels, and then flung herself through the open gate of a vast Gothic church. Beggars sat under its eaves and gargoyles watched from its buttresses, but the place was otherwise quiet.

"Get inside," Gladys managed, as she blundered up the steps staggering and weaving like a drunk bison. "I think I might be dying."

She wasn't just being dramatic. She genuinely didn't know. Yes, she was tired and had fallen, but could that possibly make you feel this miserable? Surely not. This had to be the first footfall of the Reaper.

It wasn't. It was merely physical discomfort of the kind that humans soldier through daily. Xavier said as much, snapped it actually, which Gladys felt was uncalled for. She shot him a dirty look as she eased herself through the church door.

Inside it was cool as only large stone buildings can be, its nave lined with columns and statues, mostly decapitated by zealous protestants a few years earlier. There was a tower, which must have given a spectacular view of the area from the South Bankside with its theatres and stews, down to London Bridge and across the river to the city proper. There were monuments and sarcophagi but no crypt she could see. Gladys made for the eastern side, which was impressively vaulted with great radiating arches and was, most importantly, empty.

Light in the great church was low and amber, coming from candles, though there were narrow lancet windows arranged in trios whose glassed slits looked out into the street. Beneath the windows were little side altars. The stone flagged floor was inscribed with the names of the dead, and as soon as he realized as much, Jimmy had taken to picking his way around, tiny steps interspersed with great strides as if afraid of violating the bones beneath his feet. Xavier took up position behind one of the ornate columns and peered back toward the door.

"I think we lost them," he said.

For a minute or more, the four of them said nothing, but crouched (Rose), gasped (Jimmy), scowled (Xavier), and groaned (Gladys). Then, just as they were getting back to normal, sure that the street brawl they had left in their wake had forgotten them completely, things got more seriously problematic. It began, as real disasters tend to, small.

"You're bleeding," said Jimmy, helpfully.

"I'm aware of that," snapped the angel. "How very observant of you."

"I just didn't know angels *could* bleed..." Jimmy began.

He made the remark in a conversational way, but something in Gladys' face made him pause thoughtfully.

"What?" he asked.

"Angels don't bleed," Xavier suggested. "Right?"

"Right," Rose replied, casting an inquisitorial glance at Gladys.

"Look," said the angel defensively, "I'd rather not think about that just now. Can we just get on?"

"Listen lady," said Xavier, "you're our life-line. No offense, but if you aren't gonna make it, we need to know: you see what I'm saying? You have to get us back to where we were before."

"*No offense?*" Gladys retorted. "Your concern is touching. I could be dying and all you care about..."

"Are you actually dying?" asked Jimmy.

"No," Gladys shot back. "Probably not. But I could be."

"I think the key question..." Rose began.

"Is can we still travel in time?" Xavier concluded.

Despite her irritation, Gladys considered this seriously. "Yes," she said. "I think so."

"You think so?" said Xavier.

"Pretty sure," Gladys returned. "You people are going to have to start trusting my instincts."

"And if some local with a sword comes and whacks your head off, we'll still be okay, will we?" Jimmy ventured guilelessly.

Gladys glared at him, amazed that she had ever taken him for a professor, or someone with an ounce of sensitivity. Pain was a good deal lower on her list of Things That Might Be Interesting than it once had been, but what bothered her about the question was the other questions it raised about what might come after the killing stroke or, for that matter, what might not. Could she, an angel, die? She wouldn't have thought so, but then she wasn't supposed to be able to bleed either. And if she could die, what would that mean? Would she join the line waiting for a double cheeseburger in the Transition Stage that she had helped administer—a fairly horrific prospect of itself—or would she somehow fall through the cracks? She wasn't human, so she probably wouldn't get filed with the souls of the lately departed. But there was no department to deal with dead angels. Could her spirit be extinguished, snuffed out of this rather strange temporal prison, simply ceasing to be, all consciousness ending at a stroke, or would she be doomed to haunt 1594 for eternity? And if she was treated as a human, did that mean she could be damned?

"So you're human now?" said Rose.

"How dare you!" Gladys snorted.

"Well, you're not an angel," said Rose.

"I am still an angel," Gladys retorted, "albeit one who has, judging by the blood pouring out of my head, temporarily become *mortal*, yes. Good Lord, what is that stench? It's you! All of you! Your flesh and fluids..."

She clapped a hand over her nose and mouth, then recoiled. "And it's me!" she gasped. "I reek of...*mortality*."

"Are you sure?" Jimmy asked.

"I've become mortal, not stupid," Gladys returned. "*If you prick us, do we not...*stink?"

Her mind raced. Had she been stripped of her essence by her superiors for going, as the humans said, *off the reservation*? Or was something else at work? She thought of the dark and sickly presence she had sensed earlier. There had been nothing angelic about that.

We shouldn't have come, she thought.

"But we're not stuck here?" said Xavier, clarifying.

"What?" snapped Gladys. "No! There's no reason to think I can't still move you in time, even though I'm, apparently..."

"Mortal?" supplied Rose.

Gladys moistened her lips then nodded quickly.

Xavier wasn't done. "But if you die...?" he began.

"Then yes," Gladys replied, "if I die, you're stuck here. Then you die too. Again."

Gladys let them scream at her for several minutes and then, unable to contain herself any longer, snarled, "And what about me, you self-involved little worms?! You think I want to be trapped in this pit of despair in the same semi-evolved skin suit you people fester in for your allotted three-score years and ten? You think I'm keen on slugging around in all this... *flesh*? Or perhaps you think I relish the possibility of eternal obliteration when one of your illustrious and oh-so-perceptive forefathers runs a length of steel through my spinal column because I've been seen in the company of a demon Black man? I saved your lives, you bloody ingrates."

The increasingly disappointing Jimmy gave Xavier a baffled glance. "He's a devil?" he said.

"No, you stupid bloody human!" exclaimed Gladys. "They *think* he is a devil or a foreigner, which amounts to about the same thing in this gloriously enlightened part of the universe, and *that's* why they're going to kill me."

"So now it's my fault?" Xavier shot back.

"Did someone blame you?" Gladys snapped. "My problem right now is with humanity. All of it. Okay?"

"Not really," said Xavier, but he seemed daunted by the formerly serene angel's all too human rage.

"Can't you appeal to one of your superiors?" Jimmy said at last.

Gladys went very still like a rabbit in tall grass when it senses dogs close by. Big slavering dogs. Lots of them. She reached into her wounded body, dredged up a smile, and gave it a little polish before turning it on the humans.

"Oh, I don't think we need bother any of my...*superiors* with this," she said.

She said the key word as if it might bite her.

"Why not?" asked Jimmy, who she suspected was still smarting from being called a *stupid bloody human.*

"Well," stalled Gladys, "this isn't really their kind of thing."

"Why not?"

"Well, it's all very complicated, but hierarchy in the heavens is an infinitely difficult and, well, *complex* kind of business. Very complicated."

"Couldn't you talk to some of the big-name angels," suggested Rose, delving into her Catholic school past like someone fishing for a sock under the bed. "You know, Michael, Gabriel..."

"Raphael?" suggested Xavier, uncertainly.

"Urinal..." Rose continued. "No, not urinal. *Uriel.* Wasn't he an angel?"

Gladys said nothing. At the mention of each *big-name* angel (except Urinal) she had flinched, as if someone had threatened her with something heavy, like a cathedral.

"Well?" Rose pressed.

"No, no, I really don't think we ought to bother the more exalted members of the..." Gladys' voice petered out and she opted for command instead of explanation, a strategy long utilized by heavenly powers. "Look, you are just going to have to do as I say, okay?"

"No," said Xavier. "You wanna tell us what's going on?"

The angel stared at him but then blinked and hung her head. "Fine," she said. "This mission is not what you'd call...official."

"What the hell does that mean?" demanded Xavier.

"I'm getting to it, alright?" answered the angel, testily. "We have come to find out why Shakespeare's plays seem to be vanishing from Western civilization, right?"

"God knows why we're bothering," said Xavier under his breath.

"Well, there's the thing..." said Gladys.

They waited for clarification of this oddly incomplete statement, but nothing followed. Xavier fixed her with a stony eye.

"God *doesn't* know?" he said.

Gladys took a long breath and began.

"The entity you call God, the angelic high command, my superiors," Gladys confessed, "none of them are fully *in the loop* as far as this little mission of mine is concerned."

"How not in the loop are they?" Rose asked.

Gladys' defiance buckled. Lying (except, in time honored theological tradition, by omission), wasn't an option. "Not at all," she confessed. "And if they did know what I was doing, they might not be entirely supportive."

"Wait," said Xavier. "What?"

"You're *not* on a divine mission?" Rose asked. "You're *not* following orders from the...you know, angelic executive committee, or something?"

"Not as such, no," said Gladys, shuffling.

"You aren't leading the armies of the Lord in pursuit of justice and virtue?" said Jimmy, vaguely.

"That wouldn't really be my department," said the angel.

"So, the answer is no," Jimmy clarified.

"Yes," said Gladys. "I mean, *correct*. Good job. Well done, you. The answer is, no."

"So you dragged us here with all this talk about saving a bunch of *plays*," said Xavier, "but in fact, your bosses don't care about this Shakespeare crap any more than I do?"

"Look at me!" Gladys exclaimed. "I'm bleeding, and all you lot can do is blame me for..."

"I swear to God," Rose interrupted, "you're gonna be bleeding a whole lot more if you don't tell us what exactly is going on."

The angel gave her a petulant scowl while she thought, then took a breath.

"What you have to understand," she began, "is that literature doesn't really fall strictly under the *good versus evil* category, which is what angels usually deal with. I'm afraid that Heaven has rather given up on art in general. I mean, it was fine when it was all church ceilings and statues of, well, *us*," said Gladys. "But it's rather harder to champion the idea that art raises man to acts of goodness and devotion to God, if the art in question is New Kids on the Block or 'Grandma Got Run over by a Reindeer.' Most popular music celebrates little more than drink and fornication, and the only thing more hellish than that to the ears of angels is Christian rock, which would make a saint vomit. Has done, actually. The one thing in favor of high art is that hardly anyone cares about it, but you can't build a heavenly task force around irrelevance, can you?"

"I like art," said Jimmy cautiously. "Some of it."

"Spend a lot of time in museums and art galleries, do you?" replied Gladys, knowingly. "Got an extensive collection of French impressionists in your kitchen?"

"Well, no," said Jimmy, shrugging.

"See?" said Gladys triumphally. "Who goes to art galleries these days? Hipsters and rich people who want to be seen in art galleries, thereby impressing other hipsters and rich people. And theatre! That's just the music and the art galleries glued together with the same people going to show off their mink and Armani so they can tell people that they went."

"That's crap," said Rose.

"Is it?" said Gladys. "How much of the American population would care, or even notice, if every museum and library were closed down over night? Not enough to count, the archangels tell us."

Xavier was shaking his head, but Gladys was on a roll.

"There used to be a group of angels who kept the pro-art lobby going strong," she said. "Claimed that art enriched and bettered society. But then you catch the Nazis cheerfully playing Wagner and Mozart, and the argument gets a bit thin. Xavier's right! Shakespeare, like the Bible, has been used to justify almost every atrocity committed by

Western civilization. You think the archangel Gabriel wants to ensure that some white settler will be able to have some apposite lines from *The Tempest* to say before he wipes out a Native American settlement? Not really. So we are supposed to leave the art thing alone. I hate to say it, but the disappearance of the entire Shakespearean canon would affect the heavenly powers not one iota."

"Let me get this straight," said Xavier, refusing to get side-tracked by all this esoteric decline-of-culture business. "Angels aren't interested in the Incredible Disappearing Bard. In fact, they'd actually like to see the back of him."

"Right," said Gladys. "Precisely."

"So what the hell are we doing here?" Xavier concluded.

"Ah," said Gladys. "And well you may ask."

"I am," said Xavier with a touch of menace.

"Ah," repeated Gladys, adding after a pause, "indeed."

It wasn't an easy question to address, as Gladys' ineloquence was demonstrating, because it was, paradoxically, all too simple. Gladys was acting alone, without the approval of her superiors and in flagrant disobedience of her orders. To all intents and purposes, the angel was AWOL, pursuing a private mission that was neither in her jurisdiction or in the interest of the heavenly powers for whom she worked, and Gladys was therefore acting in defiance of her superiors. The problem with this fairly straightforward analysis of the situation was that it pointed fairly squarely at REBELLION, and angels who rebelled tended to find themselves waking up with horns, a tail, and a radically different perspective on eternity. Just ask Lucifer.

It was an alarming thought, but one that, perhaps, answered her earlier questions as to why she wasn't feeling particularly angelic at the moment: she had been found out and punished. This was clearly the sense of malice and decay she had been picking up ever since the time leap. The corruption, the feeling that something was badly wrong: it was *her*. Gabriel or one of the other shining captains of God had been informed of her transgression and had acted promptly, clipping her wings, as it were, making her mortal and, for all she knew, reserving a pitchfork for her in the lake of fire when this earthly purgatory came to an all-too-rapid end. All for a few plays that no one really liked.

Hell, thought Gladys. *What a complete screw-up.*

ACT TWO, SCENE SIX

"I am as peremptory as she proud-minded
And where two raging fires meet together
They do consume the thing that feeds their fury."
(*The Taming of The Shrew*, 2.1.131-3)

London, 1594.

Belial

S hakespeare?" repeated Cathy Cornwall, thinking perhaps that
she had misheard, and giving the devil a searching look. "*Wherefore art thou Romeo* and all that crap?"

"Yes."

"Why?" she asked.

"One of my clients would have it so," said Belial, "and that is all you
need to know. I serve him, for the moment, and you serve me. So I want
you to help. I thought you'd jump at the chance."

"At destroying the works of Shakespeare? Why?"

"All that conflict," Belial tried. "All that anger and killing. Can't be
healthy for people to watch plays that are that violent."

Cathy looked at him blankly."But no one takes that stuff seriously," she said. "Movies are different because they are realistic. Shakespeare is just people in bad suits talking gibberish. No one cares. Literary types who buy into all that high culture garbage are going under like the dinosaurs."

"So, you don't want to destroy Shakespeare," said Belial, both surprised and a little disheartened.

"Oh, yes I do," Cathy answered, brightening. "Every word if I can. When can we get started?"

Belial frowned then said, "If the plays don't bother you, why are you so keen to get rid of them?"

"It doesn't matter what they're about," she explained. "What makes them so awful is that some people tell us that they're great, when in fact they're boring and impossible to read and everyone hates them. Since we're not *supposed* to hate them, we feel guilty as well as stupid. That makes us dislike ourselves. It doesn't matter what Shakespeare is about. Shakespeare is hard. Hard is bad. If we don't get it, then we are sad and we don't love ourselves properly. Shakespeare is bad for our self-esteem and therefore must be destroyed."

Belial nodded, oddly fascinated. As a devil who had fallen with Lucifer before the world came into being, he had seen, as they say, a lot of stuff. But conversations about Shakespeare with talk show hosts still had a distinct sense of the surreal. Their environment didn't help, of course. They had stepped into 1594 outside the Rose Theatre where the original summons had been performed by Edward Alleyn, but had then had to trek across the bridge and all the way to the north wall of the city. Cornwall, muffled in a suitably Renaissance cape, had cooed at the quaintness of the buildings, laughed at people's clothes, complained about the smell, and otherwise talked incessantly all the way which, if the devil walking alongside her had not generated a queasy need to be elsewhere in the passersby, might have led to some choice words from the locals about Suitably Demure Female Behavior.

They went through Bishops' Gate and moved into the suburbs of the rapidly expanding city to a grim, monastic building with bars on the windows. It was technically a hospital but, in keeping with the brutal notions of entertainment on offer in early modern England, it was also a kind of tourist attraction. Its official name was Saint Mary of Bethlehem, which had a benevolent and maternal feel to it, but the hospital was more generally known by the colloquial contraction of the name, one which would be remembered for centuries to come as a byword for noise and chaos.

Belial gave some coins to the man at the gate and they stepped inside. The coins, for once, stayed coins.

They were almost immediately approached by a ragged-looking fellow who informed them while bread was good, and cheese was good, bread and cheese together were also good, an observation he was sharing with anyone who would listen, over and over again. Then from somewhere in the depths of the building came a laugh, high and cruel and demented. Cornwall shot Belial a suspicious look.

"Is this one of those National Health places?" she asked, wrinkling her nose. "I've heard about those. This is what happens when you give up a perfectly good insurance system for some single payer..."

"It's a madhouse," Belial inserted.

And right on cue the place exploded with noise, as a wild-eyed woman came shrieking and drooling towards them.

"Get away from me, you crazy bitch!" Cornwall yelled. "You know what I paid for this suit?"

Belial hurried her through the draughty corridor, and the wild, frightening laugh got louder with each step. They rounded a corner into a dank little dungeon where a lunatic in a cage flapped hopelessly round as if trying to take flight. Sitting outside the cage was Robert Bliss. He was tearing pages from the books at his feet and pushing them through the cage. The bird-man inmate snatched the paper and stuffed them into his mouth, chewing furiously.

"We should rent this guy out as a novelty shredder," he observed. "I know lawyers who'd pay through the nose. It's too bad we can't get cameras in here. Live stream a place like this on cable. We'd blow all that daytime talk crap off the air..."

Whereupon he recognized one of the prime purveyors of that daytime crap loitering in the doorway in a cape.

"Talk of the devil," he remarked. "Cathy Cornwall! Well, who'd have thought it!"

"And you are?" she said, appraising her fellow devil-worshipper with a tight little smile.

"In charge," said Bliss. "My name is Robert Bliss."

Cornwall shot Belial a look.

"I don't know who this person thinks he is," she said, "but if you think someone of my standing and cultural influence is going to take orders from the likes of him, you've got another thing coming."

"Think of it as just another show," said Belial. "Just a gig."

"I don't do *gigs*," Cornwall replied in high dudgeon. "I *help* people!"

"Don't start with me, lady," Bliss fired back. "Your moral high ground vanished in a puff of brimstone the moment you stepped into this medieval pit on the end of a demon's leash."

"Renaissance," sighed Belial, thinking that this was going to be a long day. "Not medieval. Didn't you have any education at all?"

"This is what I'm talking about!" said Cathy Cornwall, turning on Belial. "You are using education to intimidate and devalue his sense of self. It's just like Shakespeare. You should value Mr....?"

"Bliss," said Bliss.

"Mr. Bliss for who he is," she continued, not missing a beat, "not who you think he should be."

The speed at which she had changed her attitude to Bliss made Belial's head spin.

"Please," said Bliss, smiling suddenly at Cornwall, "call me Robert. You could learn from her, devil," he added to Belial. "You don't boost my self-esteem anywhere near enough."

"Maybe you should earn your self-esteem," said Belial petulantly. "We need to move on from 1594."

"Can we get *Macbeth* now?" asked Bliss, his face lighting up like a child who has just been promised a flame-thrower.

"That's one of the worst," agreed Cornwall. "People are always quoting it, answering questions about it on game shows..."

"Yes, yes," Belial said, "we have established how much Shakespeare erodes our sense of self-worth."

"And have you ever read *Romeo and Juliet*?" Cathy added. "When you decode all the poetry and crap, it turns out she's thirteen! Romeo gets off way too easy."

"I believe he dies at the end," Belial remarked.

"Waaay too quickly," said Cornwall. "I gotta say, I'm amazed you are going about the problem this way, moving from year to year collecting plays after they are printed. Why not cut the source off at the head?"

"Meaning?" said Belial, not really wanting to know.

"Kill Shakespeare," she replied simply.

"Interesting," said Bliss. "From a time and motion standpoint, she's right."

"You can't enter a prior time stream and kill people!" said Belial.

"Why not?" asked Cathy Cornwall, as if she had been denied an ice cream.

"Because!" Belial exclaimed.

"Not a reason," Bliss said.

"Because it breaks all cosmic law," said Belial. "Okay? Because both heaven and hell will come down on us like a ton of bricks, wipe us out, and reset the timeline. We are very limited in what we are allowed to do in a period that isn't our own."

"What if we got someone else to do it?" Bliss mused. "Delegation is the core of management. We can't kill him, but one of the locals could. We just need to provide some incentive."

Belial stared at him.

"Well?" said Cornwall, suddenly all bright eyed and bushy tailed. "Or is that forbidden too?"

She said it as if Belial was being childish and cowardly, and maybe he was a little. They had hit on a solution he had hoped wouldn't occur to them for a while, and they had done so within moments of meeting each other.

A tactical error, he thought.

Belial shook his head. "It would lead back to us," he said. "The rupture in the timeline would immediately attract celestial attention. The circumstances of his death would be investigated, and the moment our hand was discovered…"

"So, we make sure they don't know it's us," said Cornwall, refusing to let go of an idea she clearly liked.

"How?" said Belial. "The investigative committee can see in time, space, and a host of dimensions you couldn't possibly comprehend."

Cornwall opened her mouth to complain, but before she could respond, she was interrupted by the caged lunatic who, without preamble, began screaming and pointing.

"The fiend!" he bawled, indicating Belial. "The foul fiend of the pit!"

"Even a broken clock is right twice a day," Bliss observed.

The screaming persisted.

"Can we get out of here, please," Belial asked. "It's..."

"Bedlam in here, isn't it?" Bliss inserted delightedly.

In sharp clarity Belial suddenly recalled just how many millennia he had been alive and marveled that this particular day seemed to be taking about as long as the rest combined. And thanks to his blunder of involving Cornwall's specific brand of rat-like cunning, it was going to get worse before it got better.

"This would all go a lot smoother," said Belial, "if you didn't talk."

"Okay, okay," said Bliss. "Keep your horns on."

"Robert," said Cornwall, with a hint of flirtation, "aren't you the wit?"

Bliss beamed and Belial sighed.

"And people think that Hell is a *place*," he remarked.

ACT TWO, SCENE SEVEN

"I prithee, give me leave to curse awhile."
(*Henry VI part 1*, 5.3.43)

London, 1594.

Gladys

Meanwhile, in the church known, since the reformation, as St. Saviour's—once the Augustinian priory of the church of St. Mary Overie, and, after a little jurisdictional shuffling, to be known one day as Southwark Cathedral—there was a lot of what the scriptures call weeping and gnashing of teeth.

"I was initiating a counter move against demonic activity!" Gladys exclaimed. She had been on the receiving end of a lot of what Cathy Cornwall would call *negativity* over the last few minutes and she was sick of it. "If a demon wants something, we try to stop it. If they make a move, we try to block it."

"Sounds a bit petty," said Jimmy.

"They do the same to us," Gladys shot back.

"So, not petty at all," Rose concluded dryly.

"How would you like to spend eternity trying to explain to people that they are dead and *do you want fries with that?*" Gladys returned.

"Let me get this straight," said Xavier. "What we took to be some kind of moral crusade was actually just self-promotion. You should have been a politician."

"Hey now!" exclaimed Gladys, wounded, "that's a bit strong."

"Oh, I'm sorry, your royal angelicness," snapped Xavier, "but you brought me to this city-wide Sons of the Confederacy rally. It didn't occur to you that I might not be welcome?"

"I didn't think it would be quite this bad," Gladys confessed. "It's not like there are no Africans in sixteenth-century London. There are ambassadors and consultants, former Spanish slaves from captured galleons. Some of them live here and marry into the population. I'm not sure why there seems to be such hostility toward you."

Xavier rolled his eyes. "You really don't understand white people," he said.

"Hey!" said Rose and Jimmy.

"Don't start with that Not All White People stuff!" he shot back warningly. "Not today."

"It is curious though," said Gladys, glad not to be the sole target of Xavier's wrath. "I mean, yes, racism and sexism are rampant in this period, but I didn't think it would flare into violence so quickly. It's almost as if..."

"What?" Xavier prompted.

"Hmm?" said Gladys.

"It's almost as if what?" Xavier pressed.

Gladys looked at him, then shook her head. "Nothing," she lied. "Just thinking aloud. I suggest we get started collecting those plays. As I said, before we had to run halfway across the city, we're going to need period clothes. Given the state of things, Tobias," she said, catching herself irritably, "I mean, *Jimmy*, I think that falls to you."

Jimmy looked up.

"You want me to steal stuff?" he asked cheerfully. "I saw what looked like a laundry on the way over here."

Gladys considered him with dull horror. "No," she said, "I don't want you to *steal stuff*. I will give you money. I want you to buy stuff. Think you can manage that?"

"I was just trying to help," said Jimmy.

"And you can," said Gladys handing him a fistful of coins. "Just don't attract more attention than you absolutely need to."

"Can he get us something to eat?" asked Xavier. "I'm starving."

"I have a tube of Rolo," said Rose, fishing in her very unRenaissance pockets.

"Not really a candy person," he replied.

"Can we get on?" said Gladys pointedly at Jimmy.

Jimmy considered the money, nodded, and said, "Okay. See you soon."

He headed for the door and Gladys watched him, wondering—too late—if she should be trusting a man like that with most of their remaining funds.

"And me?" Rose demanded. "I mean, I get that being taken for a cross-dressing whore isn't going to help us much, but since you brought me here, I figure I have some kind of role, right? What am I supposed to do?"

"Embroidery?" suggested Gladys. "You could take up the virginals. It's a bit like a harpsichord..."

Rose glared.

"I'm not sure," Gladys faltered. "Isn't that what women did? *Do*, I should say. I think you are supposed to manage the dairy if you are married," she added vaguely, "but you're not and we don't have a dairy. When you have the right clothes, you could go to the market."

"What for?" Rose replied sharply.

"I don't know," said the now apparently ex-angel, "more clothes? Things to, you know, hang round your neck...jewelry. Cosmetics: they are getting very popular in this period, I believe. The puritans are always complaining about painted women."

Rose's glare was an acetylene torch.

"Or," Gladys concluded, "you could wait until we're ready for you to do something useful and in the meantime get off my back for two minutes."

Rose turned down the torch so that it was merely orange and hot rather than blue-white and terrifying.

"You know," she said, "you're getting the hang of being human quite well."

"Meaning I'm angry and confused all the time?" said Gladys. "Excellent."

ACT TWO, SCENE EIGHT

"Think you there was or might be such a man
As this I dreamt of?"
(*Antony and Cleopatra*, 5.2.92-3)

Shoreditch, 1598.

Shakespeare

A t almost the same moment that the angelic team were reflecting on their disconnected lives, two men left The Curtain theatre in a hurry or, to be more accurate, one left and the other tagged behind him like a kitten following its mother. Actually, the relationship was probably more like that of a kitten following what it had assumed to be its mother but was now starting to look like a horse, or maybe an armadillo. The kitten (and this was about the only situation in which the analogy could be called accurate) was Richard Burbage, actor, entrepreneur, and son of the theatrical impresario James Burbage. The first man out of the theatre (our armadillo/horse), whose irritation was showing through the mask of distance and calm he habitually wore, was the writer and he was tired of having this conversation.[1]

"And I've told you, Richard," he said, crisply, "that you need a new theatre. If you don't get one, our investment..."

"I have a theatre!" Burbage replied. "My father's."

"Mired in lawsuits," the other returned.

It was true. Burbage's theatre, imaginatively titled The Theatre, was under threat. Whether the owner of the field where the theatre stood just really hated plays (and there were plenty of high-minded men in London who thought them as fast a route to Hell as man could devise), or whether he hoped that raising the rent exponentially would leave the building for his own theatrical uses, wasn't clear. But it *was* clear that he wanted Burbage and The Chamberlain's men off his land.

"So we'll use the Rose," said Burbage.

"Even if we were prepared to trust our financial future to Philip Henslowe, we can't," said the writer. "It's occupied."

"Langley's Swan is ripe for picking. Your words will sound as full there as they ever did at The Theatre..."

"It's not about my words," the writer explained precisely. "It's about my *purse*. That's what I need to keep *full*. If I die poor, Burbage, every night my ghost will harrow up your soul, freeze your young blood, and make your hair to stand on end like quills upon the fretful porpentine."

"What's a porpentine?"

"Big spiky animal."

"Like a porcupine?"

"Yes. Same thing."

"Then why didn't you say so?"

"Mine sounds better. Anyway, is my point clear?"

"Crystal," said Burbage, a little stung. "What else?"

"Meaning?"

"You seem... I don't know. Strange. Sad. Anxious."

"It's the playhouse," said the writer, glancing away.

"If you say so," said Burbage with a shrug.

"Really, it's nothing," said the writer. "Except." He hesitated.

"What?"

"Imagination is a powerful thing," said the writer.

"Yours in particular," said Burbage.

"Right," said the writer as if this was a crucial point, but one that pained him. "You have often said so."

"Some writers give me lines to say," said Burbage with a smile. "You give me a person to be."

The writer nodded quickly and gratefully, but he wasn't done.

"And if that person was drawn just right, if his voice sounded true, honest—even if much of what he said was poison—maybe *because* of that, if I wrote him as well as has ever been done, do you think he could walk out of the page and into the world?"

As soon as the words were out of his mouth the writer recognized them as madness.

"The words speaking themselves?" said Burbage. "Without, you know, *us*?"

"I know," said the writer. "It's ridiculous."

"Yes, it bloody is," said Burbage feelingly. "Theatre without actors? I'd be out of a job. Come on, Will; what's this about?"

The writer considered him for a moment, then said, "The other day, just down the street there, I saw a blackamore."

"Like, an Ethiope?"

"Tall man, of goodly form and a commanding eye."

"Yes? He's not the only one in the city. So?"

"He was with a white woman, young, pretty."

"And?"

The writer frowned and shook his head. "Got me thinking, is all," he said vaguely.

"I don't understand," said Burbage.

Shakespeare looked down as if embarrassed, then met his friend's eyes and smiled. "It's nothing," he said. "Writer nonsense. I'll be fine."

"You sure?"

"I'm going," said the writer, pointing.

"Where?"

"To write," Shakespeare pronounced without looking round. He strode off, leaving Burbage in the street. "Somewhere I won't be disturbed!"

And, turning a corner, he vanished, in search of his private spot, leaving the kitten to find a new armadillo or, and this was more likely, to grow rapidly into a Siberian tiger that would set upon the first hapless actor he found who couldn't read a blank verse line without sounding like he was falling down a flight of stairs.

For his part, the writer did not write. Instead he walked around the city, listening to the ends of conversation as he passed, heading up river till the light softened and faded, and he found himself in places he did not know, which loomed suddenly dark and sinister all around him. He took a drink in a tavern, then trekked back to his lodgings.

Still he did not write. He did not think he dared.

Perhaps a comedy. Something light and playful.

But even comedies had villains, some disgruntled figure who lurked in the shadows and took pleasure in ruining other people's lives. He had written such men before. Why did this one feel so much worse?

He thought of the virgin warrior goddess Athena springing whole and fully armed from the head of her father, Zeus, the parthenogenesis for which her temple in Athens was known. It was a miracle, and the perfect image of mental creation.

It was just a myth, of course. A story.

But then what was more powerful than story?

In other circumstances, that thought might have cheered him, but not today, and as the shadows deepened to blackness throughout the city, the writer found himself studying the darkest crevices and alleys for those hateful, watchful eyes. If by some impossible means he had birthed something into the world straight out of his head and the noxious pits of humanity into which he had delved—less a miracle than a foul and unnatural act— what had emerged was no virgin warrior goddess but a monster that mocked the meat it fed on...

"But that's a fable," he said aloud, as if to make it true. "There's no such thing."

He shuddered and looked guiltily round, sure for a moment that beneath the perennial stench of the city was a new and loathsome sourness.

ACT THREE

"This is the silliest stuff that ever I heard."
(*A Midsummer Night's Dream*)

ACT THREE, SCENE ONE

"Our remedies oft in themselves do lie
Which we ascribe to heaven. The fated sky
Gives us free scope, only doth backward pull
Our slow designs when we ourselves are dull."
(*All's Well That Ends Well*, 1.1.216-9)

London, 1594.

Rose

Putting on the clothes Jimmy had acquired was like doing a three-dimensional jigsaw, one whose box had been left in the basement when it flooded so that the picture on the front was bloated and faded into uselessness. Rose knew that the various bits of fabric and cord in front of her somehow compiled a dress, but figuring out what went where and how took her the best part of an hour, and even then, she needed the others to strap her in to the corsetry, hoop skirt, and rigid triangular panel the angel called a stomacher. There were several parts they didn't know what to do with, reminding her of when her father took appliances apart to fix them and always ended up with bits left over, which he tried to sweep away before anyone noticed.

As Xavier tied the last bow and cautiously removed his hands, poised to leap back into action if something crucial fell off, Rose felt like a Formula 1 car being tended by its pit crew, or would have, if the fabric—braced as it was with wood and whale bone—didn't leave her feeling less like a race car and more like a tank.

"You look very nice," said Xavier, looking over the ensemble.

"I'm a Transformer," she answered, rotating carefully in place, arms crooked in front of her like a T Rex. "Only instead of turning into a car, I've turned into a building."

"A classy building," said Xavier. "A building that blends in."

Rose managed a wan smile. It had been decided that, until they were sure that Xavier wouldn't be greeted with more hostility for the charge of, well, being Black, alive, and here, he was going to stay in the cathedral. He wasn't happy about it.

"You'd better go," he said.

"I'm sorry about this," said Gladys. She was sitting on a stone sarcophagus looking scared and miserable.

"Yeah," he replied. "No doubt."

The angel hesitated but apparently couldn't think of anything to add. She nodded and hung her head.

"I'd really feel better if you came with us," said Rose to Gladys. "We don't know our way around and..."

"I can't," said the angel. She looked pale and sick with terror. "I could get... Anything could happen!"

"Welcome to mortality," said Rose.

"Yes, thank you," said Gladys. "I think I'll stay here."

"And if we can't do it without you?" Rose shot back, feeling herself blushing hot with sudden anger.

The angel shrugged. "Then you'll die here," she said. "I'm sorry. That's just how it is. You should get going."

Rose turned to Xavier. "This sucks," she said. "All of it, including the part about you being stuck here."

Xavier managed a bleak grin. "Yeah," he said. "Not your fault. Your ancestors on the other hand..."

"Yeah," said Rose.

"Go," he said. "I don't fancy your chances of catching them up dressed like a wedding cake."

"Oh thanks," said Rose, mock offended. "Bye," she added. "We'll figure out how to get you..."

"Go," he said.

She did, navigating the doorway like she was carrying a pair of large suitcases. The farthingale tipped up at the back and was as wide as the lintel, so she couldn't see her feet and had to squeeze out like a barge pushing through a canal.

"Hey, book nerd," said Jimmy as she emerged from the church. "Let's move it along. We have a ways to walk."

"*Book nerd?*"

"Student," said Jimmy with a slightly sour grin.

"I'm assuming you never went to college?"

"Never got that chance, no," said Jimmy. "Had to make my own way in the world."

"Yeah?" said Rose unflinching. "Me too."

"By studying Shakespeare?"

"Among other things," said Rose.

"Good thing mommy and daddy are so supportive."

"They are, actually, yes," said Rose, defiant. "But my dad's a teacher and my mom's a nurse, so I do work-study for the English department office, wait tables at Henrico's on Boylston every other night, and am still mortgaging my future with student loans, so spare me the Working Class hero stuff."

"Maybe you should have been a plumber or an electrician," said Jimmy undaunted.

"Or a thief," said Rose.

Jimmy flashed her a look of amusement.

"Feisty," he said.

"You bet your ass," she replied.

Rose had remarked that London seemed to resemble one of those reconstructed eighteenth-century villages or Renaissance festivals dotted around the United States where hammy actors and handicraft experts chuckled warmly to you, asked "where thou haileth from" and then showed you how to work a foot-powered lathe making little dolls (available from the surprisingly expensive gift shop). A closer look, however, revealed nothing of the kind, not least because part of the charm of those reconstructed villages and Renaissance festivals is that you can leave. By contrast, Rose felt like a tourist trapped on some nightmare excursion where the guide periodically announced "and on your right you can see the sixteenth century. Still."

One of the unexpected difficulties of strolling around the past came down to language. Grammatically, Renaissance English was not—as Jimmy kept saying—Old English, as modeled by such foreign, rune-dotted texts as *Beowulf*, nor was it even the Middle English of Chaucer. As the real professor Lestering had taught her, the language of Shakespeare, though it featured lots of unfamiliar words, phrases which had evolved or dropped out of usage entirely, was modern English. It was therefore disheartening for Rose to find that she was only getting about one word in five and the general gist of most conversations escaped her utterly. Apart from anything else, the words didn't even sound English, or at least not like any English she knew and certainly not that currently mouthed by the twenty-first century inhabitants of Buckingham Palace (which, as if to prove the point, hadn't been built yet.) The dialect was hard and strange and quite the opposite of that subdued TV Englishness pronounced by actors determined not to open their mouths more than was absolutely necessary. Shopkeepers, street preachers, and market traders called out great rolling swaths of meaty, chewable words that stiffened the sinew and set the nostrils wide, but whose gist was often impossible to glean. Since Jimmy's unmasking, Rose had become the closest thing to a scholar in the group, and without Gladys' admittedly patchy knowledge of human history to help them, Jimmy clearly expected her to explain what the hell was going on around them; she felt like she had taken a year of high school Spanish and then found herself accidentally appointed Ambassador to Uruguay. After a few failed attempts to ask directions to the shop in question from a cheery and completely unintelligible group of cobblers in the St. Martin's district of the city, Rose opted for a lot of smiling and nodding, followed by anxiously worrying about what she had just agreed to.

It went without saying that they didn't want to encounter the opposition, regardless of how dismissively (and wrongly) Gladys had mentioned the "minor devil" who was "no match" for her. It therefore followed that the task at hand had to be performed efficiently and naturally, arousing suspicion in no one. It probably would have been better, then, if Jimmy had not begun their purchase by asking for "the Shakespeare play." The shopkeeper looked confused and a mite suspicious.

"Master?" he said.

Rose stepped in hurriedly.

"His name isn't on it," she muttered, turning to the shopkeeper and giving the wordy title under which the play first appeared. "The first part of the contention betwixt the two famous houses of York and Lancaster..."

The shopkeeper smiled and indicated a quarto edition a little larger than a paperback novel. He smiled still further when Rose laid down a gold coin, and beamed from ear to ear when he looked up from counting out the change to find Jimmy glancing with alarm at the pocket watch Gladys had loaned him and saying, "Forget it. We don't have time."

And so they left.

Actually they took off like the proverbial (and thoroughly inappropriate) bat out of Hell, colliding with another gentleman, medium height, brown, thinning hair, and curiously blank eyes. In her continental dress (named less for its Franco Spanish design than because it was about the size of Europe), Rose was a rapidly moving wall. She cannoned into the arriving customer and sent him sprawling in the mud. Her first impulse was to help the man up, but Jimmy was already pulling her away.

"*It's him!*" he hissed, his eyes down. "Go!"

"God damned Dark Age idiots!" shouted Robert Bliss as they ran away.

And had they stayed and listened, they would have heard the following exchange as Bliss entered.

SHOPKEEPER: Now, master, what do you lack?

BLISS: What? Oh, you sell plays, right? Drama. Theatrical texts. You speak the goddamned English language?

But Rose and Jimmy were too busy taking a much-needed breather in a nearby alley.

"That was close!" said Rose.

"But we got one," said Jimmy. "Eighteen to go. I had no idea being dead would be so stressful."

Rose took the quarto gingerly.

"Amazing," she said. "To think this will be the only one to survive. You think we should have gotten another?"

"The angel said we only need one," said Jimmy. "The fewer we take, the less likely it is that the enemy notice."

"That sounds like the voice of experience," said Rose, smiling to show she didn't mean it critically.

"You could say that," said Jimmy in kind, his eyes moving to the little book. "So this is *Henry VI part 2*? I feel better about the future already. Why didn't we get part 1?"

"I think part 2 came out first," said Rose doubtfully. "Part 1 was written later as a kind of prequel, I guess."

"Like those *Star Wars* movies," said Jimmy, moving quickly from pleasure at supplying a workable analogy to disappointment. "Oh."

"Come on," said Rose. "We'll get *Titus Andronicus* on the way back to the church. I hope Xavier and Gladys are managing to stay out of trouble."

As they walked, Jimmy gave her a sidelong look. "So you really like this Shakespeare stuff?" he asked.

"I do, actually," she replied.

"Why?" he asked, aghast.

"The poetry of them, I guess. The phrasing."

"Book nerd," said Jimmy again, grinning.

"I guess," she admitted. "But..." An image came to mind, unbidden, unwanted, but instead of dismissing it, she let it settle like a down comforter spread over a bed, giving it a second to become still. She hunted for the words, then laid them out as much for herself as for him. "A cousin of mine died quite young last year. Cancer."

Jimmy gave her a quick, shocked look.

"I'm sorry," said Jimmy.

"Thanks. I had always liked him, but when he died, I was just sort of numb, you know? Like I just couldn't really process it. I thought that was because I'd known it was coming and had sort of used up all my sadness, but it felt wrong. Disloyal. Then at the funeral, Juliet's lines on Romeo came into my head:

When he shall die take him and cut him out in little stars
And he will make the face of heaven so fine
That all the world will be in love with night

And pay no worship to the garish sun.

"So beautiful. I would never have thought anything like that, but in that moment in the church the words came and they were just...right. I lost it completely. All the grief I hadn't been able to find came out in this long rush, like I'd been holding my breath and had to let it out before I could breathe again. Anyway. I wish I could write like that."

She fell silent, embarrassed to have said so much to a stranger, wiped her eyes, and then gave him a shrugging smile. Jimmy looked awkward and terrified, unsure of what had just happened.

"Sorry," she said. "You're not a fan, I take it?"

"Never really had chance to be," he said. His accent was pure Boston with just a hint of Irish musicality, as if he might have lived there briefly or, more likely, been raised among immigrants. "Those lines from *Macbeth* that I remembered on the train platform is the only bit I can remember reading. I left school at sixteen seeking my fortune. That went well, obviously. He writes a lot about death then, Shakespeare?"

Rose frowned. "Comes up a lot, I guess, yes. But he does write a lot of tragedy. And I think the life expectancy in his day—now, I mean— was a lot lower. Forty maybe, or less."

"Jesus!" said Jimmy.

"I mean some people lived longer than that, but medicine was mostly crap and lots died in infancy or childbirth, so that probably pulls the average down. Shakespeare died at 52."

"*Jesus*," said Jimmy again, this time with something like shock.

"What?"

"I mean...Jesus."

"Yeah," said Rose, baffled by the extremity of his response.

They walked for a while in silence.

"You know what I was thinking before?" he said. "We were strolling along the street, and I was looking at all these people, men, women, old, young, children, babies, you know? And I thought: they're all dead! From our perspective, like. You know? If we can do what the angel wants and we go back to our lives, all of these people will just die. Will have *been dead* for hundreds of years! You thought about that?"

"Not really," said Rose truthfully. "I guess that's life. We age. We die. Passing through nature to eternity."

"Yeah, but not really. Other people die. I've seen that. I know it. But the idea that *everyone*, me included, just gets a few decades and then... You're done. And we're already dead! You and me and Xavier. I mean, we're walking around in the past, but in the present we're already gone. Run over by something that won't be invented for hundreds of years! It does your head in."

Rose gave him a look, bothered by his earnestness.

"I can't think about that," she said.

"No," Jimmy agreed. "But all these people keep looking at me and saying 'good morrow' and what have you, and all I can think is *you're dead. I'm* dead."

"Okay," said Rose. "Change of subject time."

But Jimmy had come to an abrupt halt and was now standing in the rutted street, his face upturned, sniffing the air with a sour expression on his face. Rose paused, worried that she had offended him by not running with his existential mood.

"We can talk about it some more, if you like," she said cautiously.

"You smell that?" he asked, his eyes half closed.

Rose gave him a disbelieving look.

"I'm trying really hard not to," she said.

"No," said Jimmy. "Not the usual nasty Renaissance London stuff. *Under* that."

Rose's brows wrinkled, but before she could ask how he could possibly identify anything beneath the body odor and rotten vegetable, the raw sewage, standing water, and animal manure that reeked from every corner, she found it, a little nugget of foulness lurking almost out of sensory reach. She turned suddenly, scanning the streets, feeling not just revolted, but strangely and bafflingly afraid.

It didn't smell animal, vegetable, or human. Not exactly. It smelled like something else entirely, something that didn't normally have a smell, so that Rose began to think that her brain was confused, was processing as scent what was actually the trace remains of some powerful emotional or spiritual presence. For a second, she could almost see it in her mind's eye, swirling like black, noxious smoke. It felt like nothing she had ever encountered before, but she shrank away from it instinctively, as if sure it would infect her, not with disease but with...what?

Hatred. Malice. A hunger to tear down, to revel in cruelty and destruction.

Yes. It made no sense, but she was sure of it.

Something was prowling the streets. Something that should not be here.

"Is that...the enemy?" she wondered aloud.

"Not sure," said Jimmy, "but I'd really like to be...somewhere else."

ACT THREE, SCENE TWO

"'Tis but an hour ago since it was nine
And after one hour more 'twill be eleven;
And so from hour to hour we ripe and ripe,
And then from hour to hour we rot and rot,
And thereby hangs a tale."
(*As You Like It*, 2.7.24-8)

London, 1594.

Gladys

In the cathedral, Gladys considered the copy of *Henry VI part 2* without much enthusiasm.

"Well," she said, "it's a start."

"What's next?" Jimmy asked.

What indeed? thought Gladys miserably. The original plan had been simple enough: step forward a year to get the sequel to the one they had already collected and then on to 1597. This all depended on Gladys still being just angelic enough that she could open the temporal portals, something she had not dared to try. The others, as if sensing her trepidation, were watching with varying degrees of hope and skepticism.

"Would you mind not watching while I did this?" said Gladys. "I feel a bit...self-conscious."

Xavier opened his mouth to say something, and Jimmy gave a dismissive snort, but Rose—optimism making her kind—took both of their arms and turned them abruptly to face the wall.

Okay then, thought Gladys. *Here goes. The moment of...well, something.*

She consulted her pocket watch and drew a door-sized rectangle in the air with her right forefinger.

For a moment the outline sparked alarmingly, and Gladys' eyes flicked to the others who—mercifully—still had their backs turned, but as she completed the shape, it rippled into golden life.

"Perfect," she said, her relief making it almost true. "And not just because it means I'm not entirely human. No offense."

She drew three more doors, and they, for once, marveled.

"Very cool," said Xavier. "But what makes you think I'll be less likely to cause a riot by showing up a year or two on from where we are now? I don't see London getting more enlightened for a whole lot longer than that."

"You're right," said Gladys. "But it can't be helped. If you sit this out, we won't get finished in time. Wrap yourself up as best you can, keep a low profile, and don't get into any arguments with the natives. Hopefully the hostility you encountered before will prove to be an aberration."

She didn't quite meet his eyes when she said that, though that was partly because her mind had drifted back to that strangely noxious almost-smell she had been trying not to think of.

"By myself?" said Xavier. He sounded almost plaintive.

"For now," said Gladys. "If we can get a few under our belts, then we can go back to working together, but we're behind and..."

"Okay," said Xavier. "Whatever. Give me some cash."

Gladys dealt out some coins and pointed out their target destinations on a frail-looking map covered in crudely drawn buildings.

"When you're done," she added, "just get out of sight and say 'Door!' loud and clear. One of these will open beside you. Go through and it will bring you to wherever—and whenever I am. Easy peasy." This was supposed to lighten the mood, but the appearance of the temporal doors had rather stripped the moment of whimsy. The three humans were gazing at them in nervous apprehension.

"Okay," said Gladys, trying to sound calm and in control. "I'll get the third part of *Henry VI* from 1595. "Rose? You'll be getting the first quarto of *Romeo and Juliet* from 1597."

Rose nodded, eyes front like a sprinter staring down the track as she awaited the starting gun.

"Romeo, Romeo wherefore art thou, Romeo," she muttered to herself. "Deny thy father and refuse thy name. Or if thou wilt not, be but sworn my love and I'll no longer be a Capulet."

It sounded like a mantra or prayer.

"Yes," said Gladys, disconcerted. "Quite so. Xavier? You're on *Richard III*. And try not to attract attention."

"Now is the winter of our discontent," Xavier recited with a sideways look at Rose, "made glorious summer by this son of York."

Rose broke her death stare on the shining doorway in front of her just long enough to shoot Xavier a curious look, but he offered no explanation for why he knew the words.

"Jimmy," said Gladys, "you can get *Richard II*."

Jimmy frowned then ventured, "To be or not to be...?"

"No," said the other three all at once.

"Whatever," said Jimmy. "Fine. Yes. Richard the god-damned second. A massively important portion of literary culture, I don't doubt."

"Now, please," said Gladys.

The three humans swallowed, steeled themselves, and stepped through their respective doors into the future.

September 24, 1597. Time remaining: 20 hours 52 minutes.
Plays to be saved: *17 +Folio.*

Jimmy

It was hardly surprising that Jimmy wasn't familiar with *Richard II*. The play was an academic favorite, particularly with those of a historicist bent who were excited by the probability that it was this play that the Earl of Essex paid Shakespeare's company to stage the day before his ill-fated 1601 rebellion. The play was packed with grist for the scholarly mill on early modern subjectivity, self-fashioning, performance, king-ship, homoeroticism, gender, rebellion, and so forth, all of which—though fascinating to Tobias Lestering with whose identity Jimmy had briefly absconded—Jimmy would have found baffling and pointless.

So he found the Angel tavern in Saint Paul's churchyard, paid for the quarto of *Richard II* after a cursory glance to make sure it had all its pages, and went to rejoin the others, without really knowing why he was bothering. The future would get to keep its Shakespeare so that girls like Rose could pay for the privilege of studying it and, in turn, he would get his solitary, criminal, pointless life back.

"Door!" he said, rounding a corner into a deserted alley.

The temporal gateway opened in a shimmering rectangle of golden light.

Well, he thought bleakly as he stepped through it, *ain't that a kick in the head?*

~

October 2, 1597. Time remaining: 20 hours 49 minutes.
Plays to be saved: *16+Folio*.

Rose

ROSE HAD JUST enough time to get to Cheapside when the cart came into view. She let it pass and began to cross the street at precisely the moment that one wheel struck a deep rut. The cart rocked and a crate of newly printed quartos fell off the back. Barely breaking stride, she dipped, picked one from the splintered crate, and kept walking. By the time the carter had clambered down from the front and come to the rear to gather up the spilled papers, Rose had already summoned the temporal door and disappeared through it.

And thus was the first—admittedly patchy—first quarto of *Romeo and Juliet* saved for a posterity who would love it, loathe it, memorize it, act it, film it, set it in a picturesque Renaissance Italy or a drugged and violent Los Angeles, write essays on it, quote it to boyfriends and girl-friends, parody it in TV commercials, immortalize it in internet memes about the body count and the ages of the protagonists, celebrate it, revile it, and otherwise absorb it into what Xavier would call the white Western cultural (probably imperialist) machine.

"Never was a story of more woe," said Rose, smiling at the thought, "than this of Juliet and her Romeo."

~

November 17, 1597. Time remaining: 20 hours 32 minutes.
Plays to be saved: *15+Folio.*

Xavier

XAVIER, heavily muffled, read the title: "THE TRAGEDY of King Richard the third. Containing, His treacherous Plots against his brother Clarence: the pitiful murther of his iunocent nephewes: his tyrannicall vsurpation: with the whole course of his detested life, and most deserved death."

"Way to stay impartial," he muttered.

At the shop by the Angel tavern, he put a coin on the counter and picked up the quarto. The shopkeeper peered at him, his eyes narrowing as he glimpsed his customer's skin under the wraps and scarves. Xavier considered offering another coin, decided against it, and snatched the book from the shopkeeper's grasp. He was almost out the door when the shopkeeper said something under his breath.

Xavier didn't catch the words, but he got the gist. Unable to help himself, he pivoted on his heel and stared the man down, plucking the scarf from his face as he did so.

"You got a problem?" he demanded.

The shopkeeper, a pale, wiry man about his own age with a shock of red hair was mouthing what Xavier took to be curses, though the words were muffled and ran together, like a stream of vicious bile. His eyes were fixed and staring, his lips flecked with spit as if he were having a seizure, and his color was rising through pink to red.

And there was a smell.

Xavier had taken a half step toward the shopkeeper when he caught it and it stopped him like a wall, not because it was deeply offensive—though it was—but because Xavier had the distinct if inexplicable feeling that it wasn't actually a smell at all. He hesitated, stymied by the strangeness as much by its repellence, and suddenly he wanted nothing more than to be elsewhere.

"Whatever, man," he snarled as he left the shop and, with barely a look to see if the coast was clear, barked, "Door!"

The temporal portal shimmered open, and Xavier stepped through it, taking with him a part that would be enacted by actors from Burbage to Garrick, Kean and Irving, Olivier, Kingsley, Pacino, McKellen, Tony Sher, Fayaz Kazek, Benedict Cumberbatch, and Kathryn Hunter.

Hell, he thought as he went to join the others. *At least he hadn't saved* Othello.

ACT THREE, SCENE THREE

"If this letter speed and my invention thrive...
I grow, I prosper.
Now, gods, stand up for bastards!"
(*King Lear* 1.2.19-21)

November 18, 1597.

Bliss

The temporal door opened outside the printer's shop three hours after sundown, when the streets were dark and already deserted. Bliss' breath smoked and frosted as he checked over his shoulder and applied the crowbar Belial had given him to the door hinges. They popped off easily, held in place not by screws but crude, angular nails with square heads. It was pitch black inside, but Bliss flicked the lamp on his cell phone on—practically its only use since the closest cell tower was four centuries away—and scanned the shelves.

"This would all be so much easier with a Molotov cocktail," he remarked, but Belial had warned him repeatedly about setting the town ablaze. Eventually, he'd come up with an alternative strategy. *Robert*

Bliss was nothing if not resourceful, he thought to himself, using that odd third person voice that people use when they think no one is listening.

He found the stack of *Richard III* plays and dumped them into a hessian sack brought for the purpose, but before he left with his winnings, aiming to dump them in the murkiest part of the Thames he could find before calling for Belial's door, he left a carefully worded note on the counter. It was, thanks to some demonic chicanery from Belial, hand lettered and adorned with an impressively ornate wax seal from which red ribbons hung. It probably wasn't exactly right, but it looked right, and that was what mattered. Perception, as Bliss was fond of saying, was nine tenths of the law.

It read:

"To the printer, Valentine Sims, and the publisher, Andrew Wise, on their selling of the most seditious and libelous tragedie of Richard Crookback by Master Shakespeare. The propertie is confiscate by Her Majestie the Queene, as ordered by the Privy Council, for manifest injuries therein containd which do harme the name of the Monarch in this realme of England, contrarie to Good Judgemente and the Wille of Godde. Whereof sale of such ungodlie books will result in Arrest and Consequences Most Severe for all therein involved. We are watching. Telle thy friendes."

Bliss had insisted upon that last line, not because he really thought it would help deter other printers from cranking out more of these damned plays, but because he liked that personal hint of menace. A good business letter, he felt, should always make the receiver just a little anxious, and the best kind of anxiety was the kind you shared.

It warmed his heart almost as if he had set the place on fire.

ACT THREE, SCENE FOUR

"To hell, allegiance! Vows, to the blackest devil!
Conscience and grace, to the profoundest pit!
I dare damnation."
(*Hamlet*, 4.5.134-6)

April 14, 1598. Time remaining: 20 hours 23 minutes.
Plays to be saved: *14+Folio.*

The Angelic Team

The three temporal doors opened, and the humans joined Gladys on the South Bankside once more. The former angel checked each quarto and smiled.

"Good," she said, apparently content with her mortal lot for the moment. "Welcome to 1598. Jimmy, you're getting *Love's Labours Lost.* Xavier, *Merchant of Venice.* Rose, *Henry IV Part One.* Your doors."

"Can we catch our breath first?" asked Jimmy, as the angel opened three new portals in front of them. "I just schlepped halfway across..."

"No," said Gladys. "We are on the clock. You can rest when we're done."

"You sound like my mother," said Rose with a resigned sadness that got her a sympathetic glance from Xavier. "Every Saturday morning cleaning the house from top to bottom. It was like being conscripted for war except that instead of a rifle you were handed a mop and a duster."

"My mom was the same," said Xavier. "Except that it was about feeding half the neighborhood. Stewing beans and shucking corn while my father fired up the grill, Marvin Gaye on in the background. That was his jam. I was all 'Play some Prince! Play some Snoop!' But Dad was all 'Just listen to this'..."

He smiled wanly.

Rose gave him a shrewd look. "What?" she asked.

Xavier looked down and shook his head slowly.

"Your dad's okay?" she said. "Right?"

Xavier blinked and stared. "Yeah," he lied breezily. "Just, you know, not as close as we were. But yeah. He's fine."

Rose hesitated. "That's good," she said, then, to smooth over the momentary awkwardness added, "my mom says you should be able to see your face in the counter tops," said Rose. "It's what her mother used to say to her. No Marvin Gaye for us though. My mother is into country music. Not bluegrass: the poppy stuff. Garth Brooks and Shania Twain. I have no idea why. No one we know is into that. Just her. It's so weird..."

"If we can get off the nostalgia bus," Gladys remarked, "the Get Your Life Back Express is about to leave."

"Funny," said Xavier darkly.

"And, as with all good comedy," said Gladys, nodding at the temporal portals, "it's funny because it's true. Go."

~

Jimmy

HAD Jimmy been trying to reach the Royal Exchange—site of Cuthbert Burby's print shop—in what he thought of as the present, we would have strolled across the Millennium Bridge to St. Paul's Cathedral and then headed east toward Bank in what was still known as The City. As it was, however, he had to navigate London Bridge—the one and only way to cross the Thames on foot—beginning with running the daunting gamut of a fortified gatehouse bristling with the tarred heads of traitors spitted upon pikes. For someone of Jimmy's checkered past, it was a bit of a facing.

He kept his eyes down and tried not to look shifty, but this only got him jostled and blocked by the constant tide of people and carts competing for the thin ribbon of roadway passing between and under the buildings that cluttered the bridge. He felt like a salmon swimming up river, except that there were hundreds of other salmon coming right back at him, and none of them were giving him an inch. Some—and here the salmon metaphor breaks down—wore fancy clothes, swords and the look of haughty righteousness that parted the seas before them, but Jimmy—ordinary, underdressed, and unarmed—was given no such privilege. English politeness, one of the few assumptions Jimmy had felt he could trust about coming to this damned country, had clearly not been invented yet, and the packed throng positively hummed with the threat of violence. Twice he was shouldered aside with looks which said that, should he choose to object, his opposite was keen to test his rapier on Jimmy's mid-section. As he labored toward the timber-framed and tulip-turreted four-story monster that was Nonsuch House, Jimmy came to a grumbling and ominous realization.

He wasn't going to make it to the book shop on time.

He began to run, muttering apologies as he blundered past people, spearing through the crowd as if he had spotted a squad car just as he dropped from a window in his mask and with a bag labelled "swag" over his shoulder. Someone shouted indignantly behind him, but he kept going, faster now, sweating through the unfamiliar clothes.

It took him the better part of an hour to reach the Royal Exchange, most of that spent on the damn bridge, but he made it in time. Just. He burst into Burby's shop anxious and sweating. He scanned the dim interior desperately, ignoring a single female customer who was perusing the wares, and set to rummaging through the stacks of books and pamphlets.

Where the hell was it?

He considered one after another, their titles bizarre and unfamiliar, and then his eye fell on a little teetering heap next to the woman.

"A

PLEASANT

Conceited Comedie

CALLED

Loues Labors Loft.

As it vvas presented before her Highnes this laft Chriftmas.

Newly corrected and augmented

By W. Shakefpeare."

"Thank God," he muttered.

"That's the Shakespeare?" the woman asked. She was cute in a polished sort of way. Good teeth for the period.

"Yep," said Jimmy, his relief making him stupid. He gave the pretty woman a roguish smile. "Came pretty far for this."

"Far?" said the woman, pouncing cat-like. Jimmy gave her a puzzled look. She hadn't just repeated his word, she had repeated it the way he had said it.

Fah.

"Yeah," he said, smiling flirtatiously. "I'm not what you'd call local."

"I guess not," said the woman, fluttering her eyelashes. "Did you also pahk the cah in Havard yahd?"

Jimmy grinned, then felt the chill of his own idiocy stealing over him.

"What?" he sputtered. "No, I'm from...Manchester. In England, not you know..."

"New Hampshire?" said the woman. Her smile had grown wolfish.

"What?" Jimmy said again, his face hot. "No. What's New Hampshire? I mean, nay forsooth, thou art verily mistaken, my fine wench..."

"Too late, loser," she said, grabbing the pile of plays and marching towards the counter purposefully.

"It's you!" said Jimmy, aghast. "You're..."

"...gonna burn this fucking nerd-fodder?" she completed. "You got that right."

"Burn it?" Jimmy exclaimed. His brain—rarely at the front of the line —was struggling to catch up, as if he'd left it stuck in traffic on London Bridge.

"And good riddance." She grinned coolly, looking him up and down

139

with utter contempt. "I don't know who you are, but if we were back home, in our own time, you'd see I was out of your league in every possible way, so you should give up whatever crazy-assed mission you think you're on because—and you can take this to the fucking bank— you're gonna lose, and it's gonna hurt."

"Is that right?" Jimmy spluttered. "Well...I think you'll find...that in the long run..."

But he knew she was right. She was classy and smart and he was... neither. Jimmy had no idea how someone like him was supposed to defeat someone like her in either the long or the short run. He faltered, but the gleam of smug victory in her eyes was more than he could bear. Words failed him, but Jimmy had always been more a man of action, albeit badly thought out and frequently incompetent action. He swiped the top play off the stack and ran with it.

ACT THREE, SCENE FIVE

"I am sorry I should force you to believe
That which I would to God I had not seen."
(*Henry IV part 2*, 1.1.105-6)

The Bear Garden, London, July 5, 1598.

Bliss

The most brutal form of entertainment the age had to offer, and by that I mean something that was designed to be nothing but entertainment as opposed to public executions that were supposed to serve some higher function on the part of the state, was bear baiting. The logic of this subtle sport involved chaining a bear (or sometimes a bull or other large animal) to a stake and setting dogs on it. Bets were placed, blood and carnage ensued, and the populace found it all terrifically diverting. The bears usually lived to fight another day, and many became local celebrities known by name to the populace. The dogs generally fared less well, but people considered themselves entertained, and that was what counted.

In twenty-first century Boston, Robert Bliss would have found the prospect of such a thing faintly distasteful, but presented with the reality of it in a world in which no one seemed to be carping about cruelty to animals, he found that his residual guilt burned off like a morning fog. Once he relaxed into it, he thought it all rather fun and was soon laughing and cheering along with the locals, and not just because some of what the frenzied animals were chewing up were balled up pages from *The First Part of Henry IV*, which he had been pelting at them since taking his seat.

"Woof woof, Falstaff," said Bliss, barking like the ravaged hounds. "Still think you're funny, you fat bastard?"

And then he laughed, the high, wild laugh he had picked up in Bedlam like it was a communicable disease. He could sense Belial watching him uneasily.

"Oh, lighten up," he said to the devil. "Just letting my hair down a little is all."

Bliss had come into Renaissance London with a profound sense of distaste for this world without cell phones and elevators and BMWs: he despised these people with their absurd dialects and their stupid clothes, but—he had decided—they did know how to have a good time. You couldn't spit without hitting a church, but they didn't seem to let all that holiness cramp their style where it came to good, old-fashioned blood sports. There was no whiney PC BS about how mean it was to fasten razor-edged spurs to a couple of roosters and watch them rip each other apart. It was fun and everyone knew it. Better yet, it was profitable. Some serious coin changed hands at these places, and Robert Bliss, first and foremost a businessman, had to admire that.

Even before striking his deal with Belial, he had been only nominally religious, but he had absorbed one of the core suspicions that haunted a lot of organized religion, that regardless what scriptures said to the contrary about the virtues of poverty, it was the rich who seemed to have God's favor. Yes, the poor were promised cake after they kicked off, but for the wealthy, cake came early and often. Since no divine power ever stepped in to hold up delivery for those who could afford it, it seemed safe to assume that Heaven would maintain the supply. Bliss' religion was capitalism, and if that might once have set him at odds with other religions, those days had long gone.

"How many of these people will go to Hell?" he inquired of Belial, as if he were asking whether it would rain later.

"Other than you?" said Belial.

"Funny. Yes, other than me."

"I can't say."

"You mean you don't know or you refuse to tell me?"

"Both," said the devil. "I don't make those determinations, and even if I did, I wouldn't know where a soul was going to spend eternity until the body connected to it had breathed its last."

"In case they repent at the last second?"

Belial shrugged. "That's easier said than done," said Belial, "especially if you've racked up some serious sin in your life, but yes, it's possible. Of course, words alone won't get it done, but evil can always be countered with good in ways providing a path to salvation."

"So you might not get me after all," said Bliss with a grin. "Despite our little agreement."

"I wouldn't hold your breath," said Belial. "As usual I am amazed at your flippancy. How can you sit in a place like this, stinking of death, and not reconsider *our little agreement*? Do you feel no terror at what you have done? At what will happen to you?"

Bliss was unmoved. "Eh." He shrugged. "What are you gonna do?"

"It's just inconceivable to me," said Belial, unable to stop himself, "that someone can be so cavalier about the most important thing in his existence! It's not all Transitional Stage Burger Bars, you know. That's just where you go to adjust. After that it's your own special eternity, and yours, my friend, does not look good."

Another shrug. "Something will turn up," said Bliss.

As if on cue, someone tapped him on the shoulder. It was Cathy Cornwall. She was holding a stack of quartos, but she looked livid and her face was a mask of grim resolution.

"Cathy...?" he began.

"We have a problem," she said.

ACT THREE, SCENE SIX

"This is the fairy land. O spite of spites!
We talk with goblins, elves and sprites.
If we obey them not, this will ensue:
They'll suck our breath or pinch us black and blue."
(*The Comedy of Errors*, 2.2.188-91)

March 18, 1599. Time remaining: 19 hours 06 minutes.
Plays to be saved: *11+Folio.*

Gladys

Gladys and the humans had gathered in a glade of young birch trees above the South Bank of the river to consider the alarming new wrinkle in their situation. It was cold and there was snow on the ground. On a tree stump, they had piled the plays they had collected thus far along with Jimmy's/Professor Lestering's *Complete Shakespeare* and Gladys' golden stopwatch.

"And you're sure it was the enemy?" Gladys confirmed.

"No question," said Jimmy. "Actually, she looked kind of familiar, like I might have seen her on TV or something."

"A movie star?" asked Gladys, thinking she wouldn't be the first who owed her career on the big screen to the machinations of Lucifer.

"I don't think so," said Jimmy. "More like a news anchor or a meteorologist or...*a talk show host.*"

"Cathy Cornwall," said Rose. It wasn't even a question.

"Yes!" said Jimmy. "I'm sure."

"I knew it!" said Rose. "I always hated that smug bitch."

"This is bad," said Gladys. "We were struggling to keep up as it was. If they know we are following them, they'll get the plays even quicker than they have been. Heavens to Murgatroyd!"

"Will you stop saying that?" said Jimmy.

"God damn it then!" Gladys exclaimed most unangelically. The humans exchanged worried glances, but Gladys had other things on her mind. "How do you people function like this?" she demanded.

"Like what?" asked Rose.

"Inching forward through time sequentially, one second after the next!" said Gladys, rubbing her temples. "It's insufferable. I feel like a rock waiting for continental drift to give me a change of scenery."

"Can't you, I don't know, slow things down or speed things up?" Jimmy said. He wasn't sure which would help and his confusion seemed only to exacerbate Gladys' frustration.

"I've told you," she snapped. "The rules for time travel are very precise! We can't go back, we can't re-enter the same moment more than once. We have to keep moving forward. We're just going to have to be much quicker."

"I thought this was all going to take no more than a couple of hours?" said Xavier, nettled by the angel's contempt.

"Well, if you could go directly to where the plays are for sale instead of wandering the city like lost tourists..."

"We are lost tourists!" Rose shot back. "Your map is garbage and we hardly dare risk asking directions for fear of being arrested as foreign spies!"

"Yes, I'm sure it's all very hard," Gladys returned in her best Disappointed Nun voice, "but if you want your lives back..."

"Yeah, yeah," said Xavier. "But I'm beat. And frankly, I could use a bathroom."

"There's no time," said Gladys. "Use the woods like everyone else."

"The woods?" said Xavier. "What do I look like, a bear?"

"The height of urban sanitation right now is a bucket," Rose suggested, "so I wouldn't turn my nose up at the woods. No pun intended."

"I think I'll hold it," said Xavier.

"Can we go?" demanded Gladys. Things were slipping away from her, she knew. In fact, the whole thing was starting to look not just impossible but preposterous. "There are a lot of plays published in 1600. Rose, start with *Much Ado,* then get *Henry V.* Jimmy you get *Midsummer Night's Dream.* Xavier, *The Merchant of Venice.*"

So saying, she began opening doors and the snow reflected their bluish light so that the trees threw precise, charcoal shadows like the spokes of a wheel around them.

"Can I trade with Rose?" said Xavier.

"Why, pray?" Gladys asked with a beady look.

"As a rule I try not to add to the world's store of racist literature," he said.

"Must we go over this again?" said Gladys. "If we don't maintain the whole canon, the timeline will rupture irreparably. *The Merchant of Venice* is a significant historical and cultural marker..."

"Yeah," said Xavier. "I believe the Nazis loved it."

"I don't think Shylock's the bad guy," said Rose. "He's reacting to years of mistreatment by the Christians..."

"Lots of good Jews in the play other than him?" Xavier shot back.

"There's Tubal," said Rose. "He's a good guy. Or not clearly a bad one."

"A ringing assault on antisemitism," said Xavier dryly.

"How about we save the fascinating literary debate till we are sitting in some cozy Boston library," Jimmy inserted, "where the plays are safely on the shelves and we are, you know, alive?"

Xavier gave him a *whose-side-are-you-on?* stare but then said, "Fine, but I'm trading with Rose."

"Suits me," said Rose.

Gladys sighed. They were all getting irritable.

"Ready?" she demanded. "Or do you need to relieve yourself in the woods?"

"I said I'll hold it," said Xavier sulkily, "but if this does serious damage to my gastrointestinal tract..."

"More damage than, say, a train?" Gladys prompted.

Jimmy scowled and stepped through. Rose gave Xavier a sympathetic look then followed suit.

"You'd better know what you're doing," said Xavier to Gladys. He did not wait for her response before stepping through his portal, which was just as well because she could think of nothing to say.

ACT THREE, SCENE SEVEN

"My brain I'll prove the female to my soul,
My soul the father, and these two beget
A generation of still-breeding thoughts;
And these same thoughts people this little world
In humors like the people of this world
For no thought is contented."
(*Richard II*, 5.5.6-11)

April 24, 1599.

Shakespeare

Only yards from where Gladys' angelic little covert ops squad had just stood, the writer, Richard Burbage, and the rest of the Chamberlain's Men were ferrying the timbers of their old theatre (AKA The Theatre) from a warehouse near Bridewell across the Thames to a spot on the South Bank between the old Clink prison and the church of St. Saviour.

Burbage was supervising the construction, or trying to. But the workers had as many actors among them as carpenters and builders, and it seemed unlikely that the structure would ever get finished. This fact was nicely emphasized by the scene playing out in front of him now, a scene in which a handful of the workers got their instructions confused, tripped, bumped into each other, and found three lengthy and therefore expensive beams of good English oak slipping from their grasp. They slid down the bank and, among a general and ineffectual cry, sploshed heavily into the river.

Burbage roared and there was another cry of accusation, a volley of pointing fingers and another dull splash as yet another timber vanished beneath the muddy surface of the Thames. Shakespeare leaped to his feet.

"You know what those timbers cost!?" he bellowed.

"Shouldn't you be writing?" said Burbage.

"That would be easier if I wasn't continually distracted by the world's stupidest builders busily DROWNING OUR INVESTMENT IN THE THAMES!"

This last was roared out for all to hear. The laborers lowered their eyes and muttered to each other about artists.

"Seriously, Will," said Burbage. "You are not helping. How's the new play coming?"

"Slowly."

"Well maybe you should spend less time here and more time in your study. Not much point building a theatre if we don't have new work to stage in it. A Brutus and Caesar play, yes?"

"That's almost done."

"I thought you said..."

"I have this other idea I want to get to," said the writer.

"What's it about?" asked Burbage, turning before the other could reply to bellow at the workers, "Not there! THERE!"

The men who were probing in the reeds for the fallen timbers moved three yards upstream in sheepish silence.

The writer waved the question away. "You'll see it when it's ready," he said.

"Writers," muttered Burbage. "Were you here last night?"

"Where?" Shakespeare asked.

"There," said Burbage, nodding toward the construction site. "Some of the boys said they saw someone wandering around. Thought he was looking to nick tools or lumber. When they asked him what he was doing, he stood and stared at them, like a man without a tongue."

"Does that sound like me?"

"No," said Burbage. "But... "

"What?"

"They said he looked like you," said Burbage with a nonchalant shrug, which did not entirely convince. "At first."

"What does that mean?" said the writer, laying down his pen.

"They thought it was you, and then he, sort of, looked different." Burbage spoke casually, but he kept his eyes on the building work a little too fixedly.

"You mean at first they thought it was me and then they got close or saw him in the light or..."

"Probably," said Burbage quickly. "Which is to say, that was probably what happened."

"But that's not what they said," Shakespeare prompted.

Burbage glanced at him, and his face was troubled. "It *was* dark," he conceded.

"Should I ask them about it?"

"No," said Burbage. "They have enough to think about."

"I'm going to ask them," said Shakespeare.

"What did I just say?"

"Which of them saw it?"

The pronoun raised Burbage's eyebrows.

"I mean *him*," said Shakespeare. "Which of them saw him?"

"The boys, Cooke and Beeston," said Burbage. Shakespeare made a face, unimpressed. Cooke was a child, with a child's imagination, and Beeston was as close to a snake as something with two legs could get. "And Will Kemp," added Burbage carefully.

"Kemp?!" exclaimed Shakespeare, his eyes flashing to where the company's chief comedian labored with the rest. "I'm going to speak to him."

"Will!" said Burbage as the writer moved quickly away. "Can we get through one day without you two yelling at each other like oyster wives?"

But Shakespeare was already striding toward a well-proportioned man with a full beard, a shaggy head of hair, and bright eyes.

"Master Kemp," he said.

"Master Shakespeare," the clown replied. The two disagreed so frequently of late that formal politeness was the only way they could interact.

"Burbage says you saw me here last night," said Shakespeare, failing to keep the note of challenge out of his voice.

"That I did," said Kemp, instantly cautious. "Or so I thought."

"You were mistaken," said Shakespeare.

"As I said, I *thought* I saw you."

The two men considered each other, then Shakespeare glanced briefly away.

"This man," he said at last. "He looked like me?"

"Most like," said Kemp. "Your height, your gait, your hair and—in so far as I could see them—your clothes. But then when I got close..."

"Yes?"

"It wasn't you," said Kemp, and he looked awkward, keen for the conversation to be over.

"It was someone else?"

Kemp moistened his lips, but he said nothing and his eyes flicked away like a nervous insect that didn't want to settle for fear of being swatted.

"It *was* someone else, right?" Shakespeare repeated.

Kemp's brows knitted and his eyes dropped to his feet. "I suppose," he said. "Though I couldn't make out his face."

"You approached him?"

"Yes, but then..."

"What?"

"There was this terrible smell," Kemp replied, looking up now, his face earnest. "And...it was like he wasn't really there. I could see the outline of him, but when I got close enough, his face was gray and blank, like he was made of smoke. He was as a shadow cast by nothing. Or rather," the clown added, "cast by you, though you were not present."

Shakespeare stared at him, reading the bafflement, conviction, and fear in the clown's face. In all the years they had known each other, all the debates and arguments about his brand of acting and notion of comedy, Kemp had never looked like this. The man was scared.

"He frightened you," said Shakespeare.

Kemp looked ready to deny it, but he caught himself and nodded.

"You thought he was dangerous? Unsound in his mind or just cruel?"

Kemp was shaking his head. "Neither," he said. "There was some cruelty there, but that wasn't really it."

"What then?"

Kemp looked away and then smiled at the absurdity of what he was about to say, as if it was all a joke and he didn't believe any of it. The smile didn't reach his eyes. "I said he frightened me," he confessed, "but I wasn't afraid of him. Not exactly. I was afraid...of *me*."

"Of yourself? I don't understand."

"Me neither, but it was as if he had opened up my very heart and in it, I saw such black and filthy spots that I hated myself almost as much as I hated him. And, worse, the hatred seemed to grow, like it was reaching out from my chest, my head, looking for something—someone —to hurt. Even to kill. I don't mind telling you, Will," he said, all pretense suddenly gone, honest and candid as he hadn't been for years, "it scared me. All of a sudden I was just so *angry*. I wanted to find someone to blame for everything that had ever gone wrong in my life. It was a rage unlike anything I had ever felt, and even though it was wild and dangerous, it felt cold, you know? Deliberate. Like I was capable of... unspeakable horrors after which I would walk away without so much as blanching and do more. I turned on the boys."

"You what?"

"They saw it in my face, ran before I could reach them, thank God. If they had stayed, I don't know what I might have done."

The writer stared at him. Kemp's face was white.

"You spoke to him?" said Shakespeare.

"I did. Asked him what he was doing, who he was."

"And?"

"And nothing, but then how could he respond?" said Kemp with another bleak little smile. "He had no mouth."

ACT THREE, SCENE EIGHT

"O, let the vile world end
And the promised flames of the last day
Knit earth and heaven together"
(*Henry VI part 2*, 5.2.40-2)

July 5, 1598.

Bliss

Bliss was angry that someone was trying to mess up his plans, but he had also picked up on Cornwall's resolution and was glad of the chance to stick it to someone. Or something.

"Angels," said Belial. "One angel, at least, probably with some human operatives."

"The bastards!" Bliss spat.

"So some unfunny comedy no one cares about survives!" said Cornwall. "Big deal. We just have to get to the rest before they do."

"But we can't be sure they haven't been doing something similar all along," said Belial. "They may have more than *Love's Labours Lost*."

"Then we'd better make sure they don't get any more," Cornwall said, darkly. "I told you, this would all be much more efficient if we just killed Shakespeare before he could even write them..."

"And I told you we can't do that," said Belial.

"Unless we find a willing agent among the locals," Bliss added.

"Yes," Belial conceded. "But since you aren't exactly locals yourselves, any attempt to get into the good graces of the population is just as likely to get *you* killed. It's not what you'd call an inclusive and tolerant culture."

"We could pay someone," Cornwall suggested.

Belial shook his head.

"Too quid pro quo," he said.

"Meaning?" said Cornwall.

"It's overstepping," the devil replied. "I already explained this. If you can persuade someone to do it of their own volition, fine. But paying someone makes them your employee. That puts responsibility on you, so the act will be immediately blocked by the powers that be, who will be sure to deal out some significant and terminal punishment for their trouble."

"So we just have to suggest to someone that they kill Shakespeare," Bliss mused.

"How hard can that be?" said Cornwall. "I mean, there must be thousands of people who have seen one of his shows and would cheerfully knife the guy, right?"

"And you'll find them how?" asked Belial. "It's not like you can start a *Let's Murder Shakespeare* Facebook group."

"You think we should keep doing what we're doing," said Bliss, eyeing the devil unhappily.

"Until a better option presents itself," Belial replied, "yes. We'll have to be faster and find ways to get each play as soon as it is completed so they can't beat us to it."

"Can you do it, devil?" asked Cornwall, who was clearly disappointed that they had shelved the assassination option.

"Of course I *can*..." Belial said.

"Yet here we are still, *not* doing it," said Bliss, with a hint of menace.

Belial shrugged, resigned and a trifle exasperated.

"Right," he said simply. With no enthusiasm whatsoever, he

snapped open a pair of temporal doors. "*A Midsummer Night's Dream*," he said.

"That's the one with the fairies, right?" asked Bliss.

"Oberon and Puck, Titania..." Belial began.

"Yeah, I thought so," said Bliss. "You want to explain to me why we teach kids stories about fairies, for God's sake? You think that's going to help them get jobs, pay their bills, put their kids through college?"

"Perhaps there's more to education than..." Belial began.

"I thought we were in a rush?" said Cornwall.

"An excellent point," said Bliss.

Belial glared at him then nodded at the glowing doors.

"Just go," he said.

ACT THREE, SCENE NINE

"So minutes, hours, days, months and years,
Passed over to the end they were created,
Would bring white hairs unto a quiet grave."
(*Henry VI part 3*, 2.5.38-40)

September 25, 1600. Time remaining: 15 hours 23 minutes.
Plays to be saved: *8+Folio.*

Xavier and Rose

The Rose had seen better days. In a couple of years, it would again play to enthusiastic audiences with Worcester's Men strutting and fretting upon its stage, but now no flag flew above the silent theatre and it showed signs of disrepair. Burbage's Blackfriars Theatre—one of the indoor "Hall" playhouses—was finally in use by a company of boy actors, and the Chamberlain's Men had taken up residence at the newly completed Globe a little ways down the South Bank. Langley's ill-fated Swan was functioning only sporadically, and Philip Henslowe and the Admiral's Men had moved north of the city to The Fortune, escaping the competition of the South Bankside.

Xavier and Rose liked the old theatre. It felt expansive and yet intimate, as the best theatres always do, and it made you want to act. Rose stood up and, standing center stage as no other woman had done to date, looked at the open quarto she had been ready to add to the pile and pronounced loudly: "*Once more unto the breach dear friends, once more, or close the wall up with our English dead!* Cool."

She grinned at Xavier, but he rolled his eyes.

"Give me *Star Wars* any day," he said.

"I saw a movie of this," she said. "*Henry the Fifth*. It was…"

She sought for a word and Xavier supplied a couple. "Self-indulgent?" he suggested. "Elitist?"

"Have you even seen it?" said Rose, piqued.

"Yes, actually," Xavier replied. "I'm just saying…"

"I know what you're saying," Rose returned, needled. "You've been saying it ever since we started this. And I'm tired of hearing it."

"It's just hard to have to spend my time working to save this stuff when I think the world might be better off without it."

"Because you think it's racist," said Rose, conscious that she was inching out over a very narrow bridge but determined to take the bull by the horns. On a narrow bridge.

"I think it's a brand of culture whose day has passed," said Xavier carefully. "But since you ask, yeah, I think some of it is racist."

"*Othello*."

"Give the lady a prize."

"But *Othello* is a play *about* racism!" Rose exclaimed. "Iago speaks for a culture that didn't accept a Black man even though he's the head of their army!"

"And that Black man," said Xavier. "What does he do at the end?"

Rose flushed but did not dial down her defiance.

"He kills his wife," she admitted, "but…"

"His white wife."

"Yes, but…"

"For a crime of which she is innocent," said Xavier, pounding the point home.

"Because Iago exploits his insecurity and fills his head with misogyny. Othello's Blackness is irrelevant. The play isn't about race; it's about gender."

"Can we go back to what Othello does to his wife when he—mistakenly, stupidly—decides she has been having an affair?" said Xavier, not giving an inch.

"I don't deny that he's..."

"A noble savage?" said Xavier bitterly. "A barbarian dressed up like a civilized person like a horse in a hat? Worse, he's a wolf in sheep's clothes. He looks like one of you, but the wolf was always gonna come out."

"One of you?" said Rose, indignant.

"A white man's Black man, played on this very stage or one just like it by a guy in blackface. It's a case study in the unnaturalness of a white woman marrying a Black man."

"Well, I don't see it that way," said Rose.

"Of course you don't!" said Xavier. "Because it isn't you!"

Rose hesitated, but she couldn't let it go. "Shakespeare didn't say all Black men were like that," she said

"He didn't have to! He wrote this one, and he stands in for the rest. Where's his Black Hamlet? His Black Orsino? He writes one Black guy, and it turns out that underneath all the nobility, all the borrowed civilization, he's still a savage, still a monster. And because he's the only Black man in the play—in practically any of the plays—he stands in for the rest. For all of us. That's what the audience takes away. You don't think that's racist? This play has hung around the necks of Black men like a sign for four centuries. Like a noose. Must be true, because it's Shakespeare! Who doesn't know humanity better than the Bard?"

"I don't think it's that simple," said Rose, less sure of herself.

"No? You don't think that among the lynch mob who killed Emmett Till there was someone who had read or heard of that fucking play? You don't think that felt like evidence of a Black boy's crime? Like Proof?"

Xavier's voice had maintained its level calm, but his eyes were wide and shining with rage. And grief. Rose stared at him, mouthing nothing in the sudden silence. When at last he broke his hollow stare and seemed to study his own hands, she nodded.

"Right," she said in a small voice. "I see what you mean."

"And the angels want us to save it," said Xavier with bitter amusement. "The guardians of holiness and virtue think that what the world really needs is another high literary excuse to make Black men the world's whipping boy."

"I'm sorry," said Rose. "I hadn't thought of it like that."

"Why would you?" said Xavier. He made a vague gesture, then added, softer this time, "It's not about you."

"I see that. I'm sorry."

"It's fine. It's not your fault. It's not like I hate every part of the play... But that ending, man. I can't get past that."

There was another loaded silence and Rose sat heavily. "I want to go home," she said. As soon as the words were out, she laughed at them.

"Right there with you," said Xavier.

"You think we ever will?"

She hadn't admitted to herself just how much she had begun to think she wouldn't.

"Sure," said Xavier. "With our crack team of intergalactic specialists, or whatever the hell we are? What could possibly go wrong?"

Rose smiled faintly.

"I'm really sorry about before," she said.

Xavier managed a grin.

"It is what it is," he said. "Hell, I can't even really blame Shakespeare. He's just a guy from, you know, *here*, loaded up with the bigotries and ignorance of his age. I mean, have you looked around you at the golden age of Western culture and sophistication? Hanging witches, burning heretics, massacring the Irish, gutting the political opposition, and sticking their heads up on spikes like Christmas decorations? It's like *Lord of the* fucking *Flies*. And this is where he lives, the world he writes out of. It's amazing every word Shakespeare ever wrote doesn't turn my stomach."

It took a second for Rose to register what he had just said. "You like some of it," she said.

"What?"

"Shakespeare. It drives you mad and some of it you hate..."

"Absolutely."

"But some of it..."

Xavier glanced away.

"Some of it," Rose repeated.

"Yeah, okay," said Xavier grudgingly. "Some of it is pretty good, though that's not the point."

"What's the point?"

"That art can be good—great even—and still celebrate values that are messed up, outmoded, disgusting to other periods and cultures."

"So you throw it all out? Bathwater, baby, the works?"

"If, on balance, the effect does more harm than good, yes."

"And you think that's true of Shakespeare?"

"I think he takes up space that could go to work more clearly relevant to the present," he said. "Like, in school. Kids need to see themselves in what they read. Otherwise books are just another set of hoops to jump through on your way to graduation."

"Isn't reading also about seeing through the eyes of people who *aren't* you? Sounds pretty limiting that the only thing worth reading is whatever represents the experience you already have? Reading is about empathy, right?"

"Maybe I don't want empathy. Maybe I want justice. And maybe you think that way because your experience is already represented pretty fully in schoolbooks."

"Because I'm white?" said Rose. "You think Shakespeare represents the world of a twenty-year-old in twenty-first century Boston if they're white? The beauty of Shakespeare is that he doesn't represent *anyone's* experience anymore because the people he wrote for have been dead four centuries..."

"Present company excepted," said Xavier, glancing around their pointedly Renaissance surroundings.

"True," said Rose, grinning. "I mean, if we were home. What I'm saying is, he's up for grabs. He's not mine any more than he is yours or anyone else's. I read him the way I want to. I find what interests me, not what represents me."

"And what about the kids who feel that Shakespeare is just a stick to beat them with, a way of reminding them that they aren't sophisticated enough?"

"It's challenging. But school should be challenging, shouldn't it? It's supposed to stretch you, make you think."

"So it's hazing. More hoops to jump through."

"No! The richness of the work justifies the difficulty," said Rose.

"It's not just about difficulty," said Xavier, raising a warning finger but grinning. "Lots of books are rich and difficult. The assumption that Shakespeare is the richest is lazy and, yes, colonial."

"So you want a balanced curriculum in schools. I have no problem with that."

"Okay then," said Xavier. "Good. But then the teachers have to know what they're doing in school, and I still wouldn't be giving some of this stuff to little kids."

"Okay," said Rose.

"And school isn't the same as theatre," said Xavier, gazing round the building. "In a classroom you can talk this stuff through, interrogate it, contextualize it, and so on. You can't do that here. There's no pop-up footnotes to explain the subtext while the story is happening in front of you. That's different. Makes it feel...real. Or at least endorsed: like, this is how it is and we're not going to explain it. Study it critically by all means, talk about it, but don't stage *Othello* and expect me to just sit there and drink it in, okay? Not gonna happen. Not *Othello*, and not *The Merchant of Venice*."

"Or *Taming of the Shrew*," said Rose a little sheepishly.

"Yeah?"

"Yeah," she admitted. "I had a teacher who kept trying to read the ending like it was a feminist joke, but it still feels like a play celebrating spousal abuse to me."

"The other women don't bother you?"

"Sometimes," said Rose shrugging. "The *I'm so weak, whatever shall I do?* stuff. But there's a lot of tough, kickass women too."

"Lady Macbeth?" said Xavier. "She's quite the role model."

"Who's looking for role models in the books I read? Not me. I want compelling characters who do interesting things. And what about Viola and Rosalind, Titania, Imogen, Beatrice? Women who take charge and go after what they want, what they need. Yeah, they are of their time, but I don't think it's reasonable to expect history to always reflect twenty-first century values, do you?"

"No, but then we shouldn't assume the plays speak timeless truths."

"We don't!" said Rose. "Art is of the period that made it. My professor said that."

"That would be the professor who is pointedly not Jimmy and is currently looking for his wallet?"

"That's the one. Anyway. Yes, there are issues..."

Xavier grinned almost in spite of himself. "Some of the other stuff though," he conceded, letting the sentence hang unfinished.

"Some of the other stuff," Rose concurred, grinning.

"Don't tell anyone I said that."

"And if I do?" she asked, managing a smile that was almost playful.

"I won't watch the movie with you."

"What movie?"

"*Henry the* Goddamned *Fifth*," he explained. "I'll watch it. When we get back."

"Oh," she said, trying to hold onto some of her defiance, but feeling it dissolve into gratitude, less at the prospect of finding common ground over Shakespeare and more that he had taken it for granted that they would, eventually, get back. "I'll hold you to that."

"Fine." He smiled, then caught himself and looked suddenly pained. "But you hear what I'm saying, right? It isn't a little thing. I don't just have a chip on my shoulder or something. You know? It's huge. It's history. It's social conditioning, and people—my people—have died for it. Still are doing."

"Yes," she said.

"Okay then."

Rose blushed and looked down, not knowing what to say, relieved when two temporal portals flashed open almost simultaneously. Gladys emerged from one with a slim volume in her hands. Jimmy came through the other, but his eyes were full of panic and his hands were empty.

"*Midsummer Night's Dream*!" he exclaimed. "It's gone!"

"What?" gasped Rose.

"I got there but they had already taken the lot."

Gladys put the heels of her palms to her temples and pressed hard, her eyes shut.

"Can't we just go back a few hours earlier," said Xavier. "Get one as they leave the printers or something?"

"Can't," said Gladys, joining them in the pit. "Remember the second twenty-four-hour rule? We only get one shot at each day. We missed."

"You think it's a big one?" Jimmy ventured hopefully.

"Lord what fools these mortals be," said Gladys.

"Hey!" Jimmy replied. "That includes you, now!"

"I was quoting," Gladys clarified. "The course of true love never did run smooth. Though she be but little, she is fierce. The lunatic the lover and the poet are of imagination all compact..."

"Okay," said Rose, but Gladys wasn't done.

"If we shadows have offended," she went on, "think but this and all is mended..."

"I know a bank where the wild thyme blows," said Xavier unexpectedly, "where oxlips and the nodding violet grows, quite over canopied with luscious woodbine, with sweet musk roses and with eglantine..."

He stopped and the others stared at him.

"You can quote all that?" said Rose, stunned.

"Used it as an audition piece in college," said Xavier with a confessional shrug. "I was...a bit of a theatre geek. It was supposed to be good training for public speaking. Anyway. I had to have some classical speeches to prove I could do them. Show directors I was, you know, a person."

He said this pointedly to Rose, who lowered her gaze again. Gladys went on oblivious.

"It's taught in schools and colleges all over the world! It's been staged by almost every major theatre company for four centuries as well as by high schools and community theatres. It has spawned ballets, operas, and movies. It has been adapted for novels and comic books..."

"Okay," said Xavier and Rose simultaneously.

"I'd say it was fairly important, yes," Gladys concluded. "Without it..."

"We fail," said Xavier, his voice low and hollow as the bell in a distant temple. "The future—our future—unravels and we wink out of existence."

"What are we going to do?" Jimmy asked.

"I don't see what we *can* do," said Gladys. "If the entire print run has been destroyed, we're..."

"Screwed," said Xavier, hollowly.

"As you say," said Gladys. "Screwed."

ACT THREE, SCENE TEN

"Love is merely a madness and, I tell you, deserves
as well a dark house and a whip as madmen do;
and the reason why they are not so punished and
cured is that the lunacy is so ordinary that the
whippers are in love too."
(*As You Like It* 3.2.390-4)

London, October 1600.

Belial

B liss and Cornwall were, of course, delighted. Not only were the angelic team, as they had just realized, screwed, the means to said screwing was itself a delight. They were burning the last copies of *A Midsummer Night's Dream* each lost in their own joys, but Belial knew their minds better than they did themselves. Take Cathy Cornwall, for instance. She had loathed this particular play since reading it in high school, and not just because not understanding it had harmed her self-esteem. It wasn't the fairy stuff Cornwall hated so much as the way it used magic to tidy up the problems of the world: magic and love.

Cathy Cornwall hated love. She had learned to keep that particular sentiment out of her books and TV broadcasts, but it was one of the passions that lit her from within like a blowtorch. Romantic love was the grand illusion as far as she was concerned. It was a myth perpetuated by Hallmark and Hollywood to distract people from their bleak and empty lives, promising to one day fix and make sense of everything. It was a lie. There was sex, which was fun, and alliance, which was useful, and even friendship of a sort, which thwarted loneliness, but love? No. That was a ruse. It put money in the pockets of the popstars and filmmakers, but it was no more real than Bigfoot and far more dangerous. Love and the pursuit thereof was the great self-deception and that was anathema to Cathy Cornwall. Like the song said, the only thing worthy of real love was yourself, the greatest love of all. Every morning Cathy Cornwall considered herself in the mirror and with the fervor of a saint bowing before the divine, whispered, "*You* are what matters, *your* feelings, *your* pride. Everything else is secondary. Love yourself. Love yourself to the exclusion of all others. Love yourself beyond riches, beyond virtue or principle, beyond human connection, beyond life itself."

And she believed it. Belial could look into the space where her soul had been and he knew this as surely as he knew Bliss' desire to show the world he was a Big Man and spit in the eye of the culture that derided his brand of success. He knew she believed it because she wanted to, because that made all the hurt and loneliness bearable.

Or very nearly so.

"Love looks not with the eyes but with the mind," said the play, "and therefore is winged Cupid painted blind." Bullshit, thought Cornwall; Cupid was blind because love was arbitrary, a simple matter of hormones and urges satisfied by whoever happened to be available. It wasn't about a connection. That was nonsense, a fantasy as stupid and fruitless as hunting unicorns.

But then she had been telling herself that since she had sat in a high school classroom with her battered copy of the play on her desk, eying Richy Sacramento whom she had been dreaming about for months and who studiously ignored her. God, how she had hated herself, her slightly crooked teeth and the heavy glasses her mother had insisted on buying instead of springing for the cool ones with the delicate blue frames. How her insides had writhed when she had glimpsed Richy holding hands with blond, leggy Darcy Holden.

Where were the fucking fairies then? Where was the magic flower that might anoint Richy's eyes till they couldn't stay off Cathy as she walked by? Where was the comic resolution, the joy, the connection?

Nowhere.

So it was her face the devil watched, lit by the flickering light of the burning plays. Belial saw more than satisfaction there. He saw glee, the thrill at torpedoing one of the flagships of her great enemy, and underneath it, deep, deep down, so far beneath the surface that she was almost certainly unaware of it, he saw the tiny fissure of loss and grief that opened up as she accepted what would never be.

He opened his mouth, determined to say something, to offer an alternative, a way back before it was too late, but before he could find the words, he felt the insistent pull in his mid-section and saw his right hand fading, turning to dust and blowing away. His arm followed suit, painless but relentless, as if it was burning at so high a temperature that it was vaporizing bit by bit.

"Belial?" said Bliss, staring in horror. "What the hell...?"

Belial opened his eyes and mouth wide, a silent cry of despair and terror, and then he was being sucked out of the English Renaissance, out of the world entirely, and where he was going there was only *Him*.

Waiting.

ACT THREE, SCENE ELEVEN

"And thus I clothe my naked villainy
With odd old ends stolen forth of Holy Writ
And seem a saint when most I play the devil."
(*Richard III*, 1.3.136-8)

Belial

B elial opened his eyes cautiously, glanced quickly around him, thought better of it, and shut them again. He was in an immeasurable stone cavern lit from beneath by a dull, crimson glow that drifted up from an indescribably immense lake of flame, though from this tremendous height he could see only the blurring heat-haze and the fog-like smoke that flared erratically with light from the geysers of fire below. He was perched like a nesting osprey on a stone crag, which rose hundreds of feet out of the burning lake like a broken tooth, and above him, roosting on a slightly higher pinnacle, bat wings spread in a great canopy of blackness like the umbrella from Hell, sat Beelzebub.

Belial shuddered, feeling simultaneously a rush of awestruck horror and a hint of disdain that his demonic superiors always went for the awestruck horror thing like a heavy metal band selecting album covers.

"Belial, me old mate," croaked Beelzebub in a voice that, were Belial a mere mortal, would have sent him diving into the lake of fire. As it was, he merely swallowed hard and looked up apprehensively.

"Yes, lord," he said.

"You've been summoned to report on your doings," said Beelzebub, pleased by the effect of the whole giant-bat-horror guise. "But, before you answer, right?" he continued, "you oughta know that HE has been asking about, shall we say, the value of your recent activities. Funny really. Always wanted to get noticed, didn't you, Belial, old pal? This probably wasn't what you had in mind though."

"Quite," said Belial, hating Beelzebub as only a devil can hate one of his own kind.

"But perhaps there's a perfectly reasonable explanation for you spending all your time in the past, messing about with history and what not, instead of, you know, Garnering Souls and Enlarging The Infernal Kingdom."

"Absolutely," said Belial, his mind racing.

"So why don't you explain to me what's been going on," said Beelzebub in that slow, insinuating way of his that sounded like one of Jimmy's less savory acquaintances suggesting that you pay the extra thousand and keep the other leg unbroken. "I'm sure you can clear all this up to everyone's satisfaction. You see, when people don't help me out, then I can't tell HIM what he wants to hear, and his Hellish Lordship gets a tad irritated, you know what I'm saying, Belial? So it's in my best interest to have what we like to call *full command of the facts at hand*, if you follow my drift. But when certain parties hold out on me, depriving me of the capacity to complete my task according to instructions, as it were, I'm put in a sticky situation with HIM, and I really don't like that. I fuckin' hate it, in fact. I hate it so much that them parties that don't give me what I want tend to suffer all kinds of Nasty Accidents. 'orrible, it is. I can't think why they do it, but there it is. One minute a helpful little devil is having trouble remembering what he's been up to, and next thing you know he's nothing but a little heap of bleeding limbs that keep catching fire while he screams his head off. I can't think why, but it does seem to happen."

He paused for effect and changed tack.

"Now you: you're a smart little demon aren't you, Belial?" Beelzebub oozed. "Too smart for your own good, some might say, but not me. Me, I say, he's a bright one is Belial, not the kind of devil to go about having Nasty Accidents and getting himself involved in eternal torment. Not Belial. So why don't you prove me right, me old mate, and straighten all this stuff out, and I won't, just for instance, make myself some earrings out of your eyelids?"

Belial waited the customary preamble out with a submissive look on his face while his brain sifted through Strategies Least Likely To Get Him Minced.

"Well," he said, when Beelzebub had finished flexing his wings and tapping his murderous talons on the edge of the rock, a kind of rhetorical punctuation he always used to end his Menacing Speeches, "it's all quite straightforward really."

"Oh," said Beelzebub with a benevolent smile, "I am so very pleased to hear that. Very pleased indeed. Why don't you fill me in on the details and then we can all get right back to work?"

He probed between his fangs with one of his eight-foot, needle-like claws and then looked at it pensively, as if wondering where he might insert it next.

"Very simple, really," Belial replied. "I've enslaved a couple of twenty-first century humans and, in return for their eternal souls, I'm doing them a few favors."

"One of which involves going back in time and changing stuff, does it?" said Beelzebub, still considering his talon.

"Yes. You see, Mr. Robert Bliss who has signed his soul over to me wanted..."

"Now hold on a minute," said Beelzebub slowly. "Let me get this absolutely right, 'cause I wouldn't want to make a mistake on something like this. You, Belial, have gone back in time, what? Four hundred years? And taken a couple of humans with you, and started messing with history, stealing art and stuff, for the sake of one soul?"

"Right," said Belial. There was a long pause and Beelzebub let out a deep breath that turned into a jet of yellow flame that spouted a hundred yards over head.

"Now, we've got a couple of problems here, haven't we, Belial, me old mate?" he said. "First, this is a lot of trouble to go to for one soul."

"Two," Belial inserted.

"Two," said Beelzebub magnanimously. "I stand corrected. Now I respect your energy in the matter, but a lot of demons are gonna say that this is not what you'd call a productive division of labor when you could be inspiring acts of genuine Evil. But we'll leave that for the moment. The second thing—right?—is that you're messing with history. Now, that's a big no-no, isn't it, Belial? You can't just walk into the 1590s and start messing things about. It don't work like that. Any demonic activity in another time requires a direct summons..."

"I had one," Belial cut in.

"What?"

"I had a direct summons, an invocation," Belial explained. "A human in 1594 called on the devil, performed all the usual rituals, blasphemed the name of God and everything. The works. It was a textbook summons, so I went. Once I was in, I could do what I wanted, right?"

Beelzebub thought. "A textbook summons?" he said. "You sure? 'Cause it never showed up in the ledgers."

"Must be an oversight," said Belial cheerily. "Textbook, it was. A mister Edward Alleyn in the Rose Theatre"

"I can't say I know the name," said Beelzebub uncertainly, "but if it was a real summons then I suppose you're alright."

As before, Beelzebub's gigantic wings flickered slightly and, as a strangely uncertain and irritated light came into the demon's great eyes, he managed a rather unconvincing smile.

"Right," said Beelzebub. "Then everything should be alright. Good for you, in fact. All power to you. Use the summons to cause as much misery and devastation as you can."

"My thoughts exactly," said Belial.

"So what misery and devastation have you actually caused there?" said Beelzebub, recovering some of his poise.

"Oh," said Belial. "Well... I've been stealing the works of Shakespeare and burning them, like my man wanted."

"Shakespeare? Playwriter bloke?"

"And poet. That's the one."

"What else?"

"So far?"

"As you say."

"Er," said Belial as if poring over a lengthy mental list. "Well, so far, that's about all."

"That's it?"

"Pretty much."

"And that's your idea of devastation, is it?" said Beelzebub, pleased that his role was becoming clear again.

"Culturally, yes," Belial answered.

"Culturally? What the hell does that mean?"

"Well, the twenty-first century has rather lost interest in good and evil," Belial explained. "There's no sacrificing of virgins or anything anymore. There's plenty of hatred and evil, of course, but it's usually small-scale *human* evil, you know: bad mouthing your co-workers to get in good with the boss, waiting till the last second and then forcing your way into the exit lane when there were signs telling you to get over half a mile back, voting for your own pay-raises and tax breaks while other people struggle to feed their kids, making fun of what people like on social media—actually almost anything on social media—not flushing public toilets, things like that. The problem is that the heavenly powers determined long ago that no one should be damned for things they didn't understand are evil. And that used to be fine. Religion and codes of behavior were built around the importance of the community made sure that people knew what right and wrong were supposed to be."

"And now they don't?"

"Society has changed. Goodness is in the eye of the beholder because what people used to call selfishness is now wholesome self-advancement. Even religion is in on it, telling people they can pray for windfalls, and that owning fancy cars and mansions is a mark of divine favor. *Ambition* used to be a dirty word. Now it's just a sign of healthy self-actualization."

"Self...what?"

"The community is less important than the individual," Belial continued. "Blessed are the poor? Forget it. The poor are just the refuse who haven't pulled themselves up by their bootstraps. The homeless, the migrant workers, and refugees, people about whom the New Testament has a lot to say, are now the irrelevant dregs of a culture that uses phrases like 'wealth management' unironically. Going to church seems to make no difference to what people do with their time, what they value, or how they vote. People today are almost impossible to damn because they think they are essentially virtuous no matter what they do."

"But isn't there plenty of rape and murder in the twenty-first century? Fornication, stuff like that?"

"Oh yes, never better," said Belial airily. "But a lot of it isn't sin any more. Take fornication, for example. In the old days you could catch some guy checking out a girl's ankle and then whisper in his ear how evil he was and he'd believe you. He thought it was a sin, so it was. Nowadays, everyone's cheerfully copulating all over the place and it's not sin, it's Healthy Living."

"Really?"

"Oh yes. I mean, of course you have the religious nuts for whom pretty much everything is a sin, but you can't prosecute that, can you?"

"Can't you?" asked Beelzebub.

"Nah. These are the kinds of people who spend their high school years counting the bad words in *The Catcher in the Rye* and then trying to get *Harry Potter* banned from the library. They're a kind of moral police force, but they're too delusional to take seriously, and half of them work for us anyway. The thing about evil in the twenty-first century is that it is reserved for Other People. In the Middle Ages," said Belial, sensing he had his superior on the run, "evil was lurking round every corner in a woman's hemline, a missed liturgical service, a thought about the lord of the manor, and so on. Everything was sin. Now, it's just things that 99 percent of the population never do, like killing or raping people, and if you're entitled enough, you can even find justifications for those. There are real villains, monsters who knowingly do terrible things, but they just make the rest of humanity feel pretty good about itself morally. *See?* they say. *At least I'm not that guy.* They think they are all Good People just as they think they are above average drivers."

"So we need to explain things to them, do we?" said Beelzebub, unsure of himself for the first time in eons.

"No point. The humans have developed a global communication technology designed to contain all knowledge."

"That must have made them smarter."

"You'd think so, wouldn't you?" said Belial. "The reality is that all it means is that there will always be someone out there who will argue that black is white, and you can decide to listen to that and that alone. Morality is always muddy because you can choose who to believe, thereby validating your view of the universe and your place therein. I had always assumed the internet was one of ours, no?"

"Never heard of it," said Beelzebub.

"Pity," said Belial. "Anyway, it means that they can justify practically anything to themselves. Competing notions of morality are just fake news."

Beelzebub's wings drooped a little. "I don't understand," he said. "What does what they think have to do with anything? Sin is sin. The fact that they don't *think* it's sin...well that's *immaterial*, ain't it?"

"There's two men," said Belial. "One of them parks his car on a hill but forgets to put the brake on. He walks away and the car rolls down the hill, hits a pedestrian, and kills them. Got that?"

"Got it."

"Another man is driving his car..."

"Same car?"

"Different car."

"Right."

"And he deliberately drives into a pedestrian he sees crossing the road..."

"This is a different pedestrian than the one who got hit by the other car?"

Belial hesitated, his eyes narrow, then pressed on. "Yep, different car, different pedestrian."

"And a different *driver*," added Beelzebub, as if Belial might have forgotten.

"The point," said Belial, gritting his teeth, "is that both men killed someone. But are they both guilty of the same crime?"

"Tricky," said Beelzebub.

"It is," said Belial, the teacher encouraging a child who is about to get the answer wrong but has at least stopped eating the crayons. "The first man might be accused of stupidity and negligence, while the second is a murderer. Same outcome, different crimes, and very different from the guy who hides in his neighbor's house for three hours and then hits them with a piece of pipe when they come home."

"Which one is he?"

"It doesn't matter," said Belial. "I'm just saying that you can do lots of things that lead to someone's death, and they aren't all equal in the eyes of divine justice."

"Don't seem right, do it?"

"No, but that's where we are. You can't sin without knowing it. You have to be aware that you're doing wrong to be considered guilty when you come to judgment. Part of the Mercy of God, isn't it?"

"Language!" said Beelzebub genuinely shocked. "So you're saying that if they don't believe what they are doing is wrong, we can't prosecute them for it?"

"'Fraid so."

"That's a fucking outrage, that is!" said Beelzebub, shooting another jet of fire out over the lake.

"Nature of the beast, I'm afraid."

"Where?" said Beelzebub looking around anxiously.

"Not *The Beast*," said Belial. "Just a turn of phrase."

"Thank Lucifer for that. Okay, but what's this got to do with Shakespeare?" Beelzebub demanded.

"Partly it's just giving people like Bliss and Cornwall what they want, partly it's to impoverish culture."

"You mean that if you take away all the high points of art, literature, and stuff, people's lives will be so miserable that they'll turn to us for power and pleasure?" said Beelzebub, hopefully.

"No."

"Oh. What then?"

"We have to think long term," said Belial. "Our ideas of sin have always been rooted in *active* thought or deed: deliberation. What we have to do is make the absence of active goodness and spirituality a sin."

"Huh?"

"Remember the old sins of omission: not doing something you should have, not speaking the truth even though you didn't actually lie? Not sending money to the starving millions in one of those hot countries the west has been milking of resources for centuries? Not chasing after someone who drops a twenty dollar bill? Religion used to offer a continual sense of everyone's essential sinfulness. Not anymore. Guilt is pretty much out."

"I don't like this," said Beelzebub.

"No, and neither do the opposition," said Belial. "HEAVEN is starting to think that simply not being bad by twenty-first century standards isn't enough to get you through their pearly gates. A lot of saints and angels are looking at Earth and seeing people just drifting along without ever making a moral choice in their life and then coming straight up for an eternity of harps and clouds, and it's starting to piss them off. Rules are going to change. They are going to make apathy a sin. When they do, our kingdom will open up like a Las Vegas buffet."

"I still don't see what this has to do with Shakespeare."

"We have to encourage that apathy if we are going to win souls, see?" he said, as if it was blindingly obvious. "We strip culture of anything that might challenge, anything that pushes people to think, to feel deeply, to contemplate *anything*, because so long as those options are there, we don't have them as passive as we want them. Once they are deprived of the things that lead to passion, conviction, intellectual analysis of any kind, they become vegetables, devoid of reason, devoid of the power to act, devoid of the power to reach out to God or man in any meaningful way. They'll be damned by their inaction and we, Lord, will be sitting pretty."

Beelzebub nodded thoughtfully, his eyes narrow, and Belial held his breath. At last, the great bat-demon nodded and smiled.

"I knew you were a smart one, Belial, old son," Beelzebub remarked. "You just keep at it, and I'll watch your back for a while."

"For which, when all this comes to pass, I'm sure our mutual Lord will reward you most fulsomely."

"Yeah," said Beelzebub, grinning hideously. "*Fulsomely*. I like that."

"I thought you might."

"There is one other thing," said the great bat-like demon, leaning forward so that even in victory—or at least temporary survival—Belial shrank back a little. "You didn't tell me about any of this before you started, and I don't like that. *Where's Belial?* someone says and me, I can't answer. Makes me look less than wholly in charge of the facts. Can't have that, can we?"

"Absolutely not. My oversight. I'll keep you in the loop from here on."

"Make sure you do. And while you're there... Hold on," said Beelzebub. He snapped two of his massive talons together, and in a puff of noxious smoke, a massive and ancient book appeared. The devil flipped the pages with his claws and peered at the countless lines of hand-lettered text. He lingered over one set of entries and then extended a long, forked tongue to the paper. He licked the page reflectively and considered the taste. "Yeah," he breathed at last. "I thought so. The turn of the seventeenth century was a very odd time in London."

"Lots going on," Belial agreed vaguely.

"One thing in particular," said Belial, stabbing the book with his needle-sharp talon. "Here, and here, and here again a few years later. Very odd, this is."

"What's that?" said Belial. He was starting to sweat, and not because of the lake of fire.

"Not sure," said his superior. "Little flare ups of demonic activity all from the same source."

"We have other devils working the period?"

"We do not. There's plenty of human evil, of course, all over the place, but then here and there there's this other stuff, different whatdy-acallit: *ambience*. Yeah. Not human, but not devil either. Every few years in the fifteen nineties and early sixteen hundreds, we get this new source of evil: the genuine article. Not your Accidentally Leaving The Brake Off stuff. This is someone or something who not only wants to run people down but gets other people to do it too. That's talent, that is. I just can't get a fix on him. It's like he just appears out of nowhere and gets stronger over a few weeks or months till he's like a cloud of poison or something drifting round the city. Then, just like that, he's gone." Beelzebub snapped his massive talons. "What you make of that?"

"No idea," Belial lied. "People sometimes change their minds, I suppose..."

"But this isn't a person, like I said. Not a devil either. So what is it, and why does it keep running out of juice just as things are getting interesting?"

"Couldn't say," said Belial. "It gets stronger over a few weeks or months and then vanishes without warning?"

"Right and correct."

"And it's gone for a year or two but then comes back and repeats the process?"

"Comes back weak—maybe a bit stronger than when it appeared the last time, but not much—gets stronger, then disappears."

"Most mysterious."

"Yeah?" said Beelzebub, giving Belial a probing look that promised other kinds of probing if he didn't get what he wanted. "But in this timeline, the one you've been fiddling with, it doesn't go away."

Belial stared a fraction too long then made a puzzled face.

"No?"

"No," said Beelzebub. "In all the other timelines it flares up, then goes. This time, it sticks around. Gets stronger. But you knew nothing about it?"

"Not a clue. Just, you know...coincidence, I guess."

"Coincidence," said Beelzebub thoughtfully, his eyes hard. "Right. Well, keep your eyes peeled, as they say," he concluded, grinning at the literal possibility. He always liked to keep creative punishments to hand for special occasions. "Coz if we could find out what this was, we might protect it, like, nurture it in the ways of real Evil. More to the point, we could make sure it didn't keep disappearing. If we could keep whatever it is alive and growing, that could unleash all kinds of havoc on the future."

"Really?" said Belial with a terrified attempt at enthusiasm.

"Oh yeah," said Beelzebub. "Whatever this thing is, the power of it is just off the scale. I can taste it. It's like pure hatred walking around, contaminating everything it touches. It's a thing of beauty, mate. Properly looked after and let loose on the world..." He broke off and chuckled to himself, delighted by the horrors blossoming in his head. "War, devastation, genocide... You name it, this could grow it out of nothing. I tell you, Belial, get this right and your humans might not have a twenty-first century to go back to."

"Right," said Belial, suddenly cold despite the flaming lake. "Excellent."

ACT FOUR

"Up and down, up and down
I will lead them up and down.
I am feared in field and town
Goblin, lead them up and down."
(*A Midsummer Night's Dream*, 3.2.395-9)

ACT FOUR, SCENE ONE

"Brutus: Art thou some god, some angel or some devil
That mak'st my blood cold and my hair to stare?
Speak to me what thou art?
Ghost of Caesar: Thy evil spirit, Brutus"
(*Julius Caesar*, 4.3.281-4)

November 4, 1599.

Shakespeare

Where the hell is Kemp?" the writer demanded, bursting into the empty, freezing theatre. "We only have one ensemble rehearsal, for God's sake! Is it too much to ask that...?"

"Kemp's gone," said Burbage.

"What do you mean *gone*? Gone where?"

"Left the company," said Burbage. "Took what he was owed and packed his bag. Says he needs a change of pace. Going back to Morris dancing."

"*Morris dancing*!" Shakespeare exclaimed. "Poncing about with bells and handkerchiefs? Are you serious?"

"Never more so. I'm already auditioning replacements."

Shakespeare sat down heavily in one of the stalls, staring at the empty stage. "He's really gone," he said.

"For good this time. He said to say farewell for him, but he didn't want to wait."

"What was the rush?"

"He's been out of sorts for months, Will. You knew that. Angry. Quick to quarrel. Couple of times I thought he was going to draw on me."

The writer looked down, frowning.

"Don't blame yourself," said Burbage.

"I don't!"

"And you shouldn't."

The writer heard the unspoken subtext. "Kemp blamed me?" asked Shakespeare, quieter this time.

Burbage shrugged expressively. "Only when he was in drink."

"Most of the time, then."

They both laughed at that, albeit a little sadly.

"So, you are already looking for a replacement?"

"Not for a sharer," said Burbage. "Just a journeyman actor. We should offer Kemp's share to one of the regulars."

"Seen anyone good yet?"

"Not yet," said Burbage, cheering quickly. "Certainly not a comedian like Kemp. There's Robert Armin with Chandos' men. Might be persuaded to switch. For now we just need a capable body who can do the lines set down for him..."

"And no more."

"And no more," agreed Burbage.

"And Kemp said nothing about why he was leaving?" Shakespeare pressed.

"Nothing that made sense."

"Meaning?"

"I don't know." Burbage shrugged. "He was getting superstitious. Spent half his time in church. Didn't like to be alone in the theatre."

"Why?"

Burbage just shook his head, but Shakespeare gave him a steady look till the actor spat and sighed. "Haunted," he said. "Or something. A faceless, hooded presence that stalked the stage at night. There and not there."

Shakespeare went very still. "What else?" he prompted.

"Nothing!" Burbage blustered. "It's all rubbish. We're better off without him."

He was avoiding Shakespeare's eyes.

"*What else?*" said the writer quietly.

Burbage sighed again, weary and troubled this time. "He said it came from you," Burbage confessed. "That it looked like you, but it stank like graveyard carrion."

Shakespeare got up and began to walk away.

"It's nonsense, Will!" Burbage called after him. "A kind of madness, or an excuse to leave. You should pay it no mind."

But Shakespeare did not turn back.

ACT FOUR, SCENE TWO

"O, for a Muse of fire, that would ascend
The brightest heaven of invention.
A kingdom for a stage, princes to act,
And monarchs to behold the swelling scene."
(*Henry V*, Chorus 1-4)

September 4, 1601.

Gladys

Even as a fully fledged and—more importantly—immortal angel, Gladys would have been daunted by what she was about to do. As one who might die at any moment, she was terrified. Her options were, however, limited. She had used her residual mystical abilities to scan the files of history and discovered a lifeline, albeit a lifeline made of finest gossamer and attached, in accordance with the laws of cartoon physics, to an anvil suspended over her head.

"I found one," she said, smiling as if each corner of her mouth was being pulled with wires. "One copy of *A Midsummer Night's Dream* left the printer's before the enemy got the rest. Special ordered."

"Awesome!" said Jimmy, getting to his feet. "Where is it?"

Gladys' smile hung there like a china plate six feet above a stone floor. It was going to fall, and it was going to smash, but for now—and according to the aforementioned cartoon physics—it hung there by sheer force of Gladys' will. Xavier and Rose, who could see how this was going to end, rose slowly, instantly suspicious.

"Where is it?" asked Xavier.

The smile fell and shattered.

"Well," said Gladys, "it dropped off my radar, so to speak, for a year, so we have to move forward some fourteen months or so, and I can't be absolutely certain it will still be there when we get there, and I'm not sure where exactly..."

"Gladys," said Rose. "Don't stall. Where is it?"

"Well," said Gladys, "I've set something up, but you're not going to like it."

Her eyes rested on Xavier significantly.

"What?" said Xavier, warily.

"The upside," said the angel, "is that you don't have to hide in the church or wrap blankets round your head or..."

"And the downside?" asked Xavier.

Gladys took her hands from behind her back and showed what she had rented from the Globe Theatre's tiring house. It was a suit of clothes of the kind you might wear on Halloween if you were given to that kind of thing. It was large and silky, flamboyantly colorful, and studded with semi-precious stones. The hat was a kind of turban with a crest of outlandish feathers, and the overall effect suggested that the tailor had been fired at great velocity into a roomful of peacocks.

"You've gotta be kidding me," said Xavier.

"All hail," said Gladys, not very convincingly, "to the Barbary prince."

"The what?" said Jimmy blankly. "Where are we going?"

"As I said," Gladys repeated, opening the temporal doors, "you're not going to like this."

～

November 8, 1602.

185

Xavier

AND SO IT was that the angelic team walked down to the Thames, paid a considerable sum to two pairs of skeptical oarsmen, and were ferried close to ten miles upstream to a landing near Kew where they turned south toward the gatehouse of Richmond Palace. The approach bristled with men armed with halberds[1] whose grim faces more than compensated for their silly trousers. As they approached, Gladys transformed.

The transformation should, Xavier felt, have been a big moment, a jaw-dropping demonstration of the angel's lingering mystical power which left him thrilling to the breathtaking strangeness of the universe, but his attention was on the sparkling tips of the halberds, which were clearly designed to make interesting patterns out of your intestines. Gladys turned not into a towering Seraph with wings like driven snow and a lethal, if elegant-looking, sword. No such luck. Instead, she became an elderly man in a black fur-trimmed robe with a satchel of documents bound in ribbon, which she sorted through when the first of the halberdiers demanded to know his/her business.

Xavier did his best to look imperial, as instructed, staring about him serenely as if he owned the place. Jimmy had been supplied with an ill-fitting blue coat, which Gladys said made him a servant, and Rose was loitering as a kind of waiting woman, though what precisely she was waiting for, no one seemed to know. Xavier himself had donned the hose, the flowing robe belted with a silken sash from which hung a jeweled scimitar, and even—after much protest—the feathered turban. Jimmy said he looked like a drag queen.

"Very regal," Gladys agreed, pleased with her handywork.

"No, a drag queen is..." Xavier had said.

"Very Shakespearean," said Rose with a knowing grin. "I knew we'd have to cross dress at some point."

Gladys looked bemused from her back to Xavier.

"What?" she said.

"Never mind," said Xavier.

And now here they were, staring down the guards while "Gladys" proffered faked paperwork presenting Xavier as an emissary from some imaginary African nation sent as an ambassador to one of the most volatile, paranoid, and capricious monarchs in English history. Awesome.

He shifted under the scrutiny of the guards and tried not to think about how badly he wished he had gone to the bathroom before they set out. This was all taking much longer than Gladys had promised, but in all their wanderings about the city, they had still seen only one actual toilet, a foul, fly-thronged, nightmare latrine of planks with holes in them sticking out over the river from London Bridge. They had taken one look and fled. But now, with his insides roiling at the prospect of a royal audience, instant death hanging over them if they said or did the wrong thing (and far from clear what the wrong thing might be), he wished he had bitten the bullet.

The palace sat on the riverbank among walled gardens and an extensive deer park where it was said the Queen had loved to hunt in her younger days. Constructed by her grandfather in the latest Tudor fashion from the remains of a stately home built by Henry V, it was an imposing brick and stone confectionary of octagonal towers, tall pepper pot-capped chimneys and brass weathervanes. More than anything they had seen so far, the palace balanced opulence and power. It was, Xavier thought, the architectural equivalent of the guards' shining and deadly halberds.

Gladys had admitted that her plan, such as it was, was risky and hung on the fact that there was no one in the city who knew anything at all about the culture, religion, and social hierarchy of central Africa. She had assumed, to Xavier's irritation, that he might, and was clearly baffled and irritated that he didn't.

"I'm an American," he said. "My family have been Americans—whether they wanted to be or not—for generations. I've never been to Africa and it's not a major factor in my culture."

"But surely," Gladys had said, "Black music and dancing and..."

Xavier had gritted his teeth, and the other two twenty-first century humans had, while staying exactly where they stood, done remarkable impressions of people running for cover.

"Black American," he had said in the distinct and careful tones of someone not interested in explaining himself further, "not African."

"Oh," Gladys had replied with an *if-you-say-so* shrug, which said how little she realized she was standing on the edge of the volcano crater. "Well, no one else will know anything either, so just make some stuff up."

And so far, it seemed to be working. The guards consulted and sent their "credentials" to some administrative flunky in the palace, and eventually the gates were opened and they were escorted inside. They passed through the entry arch into a square courtyard where a fountain played and servants paused to watch their approach. Xavier nodded to them and said, "Hey, how you doin?" till Gladys' death stare made him stop. They crossed a bridge over a moat and entered the privy apartments, moving via long galleries of portraits and tapestries lit by huge, latticed windows, to a kind of anteroom where they waited for the best part of an hour—still with no bathroom break—before being summoned into the presence chamber.

In front of them, seated in an astonishingly ornate throne, was Queen Elizabeth I. She looked upon them and they wilted.

Fear gripped Xavier's stomach and bowels like a gauntleted fist. No, let us call things as they are. It was stark, bladder-stretching, blood-draining, bile-pumping terror. He was passing himself off as an African Prince in front of one of the most potent, most autocratic, and most temperamental monarchs the Renaissance had produced, the monarch responsible, he reminded himself, for the heads that grinned down from the spikes of London Bridge. And for what? A play? A stray copy of something about fairies and lovers and a man with the head of a donkey. It was madness. Worse still, according to Gladys, the Queen had, with a whimsy as famous as her ruthlessness, ordered a copy of the play to be sent to her directly from the printers because she had seen it performed a few years before and had found it "pleasantly diverting." And now Xavier was here, in disguise and lying through his teeth, to steal it from her.

Maybe he should just stab himself now and have done. Someone would probably lend him a halberd...

She sat in front of them, shadowed by Robert Cecil, her small and hunchbacked private secretary, with guards and courtiers and ladies in waiting in flamboyant attendance. She looked like she had been expecting them, but Xavier, no student of Renaissance fashion, thought she also looked like she was ready for bed. It was, not to put too fine a point on it, disconcerting.

She wore a cloth of silver gown with a high collar so loosely belted at the front and arranged with such apparent carelessness that her breasts and stomach were clearly visible. She was pale and made up to look more so, which made the red wig on her head garish to the point of clownishness. Her face was lined with age—she had to be in her late sixties—but her eyes were bright and playful. Almost flirtatious. Flustered, Xavier looked down. When he glanced up again, he caught the flicker of a smile on the Queen's face. It was more than amusement. She was enjoying his discomfort, and it occurred to Xavier that her oddly unselfconscious appearance was carefully staged. It was quite a trick—this elderly woman using her body to affirm her control of the situation —and if he hadn't been pretty sure she was about to kill him, Xavier would have been impressed. As it was, he stood there, like a man on a very narrow ledge thousands of feet above some unusually jagged-looking rocks, and waited.

"Your honor is most welcome," said the Queen at last, her lips pursed slightly so that she seemed to lisp a little. She was missing most of the teeth on the right side of her face and those that remained, coyly concealed with curious rabbit-like motions of her lips as she spoke, were discolored and irregular. "Your arrival has been made known to us these several days," she continued, pausing for a narrow, playful smile that might have graced a sixteen-year-old, "and We should scold your tardiness in visiting us, but that I am hungry to hear of foreign places, the stranger the better. And so draw near that we might hear of your home and all the wonders you have seen i'the wild and barbarous lands you have traversed to behold Our royal majesty. Stop at nothing, but relate all details of your travels, the cannibals that each other eat, the Anthropophagi and men whose heads do grow beneath their shoulders. To these wild tales we will most seriously incline with greedy ear devouring up your discourse. Thereafter will we proceed to matters of state and the most blessed occasion of your visit."

There was a pause. Gladys shot him a look of alarm.

"My travels," said Xavier, stalling. "Right."

The room fell utterly silent, the various glittering attendants and courtiers fixing him with an attentive gaze as if he were a street magician brought to a kid's birthday party. He swallowed. Gladys had told him to look commanding and "foreign"—as if he had a choice—and to blame his poor command of the language if he was asked more than he knew or could invent. He had expected to nod and bow, and sign things, and gesture to Rose who had a box of exotic gifts brought for the Queen, though what was inside he had no idea. That, at least, would buy him some time to think.

"First, your highness," he said, "allow me to bestow upon your majesty these humble presents."

Rose gave him a wild look saying in no uncertain terms that she thought this a bad idea. Realizing that she knew what was in the box, Xavier panicked.

"Unless you'd rather..." he began.

"You may approach," said the Queen, inclining her head to Rose, who shuffled reluctantly forward, pulled off an awkward courtesy, and extended the box.

The Queen took it and, as Rose withdrew looking miserable and terrified, she opened it. Xavier watched open mouthed as the most powerful person in the nation reached inside and gingerly removed...

A tube of Rolo.

Oh God. Oh God. Oh God, he thought. *We are so going to die.*

The Queen considered the candy curiously, then slid the paper wrapper from the outside, marveling at the delicacy of the gold foil within. Her expression stalled, however, as she eased that open to reveal the little brown column within.

"And these are...?"

"Chocolates, your highness," Xavier managed. He didn't trust himself to look at Rose.

"*Chocolates?*" said the Queen, sounding out each unfamiliar syllable.

"A kind of sweetmeat, your majesty," Gladys inserted.

"Ah," said the Queen.

"I will summon the taster," said the secretary at her elbow.

The Queen held up a languid hand.

"Not necessary, pygmy," she said. "I will trust the gentleman."

Xavier's insides squirmed. He watched as she fastidiously freed one of the little sweets from the rest of the tube, sniffed it, frowned with curiosity, and then popped it into her mouth. For a second, there was no response, and then her face blossomed with pleasure and she became the sixteen-year-old he had glimpsed in her manner earlier. She began

190

to chew carefully, sparing her rotten teeth by using only one side of her mouth. For a long moment, nothing happened. Her eyes closed and she seemed almost entranced. At length she swallowed and her eyes opened once more.

"This is a most kingly gift," she pronounced, generating a patter of (faintly relieved) applause around the room.

"Yeah?" said Xavier, forgetting himself in his relief. "Cool."

"Such delicate and distinctive sweetness," said the Queen.

"Well, you know," said Xavier. "Rolo..."

"This is a delicacy of your homeland?" said the Queen, taking another. "It must be a remarkable place."

"Yeah," said Xavier, still stunned but keen to maintain a sense of agreement. "Wakanda has vibranium. We have Rolo."

"And now," said the Queen, eying the box as if to see how many more tubes of chocolate there were, "since your gift has pleased Us, you may now recount your travels."

"Ah," said Xavier, smiling against all possible odds like a man who has been told that he may indeed enter the cage of an unusually belligerent tiger "to get a better look." "Okay." He could feel every eye on him and the Queen's most of all. The rocks below were still distant and spiky, but a slender wire had been extended across to the cliff on the other side. He just had to walk across it. It occurred to him that not all the eager spectators were hoping he would succeed.

"Well, we were going through the er...jungle..." he began.

"Jungle?" said the Queen.

"Like a really dense forest," said Xavier, glad of a question he could answer, "full of strange animals and birds."

"I see. Pray, continue."

He hesitated, thinking desperately, feeling like an actor on stage in front of a packed house, or in one of those costume drama movies no one went to but always snagged an Oscar. Suddenly his brow cleared and his eyes, which had been dull and almost closed, snapped open, shining.

"And we'd stopped for a drink of water," he resumed hurriedly. "Now, I'm sitting there looking at this glass of water when suddenly there comes this sort of thud, distant, like thunder. But the water in the glass ripples. I find myself staring at it, watching the water, and while

191

I'm watching... *Crash*! Just like that. And the water ripples again, but more this time. Then it does it again and now I can hear something coming. I look up and there is this huge dino... well, kind of this big-assed lizard, right? Only thirty feet high and with teeth like kitchen knives, and it comes smashing through the trees roaring at us..."

The audience was spellbound. The Queen and her advisors leant forward, their eyes fixed on Xavier as he warmed to his theme and threw body and voice into the part. Gladys bit her lower lip hard and said nothing.

"Later," Xavier proceeded, "we found these egg-things: looked like melons or something but all crusty on the outside and covered over with a ground mist. Now, as we are looking at them, they start splitting, opening up like ugly flowers or something, and when one of my men bends down to look at it, this thing like an octopus that was inside the egg clamps itself over his face and whirls its tail round his throat real tight. Now, we tried to cut it off him, but it had acid or something instead of blood so we didn't dare kill it. But then all of a sudden, it just dropped off like it was dead. We thought everything was fine, and everyone was happy, but that night, while we were sitting together having dinner..."

And so it went on. Xavier recounted his Great Moments from Hollywood and Gladys stood motionless, her eyes glassy and her smile fixed and horrified. Rose and Jimmy just stared in disbelief, but the Queen and her courtiers listened to every word, and whether or not they believed him seemed less crucial than whether they considered themselves entertained.

They did.

"Theatre geek, huh?" said Rose out of the side of her mouth as soon as he stopped being the focus of royal attention. "I see that now. You have a flair for the dramatic."

"Thank you?" said Xavier, unsure.

"Oh, it's definitely a compliment," Rose clarified. "I mean, we are still alive, which, in the circumstances, seemed unlikely. So yeah. Good job."

"Under the heart-stopping terror," Xavier admitted, "it was quite fun. A long way under, but still."

"You have a gift. Seems wasted in banking."

Xavier's heart sank. Rose saw and tried to recover.

"I mean, I'm sure it's an important job and all," she said. "I just meant..."

"I know," he said, smiling faintly. "And it is. But I do miss the performing. Even the Shakespeare, or some of it. I like modern pieces because they feel real, but Shakespeare is bigger and richer than life, you know? When you feel like the words are yours, you feel bigger and richer too." He paused, catching Rose's smile. "Too bad folk like me were never meant to own them."

"You can now, surely? I mean, not *this* now. Our now."

Xavier made a doubtful face, but before he could say anything, Jimmy had joined them.

"Dude!" he said. "Good job on the movie thing. Is there a bar? I'm parched. I went looking, but these guys with the big spiky things started following me like I was looking to lift something."

"Tell me you didn't," said Rose.

"Steal anything?" said Jimmy. "Nah. All this fancy jewelry and shit is too hard to fence anyway."

"The triumph of virtue," said Rose dryly.

Jimmy nodded as if she'd agreed with him.

"On your travels, you didn't see anything like a toilet, did you?" asked Xavier.

Jimmy shook his head.

"As luck would have it, I went right before we got ploughed by the train," he said. "Every cloud, right?"

"Right," said Xavier miserably.

The evening progressed apace, sliding into the kind of masqued ball usually enacted during high school productions of *Romeo and Juliet*. The Queen danced briefly with Xavier, an honor he would have appreciated more if he wasn't trying to learn the dance while doing it. Fortunately the elderly Queen soon tired and sat down, entreating him to continue the dance with a lady of his choosing. He chose Rose on the grounds that, not knowing what a galliard was any more than he did, she wouldn't make him look bad. After a couple of goes round, he settled into it and added a few flourishes of his own so that Rose laughed with relief that they were still alive, and the other courtiers followed suit, till he felt like a Black Heath Ledger rocking out to David Bowie in *A Knight's Tale*.

"How are we supposed to find *A Midsummer Night's Dream*?" hissed Rose.

"No clue," Xavier said. "And right now my priority is getting out of here with my head intact, pausing only to find a bathroom that isn't a plank with a hole in it."

"The Queen's still watching you," said Rose. "I think you've got a fan."

"Better than the alternative, I guess."

~

Gladys

GLADYS TOOK a step toward where the Queen was seated, fanning herself lazily, her eyes on the dance floor. When Cecil gave an approving nod, Gladys said, "Your highness has treated his Lordship and his humble servants with much kindness. We are most grateful for your audience."

"He is a most impressive gentleman," said the Queen, still watching Xavier. "Is it common among his people for a man of his standing to be so familiar with his maid?"

Gladys blinked, sensing an oncoming hurdle. "It is."

"Remarkable."

"As you say," said Gladys, whose sense of the hurdle was shifting in ways that made her newly acquired insides tie themselves in knots. "He is a most generous and tolerant master."

"And handsome," said the Queen, giving Gladys a flinty stare.

The hurdle was now less a hurdle than it was a wall, high, concrete, and—for reasons that weren't immediately apparent—coming towards her at a high rate of speed.

"I wouldn't presume to say," said Gladys.

"No," said the Queen. "Though I might. And I am sure you could tell me more of him."

"Majesty?"

"His tastes and interests," said the Queen airily, "in case I should send a gift after him."

Gladys blinked, then blurted, "Drama!"

"I beg your pardon?"

"Plays," said Gladys. "He has heard tell of London's famous theatres and of one writer in particular..."

"We have no performances this night," said the Queen. "Though something might be arranged in a week or two. How long will his Lordship reside within our court?"

Gladys could almost feel the ticking of the watch she had secreted beneath her robes.

"Alas, your Highness, we must away this night," she said.

"Nonsense," said the Queen. "I won't hear of it."

"His Lordship has other matters of state commanding his attention elsewhere."

"Matters more vital than the companionable presence of my royal self?" asked the Queen in a low and dangerous voice.

Gladys swallowed. "Nothing could be more vital than that," she said.

"Excellent! Then arrange to stay a month longer. Cecil!" she added over her shoulder to the loitering secretary, "see to it."

Cecil stooped toward her and muttered in the Queen's ear.

"Are you sure?" she replied, her face baffled and surprised.

"It seems the prince is curious to see your godson's latest...*invention*," said Cecil.

"What?" said Gladys, anxiously glancing over to Xavier and wondering what in the name of all that was holy he had asked for.

The Queen ignored her but smiled.

"We thought," she said, "Our Self was the only soul on Earth who did not think Harrington's contraption a device of the utmost absurdity."

"He is most desirous to inspect it," said Cecil, "since I mentioned that your majesty's palace leads the world in...*such matters*."

"What matters?" asked Gladys, conscious that her voice had risen in pitch and volume.

"Does he by God?" said the Queen, turning her attention to Xavier again and beaming benevolently. "Then lead him to it, pygmy. But see that he alone *avails himself* of it."

"But of course, your majesty," said Cecil, bowing and backing away.

Gladys followed, jogging a few steps to catch up.

"Great," she said to Cecil's hunched back. "So...what's happening?"

Xavier

"WE ARE STAYING *HOW LONG*?" said Xavier as soon as the makeshift dance floor had been cleared and Gladys had gathered the team together under the watchful but respectfully distant eye of Robert Cecil. He seemed to be waiting for them.

"Well, obviously we aren't going to actually stay a month," hissed Gladys. "We're running out of time in our allotted twenty-four hours as it is. We just have to, you know, pretend."

"And then sneak out while no one is looking?" demanded Rose in a hoarse whisper. "There's an army in here!"

"I think they mostly concern themselves with people trying to get *in*," said Gladys.

"This is crazy!" Xavier mouthed.

"There is an upside to being here," said Gladys.

"Yeah?" said Xavier. "And what's that?"

The angel nodded significantly toward Cecil, who bowed and began walking away.

"Follow him," said Gladys. "The rest of us will keep looking for that play."

God, thought Xavier. The all-important *Midsummer Night's Dream* quarto. With all the ridiculous pageantry and lying, he had almost forgotten. The play was why they had come, but they had seen no sign of it.

"We passed a library before we reached the waiting room," said Rose. "Maybe we can get permission to browse a little..."

"Go," said Gladys.

"Let's just hope it's not sitting on the Queen's bedside table," Jimmy observed.

"I think," said Gladys, "that we have enough real problems without dreaming up more. Xavier, come on. They are waiting."

With a gaggle of courtiers in tow, Xavier left the rest of the team and walked along a corridor toward a heavy wooden door. Waiting women watched, giggling behind their hands, and with a leaden feeling in the pit of his stomach, he said to Cecil, "So, where are we going?"

Cecil merely smiled cryptically, stopped beside the ominous door, and from the purse attached to his belt produced an impressive key. He put it in the lock, turned it, opened the door, and stepped aside.

The room inside was no larger than a closet, but it featured a throne-like seat on a raised platform, a throne with a hole in the center of the seat beneath which was a pan of water. Behind the throne was an elevated cistern also full of clear water, and with a handle beside the seat. Xavier stared. Against all the odds, he had found one of Europe's two flushing toilets.

"Oh, thank God!" exclaimed Xavier.

"A most commendable sentiment," said Cecil.

He smiled his shrewd little smile again, inclined his head, and the procession retraced its steps.

Xavier closed the door and settled contented onto "the throne," pleased by the idea that the term was, in this case, more than usually metaphorical. Just as he would have found in his Boston apartment, there was a little stack of reading matter at his feet, though here it apparently doubled as toilet paper. He took a pamphlet off the top of the pile, opening it, somewhat perversely, to the last page.

"*If we shadowes haue offended,*" he read, "*thinke but this (and all is mended), that you haue but slumbred here while, these visions did appeare. And this weake and idle theame, no more yielding but a dreame.*"

He checked the cover: "*A Midsommer Nights Dreame.* As it hath been sundry time publickely acted, by the Right Honorable, the Lord Chamberlaine his seruants. Written by W. Shakespeare. Imprinted at London, for *Thomas Fisher*, and are to be soulde at his shoppe at the Sign of the White Hart, in *Fleetstreete.*1600."

Xavier grinned wide.

When he returned to the others, there was much suppressed rejoicing.

"Now can we get out of here?" said Rose. "This place is cool and all, but it gives me the willies."

"Also," Jimmy added, "have you seen all these little jewel-studded knickknacks all over the place? I don't think I can stay here much longer without stealing stuff. Just sayin'."

"Let me make our excuses," said Gladys. "We'll say we are going to bed and will then make our next time jump."

"The Queen will love that," said Rose darkly.

"Yeah," said Xavier. "We had better make sure we don't cross paths with her again."

"Won't be a problem," said Gladys airily. "She'll be dead within the year."

There was an odd, stunned silence as the humans stared at the angel, then at each other, then at the frail, if resplendent woman still presiding over the last of the courtly games and entertainments.

"She's about to die?" asked Jimmy. He looked stunned, appalled.

"Not, like, in the next few minutes," said Gladys, "but by late March..."

"She'll die?" said Jimmy.

"In this very building," said Gladys. "To be succeeded by James I, son of Mary Queen of Scots, her cousin."

The humans continued to stare.

"What?" said Gladys, finally detecting the change in the atmosphere. "Oh, right. Yes. Very sad."

"We should do something," said Jimmy vaguely.

"Like what?" Gladys replied.

"I don't know," said Jimmy. "This just feels...wrong."

"I'm gonna say goodbye," said Xavier.

"Yes," said Jimmy, who still looked a little manic. "I'll come too."

"Make it good night," Gladys reminded him. "She doesn't know we're leaving."

Xavier gave her a hard frown then nodded.

"What?" said Gladys again.

Ignoring her, Xavier stepped toward the throne where the Queen was sitting, considering her finger ends, only just awake. He eyed the guards and attendants who were watching him, alert and ready to defend their monarch should he so much as breathe on her, and when they give him the nod, he approached, bowing, and spoke softly.

"Your majesty. We are about to retire for the evening. I just wanted to say..." he hesitated, suddenly unsure, cleared his throat and ended lamely, "thanks. For welcoming us into your home. It's been...really great." He swallowed, reaching for something more significant, more resonant but, finding himself unexpectedly upset, said simply, "I won't forget it."

"I doubt it not," she said, with a sleepy smile. "But you will grace us with your presence once more tomorrow evening."

"Tomorrow," said Jimmy, nodding in agreement. "And tomorrow and tomorrow."

The phrase changed her. She seemed suddenly both more awake and more reflective as she considered Jimmy, then turned back to Xavier. She held him long in her gaze before she said:

"My Lord, We see your visage in your mind and to your honours and your valiant parts We do Our soul and fortunes consecrate. Come back and see us soon, for I am old, and few things give me pleasure."

ACT FOUR, SCENE THREE

"O, beware, my lord, of jealousy.
It is the green-eyed monster which doth mock
The meat it feeds on."
(*Othello*, 3.3.178-80)

Richmond Palace, November 8, 1602.

Cecil

He is indeed a goodly gentleman," said the Queen. "Who would have thought so dark a face could mask so noble a mind? And yet methinks his blackness lacks not a certain beauty too, not of the common sort, but a kind of dignity lives in those sable looks. I never thought the Ethiope beautiful, but now I see the man and hear his stories strange and wondrous he quite o'oercomes me. Would'st think the English people could learn to love a Moor if he were wedded to their Queen? Methinks not, and yet it is no matter. I am old and marriage, which always was a dangerous fancy for me, is now mere impossibility. No heir of mine will rule in Albion. In Scotland methinks they watch like the audience at a play for me to retire to my sickbed for the last time. Then will my treacherous cousin's brat be sent for...and that also is no matter. But tell me, is the Prince not a most proper man for all his blackness?"

"He is indeed, your majesty," said Robert Cecil, her hunched and twisted secretary. "And were he faithful, pale, and here some twenty years agone, he might have made a spouse most suitable."

"Well, he is here now, not twenty years agone, and he is black as coal, but yet methinks he is faithful."

"Ay, madam, he may be."

"Is, I'm sure," the Queen repeated.

"I could not say, your highness, but were he not..."

"The point needs no considering. He is most faithful to me and to my nation."

"I doubt it not, and well it is for such as he would make most fearful foes if they should ally with the Spanish."

"Why would he do that, pray?" demanded the Queen.

"No reason," said Cecil, "unless he should prove faithless. Then who knows which way Spanish gold might draw him and his people. Then maybe..."

"What?" said the Queen, turning thoughtfully on her councilor. "Come, sir, speak your thoughts."

"Madam 'tis not my place."

"I say it is and you, pygmy, are mine to command."

"Indeed, madam, but some things should not be spoken, and besides, the prince no doubt is faithful to your highness. If other women look upon him, how is he to blame?"

"Other women?" the Queen stuttered. "What other women? Come, pygmy, and unburden yourself more plainly."

"None, I am sure, your highness."

"And yet you said they did."

"I said that if they did it would be none of his fault, my lady, that is all."

"But yet you think they do?"

"Who I, my lady?"

"Yes, you, you most imperfect speaker. Do you think other women pursue him?"

"Do I think it?"

"By heavens the fool begins to echo me! Yes, you! Do you not think the prince has women pursuing him?"

"It could be, my lady, and yet I'm almost sure he does not look on any but your blessed self."

"Almost sure! How, villain! Almost sure?"

"Most sure, your highness. If he leans close to the Lady Rose, his serving wench, and whispers in her ear and smiles, why what is that? Nothing, my lady, but good housekeeping as a master should bestow upon his servants. No more. I humbly do beseech your pardon, Madam, I fear I have distracted you."

"It is your role to council me and I thank thee for it."

"Yet I see this hath a little dashed your spirits."

"Not a jot, not a jot."

"I' faith I fear it has. I hope you will consider what is spoke comes from my love to you: no more. My lady, I see you are moved."

"No, not much moved. I think the prince be honest to me still."

"Long live him so! And long live you to think so."

"And yet I fear I know not the mind that beats behind so dark a face..." said the Queen, abstractedly.

"Ay there's the point! As—to be bold with you—who knows what thoughts can harbour in a man so far distant from these climes of ours. They say he is a man, and yet I'm sure I've seen only beasts whose hide is black as night, black as sin, and who knows what unnaturalness might live inside a bestial mind. But yet, my lady, perchance there's no such thing. The Prince is valiant and, it seems, most honest."

"Indeed."

"And his closeness to the milk-white Rose, his maid, is perchance but the custom of his land, where closeness betwixt those of differing standing or color is but a trifle. Though he promised loyalty to you and stays t'attend your highness, what if he smile upon his Rose in public where the court can see them? And if a kiss should pass between them, then what then? It is of matter most inconsequential."

"Has there been such kissing work thinkest thou?"

"No meaning in it, I assure you. A mere billing and embracing is little nowadays."

"You have seen these actions? Speak man, why hold you your tongue when your sovereign commands?"

"My lady, I have seen but little. But guards upon the stairwells of her lodgings have, methinks, by night seen..."

"By night?"

"Perchance more morn than night, but what of that? Doubtless my lord the prince had need of some honest service from her. Most honest, doubt it not."

"I do misdoubt it, though."

"Think not upon it or else we make ourselves as like the servants and courtiers who have naught to do but whisper about such matters and, (saving your grace) the shameful dotage of their queen and mistress who could admire a man who wantons with his maid and laughs at your age."

"Say they so? Say they so?"

"Courtiers say it, who will say anything. Think not on it, I pray you."

"But is there no truth to these reports, thinkest thou, that he frolics with his whey-faced Rose and flouts me to my subjects?"

"Some truth, perchance, but why should a queen, the great and mighty sovereign of this land, care for such petty and noisome whisperings? Are not you greater than he and all his friends? Could you not have his hussy whipped for daring to meet him without your leave last evening? Could you not send the prince's head back to his father in Africa?"

"Ay, and will. Oh heavens, has there been such night-time meeting, such secret harlotry? Zounds, I'll have the minx's head, so I will, and that devil-faced prince may yet take poison 'ere he departs our shores. Deceive me? Draw secret laughter around the throne of England! He has o'er reached himself and will fall 'neath our royal heel within these next four and twenty hours."

"Madam, I fear I have offended."

"But with truth, and that can no true councilor withhold. Fear not. You shall not suffer for showing me the picture howe'er horrid it might be, how e'er mad it might make me. We will have revenge on these most vile deceivers and you will be my chiefest friend and councilor."

"I am yours forever."

So saying, Cecil left her to her dark and private thoughts, stepping out into the dim stone-flagged hallway where, leaving pointed instructions with the guards, he paused, momentarily confused.

For a long moment he stood where he was as if rooted, sucking in the night air as if he had been under water.

No, not water. Something black and viscous that filled more than his lungs...

What had just happened? He looked after the guards, wondering if he should call them back. The orders he had given already seemed strange and terrible, and though he was doing Her Highness' bidding, he found he could not recall his own part in the events that had led to her instructions.

He frowned, sensed something on the air, and turned slowly, full of apprehension.

In the shadows by the chamber door, a man stirred, and Cecil almost jumped, not because he was unfamiliar—though reminiscent of the playwright the Queen so enjoyed—but because he was suddenly aware of a curious and powerful rankness, a stench so nauseating that his bowels writhed and clenched. He doubled over, one hand clapped to his nose and mouth, baffled that a mere odor could fill him with such deep revulsion. It wasn't merely unpleasant. It was as if he had rolled over in his sleep and found himself sharing his bed with a corpse. Cold, and with the hair pricking on the back of his neck, Cecil turned abruptly to where the shadowy stranger had been loitering, but either he had slipped soundlessly away or he had never really been there at all.

ACT FOUR, SCENE FOUR

"Rosalind: O Jupiter, how weary are my spirits!
Touchstone: I care not for my spirits if my legs were not weary."
(*As You Like It*: 2.4.1-3)

June 14, 1602. Time remaining: 10 hours 13 minutes.
Plays to be saved: *7+Folio*.

Gladys

Gladys and her team stepped clear of their shimmering rectangles—which promptly closed up on themselves like folding chairs.

"Right," said Rose. "*Merry Wives of Windsor*, yes? Is it true that the Queen requested that one personally? Wanted to see Falstaff in love or something, right?"

But Gladys was still watching the place where the temporal doors had been, and she looked troubled.

"Hello?" said Rose. "Did I just become invisible?"

"What?" said Gladys vaguely. "No. It's just..." She hesitated.

"Rose was asking about the Queen," said Xavier.

"The Queen," said Gladys. "Yes."

The others waited patiently, but Gladys stood there looking distant and perturbed.

"Is there a problem?" Rose pressed.

"What?" said Gladys again. "No. Not now."

"But there was?"

"When we left the Palace," said Gladys, nodding. "I only got a glimpse, but it looked like there were guards coming to our rooms."

"I knew they wouldn't want us sneaking out when we'd said we'd stay a month," said Jimmy.

"Yes, but..." Gladys faltered. "It's just that, things were fine moments before," she said. "The Queen seemed happy. Seemed like she liked you," she said, nodding at Xavier. "So, what happened?"

"You said she was famously changeable," said Rose.

"Even so," Gladys said, shaking her head. "Did any of you smell anything as we were leaving?"

"Smell anything?" said Jimmy. "Like what?"

"Something...unpleasant."

"More unpleasant than Renaissance London usually is?" Xavier qualified.

Gladys considered him, then shrugged, smiled unconvincingly, and said, "Probably nothing. Okay. Jimmy, I'll send you into 1603 for the first quarto of *Hamlet*. As soon as you get it, call for the door and I'll move you forward a year so you can get the second one."

"Another *Hamlet*?" he said. "You sure we have time?"

"In this case," said Gladys, "we make time. The first quarto is not without its merits, but if the second doesn't survive, Shakespeare may wobble on his cultural pedestal. Yes, we need it."

"To be or not to be, that is the question," said Jimmy, pleased to be able to quote from something other than *Macbeth*.

"Not in this version," said Gladys. "That's why we need the other one as well. There," she said, opening the door. "Off you pop."

Jimmy looked daunted, but Gladys, her mind full of threatening clouds, pretended not to notice. As he stepped shiftily into nothingness, she turned back to the others.

"Now," she said, "*Merry Wives*. You wanted to know if the Queen requested it? Well, yes and no. It's actually a funny story. I'll tell you as we go."

And she did, figuring that a little royal trivia would distract them from her increasingly obvious panic. Something was wrong. She could feel it.

~

Shakespeare

As THE TEAM set to work, the author of the play in question was watching the crowd filing in to see *The Merry Devil of Edmonton*. He was counting the door take but kept glancing up at the boy who was collecting the penny admissions, behind whom was a stack of seat cushions.

"Offer them the cushions," said Shakespeare.

The boy regarded the pile and stated the obvious. "They can see them. If they want one, they give me the extra penny."

"You have to *make* them want one," said Shakespeare.

"What?" said the boy, as if he had been asked to juggle cannon balls.

"How do they know they'll want a cushion unless you *advertise* the fact," said the playwright. "We own the cushions, so anything we make on them is profit."

The boy considered this, and a haze came into his eyes. But just when it seemed the fog was too thick to lift, it cleared unexpectedly and the boy grinned.

"Oh!" he exclaimed. "Right." And without further ado he turned to the next audience member in line and said, "Cushion, sir? The seats are grievous hard and 'tis a long play."

The "sir" in question paused as if the possibility had not occurred to him before, then forked over the extra penny.

"Better," said Shakespeare. He added the coin to the box and felt its weight thoughtfully. At the same moment, a garishly made-up young woman in a similarly garish dress filed through the gate, remarking, "How now, Will. When will you lie with me?"

Shakespeare, dry, his eyes still lowered to the cash box, replied, "When you halve your prices and cure your pox," as if he'd been asked the time while standing in front of the world's largest clock. The whore, unoffended, shrugged acceptance of this and passed into the theatre, where, if the Puritan theatre critics were to be believed, she would find easier customers in large numbers.

"Are you writing at the moment, Will?" said the boy as the last of the patrons filed into the theatre.

"Always," said the writer. "Why?"

The boy's face fell. "I'm supposed to be collecting some new daggers from the smithy tonight," said the boy. "But it will be dark when I get back here."

"So?"

"So, I don't like being in the theatre at night," said the boy wretchedly. "Not, you know, when you're writing."

Shakespeare gave him a quick look. "What's that supposed to mean?" he snapped.

The boy looked away, as if looking for something: courage, it turned out. "Before he left," the boy admitted, "Master Kemp cautioned us against being in the theatre at night when you were working. Said your genius walked abroad in the likeness of a man of shadows. Said it was dangerous. All your hatreds and resentments, your little jealousies and terrible rages."

The writer considered him seriously. The boy was staring, pale in his fear, his eyes wide and shining. "Will Kemp was a fool," said Shakespeare curtly.

"He didn't blame you as such," said the boy, determined to get it all out now that he'd started, even though a tear was rolling down his cheek. "Said it was what creativity did to a body, made him draw up bad feeling like a man pulling a bucket from a corrupted well. But things come with it and they walk abroad."

Shakespeare felt a surge of anger so sharp that he almost hit the boy across his terrified face, but he fought the impulse down, marveling at the impulse even before it had completely faded.

"It's not true," he managed. "Fear not. And yet...I'll collect the daggers this evening. There is no need for you to return to the theatre."

The boy was speechless in his gratitude, nodding vigorously so that more tears spilled down his face.

"Now get thee inside," said Shakespeare, "and help the boys into their dresses. I'll not write a word till I'm far from the theatre. If you see a spirit walking the stage, strike it about the head with a stick. I warrant that will put pay to it."

The boy grinned despite himself and left. Shakespeare watched him go but went on staring sightlessly after him. When he blinked and came to himself again, he tried a rueful smile at the credulity of children, but a moment later he caught himself warily sniffing the air.

ACT FOUR, SCENE FIVE

"The time invites you. Go your servants tend."
(*Hamlet* 1.3.83)

1600

Bliss

I t was a warm summer night, and the people of London were celebrating. The harvest looked good, they had emerged from another victory over the Spanish and an apparently successful campaign against the Irish, the pointlessness and brutality of which had not yet occurred to them, and they were celebrating these triumphs in their usual manner, with a kind of festive riot.

Bliss, who had been getting somehow filthier in the course of this campaign, was wiping the mud from his face while Cathy Cornwall cranked her self-esteem up a notch: "I got every copy of *Merchant of Venice, Henry V,* and *Much Ado About* Absolutely *Nothing*," she gushed. "Yea me!"

"Yea indeed," said Belial, bleakly.

"And I got the second quartos of *Titus Andronicus, Henry IV part 2* and *Henry VI parts 2* and *3*," said Bliss, rather less enthusiastically. "We really need all these?"

"Unless you want them to survive into the future, yes," said Belial. "Now, 1603, which includes the first quarto of *Hamlet...*"

"Ugh," said Cornwall. "I *so* hated that one."

"Then just a few more stops before the Folio," said Belial.

"Which includes *Macbeth*?" asked Bliss for the umpteenth time.

"Which includes *Macbeth*," Belial said.

"About time," said Bliss. "And no sign of those sniveling do-gooders?"

"Not so far as I can tell," said Belial.

"You know, I have to ask," said the devil, picking up on Bliss' last remark. "I've given you power to move in time, to break the laws of physics, power as close to omnipotence as any mortal could ever wield, power beyond man's wildest imaginings, and all you can think of to do with it is burn a few plays?"

He stopped short before Bliss could answer.

"That's it, isn't it?" he said, speaking as much to himself as to the humans. "Power beyond man's wildest imaginings. It's *Doctor Faustus* all over again! You want the power, but you don't know what to do with it when you have it; your mind won't stretch that far. You can only conceive of a world pretty much like the one you already know, so you use your omnipotence to fiddle and embellish in ways you think would impress people if they knew it was you who was doing it. Your selfhood is completely externalized, your sense of personal wealth based entirely on what you imagine other people envy. Extraordinary!"

There was a long, bewildered beat, and Cornwall smirked as if someone had broken wind audibly at a cocktail party.

Bliss rolled his eyes. "Loser," he said.

Belial stared at him in disbelief.

From time to time the absurdity of Belial's predicament struck him with epiphanic clarity. That a demon of his standing should have been given responsibility for the soul of a man like Bliss was like asking the conductor of the London Philharmonic to teach introductory kazoo. As a devil confined for all eternity to an existence of misery and desperation, he was used to filling his time with things that were both incredibly difficult and utterly pointless, but dealing with Bliss was a new low.

The man thought he was a crusader, a warrior of hard truths improving the world with his Educational Reforms and Business Initiatives, when he was really the child at a birthday party who, already stuffed to bursting, his face smeared with frosting and cream, licks all the pieces of cake. He can't eat any more, but he'll be damned if anyone else can have any. They say people don't want to pick up a newspaper till they see you reading it. Then they badger you for the sports section or ask if you're done with the comics yet. Bliss was the guy who ignores newspapers altogether, but the moment he sees you reading one, wants to burn it.

"Well, devil?" said Bliss. "Are we going or what? Time is money."

Belial considered saying that it wasn't, that time was, in many ways, the very opposite of money, which could be accumulated, saved up, while time—at least for humans—was always draining slowly away like a leaky bucket, but he just couldn't be bothered.

"Doors," he said instead, opening them. "Go on. Do your worst."

"Oh," said Bliss grinning playfully at Cornwall. "We will."

ACT FOUR, SCENE SIX

"A time, methinks, too short
To make a world-without-end bargain in."
(*Love's Labours Lost*, 5.2.784-5)

June 14, 1602. Time remaining: 8 hours 43 minutes.
Plays to be saved: *6+Folio*.

Gladys

J immy hadn't returned, but there didn't seem to be much they could do about that, and they really needed to move on now that Rose had recovered *Merry Wives*. They stalled, drinking flat, room-temperature beer with slightly puzzled expressions, then Gladys consulted the Complete Works edition and tried to get her tired eyes to focus.

"Are you all right?" asked Rose.

"Fine, fine," said Gladys. "A little..." She made a wobbly gesture with her hands.

"How many of those have you had?" asked Xavier, pulling the mug of ale away from her.

"Three," she said.

"Three!" exclaimed Rose.

"Oh please!" Gladys slurred. "I was drinking beer when your grand-parents were the twinkle in the eyes of Neolithic Anatolians! I raised glasses with Pharaohs at the foot of the great pyramid *while they were building it*! I drank with the semi nomadic Natufians on mount Carmel before the founding of Jerusalem. I presided over the first barley harvest on the shores of the river..."

"But you were an angel then!" exclaimed Xavier.

Gladys drew herself up haughtily. "I still am!" she proclaimed.

"But now," Rose replied, "you are a mortal angel with a human body."

"A *drunk-ass* body," Xavier concluded.

"How dare you?" said Gladys, with an expansive gesture that almost threw her off her stool. For a moment she teetered dizzily with a look of baffled alarm, then Xavier was getting hold of her arm and rendering her stable while Rose pointedly shoved the rest of the angel's beer out of reach. Gladys frowned but, registering a sudden and unangelic queasiness in her midsection, opted not to object. "Right," she said. "*King Lear*. Which means jumping to... Hold on a second."

Xavier and Rose frowned at each other doubtfully. Time travel was alarming enough as it was, without feeling that their molecules were flying through the space/time continuum as charted by someone who wouldn't be allowed to drive or operate heavy machinery.

"Ah," said Gladys, oblivious to the fault lines appearing in their faith in her abilities. "Here we are, 1608..."

As she said it, a temporal door flickered open and, assuming that she had opened it, Xavier and Rose stepped through.

But she hadn't.

The slow realization of something not being quite right dawned like a timid sun in the Icelandic winter of Gladys' inebriated mind, and the color drained from her face.

"Not that one!" she gasped. "That's..."

But it was too late. They were gone and, with a sort of fizzle and a pop that suggested something malfunctioning, so was the door.

August 10, 1608. Time remaining: 8 hours 12 minutes.
Plays to be saved: still 6+*Folio*.

Xavier, Rose et al.

BELIAL HAD OPENED the door for Bliss and Cornwall. The portal was located a year later than Gladys had wanted, on the built-up dockside of the river, where stairs descended to the jetties and mooring points of the sluggish brown Thames' South Bank. It opened, and the demon's operatives were astounded to find the empty air suddenly full of Xavier and Rose, who caught them off guard and off balance, sending them sprawling in a heap, and scattering their stacks of quartos.

Cornwall, never one to take personal affront quietly, began shrieking threats and curses that most drunken sailors would have considered a trifle risqué. As Xavier and Rose tried to make sense of the situation and Cornwall's colorful blasphemies, locals began to gather.

"That little bitch punched me!" said Cornwall, a statement that was as much astonished as it was injured.

"Hardly," said Rose, rallying fast, as Xavier dropped to the pile of scattered plays and selected a couple. "I walked into you. But if you want to know what a real punch is like..."

Rose had brothers and knew something about punches.

"What disorderly women are these?" said some pompous bailiff-type in the crowd, ready to flex his patriarchal muscle.

"Oh, go back to Boston," said Cornwall, ignoring him, "bitch."

"You smug, stuck up, plastic little Barbie..." yelled Rose, warming to her subject.

"Witch!" remarked Cornwall, conversationally, her smile freezing a little.

She hadn't intended it, but the word produced a quiet panic in the crowd. There was a scattering of gasps and, with a swelling sense of the comic, Rose considered what was happening.

"You're kidding, right?" she said.

The crowd seemed unsure and for a moment everyone stood quite still. But "witch" was not a word to be thrown around lightly in this period, and Cornwall felt like someone who had tried to pass the ball and scored by accident. Her smile, cat-like in its composure, broadened.

215

At this worst of moments, there was a flash and a temporal door opened. Gladys, weaving slightly and clueless as to the unfolding drama, stepped out of nothingness with Jimmy at her heels.

"Everything alright?" she said. "I think you went through the wrong door..."

It wasn't. The sudden hush turned in to a gasp of horror as the magical word "witch" coupled in the brains of the bystanders with the appearance of a foreign-looking woman who had not been there a moment before. Clearly the good people of London were in the presence of Satanic powers. The fact that they *were* was unlikely to help the angelic team.

Someone pointed. Someone quoted some pithy Biblical verses in a tone of outrage and horror. Someone drew a weapon. They closed in, all righteous fury and thinly concealed terror.

"Is it me," breathed Xavier, "or did we just become extras in a Monty Python skit?"

"Not gonna be a lot of laughs in this version," said Rose, backing toward the embankment wall.

"The director's cut," Xavier agreed, following suit. "Excellent."

Gladys joined them, but there was nowhere to run. Struggling to shrug off the effects of the beer, the angel dithered.

"Now, look here!" she began, hoping that vague indignation would compensate for the fact that she had nothing else to say.

"Lay hands upon the agents of Satan!" shouted the bailiff as the huddle of God-fearing townsfolk balanced their shared righteousness with their equally shared terror and decided—as crowds often do—that the best solution involved a good deal of violence.

"Not this again!" bawled Jimmy. "What did you guys do?"

But then he was being yanked by Rose and Xavier, hands clasped as they vaulted the low wall beyond which was a twenty-foot drop to the murky, sucking depths of the Thames.

"Gladys!" yelled Xavier. "An exit please!"

They were already falling, Rose and Xavier clutching a quarto each in their free hands, as a shimmering rectangle of light flashed briefly across the brown surface of the river. It shifted as they fell, like an outfielder reading a drive to centerfield, and received them without a splash. They vanished beneath the surface and, as the crowd gathered hastily on the dock stairs, crossing themselves contrary to the views of their protestant churchmen, all four vanished from view and did not reappear.

∼

August 11, 1608. Time remaining: 8 hours 03 minutes.
Plays to be saved: *5+Folio.*

THE TEMPORAL DOOR opened the following day in the usual place, and Xavier, Rose, Jimmy, and Gladys, still holding hands and screaming, "fell" through the now vertical panel of light and collapsed in an untidy heap in the street.

Gladys squealed with discomfort and irritation.

"Oh good," she muttered. "More bruises. I swear by all that's holy, I don't know how you people walk around in these things."

Xavier seized her roughly by her shoulders.

"You are not allowed to drink ever again," he said. "Ever!"

"Well," said Gladys, shrugging free and testing the movement of her shoulders gingerly, "I confess it's not how I planned it, but we got what we wanted. Jimmy got both *Hamlet* quartos. So we just need to hop forward twelve months for *Troilus and Cressida* and *Pericles*... Wait. You have the fourth quartos of *Richard II* and *Henry IV part 1* here," she said, looking bemused. "Where's *King Lear*?"

"That was all they had," said Xavier. "I just grabbed one of each."

"*King Lear!*" gasped Gladys, the panic back in her voice. "What happened to *King Lear*?"

"I think he dies at the end," said Rose ruefully.

"Yeah," said Gladys, suddenly ice cold and staring at them meaningfully. "Then you'll be able to say hi."

∼

THE ANGELIC TEAM WERE FRANTIC. They had tried every bookseller in London, wasting a lot of time in the process, and found that the closest thing to the missing play in the shops was one *King Leir* (different spelling), which was clearly not Shakespeare's. They had even tracked down the printer who Gladys said had printed the play, but he informed them that on the day of the supposed transaction, he had been indisposed while his shop was, he believed, raided by foreign spies (judging from their accents). Why, he was at a loss to say. If Shakespeare's company had ever brought the *Lear* pages to be printed, he had never received them.

Gladys made the point brutally clear: "Without *Lear*, it's over. We fail, you die. Period."

"Isn't it in the Folio?" asked Rose.

"A substantially different version," said Gladys.

"Different story?" asked Xavier.

"No, but literally thousands of sentence level variants," said Gladys.

"Who cares?" said Jimmy. "Focus on making sure the Folio survives, and we're good."

"People care," said Gladys. "Academics. Editors. Theatre managers."

"I meant regular people," said Jimmy. "So there used to be two versions and now there's one, so what?"

"So the future will be different!" said Gladys. "Is this still not clear? *Lear* is a hugely important play. Every modern edition is the result of editors choosing which line, which word, they think is best. Will the world be substantially different if they can't do that? I don't know. Probably not. But are you prepared to take the chance? Any minute alteration in the intervening four centuries could lead to you not being where we need you to be at the precise moment of the railway accident."

"How could a few academics fighting over the precise wording of a play change our lives?" Jimmy persisted. "I've never even heard of the damn thing!"

"This is the butterfly," said Xavier thoughtfully. "Right? The butterfly that flaps its wings and changes weather patterns a thousand miles away. It's chaos theory. Fractals. Stuff like that."

"Microscopic variations in the timeline that alter subsequent events," said Rose.

"Oh," said Jimmy, apparently satisfied. "Right."

"Did you understand any of that?" said Gladys accusingly. "Butterflies and fractals and..."

"Chaos theory," said Jimmy sagely. "It was in *Jurassic Park*."

"Oh, well that's just great," said Gladys sulkily. "Reasoned argument about Shakespeare from a higher intellectual power makes no impression, but Xavier dips back into his Hollywood Classics series and suddenly everything is crystal clear."

"Can we move past this?" said Xavier. "We have established the potential importance of a play we don't have and can't get. Now what?"

"Maybe it's time to contact your superiors," Rose insisted. "We can't give up now. You have to get their help."

"They won't listen to me," said Gladys, who didn't bother to hide how much this was actually a relief. "I've tried."

"Well, try again!" Xavier said. "Our lives, let alone the future as we know it, *knew* it—whatever—are on the line."

"I can't get an audience with the higher powers!" Gladys explained. "I couldn't when I was an actual angel. Now I'm not even that. They have no interest in what I'm doing and are likely to cast me out of Heaven entirely for trying. I've told you this already! As far as they are concerned, I'm one of you now: human, flawed, utterly insignificant. My begging for an audience with the higher angels would be like praying to find a million dollars on your doorstep. It's just not the way things work."

Except that today, it was.

ACT FOUR, SCENE SEVEN

"The worst is not
So long as we can say 'This is the worst'."
(*King Lear*, 4.1.27-8)

Gladys

Absolutely not," said the Archangel Uriel. "You have acted contrary to your orders, contrary even to the basic principles of your angelic essence, and your status has been revoked pending a full inquiry, which could take the rest of your earthly life."

The summons had come almost as soon as Gladys had requested it, but thus far wasn't going well. The Archangel was seated in a great golden throne in a vast, white marble chamber lined with Ionic columns. He had taken the form of an elderly man who, for reasons unknown, exuded a soft, benevolent glow. His hair was white and immaculately groomed, his beard full and shapely, and around his eyes and mouth were the lines of a graceful but infinite age. All very Michelangelo. In the bright blue eyes themselves, however, was a frost that showed no sign of thawing.

"But I was protecting the works of Shakespeare," said Gladys, without much hope.

"What's that," said the Uriel, "some kind of charitable institution?"

"Shakespeare!" said Gladys. "You know, *Shakespeare.*"

"Art, or something, is it?"

"Yes, I suppose so."

"Painting and what have you?"

"No!" Gladys exploded, holding up her hands. "He is a dramatist. He wrote plays and poems."

"Plays?" said Uriel, mouthing the word as if testing marshy ground with his foot.

"You know," prompted Gladys, "theatre."

"Oh, one of those things when people pretend to be things they aren't. Like those, what do you call them...*movings.*"

"You mean *movies.*"

"Yes."

"No. Well, kind of."

"And this Shake...what?"

"Spear. Shakespeare."

"Right. He wrote movies...or *plays* then, did he?"

"Yes!" said Gladys, between triumph and exasperation.

"So?" said the Archangel. "How is this relevant? You're an angel, of a sort. Or were. How does this messing about with *plays* aid the fight against the lords of darkness and the pit? How does it save mortal souls, bring men to God, or show them the truth?"

"It doesn't."

"So what are you doing investing angelic labor into..."

"Well, it kind of shows the truth," said Gladys, improvising.

"Kind of?"

"Yes. Depending on what kind of truth you mean."

"You sound like bloody Pilate," said Uriel. "No wonder they asked me to keep an eye on you. *What kind of truth?* There is only one kind. That's what makes it true."

"But what if there is more than one truth?" said Gladys. "What if there are all kinds of human truths that we don't know about?"

"Human truths? That's a contradiction in terms if ever I heard one. And if there were human truths, how could we not know about them?" said Uriel, easily.

"Same way you didn't know what Shakespeare was."

"So this Shakespeare is a mouthpiece for Truth and I didn't know it?" said Uriel skeptically.

"Not Truth," said Gladys. "Just truth."

"That's what I said."

"No," said Gladys. "Your Truth had a capital T. I could hear it. You mean universal, cosmic, eternal Truth. This is different."

Uriel considered. "You mean some truth *about* humans," he said guardedly.

"Kind of," said Gladys, in a tone that said "not really." "*Truths*. Lots of them. Plural. Not some great insight into the nature of humanity because humanity changes from moment to moment and depends on all kinds of specifics."

"Then how can there be any truth there?"

"You sound like Ben Jonson," Gladys grinned.

"Who?"

"Another dramatist."

"There's more than one?"

"Oh yes. There are lots."

"Hell," said Uriel, forgetting himself. "And does this Benjonson throw these truths about too?"

"Oh yes," said Gladys. "Different ones, usually, but truths none-theless."

"Are you *sure*? I mean, I know I haven't been watching that closely for the last few millennia, but can they have developed to this extent, that they can be dealing in Truth, sorry, truth…"

"Truths."

"Right, truths, that we have no knowledge of?"

"We don't know them because they are truths about them, not us, not the universe, not HIM ABOVE or THEM BELOW. This particular one, Shakespeare, has all kinds of truths about, well, for example, love."

"Love?"

"And social hierarchy. You know, poverty, kingship, power dynamics, that kind of thing."

"Sound like politics," said Uriel with distaste. "We don't do politics."

"I think that's debatable," said Gladys. "But let's stick to the matter at hand."

"Shakespeare's truths."

"Yes."

"About kings."

"And identity," said Gladys. "About how people see themselves and the way their position in the world shapes them."

"There's truth about that?"

"Oh yes," said Gladys, warming to her subject. "And lots of other things: role-playing, romantic obsession, the functions of language, jealousy, ambition, the way that the smell of a certain flower reminds you of something from long ago, what happens to you when you drink several pints of beer: things like that. I hadn't realized it before," she added, thinking about the beer part in particular, "but now that I am human—kind of—it's obvious."

"Extraordinary."

"And it's not just him. Jonson, Marlowe, Dekker, Middleton, Marston, Massinger, Kyd, Beaumont, Fletcher, Heywood: there are lots of them. Most of them have been forgotten by all but a few academics, but each one talks about their world and the things that people saw and thought about in that time. That's a kind of truth, isn't it?"

"I suppose," said Uriel, unsure. "But if these truths are all about the writers' own periods, why should the twenty-first century care? And if it does, doesn't that make these truths eternal, universals? And if I don't know them, doesn't that make them lies?"

"No," said Gladys. "Firstly, like I said, just because we don't know them doesn't make them less true. We haven't been paying attention. Secondly, the twenty-first century wants to know them not because they are universal truths that speak to all people in all places at all times, but for all kinds of complicated reasons. Some of them aren't very good reasons and have a lot to do with schools and cocktail parties and game shows, but some of them are quite good reasons."

"Such as?"

"Well, in the great scheme of things the twenty-first century is only a hair's breadth from the seventeenth."

"So?"

"So things haven't changed that much. You don't have to push Shakespeare's truths too hard, once you see what he's talking about in his own world, to see how it fits the twenty-first century. Plus, the plays are ways of reflecting whoever reads them. They find in them the things their own culture finds valuable or interesting. That's what makes them neat."

"Neat?"

"Mmm. Neat. If you can put *Hamlet* in its original context, you understand the play and what it's talking about, then, consciously or otherwise, you see your own world slightly differently. It's like every experience that someone has is like a pair of sunglasses, each pair very slightly tinted, some more than others."

"Sunglasses?" said Uriel, baffled.

"Spectacles with colored lenses designed to protect your eyes when the sun is bright."

"And reading Shakespeare is like wearing these...*sun glasses*?"

"I mean they change the way you see." Gladys hesitated like a woman on the top of a very tall ladder who could hear the woodworm tucking into the lower rungs, but opted to persist with what was, fairly clearly, a terrible analogy. "Actually, Shakespeare is like lots of different pairs of sunglasses. For some people, *Hamlet* makes very little differ-ence. For others, it's life changing. And, and this is the *really* neat bit, different people can read *Hamlet* and come out with different colored sunglasses, which is especially neat because that's kind of what *Hamlet* is about. Or one of the things it's about anyway. That's what I mean about it being true with a small t."

Uriel wondered whether it was worth asking what *Hamlet* was, and decided it wasn't. He wasn't getting much of this anyway, which was probably as well since it would have sent his identity into paroxysms, as if he had bent down to tie his shoelaces and sunglasses he didn't know he was wearing had fallen off.

"But don't sunglasses stop you from seeing the sun?" he said, falling back on the only bit of literature that had ever made any sense to him. "You know like whatshisname said: Plato. If you wear these human sunglasses, you can't see the sun, which is the real Truth."

"Ah," said Gladys knowingly. "But sunglasses protect your eyes. They allow you to see what would otherwise blind you."

"Mmm," said Uriel. "Well, I must say, this is all very interesting. We should chat about it some other time. Maybe you can show me one of these play-things."

Gladys wanted to ask about the other thing, the Thing that had been Bothering her, the Sensation, the Thing Which Stank, but things seemed, against all the odds, to be going so well; she hated to spoil it. She opted for something lighter.

"And I get my angelic status back?" said Gladys with breezy confidence.

"Oh no, my dear," said Uriel, surprised. "Is that what you thought we were talking about? Oh, dear me, no. That is quite a separate matter and is being processed by the Tribunal on Rebellion even as we speak."

"The Tribunal on Rebellion!" Gladys exclaimed.

"I'm afraid so," said Uriel. "Defiance of orders, acting on one's own authority, all that kind of thing is very clearly their jurisdiction."

"But those tribunals take years to produce anything!" gasped Gladys.

"At least," said Uriel. "It's a very serious business, rebellion. I'd keep the next century or two open if I were you."

"But I'll be dead by then."

"Mmm," Uriel mused. "Quite. Well, I suppose we'll just hold you over in that rather nice little hamburger establishment that you helped design for as long as it takes..."

"And *King Lear*?"

"That's the play you lost, is it?" said the Archangel.

"Yes," said Gladys, forcing herself not to scream.

"Gone, I suspect," said Uriel, cheerily. "Can't be helped."

"But that's the end!" Gladys wailed, trying to make him understand. "If we lose that, it's going to change everything. We won't have saved enough of the important stuff to count and my team will die and the future will go all...*weird* and..."

"Not really my problem, I'm afraid," said Uriel. "And in the grand scheme of things, I really don't see what difference it makes. People come and go. We continue. Our Truth—capital T—continues. No wonder you lost your angelic status. You have started to think like one of them."

Gladys closed her eyes and let out a low, dragging moan. She was still doing it when she opened her eyes to discover that the marble and gold splendor of Uriel's audience chamber had been replaced with the altogether more earthy and mundane environs of London in 1608 and the faces of her human team who, it seemed, would be dead within the next few hours.

ACT FOUR, SCENE EIGHT

"We are not the first
Who, with best meaning, have incurr'd the worst."
(*King Lear* 5.3.4-5)

August 11, 1608.

The Angelic Team

G ladys' team read her face instantly so she was spared having to explain their predicament. Instead, she said, with absolute sincerity, something that had been worrying her for a while.

"Look, I'm really sorry. This whole thing has been a cock up from first to last and it's all my fault. I should have left you under the tram."

There was something about that last detail that energized Xavier. It was absurd and he resented the hell out of it, but he was damned (ha!) if he was going to leave it at that.

"There has to be another copy of that play somewhere," he exclaimed. "Maybe the new King ordered one like the Queen did with *Midsummer Night's Dream*?"

Gladys shook her head.

"Hold it," said Rose. "We're thinking about this all wrong. They aren't novels; they're plays."

"Same diff," said Jimmy.

"No," said Rose, and a glimmer of hope was beginning to show in her eyes and her flushed cheeks, "the author doesn't finish writing it and take it straight to a printer! Printing it is an afterthought. He wrote it for the stage. If he can write it *for* the stage, we can write it *from* the stage."

~

August 17, 1608. Time remaining: 7 hours 51 minutes.
Plays to be saved: *4+Folio.*

Gladys

GLADYS HAD LOCATED a staging of *King Lear* at the Globe and, with the usual furtive stepping in and out of temporal doors while no one was looking, the team had made their way into the uppermost gallery of the theatre. Now they waited, poised like greyhounds in the slips, pens in hand. As the stage filled with actors, the house quietened, and Gladys' team began scribbling for all they were worth.

They had worked out a kind of system whereby each of them was to claim responsibility for one character as they came on and would focus on getting down whatever he said, leaving all intervening dialogue to someone else. Things got sticky immediately when there were too many people on stage to track, and the twenty-first century scribes began whispering "mine!" like curiously furtive soccer players calling for the ball. This might have got them into trouble with their fellow audience members, except that the audience were too busy commenting among themselves, cheering the characters they liked, booing the ones they didn't, till the soccer ground analogy felt significantly less far-fetched. Indeed, far from distracting the other play goers, the angelic team were soon struggling to hear over the noise around them.

"Do you mind?" said Rose, huffily. "Some of us are trying to plagiarize."

The audience already knew the story, or so they thought, and had come in waiting to be entertained. Their mood was initially frivolous, as if they almost wanted the tragedy to fail, to collapse into comic misadventure. But something happened early on in the show and, periodically, it happened again: a sense of both the story, and the audience being pushed beyond their limits into new and dangerous territory. The last and most brutal stroke, more brutal even than the blinding of Gloucester, was Lear's final entrance with his youngest daughter, Cordelia, the daughter who had been honest and loving, the daughter expected to pull the fairy-tale happy ending out of all this death and misery, the daughter who the audience knew was supposed to take the throne and reign after her father's death. Shattering all foreknowledge, all sense of cosmic justice, the aged King staggered under the weight of his dead child, hanged because no one thought to intercept the executioner in time.

The audience's shock was palpable. There was not a sound in the theatre.

"Howl, Howl, Howl!" said Burbage as Lear, wild eyed, hollowed out by grief. "O you are men of stone! Had I your tongues and eyes, I'd use them so that heaven's vault should crack. She's gone forever! I know when one is dead and when one lives; she's dead as earth."

Gladys blinked, hearing the words, no, *feeling* the words drive through her heart so that her pen slowed to nothing. Not long ago it would have meant nothing to her, all this ruminating about mortality, but she got the play's grim little conclusion now all right. It was the bleakest image of life and the universe that Gladys had ever come upon and she wrote miserably, hating it.

"No, no, no life!" mused the staged King to the corpse of his child. "Why should a dog, a horse, a rat have life and thou no breath at all? Thou wilt come no more. Never, never, never. Pray you undo this button. Thank you, sir. Oh!"

And Lear died.

Long after the applause died down, after the bizarre little dance the cast performed, after most of the house had filed out in their varying states of contemplation, Rose, inky and exhausted, finished the last lines.

"*We that are young, shall never see so much nor live so long,*" she said.

"That's it. Thank God! My wrist! I mean, it's great and all, but why couldn't he write something shorter?"

"Haiku?" Xavier suggested. "Limericks..."

"I can't believe Cordelia died," said Jimmy. He was still staring at the empty stage, his face blank.

"Pretty bleak," Xavier agreed.

"No, but I mean, she *died*," said Jimmy sounding stunned. "She was the good one. And she died! Don't seem right."

"That's life, I guess," said Rose, not unkindly. She reached over and patted Jimmy's hand.

He stared at her. "I guess," he said, not liking it.

Gladys consulted her watch. It had been a long play and they were running out of time. It also looked likely that large sections of what they had transcribed was garbled, misheard, illegible, or missing.

"I think we just invented the Bad Quarto," she said. "Well, something is better than nothing. We need to get to a printer, then move on."

"Good play?" said Rose to Xavier.

"A laugh riot," he replied, turning to Gladys with an accusatory look and quoting. "As flies to wanton boys are we to the gods. They kill us for their sport."

"I wasn't driving the train," said Gladys testily. "I just picked up the...er...the bits."

"Can we go?" said Rose.

"Don't panic," said Xavier. "We're as good as finished." He paused to consider the implications of what he had said and added lamely, "But in a good way."

ACT FOUR, SCENE NINE

"Excellent! Your lordship's a goodly villain.
The devil knew not what he did when he made man
politic; he crossed himself by it, and I cannot think but
In the end the villainies of man will set him clear."
(*Timon of Athens*, 3.3.29-32)

London, 1623.

Henry Condell

The ominous implications of being "finished" would have resonated more darkly still if they had realized just how much the delay at the *Lear* performance had cost them.

Indeed, it may well have cost them everything.

There was no denying that *King Lear* was extraordinarily important as Shakespeare's canon was concerned, but it paled in comparison to a single publication that was printed in 1623: the first Folio, an expensive collection of Shakespeare's plays which contained, as well as those already printed in earlier quartos, eighteen plays that would have otherwise disappeared including *The Comedy of Errors, The Taming of the Shrew, As You Like It, Twelfth Night, All's Well that Ends Well, Measure for*

Measure, King John, Henry VIII, Antony and Cleopatra, Julius Caesar, Coriolanus, The Tempest, and *Macbeth.* To lose the Folio would mean not so much failure as abject and total disaster that would radically alter human culture.

But this was beginning to look likely. For while Gladys was hastily moving her team into 1609 so that they could collect *Troilus and Cressida* and *Pericles*, Bliss, Cornwall, and Belial had already made their way to a printer's shed in 1623 where the presses were being set up to begin their first run of the world's most famous secular book.

Henry Condell had acted with Shakespeare and the King's Men for years. Together with his old theatrical comrade in arms John Hemmings, Condell had come up with the idea of printing a Folio volume of their old friend's plays as much as a tribute to him and their work on stage as to make money. In truth, it was far from clear that they *would* make money. The volume was going to be expensive, and the idea of people buying plays as if they were literature instead of throw-away trash, was novel to say the least. Only Ben Jonson had done something similar, and he had needed all his pugnacity to brazen it out when the gallants and intellectuals of London had poured scorn on the idea that drama might be read as if it were poetry.

So Condell had a lot on his mind when he heard the tap at the door and was in no mood to barter with hawkers or preachers.

"We really are most busy..." he began as he opened the door.

But there was something about the three people outside that troubled him. It wasn't just their clothes, which were almost in fashion but not quite, nor the fact that they were a little taller than the average (including the woman). No, it was something in their eyes or, as he later reported to Hemmings, something that *wasn't* in their eyes.

"Cold night," remarked the nondescript fellow at the front who seemed to be the leader.

"Indeed," said Condell, cautiously.

"You're printing Shakespeare's Folio?" replied the man with frightening congeniality.

"We are printing the comedies, histories, and tragedies of Master Shakespeare in folio, yes," said Condell, now doubly suspicious. "How did you know?"

"We are concerned citizens," smiled the woman. "It's our business to know."

"Were you hoping to purchase a copy of the printing?" ventured Condell without much hope.

The blank-eyed man grinned.

"No," he said. "We thought we'd help you out."

"I think everything is in order..." Condell began, anxious to get rid of them for reasons he couldn't quite fathom.

"Really?" the other replied, jamming his foot in the doorway before Condell could close it. "You see, I don't think it is. Do you, Cathy?"

"I don't, Robert," said the woman, smiling wolfishly. "Not at all."

1622. Plays to be saved: 1+ *Folio*.

Gladys

THE ANGELIC TEAM were one play short. The last quarto to be published before the Folio had proved a sticking point and they were wasting valuable minutes arguing about it.

"The future doesn't need *Othello*," Xavier said.

"They are gonna get it," said Jimmy. "Right? If it means we get our lives back?"

"It's in the Folio," said Rose, "so they'll get it anyway."

"Then I don't see the issue," said Xavier. "Leave the quarto edition and move on."

"You're hoping that if all the quarto copies are destroyed, *Othello* won't make it into the Folio either," said Rose.

"Is that possible?" Xavier asked Gladys.

"I suppose so," said the angel, squeezing her eyes shut in an agony of indecision. The truth was unavoidable. "We don't have time. We can't get the *Othello* quarto and save the Folio as well. If we have to choose...there's no contest."

"Gotta get the Folio," said Xavier, managing not to smile.

Gladys nodded solemnly, then flicked open a temporal door to the next year.

"Right," she said. "Fine. Now will you all just shut up and run!"

1623

Henry Condell

"WE REALLY DON'T NEED any assistance," said Henry Condell, peering round the printing shed door.

"That's because you don't know what we have to offer," said the woman, beaming.

"Oh?" said Condell. "And what's that, pray?"

"*Pray*," said the woman turning to her comrades. "Don't you just love the way they talk?"

"We're offering you exactly what you need on a cold night like this," said the man with the dead eyes.

"What is that?" said Henry Condell, not wanting to know.

"You need a fire," said the man, grinning. "Belial, will you do the honors?"

"Is that a question?" said another, older man who was, if anything, even more troubling than the other two. His voice had an echoing, slightly sibilant quality, like a snake in a barrel.

"Just do it," said the first.

The older man shook his head.

"Can't do that," he said. "Any direct interaction with physical objects within the timeline..."

"Fine," said the one the woman had called Robert, shoving his way into the printing house. A series of oil lamps were arranged around the room, bright enough to set type by. Condell realized too late what was happening. He lunged to stop the man with the blank eyes, but he had already swept two of the lamps from the desk. They exploded on the floor in a rush of flame.

Condell moved fast, but the fire spread with unreasonable haste, as if a bellows had been applied to the root of the flames. A stack of the first printing, Shakespeare's face engraved on the frontispiece looking distant and intelligent, caught fire and wilted before their eyes. Condell grabbed at it, but the heat singed his eyebrows warningly.

Fire is a living thing. It eats and breathes and tries to make more of itself. A young fire might be cautious and hesitant, and an old one might be subdued, content to smolder quietly in the corner, but a mature fire likes to run and jump, to consume and ravish, to snaffle up the world itself with no thought to its own survival. This was suddenly a very mature fire. There was no chance the printers would save the press and the typeface, let alone a single copy of the book. Condell knew they would need every second they had just to get out of the shed alive.

His lungs half full of smoke, Condell launched himself at the doorway and out, stumbling and retching into the snow as his investment burned behind him. Dimly as though his ears were as clouded as his eyes, he heard the woman speak as she and the two men walked away. Her voice was casual, amused. "See?" she said. "This way is *so* much more fun."

~

London, the same night.

The Angelic Team

GLADYS AND CO. crossed London Bridge at a run, or as close to it as the tunnel-like road, hemmed in on both sides by overhanging buildings, would permit. They had grown used to the heads of traitors and criminals, which looked down from the tops of pikes around them, but it was hard not to see them as an omen. Gladys consulted her watch and let out a little mew of misery.

Jimmy led the way. He wasn't in the kind of shape that Xavier or Rose were, but, despite having had to pause for breath a couple of times, he had found a second wind and ran like the devil was after him. Which he wasn't. The devil was in front of him, or had been, and his work was done. They rounded a corner and found what was left of the printer's shed directly in front of them.

It was no more than a blackened hulk of charred timbers and molten pools of lead. Parts of it were still burning, but mostly it just glowed and smoked and stank. No papers of any kind had survived the inferno.

"Oh no," said Rose and, inadequate though it was, there didn't seem more that could be said.

Xavier moved as far into the ruined building as he dared and squatted on the ground. The others joined him in silence.

"Well," said Gladys, bleakly, "that's that."

There was a long silence and then someone concurred.

"A tragic loss," said a voice.

They turned to find an immensely tall man looming over them. He was dressed in the mode of the day and wore a long heavy cloak against the cold. He was old and somber and they didn't know where he'd come from.

"You have no idea," Xavier said, without looking at him.

Rose put her head in her hands and wondered how it would feel to truly die and when she would feel it start. Or stop. She did not cry, but she could not speak, and she dared not open her eyes.

"But all things have their endings," said the tall man distantly, "passing through nature to eternity."

The lines chimed dimly in Rose's head, and she looked up, puzzled.

"After all," said the stranger, "all the globe's a stage, and all the men and women merely players. They have their exits and their entrances and one man in his time plays many parts."

"World," said Rose, too close to despair to be irritated by either the patronizing sentention or the misquotation. "All the *world's* a stage. Not globe."

"Are you sure?" said the tall man. "I could have sworn it was *globe*."

Rose didn't feel like arguing, but she shrugged away the beginning of a sob and looked up.

Globe...

Her eyes opened, she wiped rapidly and said, "We have to get to the theatre!"

"It's over," said Xavier.

"No!" she said.

"I'm afraid he's right," said Gladys. "Any moment now you will be transported back to Boston..."

"No!" said Rose. "Shut up and listen. The theatre would have copies of the plays, right? I mean, that's the company's headquarters, and there has to be a prompt book in a theatre, right?"

No one said anything, not daring to clutch at this new straw. Jimmy got unsteadily to his feet and looked at Gladys.

"When?" said Gladys. "We can't go back..."

"Now," Rose answered.

The angel showed nothing in her face, but she opened a temporal door and, without another word, they stepped hurriedly through it.

The tall man, whose presence they had forgotten, watched all this thoughtfully and then walked away. He showed no sign of surprise and, as he rounded the corner, he actually began to whistle a little before turning into something that could not possibly have been mistaken for human.

ACT FOUR, SCENE TEN

"The Windsor bell hath struck twelve; the minute
draws on. Now, the hot-blooded gods assist me!"
(*The Merry Wives of Windsor*, 5.5.1-3)

January 24, 1623. Time remaining: 3 hours 41 minutes.
Plays to be saved: 1+*Folio* (*18*).

Jimmy

G ladys' temporal door brought them, as usual, to the South
Bankside. By now they could make the short trek to the Globe
with their eyes shut, which was as well because it was after
midnight and completely dark: a real dark without streetlamps, neon
signs, and car headlights. This was a darkness you could respect, a darkness that led the Anglo Saxons to see Grendel in the trees and dragons
over Northumbria. Technologically, little had changed since those days,
and the Renaissance night still belonged to days long past where the
only things stirring were owls and rats and foxes.

And thieves.

"Jimmy," said Xavier, scanning the heavy oak door of the theatre by
the inconstant light of a small lantern, "we're in your hands."

Jimmy considered first him, then the door.

"You probably need some kind of special tools," said Rose, trying to keep the disappointment out of her voice.

"That I do," said Jimmy, plucking what looked like a keychain from the purse on his belt. It hung with an assortment of metal spines and hooks, some thin as needles, some stocky and robust.

"You brought lock picks on a heavenly mission?" said Gladys.

"Just happened to have them on me," said Jimmy absently as he studied the keyhole. "I can't think where they came from."

He inserted an L-shaped wrench into the lock, and then selected one of the straight pins and probed cautiously.

"We don't have a lot of time," said Gladys.

"You," said Jimmy, his eyes closed, "are going to need to. Stop. Talking."

His expression in the low light became distant, his mouth slightly open and his head tilted up as if to catch the strains of faint and beautiful music. The others held their breath, and Gladys consulted her watch.

They heard the snap of the lock, the slight shudder of the timber as the door became almost weightless on its hinges.

"Go," said Gladys. "Quick!"

They crossed the apple cores and nut shells of the pit and clambered up onto the dark and silent stage. It felt like a church, a ritual space waiting for strange and magical words to ring out.

"Fucking doors are locked," spat Xavier as he tried the tiring house entrances. "Jimmy?"

"Again, I hate to say it..." Gladys began, holding up the watch, whose ticking suddenly seemed to fill the air.

"Then don't," said Jimmy.

"Can't we just force it?" asked Rose.

"Good door," said Jimmy vaguely. "Strong door. These guys knew how to build with wood." He fell silent as he worked. "Fortunately," he added suddenly, "their locks aren't worth a damn."

He pushed the door open and the team bundled in, scanning the dark backstage room. Another locked door admitted them to a wardrobe hung with elaborate costumes, bishop's robes, and courtly dresses, racks of dull rapiers and, unlocked, a cabinet of bound pages.

"El Dorado," said Jimmy.

"Oy!" called a voice from somewhere in the theatre. "Who's there?"

"Great," said Rose. "Someone must have seen the lantern."

"Just get what you can, and we'll hope for the best," said Xavier.

They heaped their arms full and, as the sound of heavy boots reached the backstage and torchlight fell upon their faces, Rose shouted, "Gladys: an exit!"

The temporal door opened as the first watchman arrived, and they dived through it. One play fluttered to the floor like a mangled butterfly: *Macbeth*. They were already through the door and into a different period, but the door stayed open just long enough for Xavier's arm to reach back through, grab it, and whisk the play back into society and culture like Indiana Jones recovering his hat.

THEY REAPPEARED a week after the tragic fire at the folio printers', staggering under the load of papers.

"Well?" said Xavier. "Did we make it?"

"The Folio will be a little delayed," Gladys mused, "but if we pass these on to the printers.... There's only one way to be sure."

She opened the Complete Shakespeare that Jimmy had been carrying and considered it. It was about half the thickness it had been on the day of the train accident, though it had been briefly no more than its end papers.

"That's just the stuff we saved earlier!" said Rose, miserably.

"Wait..." said Gladys. "Now."

And the book swelled as if soaked, doubling in size, as its contents page filled up and eighteen new plays slotted into place.

Gladys breathed out, relief momentarily taking her mind off the other business, turning to watch the humans as they jumped and sang and laughed, and the cosmos registered the change thusly:

Time remaining: 3 hours 28 minutes. Plays to be saved: *0*

ACT FOUR, SCENE ELEVEN

"To know my deed, 'twere best not know myself."
(*Macbeth*, 2.4.73-4.)

The Globe, 1603.

Shakespeare

W hen am I going to see your new play?" said Richard Burbage, catching the writer in a corner of the taproom while the boys ran lines, sitting on the edge of the stage kicking their legs like the kind of chorus line that wouldn't be invented for almost three hundred years.

"When it's finished," said Shakespeare.

"This is the thing about the Moorish general with the wife?"

"You don't like it?"

"Haven't read it, have I?"

"The idea. You don't like the idea."

"I didn't like the idea of you doing another bloody Hamlet play, but it came out all right."

"Not sure *I* like the idea," said the writer miserably. "I've been thinking about it for months. Years."

"And putting some of those thoughts down in ink, I trust?"

"Some. It's harder than usual. There's an ugliness at the heart of it."

"Maybe cast Dick Harris?"

"Not a physical ugliness," said Shakespeare. "A moral, emotional ugliness."

"Well, if it's going up any time soon, we'll need to get the parts to the cast. Maybe try out the new bloke."

"New bloke?" said Shakespeare vaguely.

"The new actor. Auditioned yesterday," said Burbage. "Honestly, Will, where is your head?"

"Sorry. But yes, there'll be a part for the new bloke. What's he like?"

"Good looking, pleasant. Blue eyes. Looks a bit like you, actually," said Burbage, "but with better legs."

"Of course."

"He's good: easy presence on stage. A natural. The words in his mouth sound true, you know? Especially yours. Plausible. Everyone liked him."

"Name?"

"Iago."

Shakespeare had been huddled low in his seat with his hands under his arms for warmth and his chin in his doublet. Now he looked up and stared.

"Iago?" he said.

"Said his parents were Italian, but I think he just made it up," said Burbage. "A stage name, you know? Not Iago Smith or something. Just *Iago*." He said it breathily and with a little flourish of his hand. "Might bring in a few punters. Yes?" He hesitated. "Will? You all right?"

HE SHOULD HAVE KNOWN. It had, after all, happened before, if not quite this badly. The first time he had been sure of it was when he'd been working on Richard Crookback. The character had evolved over the last of the *Henry VI* plays and kept on growing as the writer gave him his own story, the one that would bring the histories right up to the present queen's grandfather, and about as close to the present as Tylney, Master of the Revels, would let them. Shakespeare had sensed it happening as the character evolved from Duke of Gloucester to King Richard III, had gloried in the way the man came alive on the page, moving from stock villain to something more clearly alive, a thinking, feeling presence the writer had known would be the joy and terror of the theatre. The historical Richard had been presented on stage before, but never with this wit and boldness, the joy he took in outflanking his enemies, the flagrant self-regard, the glorious theatricality that made him as funny as he was appalling.

Shakespeare had taken a cut-out from history and fleshed him as well as Marlowe might have till he had become a giant of the stage, a glorious monster who would redefine the form of the tragic history. The writer had felt it early in the drafting, that leap in his own creative gift. It had been dizzying and heady as good wine, because he knew that he had proved his worthiness in spite of Greene and the rest who carped at him for his successes. No one could accuse him of copying greater writers anymore.

But that hadn't been the moment.

One night he had woken from a fitful slumber and written in a hot flash the scene when Richard, on the eve of the battle that would kill him and end his dynasty, was haunted by the spirits of his victims. It was mere pageantry such as Kyd might have written for Hieronimo, a procession of curses like a religious service, but then the King woke and reflected on what he had dreamed and, more importantly, who he was.

That was when it had happened, as the words poured from the writer's scratching quill, each phrase linking to the next not like the line of a portrait but the shaping of a sculpture.

What do I fear? myself? there's none else by:
Richard loves Richard; that is, I am I.
Is there a murderer here? No. Yes, I am:
Then fly. What, from myself? Great reason why:
Lest I revenge. What, myself upon myself?
Alack. I love myself. Wherefore? for any good
That I myself have done unto myself?
O, no! alas, I rather hate myself
For hateful deeds committed by myself!

I am a villain: yet I lie. I am not.
Fool, of thyself speak well: Fool, do not flatter...

And that was that. The character suddenly knew himself. It was just that complex, and that simple. One minute the evil King had been the writer's shadow descanting on his own deformity and then he had been himself and alive. Shakespeare had felt the moment when the words became a mind that was separate from his own, and the feeling had been at once sublime and horrifying. The very pages beneath his hand had throbbed with the heartbeat of the creation, and the writer had become suddenly convinced of an impossibility: that somewhere the man he had written into life was rising from his bed and stretching, thinking about what he would do...

It had been an anxious few days till the play opened and then something remarkable had happened. As Burbage spoke the character's final lines and fell before the ragged foil of the actor playing Henry VII, first monarch of the Tudor dynasty, the audience applauded, and the strangeness, the sense that he had genuinely created a monster he couldn't control, ended. The character stayed in the play, but vanished from the world. Shakespeare didn't know how that could be true, but he was sure of it. One minute the dead King had been a bunch-backed toad trying to squirm out of the writer's fist, and the next moment he was gone, confined by ink. Sometimes when they staged the play now, Shakespeare thought he glimpsed him, the man he had made, peering out from Burbage's eyes like a caged tiger, but then the applause would end the show, and the actors would just be actors again. The crook-backed killer was bound by the play.

Burbage had said it was just his imagination, but Shakespeare wasn't sure he believed his friend's calm rationality. Burbage was, after all, an actor.

And this time...what?

Iago. An actor had come to town and auditioned for the company, an actor who happened to have the same name as a character in a play that was only half written. A coincidence. It had to be. Anything else was madness.

And yet...

He thought of Kemp's tale of the shadow man who resembled him, a presence that had filled the comedian with irrational rage and hatred. And now the shadow was a real person walking and talking?

It couldn't be.

Maybe he should work on something else. Another cross-dressing comedy, perhaps, though maybe the public palate for such stuff was sated? He could always revise his *Hamlet*. Again. Something coming to life in that wouldn't be such a bad thing, he thought with a grim smile.

"Abandon *Othello*," he said aloud. "There will be other ideas. All may be well."

As he spoke, the wind shifted and he caught a reek so foul that he covered his nose and looked around, half expecting to see a dead dog breeding carrion, or a human corpse borne mermaid-like upon the waters of the Thames.

Nothing.

He glanced back toward the wooden O of the theatre, scowled, and moved off in search of a bank of violets where the world might smell less like a foul and pestilent congregation of vapors.

ACT FOUR, SCENE TWELVE

"This is thy negligence. Still thou mistak'st
Or else committest thy knaveries wilfully."
(*A Midsummer Night's Dream*, 3.2.345-6)

Boston. 12.00 a.m. Today.

Bliss

Robert Bliss, the medium height, medium weight, and utterly damned head of the Northside College Board of Regents, stepped through a shimmering rectangle of air and into his office with a spring in his step and the satisfaction of a job well done. It had taken longer than expected, and he was close to physical exhaustion, but he had been absent from the office no more than a microsecond or two, so that his disappearance might not have been observed even by someone who had been in the room with him. Nonetheless, he felt the hours of labor trudging around that antiquated sewer as if he'd been at it for weeks.

But that was it. No more Shakespeare. Gone. Histories, tragedies, romances, problem plays (whatever they were) and, the most ludicrously named of the lot, comedies. All those puns, he thought. Gone.

Burnt to ashes and forgotten. No more *Macbeth*. No floating daggers, no murdered kings, no witches, no walking forests, and no talking and talking for hours by all of the above (including the forest) for no reason. All that sound and fury signifying Jack was so much ancient smoke and ashes.

It hadn't occurred to Bliss that removing Shakespeare from history might have a knock-on effect throughout society and culture thereafter, so he was utterly unsurprised to find his office exactly as he had left it. He settled happily at his desk, picked up the phone, and dialed his secretary full of an almost childlike glee. This was going to be fun.

"Yes, Mr. Bliss?"

"Hey Kathleen," he said, conscious of how uncharacteristically chipper he sounded. He smirked to himself in anticipation and then went for nonchalant. "Come on in here and bring me a Complete Shakespeare, will you?"

She would be baffled because she wouldn't know what a Complete Shakespeare was, and then, when she thought her job might depend on her fulfilling his wishes, she'd be scared. At last she'd arrive, shame-faced and maybe a little teary, and he would be like Scrooge lying in wait for Bob Cratchit the day after Christmas, waiting for her terror to reach its height before dancing round the office, making up the fires and promising to raise her salary.

"Certainly, sir," said Kathleen blithely. "Any particular edition?"

Bliss froze, staring at nothing.

"What?" he managed.

"I mean, does it matter who the publisher is? Or is there a particular play you need to read, *A Midsummer Night's Dream*, say, or *Macbeth*? I could nip over to the college library and..."

But Bliss wasn't listening.

"Goddamn it!" he yelled, slamming the phone down in rage and disbelief. "God DAMN it! It's all still fucking here!"

Kathleen and the other office secretaries would hear through the door, but he didn't care.

"God DAMN IT!" he bellowed. "Belial! BELIAL!"

"There's no need to shout," said the devil, materializing in the chair opposite him.

"Really?" roared Bliss, his eyes wild. "You don't think there's a need to SHOUT?"

"I understand that you're upset, but it's nothing we can't fix."

"You'd better," said Bliss, calmer now, which was somehow more frightening. His skin was glistening with sweat and his normally blank eyes had developed a manic intensity. "You are my servant for twenty four years, remember that, devil? Twenty four years! During which time you do my bidding. Now, I *bade* you to get rid of every lousy Shakespeare play and yet, here they all are. Every stinking word. So tell me why I don't call Beelzebub up now and tear that soul contract to shreds in front of him."

Belial thought quickly. Bliss didn't bluff and the last thing he wanted was to have Beelzebub demanding why he had lost a potential client. He swallowed his pride (not an easy thing for devils to do, historically speaking) and sighed.

"Fine," he said. "I told you I'd take care of it. We just have to..."

He paused, his eyes suddenly vacant. He got very slowly to his feet, inclined his head, and sniffed.

"What?" Bliss demanded. "What the hell are you doing?"

But Belial wasn't listening. He looked stricken with dread and horror which, given who he was, what he had seen, what—in ancient times—he had caused, was not to be sneezed at.

"It's here," he whispered, aghast. "I can't..." He paused, his face sour, then turned back to Bliss, with grim resolve. "We have to go," he said. "Now."

ACT FOUR, SCENE THIRTEEN

"Irreparable is the loss, and Patience
Says it is past her cure."
(*The Tempest,* 5.1.140-1)

1623. Time remaining: 3 hours 07 minutes.

Gladys

Victory had seemed such an unlikely prospect to Gladys that, when it arrived, she wasn't sure how to handle it. She stared at the fully stuffed Complete Shakespeare like some stone age hermit in the frozen north who, after months of polar night, sees the faltering beginnings of a sunrise.

She was standing on a hill gazing out over the river and the teeming city beyond, her team at her side.

"We did it!" she said. "I didn't think it possible."

Xavier and Rose had embraced joyously, leaving Jimmy to perform a kind of high five with himself, but at this they both turned on her.

"You brought us all the way here but didn't think we could actually do it?" said Rose.

"It's not like you had other options," said Gladys, "so don't get all indignant on me now."

"Wasn't going to," said Rose. "In fact..." She broke from Xavier's embrace and folded Gladys into her arms. "Thank you," she said.

Gladys stared like a trapped animal over her shoulder, and Xavier, unable to resist, grinned at Jimmy.

"Come on," he said, "group hug."

And the two men wrapped their arms around their companions till Gladys' eyes looked about to pop out of her head.

"That is..." she hesitated, unable to say precisely what it was. She was hot and suddenly in need of a lie down. All that human proximity, the feelings of generosity and gratitude, coupled with the sheer physicality of the thing... It was overwhelming.

Gladys, it should be said, had never been hugged before.

"Oh my," she said, suddenly unsteady. "Yes, I see the appeal of that. Quite...touching. Endearing. Intimate in a confusing sort of way. I think I need to..." and she sat down awkwardly, staring at the others, her eyes unaccountably brimming with tears.

Those were her first too, and she dabbed at them, baffled and thrilled, till more came and ran down her cheeks and dripped onto her clothes. The humans who had been laughing were suddenly anxious and huddled around her, but their earnest compassion only intensified her tears.

"I don't understand what is happening," Gladys sobbed.

"It's okay," said Rose. "You're just happy."

"This is happy?" gasped Gladys. "It's terrible!"

"Sometimes," said Rose, smiling.

"So, what will you do when you get back?" asked Jimmy.

"Go see my dad," said Xavier.

Rose gave him a quick look, and he shrugged apologetically.

"He's sick. I haven't seen him for a while. We used to be real close, but in the last few years... You know how it is."

"Fathers and sons," said Jimmy thoughtfully.

"Yeah," said Xavier. "Anyway. Since we got stuck here, I started to think I might never..." He broke off, shook his head, and forced a smile. "What about you?"

"See Tracey," said Rose. "And my parents. Go back to school. Jimmy?"

Jimmy frowned. "Not sure," he said, curiously noncommittal.

"What?" said Xavier cheerily. "No big heists to pull?"

"Nah," said Jimmy so definitely and with such a pained look that Xavier pulled back immediately.

"I was just kidding, man," he said. "I didn't mean anything."

"No," said Jimmy. "It's cool. But I'm starting to wonder if there might be something else for me, you know? Something different. Better."

"Yeah," said Xavier considering him wistfully. "I do."

"You too?" asked Rose. "No more the high-flying financier?"

"I didn't say that," said Xavier, grinning. "I like my job and I'm pretty good at it. But I think it has started to fill my life more than I intended it too."

"Yeah!" said Jimmy, pointing at him. "That's what I was thinking. After all *this*," he said gesturing vaguely around him, "I want more, you know? Not more stuff? Not money. More...other things. I don't know what."

Rose grinned at him.

"It's not a precise career plan," Jimmy conceded.

"Maybe not," said Xavier, putting his hand on Jimmy's shoulder and squeezing slightly, "but I know what you mean."

"A curious way to celebrate," said a pensive voice.

The team turned to find an elderly man in subdued clothes watching them.

"Angels and ministers of grace, defend us!" Gladys exclaimed, rocketing to her feet and staring, her wet eyes suddenly wide and terrified.

"Who...?" Jimmy began, but Gladys cut him off.

"Belial!" she shrieked, staring fixedly at the nondescript looking man. "Oh my God! They are working with Belial!"

The devil inclined his head and smiled briefly. "Delighted to make your acquaintance," he said.

"Not the minor sprite you thought we were up against, then?" Jimmy clarified.

"It's *Belial*!" Gladys exclaimed.

"And that's bad?" said Jimmy, uncertain.

"Of course it's bad, you stupid bloody human!" Gladys shot back. "He's the captain of the hosts of Hell!"

"But you are an angel..." Rose began.

"Was," Gladys clarified with grim disbelief, "and compared to him I was understudy to the bloody tooth-fairy!"

"Ah," said Jimmy, taking a cautious step backward.

"So," said Xavier, who figured that since he was already dead he may as well be brave, "you've come to punish us for winning, I assume."

"Not exactly," said the devil. "And I'm afraid you are going to have to rethink that whole *winning* thing."

"We saved the Folio," said Rose, stepping up with Xavier, her face a mask of defiance that almost outweighed the tremble of her hands.

"And all those quartets!" said Jimmy.

Gladys winced. "Quartos," she said.

"Yes," said Belial. "Well done, you. But I'm afraid we have a rather different problem. A rather more substantial problem than the loss of a few plays."

For a second they all stared in dread and disbelief, and then one of the demon's words clunked into place like the coin that sets a fifties juke box going. It was Rose who put the question into words.

"What do you mean *we*?"

~

"You knew," said Belial to Gladys.

The angel looked sheepish, then gave a noncommittal nod. "I sensed something," she confessed.

"When?" demanded the devil. "I mean, when did it start?"

"1590s," she said. "Thought I was imagining it at first, or misunderstanding some aspect of my new body. It came to me as a..."

"Smell," said Belial. "Yes."

"Will someone tell us what is going on?" said Xavier.

"Ah yes," said Belial. "You're Xavier, yes? You played the Barbary Prince, I think. The court were talking about that one for months. And to use it as a way to get *A Midsummer Night's Dream*, of all things... Most ingenious."

This last was directed at Gladys, who smiled modestly, then remembered who was complimenting her and developed a sudden hunted look, in case Uriel or Gabriel might pop out at any moment shouting "*J'accuse!*"

"Still not explaining what's going on," said Xavier.

"Right," said Belial. "Well, there's a new evil in the world. I'm not sure how else to put it. We don't know what it is or where it comes from, but it's bad."

"How bad?" asked Gladys, not wanting to hear the answer.

"Well," said Belial, "I'm not sure how to put it."

"It's a demon?" said Rose, adding almost apologetically, "Like you?"

Belial shook his head. "I don't think so," he said. "If it is, it's one I don't know anything about. I would have called it simply a *presence*, but it seems to be able to think." He hesitated.

"So it's...?" Xavier prompted.

"A monstrous, destructive consciousness," said Belial. "It moves through time and space sewing hatred, death, and division wherever it can. It generates toxicity like a ruptured nuclear power plant, but it seems to get stronger with each passing year. It contaminates every human interaction it touches in every possible reality that connects to this particular timeline."

"What has this got to do with us?" said Jimmy.

"Well, leaving aside the fact that you are human and this thing is literally eating away at all human history leaving little piles of smoldering corpses," said Gladys, somewhat snippily, "it seems to start somewhere around..."

"Now," said Belial. "Or as near to it as makes no difference. 1604, to be precise. It has been growing for a few years but was always somehow tethered."

"Tethered?" said Rose.

"Yes," Belial replied, though he looked bemused. "To what, I'm not sure, but it was limited somehow. Weaker, but also confined to a few square miles in and around London. In all previous versions of history, it seemed to appear and then go away again before it could do real damage, but now, just in this timeline and everything that descends from it, it doesn't go away. It gets stronger, worse. And that means..."

"We did something," said Gladys. "Or you did."

Belial didn't argue the point. "Quite so," he said thoughtfully. "And I don't know what. Something happened in 1604, the 1604 we created, something that made it infinitely more powerful and, and this is the really unfortunate part, set it free."

"To go where?" asked Gladys.

"Anywhere and everywhere," said the devil. "It seems to expand like a cloud or a shadow, jumping from person to person through every possible version of every subsequent reality. It starts small: inexplicable squabbling and bad feeling over next to nothing, then people start fighting. Then they get killed. But it keeps going, spreading, intensifying like plague. When the people it infects are powerful, the results are unimaginably unpleasant. I'll spare you the details, but let's just say that it pushes people to the very worst of their capabilities. For a no-name family man, that might be rape and murder, even of those closest to him. For a king or a president, it might be war and genocide. And it doesn't stop. It's like each new act of horror feeds it, makes it bigger, stronger. It's unstoppable."

"It must have come from you," said Gladys. "Or one of your people."

"You'd think so, wouldn't you?" said Belial genially. "But Beelzebub didn't know anything about it. He felt it. But he didn't know what it was."

"So, where does it come from?" said Rose, who had gone quite pale.

"Well, as I said," the devil replied, "I think it came from...*here*."

And so saying, he opened a temporal door.

London, All Hallows Eve, 1604.

BELIAL DIDN'T SO MUCH as pause for breath.

"More specifically," he said, glancing around the tavern to where a man was sitting alone in a corner, his balding head bent over a book, "I think it comes...from him."

The group turned as one and stared at the nondescript fellow with the little beard and the earrings who was scratching with a quill pen in the margins of his book.

"Oh my God," said Rose. "Is that...?"

"Shakespeare," said Gladys.

The man looked up.

"Yes?" he said, guilelessly. "I'm sorry, did you want me?"

There was what writers call a pregnant pause, which gave birth to Jimmy waggling his hand and saying, "Hi. Big fan. I mean, not like her," with a nod at Rose, "but still."

"A *fan*?" said Shakespeare vaguely.

"Admirer," said Jimmy. "Well, not so much an admirer as...a reader, or rather...someone who has heard of you."

"Oh," said Shakespeare looking confused. "Thank you?"

"What are you working on?" asked Belial, peering at his book.

"New play," the writer said, closing the book.

"Something dark and tragic?" said Belial.

"Yes, actually," said the writer. "How did you...?"

"Something with a really great villain," Belial continued. "The kind of character who seems so much richer and more complex than everyone else, even though he's the antagonist? Someone who talks to the audience directly, perhaps, lets us in on what he's thinking and planning, but who somehow remains unknowable no matter how much he tells us about himself."

Shakespeare's smile had become fixed and anxious.

"Who are you?" he managed.

"This character of yours," said Belial, settling into the seat opposite the writer and staring hard at him till his eyes seemed to blaze with unnatural intensity, "is he the kind who feels so real, so multilayered, that he might just walk right out of the play?"

Shakespeare leapt to his feet, but Xavier stilled him with a strong hand on his shoulder.

"Will!" called a tall, bearded man from the bar in a booming voice. "Everything all right?"

"Just making conversation," said Gladys to the man whose robust self-assurance surely meant that he was an actor.

"Well, would you mind not doing?" said the actor, smiling and turning to Shakespeare. "We need those final pages for the cast."

"Rehearsing for a show?" said Jimmy.

"Next week at Whitehall," said the actor, in a tone that said they ought to be impressed. "For the King."

"New play, huh?" Xavier asked the writer, his gaze level and steely. "Want to tell us about it?"

Shakespeare stared wide-eyed at what he considered a Moor, but the words which were his stock in trade had, for the moment, forsaken him. All he could manage was, "You!"

Xavier frowned. "Have we met?" he replied.

"I saw you," said Shakespeare, suddenly sweating and breathless. "With her!"

He glanced at Rose, who gave him a blank look. And just at the moment there was a crash of furniture as a fight erupted at the other end of the tavern. A jug sailed through the air as someone bellowed in pure and unadulterated rage. The sudden stench of decay hit them before the jug shattered against the wall.

The writer looked instantly horror-stricken, and his eyes flashed to the explosion of violence in the corner.

"That's him, is it?" said Belial, following the writer's mute gaze. "Your villain. Off the page and walking around. Mr. Shakespeare," he continued, his eyes flashing with deep and improbable fire, "we need to have a little chat."

ACT FOUR, SCENE FOURTEEN

"Why, I can smile and murder whiles I smile,
And cry 'content' to that which grieves my heart,
And wet my cheeks with artificial tears,
And frame my face for all occasions."
(*Henry VI* part 3, 3.2.201-4)

London, All Hallows Eve, 1604.

Iago

The fight was nothing. They happened every night and, more to the point, everywhere he went. They happened when he released his grip on his new body, letting some of his essence leak out like oil from a ruptured tanker, the kind that left rescue workers gathering up blackened seal and dolphin carcasses for months. He wasn't always aware of when it started or why, but he knew that when it happened, when the hatred and rage spilled out, his body became a little less clearly there. Then, he could melt away and enjoy the carnage, or he could force his way back into the structure of flesh and bone that sustained and anchored him.

For now.

He was, he knew, almost, but not quite ready. He needed a little more strength, a little more control before he could separate himself from the writer who had made him, the man he hated above all others, and then the body would be of no further use. He wouldn't need to be able to walk around on these ridiculous feet or make conversation with the hole in his face. He wouldn't need the face, and that was good, because he knew he didn't always use it right. He'd be in a conversation with an apple seller or rehearsing a scene, and he'd suddenly register the panic and horror in the eyes of the person he was talking to. He'd feel them try to pull away, knowing they were fighting an urge they did not understand to run while they still could.

He didn't fully understand it, but he knew the moment was coming when he would float free of this grotesque coffin of flesh and be able to move among them, through them, seeing with their eyes, speaking with their mouths, and tearing with their hands. Before then he had to attain full, physical presence. He had to own himself. Then he had to end the link to the writer and the absurd pages of scribble that was the final chain of his prison.

He thought of those first moments of consciousness, the sense of being new and formless, still so tightly leashed to the writer that it was only in the dark and dead of night, that he could stretch and wrestle free of the author's dreams. How long it had been till he had been able to pull himself away, to leave that squalid little room and walk the streets, if only for a few minutes, he could not say. Years, he thought, but so much time passed while he was unaware of anything but the writer in his head. Or the other way around. It was hard to tell. The writer thought he had created him, but Iago wasn't so sure it worked that way.

The name had been born with him. It had tumbled from his lips the first time he could speak, when someone cowed and fearful had demanded who he was. It brought no memories with it, no tales of time past, no family or friends. He was new, it seemed. Unformed, unfinished, his sense of who he was coming unbidden as he was shaped in the writer's head and on his scribbled pages.

I am not what I am, he thought.

He watched the bar fight absently, appreciating its mean choreographic stabs at cruelty like a drowsy connoisseur savoring a dusty red wine as he drained the bottle. He couldn't not enjoy it. His love of the thing, the blood surging as tempers rose, and spattering as impulse turned to action, it was woven into the fabric of what he had in place of soul. It coursed through him like fire, feeding him and emptying him so that all he wanted was more.

As he slid back into his actor's body and felt the muscles and sinew solidify under the pressure of his endlessly yearning mind, his eyes found the writer in the corner. He was talking and writing, as usual, and that was good. It was, he knew, the words that made him. But soon, very soon now, the play would be done, and the words would have given him all they could. Then all he had to do was break free from the play before it was officially sealed with the applause that ends and binds performance.

Yesterday he hadn't known how to make that final bid for freedom, but now, as he watched the scribbling author talking to a Black man like he was a person, his hand drifted to the pommel of his dagger and he saw with instant and perfect clarity how he would escape into the world.

ACT FOUR, SCENE FIFTEEN

"I hope I shall see an end of him; for my soul, yet I know
not why, hates nothing more than he. Yet he's gentle, never schooled
and yet learned, full of noble device, of all sorts enchantingly beloved,
and indeed so much in the heart of the world and especially of my
own people who know him best, that I am altogether misprized.
But it shall not be so long."
(*As You Like It*, 1.1.155-62)

Boston, The Present.

Belial

Belial had left Gladys and her team in 1604, effecting the kind of nanosecond shift he was sure would go unnoticed by Bliss and Cornwall and not only because they were even more self-involved than was normal for twenty-first century humans. The latter, fresh from a promotional spot for her latest book *Love Me For Who I Am*, was as outraged as Bliss about the persistence of Shakespeare in what should have been the revised and improved future. "How," she wanted to know, "can we feel self-actualized and proactive if you don't give us what we want?"

260

"No soul is worth this," muttered the devil.

The three of them had reconvened in Bliss' Northside office and tensions were running high as a condor over a meth lab.

"You had one job!" Cornwall went on, wagging an accusing finger.

"Sounds to me," said Bliss, "that it's time for our backup plan."

Belial braced himself. "Back up plan?" he said.

"Kill Shakespeare!" said Cornwall, shrugging as if it was obvious.

"I see no other choice," said Bliss.

"Finally," said Cornwall. "That's what we should have done to start with. I did say so, you know."

"Yes," Belial agreed, "I think I recall your enthusiasm on the subject. But as I explained then, we can't. The moment our involvement is detected, the timeline would be reset by the guardians of cosmic law. That includes if we somehow convinced one of the in-period locals to do it for us."

"And the guardians of cosmic law work for the opposition, right?" said Bliss.

"Not exactly, but yes, the angels are generally on the side of order, while we tend to be the disrupters, the agents of chaos, so?"

"So how would they react if the rule was broken by one of their own operatives?" asked Bliss.

"I don't understand."

"What if we got someone to kill Shakespeare on behalf of the angels?"

Bliss let the question hang between them. Cornwall looked puzzled. Belial did his best to give nothing away, but he had to ask.

"How would you do that?"

"Add to their team," said Belial. "We find someone who wants to kill Shakespeare out of a sense of goodness and virtue. The celestial guardians of law won't undermine what was done in their own interests, right?"

Belial laughed with disdain and, it has to be said, relief. He had feared Bliss was onto something, but this...? This was nonsense.

"Murder a playwright out of a genuine desire to do good?" He scoffed with the kind of withering scorn that only businessmen and talk show hosts could ignore.

"Perhaps," said Cornwall, "we should talk to your friend Mr. Beelzebub about this."

Even the furious exasperation and contemptuous annoyance that flared up inside Belial was insufficient to dampen the cold shudder that name (however absurdly prefaced with *Mr.*) awoke in him. When the demonic orders put its mind to it, they could give new dimensions to the word torture. Prometheus had it bad, having a vulture peck at his continually regenerating liver for eternity, but if Beelzebub had master-minded the ordeal, the vulture would have been perched on a jukebox that played nothing but "Achy Breaky Heart." There was no Geneva Convention in Hell.

"I don't see how you could do it," said Belial.

"You have to think positive," said Cornwall encouragingly.

"No, I don't," said Belial, "and it's positive*ly*."

"Not the way I say it, it isn't," said Cornwall.

Belial returned to the core problem. "Why would the agents of righteousness want to assassinate Shakespeare?" he asked.

Bliss and Cornwall once more made knowing eye contact.

"Have you *talked* to people in the twenty-first century lately?" asked Bliss, amused by the devil's naiveté.

"Finding something tedious doesn't make murdering its creator a virtue," said Belial.

"Beg to differ on that, but there's a simpler way," said Bliss. "We'll bring some others back from the twenty-first century, explain the situation, and let them take care of it. So long as they think they are doing God's will, we can't be implicated."

"The angel and her team will know and they'll testify..." Belial began.

"Then we'll deal with them too," said Cornwall.

"All in the name of virtue," Bliss concluded.

"What?" exclaimed Belial derisively. "How are you going to convince the righteous to kill Shakespeare, an angel, and the three people assisting her?"

"Righteousness is not in the eye of the beholder," said Bliss, smirking to himself. "It's in the mind of the doer. Just watch. You'll be amazed at how easy this is going to be."

ACT FIVE

"The lunatic, the lover and the poet
Are of imagination all compact."
(*A Midsummer Night's Dream*, 5.1.7-8.)

ACT FIVE, SCENE ONE

"Shall we their fond pageant see?
Lord, what fools these mortals be!"
(*A Midsummer Night's Dream*, 3.2.113-4)

The Palace of Whitehall, November 1, 1604.
Time remaining: 2 hours 35 minutes.

Jimmy

You've seen one royal Tudor palace, you've seen them all, or so it seemed to Jimmy, who had not enjoyed Richmond and was now not enjoying Whitehall.

"Why are we here?" he asked, glancing furtively about. "If the Queen sees us, she's bound to recognize us, and we'll be for the chop. Literally."

"That would be a trick," said Gladys. "She died last year. The throne is now occupied by His Majesty James VI of the Scotland, son of Elizabeth's traitorous cousin Mary Queen of Scots, and crowned as James I of England."

"I hate time travel," said Jimmy. It might have been mere exasperation, but he looked, if anything, sad. Gladys ignored it.

"Your concern about being recognized is not, however, without merit," she went on. "Many of the courtiers here will be the same as those who attended the visit of the Barbary Prince two years ago, notably the King's private secretary, Robert Cecil."

"Then we're screwed!" said Jimmy.

"Not necessarily," said Gladys. "We'll be mostly backstage."

"I thought you said we couldn't go back in time?" said Rose. "There were rules. We had to keep moving forward. We got all the way to 1623. Now we're back in 1604. How's that possible?"

"Because," said Gladys, "I didn't move you here. Belial did." Even now it was clearly hard for the angel to say the name without twitching. "Devils play by different rules."

As she spoke, the actors traipsed into the hall with their bags of costumes and props, Burbage at their head, Shakespeare tagging along at the back like a child creeping like a snail unwillingly to school. He saw them immediately and his face fell.

"You came," said the writer, as the other actors moved into their makeshift tiring house and set about readying themselves for the show. "When I didn't see you after our...*discussion* last week, I thought it all a dream. But here you are."

He did not look happy about it.

"Not a dream," said Gladys. "But the world will get fairly nightmarish if you don't do as we say."

It wasn't a threat exactly, the angel not having much experience of Ominous Pronouncements, but it had a suitably chilling effect on what was already a cold room.

"Where's Iago?" asked Rose, who had been scanning the company as they entered.

The name sent a shudder through the author.

"He never arrives with the others," he said miserably. "No one ever sees him till the show begins and then he's just...there. Burbage finds it annoying, a kind of actorly grandstanding, stealing everyone's thunder."

"But you think he's not there beforehand because he doesn't really exist until..." said Rose.

"Until he does," said Jimmy. "Right?"

"It defies reason," said Shakespeare. "But yes. I think there is no such man, until he stands in front of us, and then there is."

"And now he's poised to leave whatever minimal connection he still has to you and to the play," said Gladys.

"So you say," said Shakespeare.

"You know it's true," the angel replied. "You feel it."

The writer held her eyes for a moment, then sagged and nodded, looking at his shoes.

"I understand it not," he said. "But I feel him growing like contagion."

"He's at the height of his powers as a person now," said Gladys, "because the play is fully written. As we said before, we have to make sure the play is staged to the end. When the audience applauds the final lines, he will be bound to it and unable to walk free again."

"You think someone will stop the play from ending?" asked Shakespeare.

"I have reason to believe so," said Gladys carefully.

"And if the play doesn't finish?" asked Xavier, who had been quiet to the point of surliness thus far.

"Then he slips free in his incorporeal state," said Gladys, "to poison the world."

"And bring hatred, misogyny, and racism," said Xavier bitterly.

Gladys frowned. "No," she said, sensing where this was going, "to intensify those things. Not to invent them."

"Yeah," said Xavier, his face still hard, "because people don't seem to need a lot of magical help where that shit is concerned."

"It can always be worse," said Gladys warningly. "We talked about this."

"Yeah, we did, and you spouted a lot of *I can see the future* stuff when all I know is that in the future, in what I called the present until about twenty hours ago, things were plenty bad as it was, and this god damned play had a lot to answer for before it spawned magic bogeymen."

"The play has to exist," said Gladys, squeezing her eyes shut. "It has to be printed to maintain the future as you knew it, and it has to be played to the end in front of an audience to bind the malevolent force it has generated. We don't have time to debate this."

"Isn't that handy?" said Xavier.

"You think the play is bad?" said Shakespeare. "That it stains my reputation?"

"Stains?" said Xavier in a dangerous voice.

"Tarnishes," said the writer.

"Mr. Burbage will be playing Othello, will he?" asked Xavier.

"He will."

"But not as a white guy, right?" Xavier persisted. "He'll color his face with something, yeah?"

"Walnut juice," said Shakespeare guilelessly. "It is a most convincing effect."

Xavier stared at him, then snatched his hand and slapped it hard against his own face. Shakespeare tried to pull away, sputtering his indignant confusion, but Xavier held the author's hand to his cheek.

"It's not makeup," he snarled. "It's not *blackface* you can paint on and wash off when you've finished entertaining people and being clever. It's my skin. It's who I am, and I don't get to change it when people leave the theatre believing what you told them I am."

He released the writer's hand, but not his eyes. For his part, Shakespeare looked shaken and unsure, but he said nothing. Rose reached over and took Xavier's hand. He glanced at her, surprised, then looked away.

"Xavier?" said Gladys.

For a moment Xavier stayed silent, staring off, seeing things only he could see, then he shrugged. "Yeah," he said. "Whatever."

"We have to assume something is about to happen," said Gladys, "something that disrupts the production. We need to anticipate it and ensure we get to the end."

"What is going to happen?" asked Shakespeare. "How do you know? You speak of the past and the future as if you have seen..."

"You're going to have to trust me on this," said Gladys. "There are other people who want to see the play disrupted. I think. That seems the most logical explanation."

"Belial said it was nothing to do with him," said Jimmy. "You think he's lying?"

"He said his team had an agenda of their own," said Gladys. "He's trying to contain them, but they have some fell purpose of which he knows not."

Jimmy frowned. "Never good when your leader goes all Gandalf-speak on you," he observed.

"Gandalf-speak?" said Gladys.

"Never mind."

"I don't understand how we can be responsible for *Othello*," said Rose. "The play existed before we came here."

"You're not," said Gladys. "But his seeing you both together charged the writing somehow."

"Is that right?" said Xavier, staring Shakespeare down.

"I don't understand!" the writer protested. "It's just a play."

"That's what we have to ensure," said Gladys. "Okay? Xavier?"

Xavier glanced away then nodded curtly.

And then the double doors behind them were opening and a pair of guards entered, halberds lowered purposefully in front of them.

"Here comes the royal court," said Gladys. "All right, people. Places!"

"Where's Belial?" asked Rose.

"He is attending to the other matter," said Gladys. She looked suddenly anxious as if an already difficult situation was slipping away from her. "They are in 1594, the site where the first temporal incursion began."

"You think you can trust him?"

Gladys faltered, her eyes flashing to where the royal party were gathering in the entry hall.

"Just make sure the play goes all the way to the end," she said. "It has to end. That is of paramount importance. You understand that, right?"

"Yes," said Rose.

"I'm just saying, because in the current timeline it doesn't and the results are..."

"I know," said Rose.

"Something bad is going to happen," said Gladys. "I don't know who will be responsible for it. Just be ready."

"You didn't answer my question."

Gladys hesitated and something fleeting went through her eyes.

"You don't trust him!" said Rose. "I knew it."

"He's a devil!" said Gladys. "How can I trust him?"

"What do you think he's doing?"

"I really have no idea, which is—believe me—worrying. I think," said Gladys, squeezing her eyes shut, "I think we're going to have to divide the team."

"Leave here?" said Rose. "What about making sure the play gets staged all the way to the end being of paramount importance?"

"Yes, I know," said Gladys. "It still is. Unless Belial and his team kill Shakespeare before he writes anything at all."

The possibility had dawned on her the moment she had learned who the devil they had been fencing with was. She hadn't wanted to believe it, and couldn't see how he might do it, but she had to face the possibility.

"Kill Shakespeare!" said Rose, stunned. "Can they do that?"

"I don't think so, but if anyone can find a loophole in a law, it's a devil. I have to find them and see what they are doing."

"And leave us here?" Rose exclaimed, suddenly panic-stricken.

"With Xavier, yes. Jimmy will come with me. Watch the actor playing Iago and make sure the play ends properly. Don't worry," lied the angel as an afterthought, "I have complete confidence in you."

ACT FIVE, SCENE TWO

"I never repent for doing good
Nor shall not now."
(*The Merchant of Venice*, 3.4.10-11)

1594

The Demonic Team. New and improved.

Bliss had told them it was going to be easy, and he had, to Belial's astonishment, been quite right. There were only three of them, all white, and Belial, whose demonic identity was now something of a secret, looked them over as they paced the streets of Renaissance London, trying to figure out what it was about them that seemed so odd.

The first was a forty-something TV evangelist who introduced himself as the Reverend Lee Boothe. His hair and his well-tailored suit were slick, and his watch cost more than most cars. He had a suspiciously even tan and great rubbery lips that continually spewed fire, brimstone, and words like "doth" and "begat." For Belial, it was all quite nostalgic. As the good reverend declared that all books but the Bible belonged in the fire, Belial thought that, clothes notwithstanding, he'd probably feel quite at home in the sixteenth century.

The second, Violet Morningside, was a middle-aged woman in a dowdy, olive-colored dress with a long skirt and buckled shoes. She had a nervous, furtive manner and a tendency to stand a little too close when she talked to you, her eyes locking onto yours and not letting go, like the better class of anaconda gamely trying to swallow a cow. Her hands were red as if recently scrubbed and she rubbed them together when Belial casually asked her what she thought of Shakespeare.

"Disgusting," she said simply. "I heard they were reading *Romeo and Juliet* in our local high school's English class, and I couldn't believe it. A story about children killing each other over a three-day infatuation! What are they supposed to learn from that? I made a presentation to the PTA."

"Banned it, did they?" asked Belial.

"No!" she replied in high indignation, stepping so close to Belial that he could smell carbolic soap. "They did not! How do you like them apples? Shut me down before I had finished my speech. It was the *Harry Potter* thing all over again!"

"Heathens," said Reverend Lee.

Violet nodded so emphatically that a passerby gave her an anxious look as if she might be having a stroke.

"I don't like to judge," she lied, "but I calls 'em as I sees 'em."

"Oh," Belial observed darkly, "this is going to be fun."

"Fun is the realm of Satan!" the reverend cautioned.

"Oh yes," said Belial. "Quite right too. Silly me."

Violet's smile got so wide and fixed that Belial took a step back. Bliss caught his eye and shot him a malevolent grin. She was perfect.

The last of the three was perhaps the oddest. Arthur Fielding was a tweedy man in his late sixties who might have been the only person in the twenty-first century who still wore a monocle. His accent was oddly *mid*-Atlantic, as if he had been raised on a rock a few hundred miles east of Newfoundland, or in a forties screwball comedy.

"And why do you hate Shakespeare's plays?" asked Belial, intrigued.

"Hate them?" repeated Fielding, aghast. "Are you insane, man? Shakespeare's work is the greatest single contribution to world literature ever penned. He is the most insightful, the most inspiring, the most..."

"So why are you prepared to kill him?" Belial interrupted.

"The writer? I'm not!" Fielding clarified unhelpfully. "I'm here to kill Shakespeare, the man from Stratford who people *think* wrote the plays. I'm not going to kill the author!" He chuckled. "The plays could hardly have been written by the son of a provincial glove-maker! The true author is, of course, the seventeenth earl of Oxford, Edward De Vere, a cultured man from whom I am fortunate enough to be descended, albeit obliquely through a bastard son."

"Ah," said Belial, who couldn't help but be impressed by Bliss' ingenuity. "That's the man who died halfway through Shakespeare's career, yes?"

"Well, clearly the chronology of the plays in conventional scholarship is wrong..."

And he was off, reciting the usual bad data and tortured play readings he had on hand for just such an eventuality. Belial switched off, but he marveled at the three of them, their ease, their certainty. They were soon chatting to each other, introducing themselves and comparing notes on their mission, all quite content and absolutely unflappable.

That was what was odd, Belial decided. Most people would be stunned by the reality of time travel, by the spectacle of a long-dead civilization alive and kicking around them, but these three were strolling around not so much unmoved by their surroundings as oblivious to them. The houses, palaces, and churches that crowded London's streets may as well have been the scenery for a high school production they had seen a hundred times. It wasn't that they couldn't see the people or hear their unfamiliar voices, it was that those things just didn't matter to them. They were the kind of tourists who wander through ancient ruins looking at their phones or debating who they liked best on *The Bachelor*. Belial saw with an almost painful clarity just how right Bliss had been. These people were capable of anything.

"It's quite an old-fashioned selection," he observed to Bliss when they were out of earshot of the others.

"These idiots?" said Bliss, nodding at his team.

"Yes," said Belial. "Given your university connections I thought you'd find some raging liberals just as bent on stamping Shakespeare from history."

"Oh, there are," said Bliss. "The problem with even the most militant feminist social justice type is that they tend to draw the line at murder. Progressives, eh? Whatyagonna do?"

"Quite," said Belial. "Most inconvenient."

"Where is the heathen, Shakespeare?" demanded the Reverend Lee in his booming preacher voice. "Where is he whose lewd and blasphemous scribblings are worshipped like the golden calf of the Israelites? He who parades the children of men upon a stage for sinners to behold and lust after, he who dresses men as women, he whose devilish work is taught in schools that should be extolling the name of the lord, he who shows our children the way to lechery with captivating words and most disgraceful stories, he who..."

"*Okay*," said Belial, "I think we get the picture."

"Get thou behind me, child of Satan," returned the reverend without missing a beat. "Thou art like unto the sheep which leaves its shepherd and falls into a ravine..."

"The man has a point, old chap," said Arthur Fielding. "Would you mind shelving the holy rhetoric for half a mo'. It rather grates on the nerves."

"Your motives are impure," returned the greasy reverend. "You do not burn with zeal for the obliteration of this Shakespeare, the blot on the virtue of our culture, this..."

"Yes," said Fielding, "I think we know where you stand on that."

"I think the reverend is sort of right," said Violet, pepping up as if someone had proposed either a bake sale or a good old-fashioned burning of Beatles albums. "You just want Shakespeare to have been someone else and leave his plays as they are..."

"Yes," said Belial, cutting in. "You all have different motives. But are you all resolved to enact what Mr. Bliss has advised?"

"It won't be nice, but I'm prepared," said Violet, "for the good of my country. It will be like surgery, you know? Not pleasant, but necessary in the long run to make the patient well."

"And the Lord will smite the unbelievers," began Reverend Lee at high volume, "and those his righteous shall raise their swords against the devil's own anointed..."

"I'll take that as a yes," said Belial bleakly. "And Mr. Fielding, you are also prepared to kill Mr. Shakespeare?"

"I am committed to the truth and to silencing the lies about this beggarly Stratfordian upstart before they take root."

"Of course," said Belial. "Where would we be without truth?"

"Right," said Cathy Cornwall, taking over, "then if you could all shut the fuck up for two minutes, maybe we can get this done."

Violet gasped and raised a dainty hand to her mouth.

"Take a weapon, please," Bliss continued, "and remember that you may have to kill more than the man himself. There are servants of the enemy at large..."

"Beasts of the pit!" exclaimed the reverend, slamming his fist down on a convenient table. "Plagues of locusts!"

"Right," said Bliss. "If that helps. I want them dead too. They've screwed me over for the last time."

Bliss had considered a range of viable weapons, but the sixteenth-century version of a pistol was a temperamental-looking thing as likely to blow your own hand off as kill your target. He had opted instead for the messy efficiency of cold steel in the form of daggers bought in Renaissance Cheapside. There would be no legal snarl-ups this time. Everything was going to be done by the book and that meant daggers all round.

"It's all very Ides of Marchy, isn't it?" said Cathy Cornwall with a wicked grin.

"Good one," said Bliss.

"Didn't think I knew that one, did you?" she whispered at Belial. "Elitist snob."

"I stand dazzled by your erudition," said Belial bleakly. This was getting well out of hand. Bliss' plan had seemed absurd to him, doomed. He'd only agreed to it as a stalling tactic. But as they swept along, buoyed by the team's sense of righteous purpose, Belial felt sure he had made another serious tactical error.

"Is this three daggers I see before me?" said Bliss, enjoying himself. "Why, yes it is." He turned to Belial. "Ready Bel...?"

Realizing who his audience was, he caught himself before saying the devil's name and amended it: "Ready *Bill*?"

Belial rolled his eyes and nodded grudgingly.

"This way," said Bliss, showing them to a door. "Enter here, oh ye righteous!"

ACT FIVE, SCENE THREE

"'Twas but a bolt of nothing, shot at nothing,
Which the brain makes of fumes. Our very eyes
Are sometimes like our judgments, blind."
(*Cymbeline*, 4.2.303-5)

The Palace of Whitehall, 1604.

Rose and Xavier

The production had begun, and everyone was watching, though they weren't all watching the same thing. The audience watched the stage action, albeit in a desultory fashion, the courtiers seeming to keep a closer eye on the King than they did on the stage, while his royal highness seemed more interested in one of the rather good-looking, dandified men lounging at his side and in the flagon of sweet wine that kept his glass topped up no matter how much he drank. And spilled. From time to time, he would applaud a line of dialogue and raise his glass to the stage in commendation, but then he'd stare off into space, start muttering to his companions, or chuckling at some witticism only those closest to him could hear.

There was a good deal of watching taking place backstage too.

Peering through a crack in the curtained section of the great hall that served as the makeshift stage's tiring house, Shakespeare was watching the enigmatic King as keenly as the courtiers whose livelihoods depended on staying in his good books. Xavier was watching Shakespeare, a spare stage rapier in his fist: it was blunt but heavy enough to deliver a hefty thump to anyone who might target the writer during the show. He was annoyed by the play, which droned on in the background, and by his having to play bodyguard to its author, but there were only a couple of hours left on the angel's watch-thingy; then it was back to Boston, back to real life, his collection of antique vinyl, hot showers, and a decent glass of red that didn't taste like it had been mixed with molasses.

Only Rose was watching the play with any great focus, and that was directed entirely at the man playing—the man who *was*—Iago. It wasn't that she wanted to watch. She just couldn't stop. He was...magnetic, fascinating. Repulsive, for sure, and every fiber of her being shrilled against him, but when he spoke, he was...plausible. Given what he was saying, it was horrifying. He glided among the other characters—or did she mean the cast?: it was hard to say—being affable, even funny. But then you'd see the disdain in his face, the loathing, and it was like leaning in for a hug and taking a dagger in the ribs, something that literally happened to his slight and gullible "friend" Roderigo.

But it was when he was alone on stage and talking to the audience that he was at his most powerful, when the mask slipped—or rather when he chose to remove it—and the audience saw the nakedness of his hatred and calculation. That hatred was directed at everyone: the dupe, Roderigo, Othello, of course, and at his good-looking lieutenant, Cassio. His scorn for the women in the play might have grown out of common or garden misogyny, but it was also personal and pathological. So was his racism, grotesque though it was, so that at times she felt herself wincing away from the words of the play. Even when Iago confessed his love for Desdemona, it seemed almost self mocking, as if he thought less of himself for being interested in her. Whatever he called it, it wasn't love. Not as far as Rose was concerned. Nor was it the obsessive and possessive passion she had once seen—and escaped—in a jealous boyfriend. This was something else entirely. Iago's love was merely an excuse to destroy what he couldn't have. In fact, that seemed to her his abiding motive. None of the reasons he offered for his behavior seemed to measure up to the scale of the carnage he was orchestrating, and it wasn't even clear who the real target was. It wasn't just Roderigo who was sacrificed along the way. Cassio, Othello, Desdemona, even Iago's own wife felt oddly like collateral damage, as if he wanted to plunge his dagger into the world itself.

"I think I'm going to be sick," she muttered to Xavier as they entered the scene when Othello was to smother his wife with a pillow.

Xavier said nothing. He was watching the audience who had grown still and focused, appalled.

"Nearly over now," she said. She spoke as if she were holding her niece's hand while she got a shot at the doctor's office and, as then, she wasn't sure which of them she was trying to console.

"Put out the light, and then put out the light," said Burbage as Othello, his face blacked up with the walnut juice.

"I can't watch this," said Xavier between clenched teeth.

"It's almost over," said Rose, gripping his hand.

But it wasn't. In a final cruelty designed to raise the audience's hopes, Desdemona seemed to revive after the smothering, only to collapse and die a few minutes later blaming herself for her death. Rose caught something of Xavier's anger, and her eyes flashed to where Shakespeare was sitting on the far side of the stage, watching.

Xavier's right, she thought. *The world might be better off without this play.*

Parts of it were wise and beautiful, full of rich poetry and rare insight, and there was no question it was mesmerizing as theatre, but the outrage welling up inside her wasn't merely about the injustice contained within the fiction. It reached beyond that, as if Iago wasn't merely a character within the story, but had penned the whole thing.

Then, just as the play was moving toward closure and the thin, pained justice, which would be Othello's onstage suicide, something happened. Iago's guilt had been revealed by his wife for which he had stabbed her, but as the by-standers ministered to her, he had slipped away.

"Tis a notorious villain," said the actor playing Montano. "Take you this his weapon which I have recovered from the Moor..."

Burbage as Othello slumped to the stage.

"I am not valiant neither..." he croaked. "But every puny whipster gets my...my sword."

And so saying, he considered his hands, which were slick and red.

Rose's mind raced. She didn't remember this part...

Burbage's face was anguished and his eyes vague.

"That's not acting," said Rose staring in horror. "Iago stabbed him before he went off. For real. With a real dagger."

There was a horrid silence on stage as the play came to a shuddering halt.

ACT FIVE, SCENE FOUR

"O, pity, God, this miserable age!
What stratagems, how fell, how butcherly,
Erroneous, mutinous and unnatural,
This deadly quarrel daily doth beget!"
(*Henry VI part 3*, 2.5.88-90)

September 3, 1594. Time remaining: 0 hours 17 minutes.

The Demonic Team

Bliss' team were mere yards from their destination, which was just as well, because they were starting to get on his nerves.

"Judgement is at hand, oh you godless!" raved the reverend at whoever fell within his line of sight. "Repent, for your hour is come! Prepare to be consigned to everlasting flames where there shall be weeping and gnashing of teeth! There will the playwrights burn for all eternity..."

"Down with negative role models!" Violet agreed, shooting Bliss a beatific smile. "Doesn't it feel wonderful to be doing something good for the community?"

"Oh yes," said Bliss with such obvious sarcasm that it seemed impossible that the woman could miss it. "I feel positively angelic."

Violet, predictably, missed it.

Belial checked his watch. "Sixteen minutes left," he said to Bliss.

Bliss nodded, thinking hard. He had been formulating an idea. He had already returned home confident of victory once, only to find he had been thwarted; he was damned if he was going to do that again. In point of fact, of course, he was damned no matter what he did, but that was a matter for another day. He didn't like this time-traveling business: too many loopholes and things he didn't understand. But a backup to his backup plan had started to shape itself in his mind: a plan C, if you like. Should the enemy manage to get in the way again, he had one last trick up his sleeve. But he would need the devil's help.

"What are you up to?" he demanded of Belial, once out of earshot of his righteous army.

"What do you mean?" the devil responded, his face unreadable.

"You're doing something, have been ever since we went back to the present and you started sniffing around like a bloodhound in heat. I can tell."

"I am a multidimensional being of inconceivable power," said Belial. "In any given moment I am doing many things."

"Yeah, but this is something to do with our mission, isn't it?" Bliss persisted. "Don't lie to me, demon. I can still report you to Beelzebub."

"It's nothing directly to do with our mission," said Belial, with a slightly hunted look.

"But it's related?"

"It may be an unintended consequence of our actions," said Belial. "But it is nothing you need concern yourself with."

"And you aren't secretly working to stop me from achieving what I want? What you promised to help me with?"

"I am not."

Bliss considered him warily.

"We are almost out of time," said Belial. "This is our last chance. If you fail to kill Shakespeare, it's over."

"No, it's not," said Bliss, deciding to play his final card. "Send me where I can do the most damage," Bliss demanded. "Just in case. As soon as we've knifed the bastard, move me to a time and place where I can wipe out as much Shakespeare as I can."

"You'll have already killed him!" the devil retorted. "How can he produce anything if he's already dead?"

"These angel types are tricky," said Bliss. "I want a contingency. Just send me to a place where—if any of these damn plays survive—I can torch as much as possible..."

"We don't have time," Belial replied, angry at having to explain this again. "No more time travel except to end the whole operation. That's the ruling, and I'm not going up against Beelzebub to suit you, so forget it."

"You won't have to," Bliss answered.

"You don't understand," said the devil. "I can move you in time only once more, and that will be back to your own period."

"I just need a momentary stop. Think of it as a layover."

"Where?" said Belial cautiously. "When?"

"Without the Folio we lose eighteen plays, right?" said Bliss, urgently.

"Right."

"Including *Macbeth*?"

"Including *Macbeth*," sighed the devil.

"And those eighteen are all in one place?" Bliss went on.

"That's how the angel saved the Folio," said Belial. "All the author's papers will be kept at the Globe, yes. Without those papers, the future may lose all eighteen plays."

"May?"

"I can't be sure. If there are other manuscripts floating around..."

"It will have to do," said Bliss.

"What do you mean?"

"Send me to the Globe on my way back to Boston. Five minutes is all I need."

"I can't do that..." said Belial, consulting his watch. "One time jump back to the present. That's all I can do."

"It will be my last request," said Bliss carefully.

Belial stopped dead and stared at him. "Hold it," said the devil, clarifying. "You want me to move you to the Globe and leave you there?"

"Yes."

"Forever?"

"If I can burn all those plays, it will be worth it."

"You won't be able to get back to the present," said the demon. "You'll die here."

"I can live with that."

"You hate this stuff that much?" said Belial, amazed.

"More than words can wield the matter."

"And this would be your final request? No more getting you diamonds and girls? No more little pink cakes that don't make you fat? No more time travel? You sure about this?"

"Yes," said Bliss after the briefest pause.

"But I get your soul, no matter what?" Belial concluded.

"Right," said Bliss.

The devil extended his hand and a vellum parchment appeared in it.

"Sign here, please," he said.

Bliss seized the proffered quill and scribbled furiously.

"Don't double cross me, devil," he said.

"The coordinates are already set," said Belial.

"I'm going to burn *Macbeth*," sighed Bliss happily.

"Not just that," said Belial, recalling the rest of the Folio's contents. "Also *The Tempest, The Comedy of Errors, As You Like It, Measure for Measure, Twelfth Night, Julius Caesar, Coriolanus, Antony and Cleopatra, Henry VIII...*"

But Bliss was hardly listening. His eyes had glazed over in obsessive delight.

"But let's kill him first," he said darkly, a cruel light in his eyes, "put the boot into all that literary crap."

"That's really it, isn't it?" said Belial. "All that crusading for a more utilitarian brand of education was just a smoke screen. It's not even the plays you hate so much. It's the people who like them. You want to take away whatever they value and grind it to nothing."

Bliss considered him for a moment, then shrugged. "So?" he said, his eyes hard so that Belial, who—as has been established—was used to some pretty grim stuff orchestrated by some pretty unpleasant people, shuddered.

"My God," said Belial. "What did they do to you?"

"I was a businessman," said Bliss with sudden venom. "A good one. I gave money to that school. And what did they give me in return? Their sneering condescension and liberal cultural bullshit. Well, I'm going to fucking torch the lot now, even if it really is the last thing I do. I'm gonna tear it from their hearts and feed it to them like I baked their kids in pies. How's that for Shakespearean?"

Belial stared at the fury in the man's soulless eyes. "Very well," he said.

"And Shakespeare?" said Bliss.

Belial looked up at the rickety two-story building in sight of the theatre. A candle was burning at an upper window. Cornwall and his three twenty-first century assassins were loitering at the street door, waiting for them.

"He's in there," said Belial. "I'll join you in a moment."

ACT FIVE, SCENE FIVE

"The baby beats the nurse and quite athwart goes all decorum."
(*Measure for Measure*, 1.3.31-2)

Palace of Whitehall, 1604.

Xavier and Rose

The audience didn't seem to have realized that something had gone wrong. Iago's wife, Emilia, still had some lines before she died, and the boy actor playing her was milking them, buying some time while the actors playing Gratiano and Montano hoisted Burbage up and helped him off.

"What happened?" Rose gasped as soon as they reached the wings. "Are you all right?"

"'Tis not as deep as a well or as wide as a church door," said Burbage bleakly, "but 'twill serve."

"The bastard stabbed him!" exclaimed one of the actors. "I never liked him. We should call the watch."

"Stop the play and tell the King's secretary what hath befallen," said the other. "There are guards enough to ensure he doth not escape."

"No," said Rose. "We have to finish the show."

"Yes!" said Burbage, but the exclamation cost him what little strength he had. "Though not with me, alas. Fetch me a surgeon and I will live, but finish the play."

"Who will play the Moor?" gasped one of the actors. "You need to be on now! There's no time to don the face paint."

With an effort, Burbage shrugged out of the exotic robe he had been wearing, winced and, as he collapsed, pushed it toward Xavier.

"Thou art Othello," he wheezed.

Xavier stared at the bloody garment, his brow furrowed with confusion. When it cleared, it was like a hot sun appearing from behind a cloud.

"Oh, *hell* no!" he said.

Rose turned to the actors who had gotten Burbage off.

"Go back on," she instructed them. "Stall."

"Stall?" said the one playing Gratiano.

"Improvise," she said. "Delay. And remember," she said, dredging up a memory from middle school drama in which she had, memorably, played two trees and an oversized apple, "the key to improvisation is saying yes!"

"What was the question?" asked one of the actors.

"Doesn't matter," said Rose, conscious that the stage had gone ominously quiet. "The answer is always *yes*. Just roll with what happens."

"Roll?"

"Just...get on!"

And they did, *aye forsoothing* and *my lording* for all they were worth.

Rose looked at Xavier.

"No," he said.

ACT FIVE, SCENE SIX

"We are all undone, unless
The noble man have mercy."
(*Coriolanus*, 4.6.114-5)

September 3, 1594. Time remaining: 0 hours 8 minutes.

The Demonic Team

Shakespeare was gazing at nothing, trying out a phrase.

"I to the world am like a drop of water," he said aloud, "that in the ocean seeks another drop, who falling there to find his fellow forth, unseen, inquisitive, confounds himself."

He mouthed the words again, silently this time, as if listening to them in his head, and had begun to write when he caught the sound of confused footsteps on the stairs. He turned to face the chamber door and it kicked suddenly open. Five strangely attired people burst in, instantly filling the tiny room so completely that they could barely move. The first three were armed with purposeful-looking daggers.

Arthur Fielding, still in tweed and monocle, took a step forwards and said, "Now impostor. Confess you scribble in the borrowed robes of the noble Earl of Oxford, then perish as the worm you are."

Shakespeare made a baffled face and glanced at the ink-stained sleeve of his smock shirt.

"These robes, I fear, are mine," he said.

"I spoke metaphorically!" said Fielding in high indignation.

"We do not waste words on sinners," bawled the Reverend Lee, raising his knife above his head. "Think on God whose name you have blasphemed and surrender to the wrath of his righteous hand. Oh vengeance!"

"Yes!" said Violet gleefully. "But first, pluck out his eyes."

Shakespeare, still confused but now seasoning his bafflement with a dose of self-preservation, got clumsily to his feet. "I pray," he said, "if this is to be my grim reckoning, that you at least unfold what wrong I have done you."

"The wrongs you have visited upon the world are too numerous to count!" roared Reverend Lee.

"Wrongs against truth!" added Fielding.

"And decency!" said Violet.

"Prepare thyself to meet the creator thou hast blasphemed," said the reverend, lunging forward and seizing the playwright by the wrist.

There was more noise on the stairs and Jimmy entered like a compact and wiry tornado. He threw an elbow that crumpled Bliss and made Cornwall flatten herself against the wall. He shoved Fielding aside, clearing a path for a battered and exhausted Gladys who clattered into the room behind him.

"Unhand Master Shakespeare!" she cried.

"Thou art unclean if thou wouldst save this sinner!" said the Reverend Lee as he turned to Gladys and lunged.

His dagger slid into Gladys' chest. Jimmy cried out, but Gladys fell heavily to the floor, her eyes showing first astonishment, then nothing.

ACT FIVE, SCENE SEVEN

"The play's the thing..."
(*Hamlet*, 2.2.566)

The Palace of Whitehall, 1604.

Xavier and Rose

What happened?" asked Belial, stepping out of the shadows and stooping to the injured Burbage.

"Iago," said Rose. "I'm trying to get Xavier to go on in his place."

"Brilliant!" said Belial.

"You want me to catch some footballs and throw in a little soft shoe routine too?" said Xavier. "Forget it."

"There's no time to argue!" said Rose.

"The play is written, and Iago is almost free," said Belial. "Only performing the play to the audience's final applause will contain him. Without that, his spirit escapes and poisons all possible futures."

"The play can do that all by itself," said Xavier.

"This new future," said Belial, "speaking from the benefit of an atemporal perspective, will be worse."

"I don't think you know what it's like as it is," said Xavier. "I don't think you've lived it."

"I have heard..." Belial began.

"No doubt," Xavier cut in, "but like I said, that's not living it. Two weeks ago, I was pulled over by a cop. And he asks for my license and registration, which are in the glove box," Xavier went on fast and quiet as the stalled play blundered clumsily about on stage. "Now, I'm thinking that if I reach into the glove box to get them, he might just shoot me because he assumes I'm carrying. And maybe he's never read *Othello*, but he's heard those kinds of stories all his life, tales of savage Black men who don't value their own lives, let alone anyone else's. Those are the stories that get people like me killed when their cars break down and they knock on the door of some respectable white lady who gets scared and blows them away. You heard that too? I *live* that. All the time. And it starts here. Ten years from now they begin chaining my ancestors and shipping them across the Atlantic. Four hundred years on, after slavery and Jim Crow and the Civil Rights era, men like me are still seconds away from dying because the people around us think they know what our skin means. That's not all coming from this play, but some of it is, and I won't be a part of it."

Belial, cowed, for once, even humbled, glanced at the stage, then said, "Iago will make it worse. Trust me. I've seen it."

"Trust a devil?" said Xavier.

"He's trying to help," said Rose.

"There's no way round it," said Belial. "I'm sorry—truly—but the play has to be performed. It's the only way to contain its influence."

"Convenient," said Xavier.

"What is that supposed to mean?" said Belial.

"It means the system is rigged," said Xavier. "Imagine my surprise."

"Right now the future stands on a knife edge," said Belial. "It could be so much worse than you remember it for people in states unborn and accents yet unknown. You can prevent that from happening."

"You notice how it's always Black folks who have to fix racism? How even though we're on the receiving end, white folks look to us to make it right?"

"Right now you are the only person who can make the future better."

"With *this* play," said Xavier doubtfully, looking round. The audience, tiring of the production's lack of forward movement were getting audibly restless.

"With this play," said Belial. "Nothing you do on that stage will affect whether the play survives into the present or not. But this production must be seen to end. And I'm sorry, but I can't stay. Everything is going wrong."

Xavier didn't seem to hear him, and he stared at nothing for a long time before he spoke. "I won't play a monster," he said. "I won't be a stage savage. If the show has to finish, it finishes on my terms. That's the deal."

Rose gaped at Belial in bafflement and apprehension as the devil took a step back into the shadows and vanished.

ACT FIVE, SCENE EIGHT

"The first thing we do, let's kill all the lawyers."
(*Henry VI* part 2, 4.2.77)

London, 1594.

Jimmy

Gladys was on her back, motionless.

Jimmy cried out in horror then leapt onto the reverend, sending him crashing heavily into the wall by the bed. The knife fell free, and the two fought furiously for a second before a thin, high voice made them still and watchful.

It was Violet. In the confusion of the struggle and the bluster of rhetoric from her companions, she had moved without fuss to where Shakespeare sat and now held her knife to his throat.

"I think we had better get this over with," she said, resigned to it as if poised to scour a wall of graffiti she would prefer not to read. Jimmy was still holding the reverend by the throat, but his hands were relaxed and his horrified eyes had strayed to where history was about to be rewritten by a stiffly coiffed woman in the kind of clothes her peers had passed on to Good Will thirty years ago.

Jimmy glanced at Gladys, and he felt a heavy, angry tear run down his cheek. So this was how it all ended.

Death, he thought stupidly. *Why was everything about death?*

As he watched, Belial materialized in the doorway. He dropped to the fallen angel, putting his fingers to her wrist, and shot an accusing glance around the room. His eyes fell on Violet, who gave an odd, puppet smile that split her face from side to side, and adjusted the grip on her knife, ready to surgically carve her version of family values into flesh and culture.

"Wait!" cried Jimmy. His eyes flicked to Gladys' watch desperately: 6 minutes left.

Violet's eyes strayed to Bliss and she paused, as if waiting for parental approval.

"You can't just kill him!" said Jimmy, unsure how he was going to follow this up.

"Sure they can," said Belial, and he seemed, for reasons Jimmy didn't understand, genuinely disappointed. "We've followed the rules for demonic time travel to the letter. Absolutely textbook: from the initial summons to..."

Jimmy's mind flailed about for something to hold onto like a man sliding over a precipice.

"What summons?" he demanded.

"He's stalling," said Bliss to Violet. "Just do it..."

But Belial held up a hand.

"The devil has to be summoned by someone in the appropriate period," he explained. "It's the only way we can alter the past legally."

"Who summoned you?" snapped Jimmy.

"Edward Alleyn made the summons," said Belial, "during a production of *Doctor Faustus.*"

"An actor?" said Jimmy. "In that devil play. Right?"

And now he had their attention, because his face had lit up with what looked suspiciously like triumph.

"Yes," said Belial. "So?"

"So he didn't *really* summon you," said Jimmy.

"Yes, he did," said Belial. "I heard the words myself..."

"But he didn't *mean* them," Jimmy insisted. "He was just an actor doing lines by someone else! If you don't mean it, it doesn't count, right? I'm no lawyer, but I've been defended by a couple and I know that in law *intent* is everything. It *sounded like* a summons, but it wasn't one because the man who made it was fictional. It was just words. And if you weren't really summoned..."

"Then we can't alter the past," Belial concluded.

"Exactly," said Jimmy. "So you can't kill Shakespeare. You can't do any of it."

"You have gotta be shitting me," breathed Cornwall with total disdain to Belial. "You aren't actually going to buy this, are you?"

"Hmmm," said Belial, thoughtfully. "Tricky. It's borderline and a bit post-modern, but until we've sought legal guidance..."

Bliss opened his mouth to protest, but Belial snapped his fingers and he, Cornwall, and the zealous assassins vanished.

Their disappearance seemed to pull sound out of the little room, and for a moment it was as if time itself had frozen. Then, as Shakespeare began to shift, his mouth opening to frame a baffled question, the devil cut in.

"Well, James," Belial remarked, "that was rather clever."

"I have a dying woman here!" said Jimmy, snapping back to Gladys as if none of the rest had happened at all.

But even as he said it, he suspected that it might not be true. A light was gathering about the fallen former angel and it had a curiously ambient quality that made one think of heavenly choirs and Handel and harps. It occurred to Jimmy that Gladys was shelving her "former" angelic status before his very eyes.

"Actually," she said, opening her eyes and sitting up as if she had been enjoying a peaceful nap, "no. I seem to be my old self again. Thank God. And I mean that literally."

"Three minutes left!" shouted Belial suddenly. "Quick!"

And he opened a temporal door.

Shakespeare stared.

ACT FIVE, SCENE NINE

"Thou speakest wonders."
(*Henry VIII*, 5.5.56)

The Palace of Whitehall, 1604.

Xavier

X avier, dressed now in the luxurious robe of Othello, considered the anxious actors on stage around him, then turned to the audience and spoke.
"My lords 'tis time for me to speak the truth.
But summon first the traitorous Iago
That I might tell the miscreant how all
His stratagems have failed. Go bring him hence!"
He nodded at the actor playing Gratiano who, seeming relieved to finally get off stage, made for the exit.
"And thou, thrice noble friend Montano, get
Thee to my wife and bring her hence, that thou
Mayst see she lies not cold and dead and did
But counterfeit; for she and I devised
All this confusion to expose this fiend's

296

Corroding hate and poison to the world.
Bring then my love and tend his injured dame the while;
despite her hurts I warrant thee she too
Will yet recover straight."

The actors stared, then Montano slunk off. Xavier watched him go into the wings where several others had gathered, each desperately scanning their script parts and checking with a prompt book, which was clearly of no further use.

"Where is that viper? Bring the villain forth," said Lodovico, striding on and pushing Iago ahead of him, his hands bound.

Iago was thrust center stage and Xavier saw with grim satisfaction that the rage and loathing in his face was not feigned.

"This wretch hath part confessed his villainy," said Lodovico, clearly glad that his lines still made sense. "Did you and he consent in Cassio's death?"

"No," said Xavier/Othello.

Lodovico hesitated.

"I'm sorry," he said, "you didn't?"

"No," said Xavier. "Except to lure this devil to the light
Where all his mischiefs would by heaven be spied
And you my lords would recognize that you
Did put your faith in one unworthy of
Your worships' trust. And lo now Desdemona
Comes to greet me full of joy and happiness!
Come here my love, and tell them what you said
Some days ago about this Iago's
Spite to me and my good Cassio."

The boy playing Desdemona, white as a sheet, eyes wide and flashing toward their royal audience, nodded. "Aye, my lord," he managed, "that is so indeed."

"And so is evil vanquished," Xavier proclaimed, beaming. "Though let me also say that even if my wife had lain with Cassio, I still would not have killed her. I mean," he added, conscious that he was losing the rhythm of the line and not caring, "I might not have been happy about it, but if that was what happened, then obviously I hadn't understood our relationship properly, right? Maybe we'd get over it, maybe we wouldn't, but I'm a person, right? We both are. You feel me?"

As if sensing that things were getting away from him, the actor playing Lodovico jumped to his final speech and turned on the wild-eyed Iago.

"O Spartan dog," he said. "More fell than anguish, hunger or the sea! Look on the...er...fairly tragic thing you tried, apparently unsuccessfully, to do, and speak now your remorse that we may yet find in our hearts an ounce of pity or forgiveness for your black deeds."

"Examine well the villain," said Xavier/Othello, "and see him brought to justice."

"Demand me nothing," said Iago, spitting in his bitterness. "What you know you know. From this time forth I never will speak word."

"Right," said Montano. "Well then, I suppose that's that." He looked wildly around, and Xavier, first shaking hands with Cassio and then embracing Desdemona, turned squarely to face the King in the audience.

"Then all is well," he said, "and add this to the score: I am a man as well as I am moor." Without waiting, he took a step toward the edge of the stage, extended his arms, palms uppermost, and bowed.

The audience broke into ragged applause, which spread and solidified, spotted with shouted praise and a hasty thunder of chair legs as the King himself rose to his feet. Dimly at his back, Xavier heard an uneven shriek, a cry of malice and frustration that faded rapidly as if the person who had made it was snatched away by a speeding train. With it came a foul and inexplicable odor that rippled across the stage, and then was gone as absolutely as the sound, vanishing so quickly and utterly that a moment later it was almost impossible to believe it had been there at all. He turned to see the rest of his stunned company, all bowing woodenly, all glad to be done and alive.

There was no trace of the thing that had called itself Iago.

ACT FIVE, SCENE TEN

"Our revels now are ended. These our actors,
As I foretold you, were all spirits and
Are melted into air, into thin air;
And, like the baseless fabric of this vision,
The cloud-capped towers, the gorgeous palaces,
The solemn temples, the great globe itself,
Yea all which it inherit, shall dissolve,
And, like this insubstantial pageant faded,
Leave not a rack behind. We are such stuff
As dreams are made on, and our little life
Is rounded with a sleep."
(*The Tempest*, 4.1.148-58)

June 29, 1613. Time remaining: 0 hours 3 minutes.
Plays to be destroyed: *37.*

Bliss and Cathy

Bliss and Cornwall stepped out of the temporal door whose coordinates had been preset by Belial before the fiasco in the writer's room and found themselves in the backstage area of the Globe Theatre. The place was packed and hushed, each audience member perfectly visible from the stage under the warm afternoon sun. On stage Shakespeare's *Henry VIII* progressed, unaware of the time travelers or how close it was to the kind of termination that would go down in history.

"What the hell is this?" sputtered Cornwall in disbelief. "This isn't L.A."

As an actor backstage shot her a reproachful, silencing glance, Bliss, assessing the layout of the theatre, muttered absently, "I arranged it."

"What do you mean you arranged it!?" she gaped. "I have so had it with this century...!"

"Shut up," Bliss said, still not looking at her. "Great things are afoot."

It was clear they had failed to kill Shakespeare, but there was a good deal that could still be wrecked. He was considering the best way to do this when he was pushed roughly aside, and a large man in deep red robes carrying an imposing, ornamented bishop's staff stepped past him and onto the stage. "You're welcome, my fair guests," he boomed. "That noble lady or gentleman that is not freely merry is not my friend."

Well, thought Bliss, he would soon put a stop to all this.

His eyes floated up to the roof and a gallery above the stage where the flag announcing the performance fluttered in the wind. There a stagehand held up a kind of long wick, burning at one end. At his feet was a brass cannon, apparently primed to fire. A sound effect. It was almost too good to be true.

The stagehand touched the wick to the cannon, it sparked and then, with a guttural belch of smoke and sparks, it fired into the air with a great booming bark.

Bliss grinned, the audience acknowledged the pyrotechnics and returned to the play proper as the stagehand began re-priming the cannon.

"You'd better get me out of here right this second, Robert..." Cornwall demanded.

"Shh," said the waiting actor, pointedly.

"Don't you shush me," snapped Cornwall.

Bliss ignored them and began to scale the ladder to the roof. The stagehand heard him coming and peered over, unsuspiciously. Bliss smiled blandly, took the proffered hand, and flipped the boy over the side. He cried out as he fell, in surprise more than fear.

The wooden floor resounded with the boy's fall, almost drowning his shout of angry pain. The play faltered and the faces of the audience turned up to the roof.

Bliss moved fast, swinging the cannon till its barrel pointed squarely at the thatched roof over the auditorium. He took up the fallen wick and touched the priming powder. The audience, still looking up and trying to make sense of what was happening, didn't even have a chance to respond before the cannon went off with a deafening roar and a shower of sparks.

A moment of silence followed, as all eyes came to rest on Bliss, who stood staring at the roof before beginning to laugh. As the smoke over the stage thickened, Bliss' amusement turned toward hilarity. The actors followed his crazed eyes and saw that the thatch was aflame and spreading fast.

"FIRE!" shouted someone in one of the galleries.

The timber-framed building kindled quickly and no one seemed ready or able to do a damned thing about it. In seconds, the place was full of shouting, pressing bodies all fighting to get out alive before the entire structure came crashing down around them. Bliss remained, laughing and dancing like a man possessed.

And at the same moment, a temporal door snapped open and Jimmy came through like some avenging angel who saw nothing but his purpose. Cathy Cornwall appeared in front of him, but he shunted her aside and made for the back room.

The audience were charging the one door that wasn't aflame, and the backstage area was fast slipping into chaos. The actors dropped their props on the spot and fled the stage. No one thought to go back for the playbooks.

"Yeah, baby!" shrieked Bliss with victorious rapture. "Whoo hoo! Burn Shakespeare, burn!"

Jimmy checked Belial's watch: 29th June 1613. Time remaining: 0

hours 1 minute. The door was smoking and, when he pulled it open, it was clear that the walls were already ablaze. But the shelves hadn't caught yet. He dived in, grabbing every manuscript in sight, feeling the heat on his face till his eyebrows smoked.

The galleries were well ablaze now and their roofs showered drops of oily fire so that much of the timber was already consumed and one great lath and plaster wall collapsed. The stage area had been the last to catch, but it was now a wall of heat, a screen of roaring flame beside which it was impossible to survive. And so it was all the more astonishing that Jimmy, now laden with playbooks and surrounded by the circle of fire that had been Shakespeare's "wooden O," could see the form of a man coming towards the edge of the stage.

It was Bliss. He had been dancing and singing, oblivious to the flames, but then he had spotted Jimmy on the stage with a stack of papers and the rage had returned. As if to manifest his hellish fury, the roof had, at that very moment, collapsed in a roar of sparks and a glut of thick, greasy smoke. Somehow Bliss landed on his feet and, as the burnt thatch disintegrated into ash and embers, he was revealed, sooty and wrathful, alone in the center of the stage. He glared at the backstage wall as it fell and Jimmy clambered through, ladened with papers.

"No!" Bliss shrieked like some primitive fire demon. "Let them BURN!"

Cornwall, who had been crouching by one of the stage doors, a cat-like vision of teeth and claws in a scorched Chanel suit, ran at Jimmy. He shifted, dodged the worst of the attack, and hung onto the papers. Cornwall snarled inarticulately and grabbed the bishop's staff. Raising the heavy metal head like a mace, she was about to bring it down hard on the back of his head when the heavy oak door beside her was flung wide and caught her squarely in the face. She dropped like a stone. From behind it, Belial emerged.

"Oh, I *am* sorry," he said politely to her groaning form. "Literary types are going under, are they, you crass harpy?"

Robert Bliss, blackened now beyond recognition, his body held together by malice alone, was a demon shuffling through the conflagration, his lidless eyes glaring at Jimmy.

"NO, NO, NO!" yelled Bliss. He came running at Jimmy, one of the assassin's daggers in his hand. With absolute clarity, Jimmy saw over the stack of papers that there was nothing between him and death.

And then Bliss crumpled, grasping his right knee with wild pain in his wide eyes and a cry on his lips. Belial was behind him, brandishing the bishop's staff. He grinned at Jimmy, whose relief was luminous, and considered the prop crosier cheerily.

"Who says art has no purpose?" Belial remarked.

"We'd better get out of here," said Jimmy, but as he did so, one of the booklets fell to the burning stage. He stooped to it and, since its facing page was uppermost, read the title: "*Love's Labours Won*, by Wllm. Shakespeare."

He reached for it, but the papers under his arm shifted. Another movement and he would lose the lot. For a split second he kept quite still, and then he concentrated on getting the stack under control. He did, but when he looked back to the stage, *Love's Labours Won* was already aflame.

As JIMMY FOUND his way out of the building with his mostly complete collection of Shakespeare's plays, Robert Bliss, raging alone in the burning building, stood up. The flames roared on all sides, but he did not seem to notice. Cornwall had crawled off and out and he was alone with his anger and failure, as his thin hair began to smoke.

"Belial!" he bellowed. "Belial you goddamned incompetent! Get over here right now!"

He glared through the heat, dimly conscious that his clothes were on fire and his skin was cracking. The last of the oak galleries collapsed, and a wave of unbearable heat scorched the flesh from his skull.

"Belial!" he roared again, a picture of limitless and insatiable wrath. "You call yourself a demon?! I'm dying up here!"

And he did. His body became a torch, burning hot and sending a stream of thick, pungent smoke up into the sky. It stood for an impossibly long moment before crumpling into the ravaged stage.

And then something else stood in its place. It was Bliss but ravaged and blackened and it lacked the substance of the physical.

"Belial! God damn it!" yelled the corpse-like specter of what had been Robert Bliss.

Belial came walking through the flames, smiling and consulting his watch as it ticked away its final seconds.

"I always said this day would come, you horrible little man," said Belial, coolly.

"Whatever, Belial," muttered what had been Bliss, scornfully. "You don't scare me."

"Really?" said the devil, interested. "How about now?"

And so saying he transformed into something vast and terrifying, something the mind of man could not look upon, something Beelzebub would have been proud of.

"Holy Christ!" gasped the former chair of Northside College's Board of Regents, sinking to what had been his knees.

"Don't you just wish," said the demon.

The spectral remnant of Bliss screamed long and high, the theatre imploded, and Belial's little watch hands clicked up to the twenty-four-hour mark and stopped.

ACT FIVE, SCENE ELEVEN

"This thing of darkness I acknowledge mine."
(*The Tempest* 5.1.289)

The Palace of Whitehall, 1604.

Xavier, Rose, Shakespeare...

With the royal party gone, and the actors packing up their things, the air of vague mystery and relief surrounding their semi-improvised production had given way to other feelings.

"You're worse than Kemp!" Shakespeare exclaimed, pointing his finger at Xavier. "You completely rewrote the bloody thing."

"A bit," said Xavier. "Posterity will get the printed versions, but here and now, the point had to be made."

"You changed the ending!" said Shakespeare, aghast. "Completely. You made it a comedy!"

"*Romeo and Juliet* in reverse," said Rose, grinning. "That one started as comedy and ended as tragedy. I like this one better."

"But you brought Desdemona back to life!" said the author.

"Again, just like Juliet," said Rose.

"But when I write a character who seems dead but isn't," Shakespeare explained as if this was a rudimentary element of storytelling, "I let the audience know so that they won't think it preposterous."

"Yeah," said Xavier, "but where's the suspense?"

"The surprise!" agreed Rose. "The not knowing."

"Audiences like to know where the story is going," said Shakespeare.

"Maybe in general," said Xavier, "but not exactly. You should think about that. A different kind of twist ending. Bring someone back from the dead. They won't see that coming."

In spite of himself, Shakespeare paused considering. "A twist ending," he said.

"Yeah," said Rose. "Defy the audience's expectations."

"And you said that if your wife strayed, you might forgive her?" said Shakespeare to Xavier. "Is not wrying from a faithful bed a monstrous thing?"

"Well, I'm not married," said Xavier, "but I think that in love all things are forgivable, and I don't think an unfaithful wife is any more guilty than an unfaithful husband. Where I come from, fidelity is important, but the relationship matters more, or should. There's always a way forward when people love each other."

"Relationship?" said Shakespeare.

"The bond between them," said Rose. "The emotional, spiritual link."

"I do not know that such generosity of spirit would please within a play," said the writer.

"Won't know till you try it, will you?" said Xavier. "Jealous husband, dead wife, ending in reconciliation and forgiveness. Sounds good to me."

"And the husband is a blackamoor...?" Shakespeare began.

"I'd leave that out if I were you," said Xavier.

Shakespeare seemed about to argue, but he caught something in Xavier's gaze, something with razor-sharp edges and a few spikes dripping with venom, and he nodded hastily.

"Aye forsooth," he conceded.

"Also," said Rose, "what he said about Moors being people first? That goes for women too."

Again the writer frowned but abandoned whatever argument first came to his lips at the flash of fire in Rose's eyes.

"No more shrew taming," she added, in case he might not have gotten the point.

Shakespeare nodded. "I fear the taste for such plays has passed," he said.

"No kidding," said Rose.

Gladys arrived, checking her watch.

"Where did you come from?" asked Shakespeare.

"Oh, I was just...*around*," she said airily. "Ready?" she asked Rose and Xavier. "It's time."

"Everything okay?" asked Rose.

"You know," said Gladys glancing around and smiling, "I believe it just might be. I died, or as near as made no difference. Strangest sensation. Everything just stopped and I was there but not, you know? Like a statue. And then I was myself again."

"A statue?" said Shakespeare, staring.

"Well, you know, figuratively speaking," said Gladys, who clearly thought she'd said too much for mortal ears. "Probably it will turn out that I only appeared to be dead but had actually taken a potion or something earlier. You know, like your Juliet."

"There seems to be a lot of that about," said Shakespeare, glancing at Xavier.

"Maybe skip the potion," suggested Rose. "If we're going for a real surprise, a sense of magic."

Shakespeare nodded pensively. "But how do I resurrect a character in ways that feel appropriate to a drama that begins in the darkest reaches of the human heart?"

The question hung in the air for a moment, and when no one spoke, the writer looked up and found he was alone. "Hello?" he said, glancing around.

But they were gone and the hall was empty. One moment they were there and the next they weren't as if the earth had bubbles and these were of them. Shakespeare frowned.

It had been an odd day.

"A play with a tragic beginning and a surprising, happy ending," he mused, then added the beginnings of a new idea. "And a statue?" The

307

wind outside picked up and the draughty palace creaked, so that he hugged his clothes to him. Shakespeare nodded thoughtfully again and said, "A sad tale's best for winter."

EPILOGUE

"Like an old tale still..."
(*The Winter's Tale*)
or
"A good play needs no epilogue..."
(*As You Like It*)

"The rest is silence."
(*Hamlet*, 5.2.360)

Boston. Present day.

The Angelic Team

Everything was motionless. Jimmy was lying on his back across the trolley tracks clasping Xavier's arm, the two men frozen in the act of falling, as Rose hung in the air, thrusting her niece out of the train's path. Time was frozen and there was no sound.

Then, quite suddenly, time restarted, or, to be more accurate, part of it did. The three humans completed their movements and, unaware of the total inactivity around them, got back to their feet. They seemed on the point of noticing the curious, unnatural silence, when the trolley horn blared and everything returned to normal. There was a squeal of brakes and the driver shouted irritably, but they were already clear of the danger. Rose seized her niece, gathered her up, and considered her as if unsure how she came to be there.

The train stopped, loaded and unloaded its passengers, and pulled away towards Brookline, but Rose, Xavier, and Jimmy all stayed where they were.

Gladys had wondered if the humans would remember their adventure and, watching from a discreet distance, she held her breath.

They did.

She saw realization and memory dawn in their faces. Confusion and panic chased through their eyes, then there was fear and shock, the wild glancing around as if still trying to make sense of where they were, and then the cautious looking to each other to see if the impossible things they remembered might be theirs alone. Seeing the same journey, the same baffled relief in each other's eyes, they were suddenly laughing and embracing, drinking each other in, old friends reunited across an immeasurable history, so that Gladys found herself almost sad, almost jealous of their fragile humanity.

Rose and Xavier embraced rather longer, new tentative tendernesses flickering through their looks, their touch. Jimmy averted his gaze and saw, on the side of the train as it slid past— "Now playing at the American Repertory Theatre: William Shakespeare's *The Winter's Tale*."

"Huh!" he said.

Gladys wanted to call out to them, to join in one of those invigorating hugs, but she found that her memory of that action, of all the earthy sensations she had felt, had already began to fade.

Like an old tale still, she thought wistfully, like rereading a story from childhood, all the intense emotions you once felt now strange and inexplicable...

Quite suddenly a heavenly light broke in upon her and Uriel was there, giving her a side-long look of displeasure.

"So you completed your task to your satisfaction," he said in a voice like a breeze through gilt-edged leaves. "Though I notice you rather messed up the timeline in the process. One of those *plays* disappeared and another appeared. Am I right?"

"Yes," said Gladys, looking down awkwardly. "*Love's Labours Won* was incinerated in the Globe fire, but Shakespeare wrote another play called *The Winter's Tale* on the advice of er...a friend."

"Bit of a cock up, wouldn't you say?" said Uriel.

"Well, yes and no," said Gladys. "I haven't had chance to read it properly, but this *Winter's Tale* thing looks rather good."

"It's about jealousy, isn't it?" said Uriel. "Putting your wife on trial so she dies of humiliation?"

"The first half," said Gladys, guessing the direction in which this was going. "The second half is about coming to terms with your sins in pursuit of forgiveness and redemption. It's about truth and reconciliation."

"And a statue that comes to life?"

"In a manner of speaking," said Gladys.

"I don't like the sound of it," said Uriel. "Shouldn't have to sit through an hour of sin and misery to get to the virtue."

"There's virtue from the start. It's just not recognized."

"That's supposed to be one of those truths with a small t, is it? Art reflecting life rather than correcting it?"

"If all art did was model virtue, no one would watch it."

"Not a ringing endorsement of human morality, is it?" said Uriel. "I'm afraid this art thing really isn't our line of work."

"Maybe it should be."

"Maybe you'd be more comfortable working for the Lords of Hell?" said Uriel nastily. "I believe they are on a recruitment drive."

"It's only a play," said Gladys shortly. "What's the big deal? People don't watch these things and then say, *Okay, I guess I can kill my wife because I can always make a statue of her that will come back to life.* They aren't that stupid."

"Lots of angels would beg to differ. And people are always saying that entertainment leads to sin: movies, videogames..."

"That argument is only used by criminals with no defense," sneered Gladys, "and politicians who figure that it's easier to change art's reflection of the world than it is to change the world itself. Which is true, but not very helpful. Guns don't kill people, theatre kills people? Right."

"But it's the trickle-down effect..." began Uriel.

"Rubbish," said Gladys, losing patience. "Let the humans work out their frustrations through art, and believe me, living a perfect life leaves you with plenty of frustrations: ask Augustine. Aristotle was right. Let some clown in silly clothes enact their murderous impulses on a stage or a big screen for them and they'll get on with their lives quite peacefully. You should try reading some of this stuff. It's really rather good."

"Well," said Uriel, changing tack. "It sounds to me like you have been doing the devil's work quite literally for once. If Belial went to all this trouble to make sure this play got written, how can it be anything but evil?"

Gladys considered suggesting that getting rid of the thing called Iago was the real achievement of the mission—angelic and demonic—but instinctively knew that that would complicate things unnecessarily.

"How well do you know Belial?"

"He is the Enemy!" Uriel exclaimed. "How well do I need to know him?"

"Better than you do right now," said Gladys. "He's quite an engaging chap once you get to know him."

Uriel's jaw dropped.

"There will be repercussions from this," he rumbled ominously. "Just wait and see if there won't.

And there were too.

~

"My hour is almost come
When I to sulfurous and tormenting flames
Must render up myself."
(*Hamlet*, 1.5.2-4)

Belial

"So," roared Beelzebub, an impressive jet of purple fire arcing lethally from each nostril, "you show your true colors at last, and it is exactly as I suspected. You have turned and you will pay the penalty!"

He sat back on his haunches and his great bat-wings fanned out behind him dripping dark slime and oozing a general purpose devilishness that only Beelzebub's limited imagination could generate.

Belial frowned. "Well, I'm sorry you see things in that light," he said, seeming slightly confused. "And I hope HE agrees with you."

"How could HE not?" bellowed Beelzebub, the snakes between his horns hissing appreciatively. "You have gone out of your way, working with angels in the process, to bring a new Shakespeare play to light, enriching culture and delighting the sons of men..."

"What?" cried Belial with mock astonishment. "Delight? Have you spoken to the sons of men lately? They hate this stuff! You want to lure souls to our DARK MASTER, hang around any high school class while the kids are being force fed *Julius Caesar*. You'll fill Hell just by promising an eternity away from iambic pentameter."

"Iambic what?" said Beelzebub, his flaming rage wilting a trifle.

"Pentameter," Belial explained reasonably. "It's a kind of poetry."

"*Poetry!*" Beelzebub coughed the word like it was an expletive. "How can they stand it?"

"They can't!" said Belial. "That's the beauty of it. It brings pain and suffering to all but a few who make a living off perpetuating the suffering of others."

"There are such people?" said Beelzebub, momentarily impressed by such gratuitous cruelty.

"Schools and theatres are full of them," Belial answered. "But I've out-done them all with this *Winter's Tale* thing."

"That seems unlikely." Beelzebub smoldered, though without some of his former conviction.

"No doubt about it," said Belial cheerfully. "It will go down in the annals of Hell as one of our greatest achievements in breaking the spirits of mankind and leading men and women all over the world to the most appalling of sins before succumbing to despair and devil worship."

"Really?" said Beelzebub, now quite at sea. "How?"

"Well, all the other plays were boring and stupid and impossible to understand, but this one is really two plays in one. Bonus misery."

"Really?" said Beelzebub, a fiendish chuckle beginning to form somewhere in the back of one of his throats.

"Oh yes. The first half is all madness, jealousy, assassination attempts, and a courtroom drama with lots of death, and the second is a sort of farce, country dances, songs, and a talking statue. One of the characters gets eaten by a bear that exists solely for that purpose. Complete madness!"

"These country dances," said Beelzebub with malicious glee, "you don't mean like Morris Dances."

"Very like," said Belial.

"Huh," Beelzebub conceded. "Anyone forced to sit through that might turn to the dark arts."

"This is what I'm saying," said Belial. "And think of the sins the play depicts: attempted murder, lust, rage, arrogance, greed, and dressing up in silly clothes! And at the end, what?: a happy ending engineered by magic!"

"Sounds absurd," Beelzebub agreed. "But does it help us?"

"When people leave a tragedy—a play or a movie—they might be sad for a bit," said Belial, "but then they realize that their own lives aren't as bad as what they just watched and they feel better. The opposite is true of comedies. They cheer you up for a while, but then you realize how much reality falls short of all that laughing and conveniently plotted solutions."

"Okay," said Beelzebub. "With you so far."

"Now imagine a play that feels like it should end in disaster, because that's what the first half promised, only to give you general happiness, reconciliation, and talking statues? It's excruciating because it's so obviously fake. *You want your happy ending?* it says. *Here you go.* But the ending is not true, and the play rubs your nose in how *not true* it is. See?"

"I think so," said Beelzebub cautiously.

"*The Winter's Tale* shows you the gap between what you want and what is real," Belial concluded, "what art promises and the way life kicks you in the privates. As such, it is a doorway to despair which, if I remember my Thomas Aquinas, is a sin against the Holy Spirit, the unpardonable sin because it refuses the possibility of redemption. It is the supreme mark of human arrogance, denying the capacity of the divine."

"Is it?" said Beelzebub, impressed. "Right. And this all comes from reading Shakespeare then, can it?"

"Absolutely," said Belial.

"Then it's a good thing," mused Beelzebub, "that I assigned you this task."

"You what, lord?"

"This Going Back In Time and Making More Shakespeare mission," said Beelzebub. "You don't remember me assigning you that task?"

As a threat from the demonic high command, this was subtler than most.

"Oh yes," Belial enthused. "I remember. I wasn't so sure when you first broached the subject to me, but now its palpable villainy is clear and I see how, in your wisdom, you will expand our Hellish kingdom."

"Exactly," murmured Beelzebub in a slow, self-satisfied manner that sent coils of smoke spiraling up from his various orifices.

"So I can go, then, can I?" said Belial.

"Certainly," said Beelzebub. "Oh, and Belial?" he added, struck by an afterthought.

"Yes, lord?"

"That little pocket of evil that didn't come from us. What did you find out about that?"

Belial's hesitation was only momentary. It could be a trap, of course. Beelzebub might have tracked Iago's presence through the alternate timeline into the twenty-first century, leaving a trail of devastation in its wake, only to see it all unravel as Iago was snuffed out at the source in 1604. And if he knew, then he was setting Belial up to lie, ready to rain down hellish vengeance on him for subverting a chance to sew hatred, death, and misery among humankind.

Unless...

"Just a glitch, lord," said Belial.

"A glitch?"

"A kind of temporal echo of our demonic incursion into the past."

Beelzebub watched him carefully. "And that was all it was, was it?" he said at last.

"If it wasn't," said Belial, "then a source of devastating malice spontaneously appeared from human beings without our assistance, something so potent and terrible that it had the capacity over time to utterly wipe them out."

"Yeah?" said Beelzebub, noncommittal.

"Yeah. And what would we do then? No people to tempt and torment? Just us down here together for eternity? We'd go mad."

Beelzebub considered, blinked, and chose to laugh. "We would at that," he said grinning. "Still, better keep an eye open for that kind of thing happening again."

Belial gazed into the monstrous devil's great yellow eyes and thought, for just a moment, that he had glimpsed something he'd never seen there before. He wasn't sure what it was, and it was there for only the merest fraction of a second, but it felt like alarm, like fear.

"Absolutely," said Belial. "I will be ever vigilant."

Beelzebub nodded and the look, whatever it had been, was utterly gone.

"Nice work," he snarled. "You just won yourself a position at the head of our Art and Culture division."

"Oh, thank you, lord," said Belial.

And as he crossed the immense lake of fire by the handy footbridge, which suddenly appeared for just that purpose, Belial smiled. He considered whistling a jaunty tune but decided not to push his luck.

~

"For ever, and for ever, farewell, Brutus!
If we do meet again, we'll smile indeed;
If not, 'tis true this parting was well made."

317

(Julius Caesar 5.1.121-3)

Boston. Present day.

The Angelic Team. And friends.

"So you're Belial?" Rose mused. "Weren't you in *Paradise Lost*?"

"I had a cameo," said the devil, modestly.

"I met you once before," said Jimmy.

"Really?" said Belial vaguely. "I'm afraid I don't recall…"

"A devil met a thief," Xavier remarked. "Very folk tale. Did he challenge you to a fiddle playing contest?"

"I didn't notice you mocking my skillset when it came to picking locks and snapping up unconsidered playscripts," said Jimmy without malice.

"Your talents were much appreciated," said Xavier, raising his beer glass.

"Invaluable," said Rose.

"Indeed," Gladys agreed. "When do you think you met him before, Jimmy?"

"I think he's mistaken about that," said Belial.

"No," said Jimmy. "I have you to thank for this."

He reached into his pocket and put a wallet on the table, ceremoniously drawing a driver's license from it and laying it down carefully where they could all read the name.

Professor Tobias Lestering.

"You!" gasped Gladys. "You arranged for Jimmy to be part of the team!"

"I merely told him that someone had left his office unlocked," said Belial prissily. "Everything else was your doing."

"Wait, you figured that the real professor would be helpful to us, so you arranged the switch?" said Rose.

"Partly," said Belial. "I did assume that the angelic recruitment system may well be foiled by a little rudimentary identity theft, yes, but that's not why I did it."

"Enlighten us," said Xavier.

"I figured a thief would be more useful than a Shakespearean," said the devil simply. "And, for the record, I was right."

"What!?" exclaimed Gladys.

"Academics are all very well," said Belial, "but take a real professor back into the past and he'd spend all his time in the theatre, or chatting to playwrights, like he was on some kind of research trip. No, you were better off with a man who could wield a lock pick and throw an elbow when the occasion serves."

"Wait," said Rose, "so you're saying you were trying to help us from the get go?"

"Of course!" said Belial. "I mean, I had to be seen to do what Bliss had asked for—that is, after all, the gig—but there was nothing that said I couldn't also thwart him."

"You thwarted your own summoner?" said Gladys.

"Oh, come on: I'm a devil! Thwarting comes with the territory. But yes, of course I was helping you. You wouldn't have saved the Folio without me."

"Which time?" said Gladys.

"First time."

"*You?*" said Gladys. "It was *YOU* disguised as..."

Belial saved himself the explanation by growing about a foot and a half and adopting the features of the man who had appeared at the site of the fire.

"All the *Globe's* a stage," he repeated.

"But..." Gladys managed, "you're a devil!"

"One man in his time plays many parts," said Belial, returning to his usual form, "some of them more hammy than others. Did the trick though, didn't it?"

"But...why?" said Gladys, even more fogged than usual. "You're Belial! Commander of the hosts of Satan! I mean, why would you help us? I don't get it."

"The official reason," Belial explained, "and the one that I have told Beelzebub, is that I have secured Bliss' soul while not actually giving him what he wanted: a combination my superiors find delightfully devilish."

"And the unofficial reason?" said Xavier.

"Probably a lot like yours," sighed the demon. "I rather like Shakespeare. He's quite perceptive. For a human."

"To a given value of perception," said Xavier, grinning.

"Fair point," said Belial. "But you can't blame the past for not being the present, can you? Anyway, yes, I enjoy them, and when you've been around for as many millennia as I have, you hang on to whatever passes the time. Not a great reason, perhaps, but there you are. I suspect you can relate."

"So the plays are saved?" said Rose, hardly daring to believe it. "And we...?"

"Can get on with your lives, yes," said Gladys.

"The same lives as before?" said Jimmy. "Or can they be different?"

"I think that's up to you," said the angel.

Jimmy was still and frowning, his eyes unfocused.

"You okay, Jimmy?" asked Rose.

For a moment he didn't seem to hear, then came back to them. "What?" he said. "Oh. Yeah. What do you call those guys who sit around thinking all the time?"

"Academics?" said Xavier.

"Nah. I mean, they wear robes, and they think and pray. Chant, maybe. Do odd jobs... Monks!" he said suddenly. "Those fellas."

"What about them?" asked Xavier.

"They have 'em in Boston?"

"What denomination?" asked Gladys. "There are still contemplative orders in the Catholic church, I think. Buddhists too. Why?"

"I think," said Jimmy, feeling his way toward the idea, "I'm gonna join up. You have to, like, apply or something?"

"You're going from thief to monk?" said Belial. "That's what I call making a hard left turn."

"You think they won't have me?" asked Jimmy, not defensive so much as anxious.

"I suspect they take all comers," said Gladys. "Are you sure you want to do that? It's basically checking out of the world entirely!"

"Yeah," said Jimmy considering the implications of that, then smiling and saying again, with more conviction, "yeah." He considered each of them in turn and nodded. "I know it sounds mad, but all this time travel and what have you... It's just made life feel different. I don't really have any skills or education," he said, with an apologetic glance at Rose, "not like you two. You can make the world better and have fulfilling lives. Me? I mean, it's not like I'm walking away from anything great, is it? I could work in a soup kitchen or something on day release, so to speak, and spend the rest of my time doing monk stuff: reading, chanting, thinking, praying. Maybe life will make a bit more sense or," he added with a self-conscious grin, "I'll worry less about losing it."

"Huh," said Xavier. "Okay then. Will we see you sometime?"

"Probably," said Jimmy, smiling. "I mean, I don't think I could handle one of those gangs that never talks or nothing."

"Trappists," said Gladys.

"Right," said Jimmy. "Them. I mean, I like the quiet, but sometimes I think I'd like to see my friends, just for a little while. And just, you know, my new friends. The rest...well, they won't miss me. Or me them." He considered their gaping faces and nodded. "Yeah," he said, a decision reached. "That's what I'm gonna do."

"And you?" said Gladys, nodding at Rose and Xavier.

"Oh, you know," said Rose. "Finish my degree and then... Not sure. I thought I wanted to be a professor..." She let the sentence hang.

"And now?" Xavier prompted.

"I think I'd rather be a writer," she said a little sheepishly.

"A novelist?" said Gladys approvingly.

"Maybe," said Rose in a *not really* sort of tone. "I kind of like the idea of writing for TV. Fun shows, you know? But smart. I don't know how to get started, and it's probably a stupid idea..."

"No," said Xavier. "It's a great idea. You should do it."

"And you?" she replied, speaking to conceal her blushes. "You will stay on at FDL Financial?"

"For a while," he said. "Maybe forever. But I want to dip my toes into other things."

"Like?"

It was Xavier's turn to look shamefaced.

"Acting," he said. "Just community theatre or something, probably. Something I can do in the evenings and weekends. I'd forgotten how much I liked it. I used to say I did it because it was good training for public speaking, for having a presence in meetings and such, but the truth is that I liked being somebody else."

"But still being true," said Belial.

"Yes!" said Xavier, pointing at him suddenly as if the devil had said something he had been trying to articulate for a while or had been too shy to say directly. "Exactly. Finding other ways to be myself, and speaking my truth through people who aren't me. Maybe that's crazy..."

"No," said Rose. "It's good."

"You gonna do Shakespeare?" Jimmy asked Xavier.

"Maybe," said Xavier. "I'd rather do Amiri Baraka, but if the right part comes along. Just..."

"Not *Othello*," said Rose.

"Exactly. Unless I can do my own patented adaptation," he added with a grin. "Oh and no *Shrew* either. Solidarity."

He offered Rose a fist bump, which she returned.

"Well, if I'm writing for TV and you're an actor..." she began playfully.

"Maybe we'll work together one day," Xavier concluded.

They laughed to say they didn't really mean it and then looked at each other.

"I'd like that," said Rose.

"Me too," said Xavier. When the silence seemed to go on a fraction too long, Xavier turned quickly to Belial and Gladys and said, with more casualness than he felt, "What about you two?"

The devil glanced at the angel.

"We have changes of our own coming," said Belial.

THAT EVENING, Xavier, Rose, and Jimmy went to the theatre to see *The Winter's Tale*. It was dark and strange, terrifying and—in the second half —funny, in a goofy sort of way. Then they got to the scene when the now elderly king, broken by the memory of what he did sixteen years before, was presented with the statue of his dead wife, Hermione, and you could feel the hushed expectation in the house. Even though most of them knew it was coming, there was an audible gasp when the statue stepped down from the plinth on which she had been standing. The staggered, desperate King took her hand and said, "Oh, she's warm! If this be magic, let it be an art lawful as eating."

Whereupon Rose, Xavier, and Jimmy, holding hands together in the dark, wept silently.

∿

"What a piece of work is a man! How noble in reason,
how infinite in faculties, in form and moving how express
and admirable, in action how like an angel, in apprehension
how like a god! The beauty of the world, the paragon of animals!
And yet, to me, what is this quintessence of dust?"
(*Hamlet*, 2.2.304-9)

IN SOME STORIES there will be characters for whom any attempt at literary closure is as illusory as it is for the reader who finishes the book but then has to get on with life, life being a narrative that is always told in media res, because being is always becoming. This is one of those stories, and it has two such characters.

"You ever wish you were human?" said Gladys, considering the humans as they said their farewells, embracing tearfully, overwhelmed by the enormity of all they had shared.

"It's part of my hell," said Belial. "I long for it. Of course, the mortality bit is limiting, but since death is just, you know..."

"A shift in the dimensional quality of your existence," Gladys supplied mechanically.

"Right," said the devil, "though that could mean a lot of things."

"And nothing," Gladys agreed.

The humans had just assumed that the burger place and the existence of angels and demons confirmed that an afterlife was an assured reality. She hadn't had the heart to tell them otherwise.

"Would I dare death and damnation to hear jazz like humans hear it," said Belial, "to taste wine, to feel drunk, to mutually enjoy the body of another, to eat roast lamb in a reduction sauce. Not sure. Why do you ask?"

"I'm not sure really," said Gladys. "Maybe it's all this Shakespeare. An angel couldn't have written that stuff. It's too faulty, too raw, too riddled with anxiety and inquisition, too desperate, too charged with passion..."

"Too human," said Belial.

"I suppose so. If an angel had written it, it would be all flawlessly metrical and sublimely beautiful but there would be no pain, no loss, no risk... I don't know, but it seems that what makes it all so intense is its fragility. Your lover might reject you. Your brother could be lost at sea. Your closest friends could die. So could you. For them, everything is marking time, lighting the way to dusty death. That's what charges everything they do and write and make, the knowledge that they may not be here tomorrow, or that whatever their happiness depends upon could, *will*, fade and disappear. We don't feel that. For us, eternity itself is laid out before us and none of us, angel or devil, will suddenly find ourselves dying or weeping beside the bed of a spouse or a child. For all our gifts and powers, age will not wither us."

Belial nodded a little sadly.

"Remember when you found out you could die?" he said.

"Oh yes," said Gladys, grinning.

"How much fun was that?"

"None, why?"

"Don't get too nostalgic for what you've lost," said Belial. "At the time you would have given anything to be immortal."

"True," said the angel. "But while I was alive as they are, I felt everything so much more sharply."

"You can't sustain that kind of intensity," said Belial. "It's like an explosion: the force that drives it also consumes it."

"I suppose so," said Gladys again.

Odd things, people, Gladys thought, though her appreciation of them had only developed when she had been staring down the barrel of her own mortality. She had always been faintly amused by—if not actually disdainful of—the way they filled their lives with trivialities, but now she saw those same thoughtless, unreflective habits as a way of staving off a state of constant anguish. She saw the heart-rending pathos of the ancient Lear, having passed through the most savage of trials, holding his youngest daughter dead in his arms, as no angel could. Howl, howl, howl, she thought, O you are men of stone!

"And what about you?" said Gladys. "Won't you have Beelzebub consigning you to torment?"

"No," said Belial, leading them into a nearby churchyard. "He's easier to play than a pipe. Gave me a new job, in fact. Meet the head of the Demonic Commission for Art and Culture. Congratulations, by the way."

Gladys smiled. Uriel had been right. There had been consequences for her actions, but, inexplicably, they had been promotion. She was, she reminded herself proudly, the new head of the equally new Angelic Commission on Art and Culture.

"We won't be working together exactly," said Gladys. "We *are* on opposing sides."

"Different, not opposing."

"Sometimes I'm not even sure how different they are," said Gladys. "Half the time I don't know who I'm working for."

"Only half?" said Belial. "I've spent years working for your lot without realizing it. I know for a fact you've done some of our dirty work in your time: though I'm sure you meant well."

Gladys grinned again and sat on a gravestone.

"What about this Shakespeare business then?" he said. "Whose scheme was that in the end?"

Belial shrugged.

"Kind of a joint venture, I think. Certainly when it came to that Iago nightmare."

"I thought your lot would love that," said Gladys. "Some nameless entity poisoning everyone it encountered with fear and hatred? Right down their alley."

"You'd think so, wouldn't you?" said Belial. "But you know what? I think it scared them. When Beelzebub first glimpsed it, he was curious, but I think it rattled him too: an impulse to destroy that didn't come from Hell? With hindsight, I think it worried him because he wasn't in control of it, and it reminded him how far humans had grown, for better and worse."

"It was purely human then?"

"Oh yes, I think so. There was some magic in its creation for sure, but it came from a human mind, grew out of his culture, and travelled mostly by words: poison through the ear. Most Hamletic."

"Maybe this is why we seem to be so much on the sidelines these days," said Gladys. "At their best, people out do the angels, and at their worst..."

"Quite," said Belial. "And for all our involvement in this escapade, it really was all them, you know? Bliss set it in motion and your people blocked it. We were just facilitators."

"You think we've been out-evolved?"

"I think we are rooted in our past," said Belial carefully. "And if I've learned anything from this Shakespeare malarkey, it's that nothing means the same once it leaves the period that created it. If we aren't careful, we'll get overwritten, turned into something else, our words and actions tweaked, inverted till we mean everything and nothing."

"Maybe we're already there," said Gladys. "Rather nice, really. Takes the pressure off."

"Funny, isn't it?" said Belial. "We spend our eternities waiting for our respective superiors to step in, force their agendas, but they never do. It's like everything has been set in motion, but somewhere along the way the humans took over."

"Ah," said Gladys sagely. "God the clockmaker."

"Perhaps. But sometimes it feels like the clock says it was half past four and suddenly it's twenty to seven, or yesterday, or an orange, and you think, *What the hell is going on here? Is someone monitoring this?* But the humans just keep going."

"Is that good?"

"I have absolutely no idea," said Belial. "Still, as with this Shakespeare business, both our sides seem happy with the results, so why inquire further?"

"I just like to know what's going on," said Gladys.

"And that, my angelic friend, is why you'd make a lousy human."

Gladys nodded thoughtfully. "So we'll be doing lunch then," she said.

"Often, I hope," said Belial. "I'll get my secretary, Mr. Bliss, to give you a call."

"That was his name, Bliss?"

"As in 'ignorance is,' yes," said Belial. "You've got to love the purity of it."

"What happened to the talk show woman?" asked Gladys.

"Still there I think," said Belial absently. "To be honest, I'd kind of forgotten about her."

"Still where?"

"1613," said the devil. "Tough place to live for anyone, let alone a twenty-first century female talk show host. She'll probably get hanged as a witch. That would make a change."

"What would?" said Gladys.

"If they actually hanged a real witch. Probably a first."

"It'll certainly make a dent in her self-esteem," said Gladys, grinning.

"You have a malicious streak," said Belial. "I like that in an angel."

Gladys grinned and Belial rose, stretching.

"Come on," said the devil. "It's time the angelic/demonic commission on art got to work. Shall we take in a show? *The Winter's Tale*, perhaps?"

"I'm Shakespeared out," said Gladys. "How about a movie where things explode?"

"Excellent idea. See? We're in sync already."

"Are movies high art or pop culture?" asked Gladys.

"Hmm," Belial mused. "Tricky one. Probably depends on the movie, but a working definition is as good a point as any for the Commission to start."

"That could take years," Gladys said.

"At least," grinned Belial. "Welcome to academia."

THE END

AFTERWORD

I usually write as quickly as possible, pounding out the story while it is fresh and exciting to me. Not in this case. I began work on *Burning Shakespeare* a quarter of a century ago. That's not hyperbole. I have been working on this book for twenty-five years. By that I don't mean that I moved forward at a snail's pace, constructing a few pages every six months or so. No. I wrote the whole thing, then rewrote it completely every few years. The version you just read bears little resemblance to most of the previous drafts. Each time I would come to it excited, remembering things about it that I liked, only to get stuck when the story went off the rails, bogged down, or otherwise failed to please. I tinkered, polished, and adjusted, but always lost interest and put it aside. The problem with revising work over a long period is that you come to know it too well, and are acutely familiar with how much time and energy you have already poured into it, and that makes it hard to make the tough edits, the broad, sweeping, wrecking ball edits that turn the plot into a blasted wasteland, transform characters so that they become unrecognizable, and rethink core ideas which had been central to the book. It took a long time for me to see that the only way to save the book was to blow large parts of it up and start pretty much from scratch. That is, as Robert Bliss might say, a tough ask, because then you have to decide whether you like enough of it well enough to do the massive amount of work necessary to make the thing as a whole work. Kill your darlings, the writing gurus say smugly: easier said than done, mate.

But at last I did, setting the bulldozers in motion late in 2018 and ploughing up and rebuilding over the next year. As I did so I realized that part of what I had found frustrating about the early drafts was that I had grown away from them, as had my subject. It might seem absurd to say that Shakespeare, who has been dead a long time at this point, has changed radically in the last two and a half decades, but if you engage with scholars or theatre artists, you'd see my point. Shakespeare is, in a way, us, and if he holds a mirror up to nature, what is reflected is as much ours as it is his, so that he evolves as we do. We find new things to interest us as our preoccupations change, and we find them in these old plays and poems. That, I think, is as it should be, or else scholars and actors are engaged in a process of archaeology, uncovering things that may have once been interesting but now look mostly like baffling old bricks and bits of pipe. We don't want to see what simply was. We want what is or might be. It seems to me that Shakespeare is still good for that.

In preparing this text I wanted to get as much right as I could—within the bounds of my story, at least—and not just in terms of matters of historical fact. I also wanted to take the temperature of some of my academic colleagues in working with some of the issues and problems raised by Shakespeare which interest us more than they did twenty-five, fifty, or a hundred years ago. One of those issues involves Shakespeare and race, so I'm especially grateful to those scholars and general readers of color who helped me navigate that thorniest of concerns by reading and sharing their thoughts: Ayanna Thompson, Sujata Iyengar, Gerald Coleman, and Kerra Bolton. Other academics and writers who read the book graciously provided insight and assistance according to their various and considerable expertise: Bill Worthen, Tiffany Stern, Peter Holland, Alice Dailey, Paul Menzer, Kirk Melnikoff, Faith Hunter, Misty Massey, and David Coe. Where there are errors of fact, judgment, or taste, they are entirely my own. Thanks also to my mother and my late father, both of whom fostered my love of Shakespeare, and to my teachers and mentors over the years, especially Bill Carroll and Jim Siemon. I am, as ever, especially grateful to Stacey Glick, my long-suffering agent, who indulges my impulse to write whatever I feel like, regardless of the marketing challenges presented by the results. I'm also grateful to this book's editor, Emily Leverett, who managed to be both keen eyed and enthusiastic enough to convince me that the story might be worth the telling, and to Melissa McArthur and John Hartness who made the book happen. Lastly, my heart-felt thanks to my family—Phaenarete Osako and Sebastian Hartley, always my target audience.

-AJH

NOTES

ACT ONE, SCENE FIVE

1. Gladys' research into US colloquialisms was not as up to date as she thought, an occupational hazard with beings who measure centuries in the blink of an eye.

ACT TWO, SCENE EIGHT

1. Rendered here in terms that suit the contemporary ear. All that "thou doth, forsooth" stuff quickly gets both absurd and exhausting. Imagine you have (*thou hast*, if you prefer) some kind of simultaneous translation device embedded in your brain, or rather between your brain and the overheard utterance, swimming like an unbelievably useful little fish in your ear canal and somehow making everything sound clear and contemporary. Yeah. Let's go with that.

ACT FOUR, SCENE TWO

1. A kind of pike with a stabby end and, just to give its owner other options for serious violence, an axe blade right next to it. Not something you want to see in the hands of someone ringing your doorbell.

ABOUT THE AUTHOR

A.J. Hartley (AKA Andrew Hart) is the bestselling author of 24 novels in a variety of genres including mystery, fantasy, sci-fi, thriller, paranormal, children's and young adult. He has written adaptations of *Hamlet* and *Macbeth* with David Hewson, and UFO mystery/thrillers with Tom DeLonge of Blink 182.

As Andrew James Hartley he is UNC Charlotte's Robinson Professor of Shakespeare studies where he specializes in performance issues. He is the author of scholarly books on dramaturgy, political theatre and performance history.

He has edited collections about Shakespeare on the university stage, Shakespeare in millennial fiction, and (with Peter Holland) Shakespeare and geek culture. He was editor of *Shakespeare Bulletin* for a decade, and is currently working on *Julius Caesar* for Arden.

He also has a YouTube channel focused mainly on Japanese rock music. You can learn more about him at www.ajhartley.net

ALSO BY A.J. HARTLEY

(As Andrew Hart)

Lies That Bind Us

The Woman In Our House

Preston Oldcorn Series

Cold Bath Street

Written Stone Lane

Will Hawthorne Series

Act of Will

Will Power

Darwen Arkwright Series

Darwen Arkwright and the Peregrine Pact

Darwen Arkwright and the Insidious Bleck

Darwen Arkwright and the School of Shadows

Sekret Machines (with Tom DeLonge)

Chasing Shadows

A Fire Within

Cathedrals of Glass

A Planet of Blood and Ice

Valkrys Wakes

SteepleJack

Steeplejack

Firebrand

Guardian

Impervious

Hamlet, Prince of Denmark: A Novel (with David Hewson)

Macbeth: A Novel (with David Hewson)

Mask of Atreus

What Time Devours

On The Fifth Day

Tears of the Jaguar

FRIENDS OF FALSTAFF

CPSIA information can be obtained
at www.ICGtesting.com
Printed in the USA
BVHW081410200322
631798BV00004B/11/J